W9-BBI-277

# Waking Up in Dixie

**Center Point
Large Print**

*Also by Haywood Smith and available from*
*¨Center Point Large Print:*

Ladies of the Lake
Wedding Belles

**This Large Print Book carries the**
**Seal of Approval of N.A.V.H.**

# Waking Up
# in Dixie

# Haywood Smith

CENTER POINT LARGE PRINT
THORNDIKE, MAINE

The text of this Large Print edition is unabridged.
In other aspects, this book may vary
from the original edition.
Printed in the United States of America.
Set in 16-point Times New Roman type.

ISBN: 978-1-60285-982-1

Library of Congress Cataloging-in-Publication Data

Smith, Haywood, 1949–
Waking up in Dixie / Haywood Smith.
p. cm.
ISBN 978-1-60285-982-1 (library binding : alk. paper)
1. Married people—Fiction. 2. Bankers—Fiction.
  3. Small cities—Fiction. 4. Georgia—Fiction.
  5. Midlife crisis—Fiction. 6. Domestic fiction.
  7. Large type books. I. Title.
PS3569.M53728W35 2011
813′.54—dc22
                                          2010040287

# Acknowledgments

My life has been pretty crazy for the past ten years, but the end of 2009 and the start of 2010 have been especially challenging. I couldn't have completed this book without the active support of St. Martin's Press; my editor, Jennifer Enderlin; my agent, Mel Berger at William Morris Entertainment; and my amazing network of friends, neighbors, and family, particularly my brothers and sisters in Christ from Blackshear Place Baptist Church in Oakwood, Georgia, and my support group in Suwanee. Without them, I wouldn't have been able to make it after my hip replacement went south and I shattered my femur.

My first and foremost thanks go to Mama, who was recovering from her own surgery when she brought me home and took care of me after my hip replacement, then provided wonderful Millie Griffith to help me when school started after my broken femur repair. (Not the best time to start college, but at my age, I don't have time to postpone anything.)

Second, my deepest appreciation goes to my mighty, fearless, and wonderful friend and Christian sister Brenda Davis for braving Atlanta traffic to get me to the doctor and the hospital.

Thanks, too, to sweet Dorene Graham and my precious "Jawja Hattitudes" Red Hats for bringing me some Christmas cheer in the hospital.

And how grateful I am to my precious daughter-in-law and son for taking me in for a wonderful Christmas with my three grandchildren as I recovered from my second surgery. There's nothing like grandchildren's hugs and kisses and visits to make the world better.

Thanks, too, to my kind and faithful neighbor Celia Dasher who brought me food and checked on me, and to my roommate, Sandi Grimsley, for keeping an ear out to make sure I was okay upstairs. My gratitude goes also to my Red Hats, and Alexis from SPLASH, and to my Bonds of Love Sunday School class for their unceasing prayers, cards, calls, and food, especially Harvey and Diane Roberts and sweet Ruth Jones and Tommy and Donna Cooper and Melinda Owenby, and Patty and Von Jennings, to name only a few. There's nothing like hard times to show what a blessing God gives us in good and faithful friends.

I also owe a debt of gratitude to my helper Callie Brooks for volunteering to push my wheelchair at school every Tuesday and Thursday, and to Pastor Dave Chappel and the pastoral care staff at Blackshear Place Baptist for making that possible. I am so blessed to be a part of a fellowship that cares so well for its members.

Thanks, too, to Dr. R. Marvin Royster and his

staff for putting Humpty-Dumpty back together again, and to Piedmont Hospital's Acute Rehab Department for wonderful care after my second surgery.

And to neurosurgeon Christopher Clare for coming in when he wasn't even on call to consult. Chris, you're definitely one of my guardian angels.

Now that I'm back on my feet (with one leg shorter than the other), I'm working on my degree and grateful for the best job in the world: writing uplifting stories for my readers. As long as I can punch two fingers at the keyboard, I'll keep on writing.

Watch for my next book, *Wife-in-Law*, in 2011, a fun story about two totally opposite best friends from across the cul-de-sac whose relationship is strained when one marries the other's ex. Can we say, *awkward?* But there's plenty of fun before the surprise finish, spiced by humorous flashbacks that send up life in the Atlanta 'burbs in the seventies and the eighties, complete with Little League baseball, ALTA tennis moms, pot-smoking protester PTA members, the "me" generation, and Young Republicans—all with a satisfying conclusion.

Last but not least, thanks to you, my readers, for making this all possible. In these difficult economic times, every book purchase makes a real difference to my career, so thank you, thank you, thank you for your loyalty in buying my new books. You're the best.

This book is dedicated to Debbie McGeorge, a kindred soul and the world's best friend and librarian. Thanks for the laughs and the "poor babies," sweetie.

# Chapter 1

There's something to be said for being married to the meanest man in town, as long as he's the richest.

Elizabeth Whittington stood in the elegant foyer of her elegant house and reminded herself that she'd gotten what she'd wanted when she'd landed handsome Howe Whittington, the crown prince of the prosperous town his family had owned for generations: respectability, for herself and their children. She'd escaped the shame and squalor of her roots. For that much, she was deeply grateful.

She told herself to be content and tried to count her blessings. In some ways Howe treated her well, despite the fact that, over the years, he'd gradually withdrawn till their lives were merely tangential, politely lived in separate rooms. She'd long since known about his fancy women down in Atlanta, but fear had kept her silent—fear of losing what was left.

At least he was discreet.

He'd given her security, too. She and the children had all the material things they could ever need, though their son and daughter took it all for granted.

She had a magnificent home that she had come to love, even though her domineering mother-in-law had refused to let her change a thing "out of respect for the Whittington ancestors." And Howe, prophetically, had refused to take up for Elizabeth with his mother.

Elizabeth told herself she should be grateful, but instead, she was lonely. Had been, for far too long. If it wasn't for her old friend P.J.'s recent attentions, she didn't know what she would have done. But as appealing as P.J. was, she would never risk her precious respectability with an affair, so their relationship had remained platonic—on her side, anyway.

Still, deep inside, some stubborn remnant of her girlhood hunger for a "happily ever after" ending still smoldered, heating the anger and loneliness she'd buried for so long. Naïve though it was, she still wished her husband would love her the way he once had. That he would want only her, so they could be happy together, the way they'd been at first.

But life was real, not fairy tales. So she'd stand by him for yet another of their annual Christmas extravaganzas and pretend she was happy, at least.

Elizabeth sighed, then pressed the electrical remote and watched with satisfaction as the tastefully opulent Christmas decorations in the tastefully opulent mansion blazed to life. And in that moment, her house, if not her marriage, glittered with warmth and beauty.

Then she frowned. She still had to speak with Howe before the party, and time was running out. For three days, she'd hoped to find just the right situation to ask him to help her friends the Harrises, but he'd been too busy, almost as if he sensed she wanted something from him. And now, here it was, only thirty minutes before everybody who was anybody in Whittington would be arriving, and Elizabeth still hadn't found the perfect moment.

Talking about work was against Howe's unwritten laws. When they'd first moved back to Howe's hometown so he could take over the bank when his father died, Howe had talked to her about the bank every day. But when he'd discovered his father's double-dealings, he'd gradually shut her out of that part of his life. At first, she'd excused it as stress. Gradually, though, he'd become more and more distant, until they were polite strangers, their lives tangential only through their children and their place in Whittington society.

She knew he wouldn't like what she was going to ask of him, but Elizabeth had to draw the line when it came to the girls in her "Sewing Circle" (which had nothing to do with sewing and everything to do with wine and whine). The bank was about to foreclose on Elizabeth's closest friend

11

Faith Harris and her husband Robert. She had to do something. For God's sake, it was Christmas! She couldn't just sit there and let Howe take away their home.

Robert Harris was the best builder in town. It wasn't his fault that the bottom had fallen out of the housing market and left him holding the bag on three huge spec houses Howe's bank had financed. Surely Howe would give Robert a break if Elizabeth asked him to.

She'd never interfered in his business before, or asked for anything this important.

Speak of the devil, Howe descended the stairway with his shirtsleeves rolled up and the jacket of his custom-made suit in one hand. Even at fifty-nine, Howell Whittington was still a gorgeous man, lean and tanned and agile from playing cutthroat tennis twice a week, without a single thread of gray in his dark, close-trimmed hair.

He scanned the foyer and the rooms around it. "Everything looks perfect," he said. Perfect was the only standard he tolerated, one he'd learned from his snidely superior mother. "I'll start the fires."

"In a minute," Elizabeth deferred, doing her best to look and sound winsome. "There's something I'd like to ask you first. A favor."

Howe's placid expression tensed. "I hope it won't take long. I want everything done before

12

the first guest arrives." God forbid anybody should catch him in his shirtsleeves. "The old ladies are always so damned early."

Elizabeth motioned to the festive living room. "It won't take but a minute. Please." She led the way to the silk camelback sofa that faced two English chintz chairs in front of the fireplace. "Let's sit."

His normally unreadable expression betrayed suspicion. It had been years since she'd tried to talk to him about anything that really mattered, and that clearly suited him just fine. "All right," he said. "But please try to get to the point, Elizabeth. No Edith Bunker, if you don't mind."

Elizabeth bristled. Was that how he thought of her? Edith Bunker?

He waited till she subsided to the sofa to sit facing her. "Okay. What's this favor?"

She licked her lower lip, her mouth suddenly dry. "It's about Faith and Robert Harris." She rushed forward with, "I know Robert's behind on his construction loans, and he used their house as collateral, but Howe, please don't foreclose on their home. Faith is my friend. You can afford to be merciful, just this once."

Howe's composure congealed. "Did Faith put you up to this?"

"Of course not," she told him, encouraged by the polite tone of the question. "She'd be humiliated if she knew."

He stood, signaling the conversation was over. "As well she should be."

Elizabeth had no intention of giving up. She rose and caught Howe's arm before he could escape. It was the first time they'd touched in months. "Howe, she's my friend, and God knows, I have few enough real friends in this town. I'm asking you to do this for me, as your wife. Please. I never ask anything of you."

"Except for your brothers' legal fees. And the condo in Clearwater for your lush of a mother," he reminded her quietly, prompting a flush of hot shame to her face.

"Besides that," she said, wounded. Howe was a master at being cruel, yet unfailingly polite. The flame of anger burned brighter deep inside her.

P.J. would never throw something like that in her face. P.J. actually appreciated her, though she'd never risk her precious respectability with an affair. His friendship had been a godsend. At least someone thought she was wonderful.

Strengthened by that knowledge, she persevered. "Howe, this is important to me."

Howe extracted his arm from her grasp, then smoothed the pinpoint oxford as he met her pleading gaze. "I can't believe you'd even ask this of me. You know I never mix personal and business matters."

"Make an exception," she insisted, sending up an arrow prayer for divine intervention. "Just this once. Howe, we can afford it, and nobody has to know. Robert and Faith won't say anything. I swear."

No lightning bolt from heaven arrived to thaw her husband's heart.

"I'm really only asking for a delay," she argued. "You know Robert will pay you back as soon as things pick up."

"God knows when that will be," Howe said, unmoved. "Elizabeth, you are so naïve."

He'd once found that attractive. P.J. still did. "Maybe," she said, "but the man I married would at least have tried to find a way to make this happen."

They'd loved each other once. Surely some shred of that was still inside him somewhere.

Howe's eyes went frosty. "The man you married was a spoiled kid who had no idea what it took to keep up the lifestyle he was accustomed to. A lifestyle, I might add, that you seem to have enjoyed over the years."

Elizabeth would gladly have sacrificed every bit of it if she could bring back the husband who'd adored her in spite of his mother's objections. But Elizabeth had long since forced herself to accept reality. "Howe, I'm begging. Please." She hated to grovel, but she only had access to her household accounts. Generous though they were, they couldn't handle this. And Howe's mother had made it clear from the

15

beginning that Elizabeth would never receive any more of the family fortune.

Howe wasn't used to having anyone argue with him, least of all his long-suffering wife. "What do you think the bank is, a charity?" he asked as if she were a child. "We're one of the few solvent entities in the state—in the country, for that matter—and it's because I never let personal feelings affect my business decisions."

As if he had any personal feelings in the first place.

Elizabeth did her best to keep her disappointment from showing. "I know, Howe, but I want this." How could she convince him? "Consider it my Christmas gift." She'd never cared about the expensive furs or cars or jewelry he always gave her, prompted, no doubt, by his guilt about the whores she pretended not to know about. "And my birthday gift. And next Christmas, too."

"I'm sorry, but it's impossible," he dismissed as cheerfully as if it were *good morning*. Crouching at the hearth with his back to her, he struck a match to a stick of lighter wood and ignited the aged hickory their handyman Thomas had laid in. "This conversation is closed," he said firmly but politely. "Permanently."

The doorbell chimed "We Wish You a Merry Christmas" before Elizabeth could ask again.

Howe stood and looked out the front window

to the well-worn Lincoln Continental parked at the curb, then glanced at his Tag Heuer watch. "Now look what's happened. Miss Emily Mason is here twenty minutes early."

"She always comes early," Elizabeth said. Miss Emily was one of Howe's mother's cronies from Altar Guild, and she invariably came early, probably trying to catch Elizabeth unprepared, so she could tattle.

"Thanks to your nonsense," Howe added in a rare glimpse of pique, "only one of the fires is lighted, and I don't even have my coat on yet." He rolled down his sleeves to button the starched cuffs. "Please don't answer the door till I have my coat on."

Furious and fighting back tears, Elizabeth headed for the foyer, accompanied by repeated choruses of the chimes as Miss Emily jabbed away at the bell.

She'd never change her husband's mind. How was she going to face Faith and Robert at the party knowing Howe would take their home from them?

Elizabeth wished she could just walk out, leaving Howe to manage without her, and drive to Atlanta to see P.J. That would teach Howe a lesson. Let him explain to everybody why she wasn't there.

Maybe P.J. could loan Robert the money. He had plenty—not as much as Howe, but plenty.

He'd made it in software after losing his shirt in the S and L crisis, so he could surely sympathize with Robert's plight.

At least P.J. wouldn't ridicule her for asking. He always made her feel special, like a desirable woman. She dearly wished she could see him.

But she didn't dare leave. It would embarrass the family if she wasn't there for the party, and she'd sworn on her drunken father's grave that she'd never embarrass her own children. So she opened the door and stayed and smiled for Charles's and Patricia's sakes, not for Howe's. But the party was a disaster. She could barely face the Harrises, who responded to her avoidance with confused concern. And Howe deliberately circulated just out of Elizabeth's reach.

Elizabeth managed to soldier on till late in the evening, when a drunken Katie Madsden—the wife of one of Howe's business associates who was nowhere to be seen—draped herself seductively over Howe and started talking about when they'd slept together, in front of everybody who was anybody in Whittington, including Elizabeth.

Conversations halted abruptly as all eyes turned their way.

Howe laughed, trying to escape and pass it off as drunken nonsense, but Katie just got louder and lewder.

Elizabeth's complexion flamed. Shocked and humiliated, she scanned the room for reactions and got a warning glance and shake of the head from Howe's mother. God forbid, she should make a scene.

But what about Howe? The scene was his, in their home! And Elizabeth had every right to react.

Their guests went brittle with anticipation of what might come next.

"Tommy," Howe called to Katie's husband. "Come get your wife! She's had so much to drink, she thinks I'm somebody else."

"Oh, no I don't," Katie insisted, grabbing Howe's crotch. "I remember you, mister, and this."

An audible gasp escaped the watching guests.

Elizabeth froze. This was too much. Nameless, faceless whores were one thing, but this woman was local, and anything but discreet.

She could have killed Howe.

How could she look the other way when everyone in town had seen this?

Heart pounding, she grimly approached her husband and his lover, then heard herself say in a low voice that trembled with suppressed rage, "Katie, I've never asked a guest to leave my home before, but I'm asking you to, immediately. Get out. You have abused our hospitality and insulted both me and my husband, and you are no longer welcome here."

Tommy appeared and grabbed his wife, pulling

her toward the door. "Sorry, Howe. She gets crazy when she has too much. It doesn't mean anything, I swear," he said to Elizabeth, then repeated for the room, "It doesn't mean anything, I swear."

"Good-bye, Tommy," Howe said smoothly. "I don't want to see you or Katie again. Our business relationship is terminated." Howe put his arm around Elizabeth's waist. "You'll hear from my attorneys tomorrow."

A wave of sympathy for Elizabeth erupted from the room behind them. To keep from crying, she took a steadying breath and channeled Miss Melly, then turned to their remaining guests. "Some people shouldn't drink at all," she said, brows lifted. She motioned toward the buffet and the bar. "Please, everyone, let's go back to the party and put this little unpleasantness behind us."

The tension ebbed as conversation resumed. Elizabeth stood rigid, a forced smile plastered on her face.

"Well done," Howe said quietly from just behind her left shoulder.

Hating him for the first time in all their long, challenging years together, she faced her husband with stone-cold anger. "You owe me for this," she bit out. "Make it right with the Harrises. Now."

He eyed her with renewed admiration. "Done. But only this once."

"We'll see," she said, then resumed her duties as hostess.

When she looked for the Harrises, she saw Howe shaking a much-relieved Robert's hand, and Faith was crying happy tears.

At least someone here was happy tonight, Elizabeth thought, and bitterly wished herself a Merry Christmas.

# Chapter 2

*The past: Greenville, Georgia*

Eleven-year-old Bessie Mae dragged the scraggly pine sapling she'd cut down in the back door of the abandoned Piggly Wiggly her family had appropriated. Once the tree was safely in, she carefully closed the door, even though the insides of the windows were coated with frost. At least the door blocked the raw December wind.

She carefully selected a battered bucket from the store's leavings and poured it half full with water from the trash cans they'd used to collect rainwater from the downspouts.

But she made too much noise. After a spate of shuffling footsteps on the broken linoleum, the sour smell of BO and cheap wine preceded her father's appearance at the opening to the front of the store. He scowled, his arms akimbo under the coats and sweaters and multiple pairs of jogging pants piled onto his gaunt frame. "What the hell is that?"

"It's Christmas," she said as cheerfully as she could manage. "So I got us a tree."

He collapsed into one of the scavenged chairs around the huge cable spool they used for a table. "Bullshit. Christmas is a hunnerd percent bull-shit," he slurred, waving a hand in dismissal. "Totally commercial. All them Jews soaking all them dumb-ass Christians for money, that's all it is." He leaned back to holler, "Jacob! Git in here."

Elizabeth tensed. If only she'd been quieter, she'd have had a chance to put on the string of popcorn and colorful paper chain her teacher had let her take home for the holidays. Then maybe her daddy might have smiled instead of gotten mad. She was his pet, after all.

"I've got some decorations for it, Daddy," she said. "It'll be real pretty. Just you wait and see."

"Jacob!" her father blared. "I said git in here! If I have to call you again, it's a beatin'!"

Daddy was always whaling away at her big brothers, even Liam, who was a strapping man at nineteen. Especially when all of them had been drinking, which was most of the time. Why Daddy spared her, she'd never been able to figure out. And though she was grateful, Bessie Mae felt guilty every time she escaped his wrath.

She let out a sigh of relief when Jacob—at six-teen, already four inches taller than Daddy—sidled into the room, his expression dark and sullen. "Whut now?"

Daddy pointed to the little tree. "Put that into the stove in my room and light it. Then git yer coat and cut some more." He glared, pulling his clothes tighter around him. "This place is colder than a witch's tit."

Jacob saw Bessie Mae's disappointment about the tree. "I cain't, Diddy," he dared to say, deliberately keeping out of their father's reach. "Gotta git to the pool hall. I'm already late. Dewey Sosebee bet me a truckload of oak against forty dollar that he kin beat me." He pulled a frayed jacket from the Salvation Army over his flannel shirt. "I'll have that wood here in less than an hour."

Their father's brows lowered dangerously. "You better, or there'll be hell to pay. And yer mama better git herself home from work soon and fix me some supper." He lurched out of his chair and started rummaging through the mess, looking for a bottle. "I'm hungry."

And thirsty.

Bessie Mae and her brother took advantage of the distraction to slip out the back door and run. When they got to the end of the street, her brother pulled a beer from his coat pocket and popped the top, then grinned. "You better make yerself scarce tonight, Annie." He called her "Annie" because she tried to talk like her teachers and believed that one day she would be rich, just like Little Orphan Annie in the musical. "There ain't no pool game," he confessed, "and no fire-wood. So we both better lay low."

Bessie Mae looked back at the dark store. "But what about Mama? And Liam?"

"They can take care of themselves," Jacob told her. "Now, go on. Git yerself to the library. You can hide when they're closin' up, then sleep there all night."

It wouldn't be the first time, and the library was Bessie Mae's favorite place, thanks to all the happy endings on its shelves. "Okay."

She felt guilty about Mama and Liam, but it was Friday—payday at the chicken plant—so Mama would be bringing home a case of beer with the weekly groceries. Maybe Daddy would pass out before he got mad, this time.

"Ya gotta look after your own self," Jacob cautioned, then headed for the pool hall.

"Merry Christmas," she called after her brother.

Jacob just shook his head in disapproval and kept on going, his shoulders hunched against the cold wind.

"Merry Christmas," she repeated, to herself. Hands fisted in the pockets of her secondhand coat, she turned toward the library.

She could find another tree. And this time, she'd hide it where Daddy wouldn't find it.

# Chapter 3

## *The present: Whittington, Georgia*

Two Sundays before Christmas, Elizabeth knelt in the pew beside Howe and prayed for help to forgive him for his greed and lack of love, then went through the motions of the service by his side, as she had for more than a quarter of a century.

When it came time for the sermon, Elizabeth settled back and tried to look interested, though she knew the message would be anything but. Father Jim's sermons had been dry as melba toast lately.

Men of the Whittington family had been falling asleep—sitting up—in the second pew of St. Andrew's Episcopal Church since their ancestors had built the place in 1793, and Howe was no exception. So Elizabeth took little notice when he went rigidly still beside her while their aged minister made a thready connection between the daily Epistle reading and the topic of global warming.

Her mind wandering, Elizabeth tuned out the priest's monotonous delivery, suppressing a sigh.

Normally, she accepted the humdrum of her weekly routines with gratitude—she'd had enough drama the night of the party to last her for quite a while—but on this particular Sunday, the minister got on her last nerve.

She looked across the aisle to see her mother-in-law focused on the priest as if he were delivering the Word of Heaven straight from God Almighty, which only annoyed Elizabeth more.

Father Jim was a kind man, but wholly ineffectual, and clearly out of ideas for his homilies. The man needed to retire, and that was all there was to it. Unless St. Andrew's got somebody livelier, the Baptists would end up with all the young people.

The Baptists might just end up with *her*—a thought that made Elizabeth smile, even though she knew she'd never dare. Her mother-in-law would disown her for sure, and there was already no love lost, no matter how hard Elizabeth had tried to win the woman's approval.

As the sermon meandered on, Elizabeth discreetly opened her purse and glanced down at her pocket calendar to review the upcoming week: Women's Club tomorrow; bring her strawberry flan.

Errands and shopping in Atlanta on Tuesday, as usual, and lunch with P.J. They hadn't seen each other since before the party, so she was looking forward to it even more than usual. Her ego really needed a boost. She wanted to tell P.J. what had happened at the party.

Nobody knew Elizabeth had been seeing P.J., and nobody needed to.

It was all innocent enough. She'd bumped into him a couple of times back in September on her regular Tuesday shopping trips to Phipps Plaza, and they'd chatted about their old high school days over lunch at Maggiano's, hitting it off immediately. P.J. lived and worked nearby, and they both loved the restaurant, so they'd fallen into splitting the huge servings every week, but lunch was all it was. Elizabeth wasn't about to risk her reputation with anything more.

Even so, people might not understand that the relationship was strictly platonic. On her part, anyway.

As the minister droned on, she focused back on her calendar. Sewing Circle Tuesday night—or "whine and cheese" as some of the husbands called it, where she offered sympathy, but never breathed a word about her own sterile marriage or friendship with P.J.

Altar Guild Wednesday; remember to pick up the altar cloths from the cleaners on the way.

Teeth cleaned and whitened on Thursday.

And her regular hairdresser's appointment on Friday; not so dark with the color this time.

Respectable. Predictable. A decent life, all in all.

She and Howe would see each other in passing, always pleasant, always polite.

Even though Howe had helped her friends, he'd only done it under duress. So she'd given him the cold shoulder all week. Now, though, guilt told her she should be happy that Howe had relented about the Harrises. She ought to be happy enough with her life.

She focused on the blessings God had given her. Their son Charles was such a darling, and even spoiled Patricia would eventually come to appreciate her as a mother one day, if only when she had children of her own.

Speaking of mothers, Howe's mother was mortal and in her mid-eighties; that was big on Elizabeth's gratitude list. Augusta Whittington would croak one day, and Elizabeth would be the one who could rest in peace. No longer would she be Princess Di under her mother-in-law's critical eye. The thought relaxed her.

Maybe next weekend Elizabeth would slip away and take a drive up into the mountains. She was free. Charles and Patricia wouldn't be coming home from college for another month—unless Patricia ran out of money again, in which case, she'd show up at the bank and wheedle it out of Howe before going back to Athens. If the weather was bad, she could read. She loved to read, as long as the books had happy endings.

Something ought to have happy endings.

The pipe organ signaled the end of the sermon and her daydreams, so she stood and opened to the hymn she'd marked with her order of service. She got through the first line before realizing Howe hadn't risen beside her. Mortified that he hadn't woken up, she gave his foot a firm poke with her own, but he remained seated, eyes closed.

Everybody in the rows behind her could see, so she tipped slightly toward him and said out of the corner of her mouth, "Howell, wake up."

Usually, the use of his name was enough to get his attention, but he didn't respond.

Elizabeth bent to whisper an adamant "Howell, wake up" in his ear, but when she did, he started to tilt toward her, his eyes still closed.

A bolt of alarm shot through her as she sat and pushed him back erect. "Howell?" she whispered, gripping his arm.

Dear God, he was pale as paste, and stiff.

But his chest was moving. He was breathing.

Elizabeth turned to see Mitt Wallace from the club on the row just behind them. She grasped his forearm and drew him toward her. "Mitt," she whispered as the choir started recessing down the aisle, "something's the matter with Howell. Help me get him out."

Her husband would be humiliated if anybody realized the state he was in. God forbid, he should have a seizure in public, or worse. His battle-axe of a mother had made it clear from the beginning that appearances must be maintained at all costs, and Elizabeth had spent the past quarter of a century seeing that they were.

So far, the recessional had distracted everyone enough to keep them from realizing what had happened. By some miracle, Howe's mother was busy mouthing for Catherine Wilkerson to meet her in the vestibule as the choir passed, so she didn't barge in and take over.

Mitt came around and helped Elizabeth lift Howell. At six one, Mitt was as tall as Howe, but even with adrenaline working in their favor, they struggled to get Howe up and out into the side aisle, then into the minister's study as inconspicuously as possible, his feet dragging across the polished stone floors.

Once in the study, they heaved him onto the velvet three-cushion sofa.

Mitt grabbed the desk phone and called 911, while a panicked Elizabeth rubbed her husband's hand and demanded, "Howell, can you hear me? Howell!"

"My friend is unconscious," Mitt told the 911 operator. "He's breathing, but unconscious. We're in the minister's study at St. Andrew's Episcopal in Whittington." Pause. "He just closed his eyes in church and didn't open them again." Pause. "No. He never drinks too much." Mitt turned to ask Elizabeth, "What medications does he take?"

"None. He's healthy as a horse." At least, he had been, till this happened.

"None," Mitt repeated, along with the rest. He scowled. "How should I know?" He immediately reconsidered. "No. No drug use. No pot, no cocaine, no nothing." Pause. "Trust me, I'd know."

Everybody who knew Howell knew he'd never indulge in anything that might interfere with his iron control of his life. The sole exception to that was his doting affection for their daughter. He'd been wrapped around Patricia's little finger from the moment she was born. But that was his only weakness. Except for the floozies, but they were just nameless sex objects, a fact that made the situation bearable.

"All right," Mitt said. "I'll be waiting for them out front. But please, ask them to cut the siren before they get here. Church is just letting out, and he wouldn't want a scene." Mitt hung up. "They're on their way. Ten minutes, tops. What can I do?"

Elizabeth shook her head. "I don't know. He's breathing. His heart's beating. He's just not responding." She laid her head to his chest, the most intimate contact they'd had in years. "It's kind of fast, but it's beating."

There had been many times when she'd dreamed about the compensations of genteel widowhood, especially since she'd been seeing

P.J. She'd imagined what it would be like not to cater to Howe's rigid habits; not to have his private peccadilloes hang over her, threatening her precious respectability. But now that she faced the possibility, panic pounced on her. "Howe," she said, maintaining a calm exterior by sheer act of will, "you're going to be all right. The paramedics are on the way. Hang on. Don't leave me." She shocked herself at how frightened she felt.

Then her husband did something he hadn't done in years: he laughed—a sharp, disjointed guffaw. One, loud, bizarre laugh, then silence.

*I died laughing* shot through Elizabeth's mind, and the panic tightened, but Howe kept right on breathing, his eyes closed to tiny slits, with no movement beneath his lids. She shook him. "Howe?"

Why would he laugh?

He couldn't be playing possum. Howe never, ever joked.

The door to the study opened, but it was only the priest. "Sorry," he said, hesitating. "I didn't know anyone was—" Father Jim registered what was going on and became grave. "What's happened? Heart attack? Have you called 911?"

"Don't know what's the matter," Mitt said. "I already called for an ambulance. They're on their way."

The priest hastened over. "I know CPR. When did this happen?" he asked Elizabeth.

"He just closed his eyes during the sermon and didn't open them again," she explained. "Out cold, sitting up. But I don't think he needs resuscitating."

"Good Lord," the priest said. "I should have listened when my wife told me that sermon was lethal." He wrung his hands. "Not that I wouldn't be in good company. Saint Paul bored a man to death with his preaching once—guy fell out the window—but he was able to resurrect him."

What?

Appalled, Elizabeth stared at him in consternation. "Joking? Are you joking?"

Mitt made things worse by letting out a shocked chortle, then, "It's like the one about the Episcopalian who died sitting up during the sermon, and the paramedics had to haul out fifteen people before they found the right one."

"Kindly do not talk about dying," Elizabeth snapped. "Howell is right here, and we don't know what's the matter yet."

"Please forgive me," the priest asked.

Penitent, the two men exchanged rueful glances, then Mitt headed for the door. "I'll go wait for the paramedics," he volunteered.

It seemed like eons, during which Elizabeth gauged every breath her husband took, but only ten minutes passed before the metallic rattle of a stretcher on the flagstones preceded the paramedics. They came in and immediately started hooking up leads and an IV as they relayed symptoms into their radiophones. After overhearing that Howe's blood pressure was elevated and his heart regular, but fast, Elizabeth tapped one of the paramedic's shoulders. "What is it?"

"We can't be sure, but my guess is, Mr. Whittington may have had a stroke," he told her. "We've administered medications to lower his pressure, but the sooner we can get him to the hospital, the better his chances for recovery."

His *chances* for a recovery. Elizabeth's heart sank. The nearest hospital was forty minutes away, and its emergency services were notoriously inadequate.

Suddenly, the sound of a helicopter grew louder and louder outside, then she heard a vehicle zoom up, then halt with a screech of brakes.

The paramedics raised the stretcher and started for the door with Elizabeth close behind, but before they got there, the side door of the church burst open and Howell's mother stormed in with four uniformed medical attendants hot on her heels, bearing a sleek, plastic patient transport. A force of nature at eighty-five, Augusta Whittington clipped out, "I heard on the scanner. We're airlifting him to Piedmont. My neurologist and neurosurgeon will be there waiting. And the best cardiologist in town."

For once, Elizabeth was grateful for her mother-in-law's interference. "Thank God. Bless you, Mother Whittington."

The woman glared at Elizabeth as if what had happened was all her fault. "This is my only son. I'll move heaven and earth to get him the best care possible." She motioned for the attendants to transfer him to their stretcher.

Clearly insulted to have their patient usurped, the local paramedics nevertheless stepped aside without comment, because nobody in Whittington —or the state of Georgia, for that matter—dared cross Augusta Whittington. But the whole scene would be grist for the gossip mill within minutes.

"I'm grateful for the medevac," Elizabeth told her mother-in-law. "I'll call your cell as soon as we find out anything."

"Call, nothing," her mother-in-law said. "I'm going with him."

The lead attendant raised a staying palm. "I'm sorry, Mrs. Whittington, but we only have room for one extra person besides the patient, and for legal reasons, it should be his wife."

Mrs. Whittington shot him a look that would shatter granite, but he didn't relent, and as Elizabeth followed the stretcher out, her mother-in-law flipped open her cell phone and dialed, then barked out, "Eddie Spruill"—the local sheriff—"this is Augusta Whittington. I'm at St. Andrew's. Howell has been stricken ill, and they're choppering him to Piedmont. Come get me this instant and take me to the hospital." She scowled in outrage. "I don't care if you're eating. The Golden Corral will be there when you get back, but if you're not here in five minutes, you'll be going home without that badge, and you know I can do it." She snapped the phone shut as Elizabeth followed the stretcher past her toward the waiting chopper.

"Don't you let anything happen to him before I get there," Augusta called after her. "I'm holding you responsible if it does, Elizabeth."

Of course.

As the chopper took off, Elizabeth watched her world grow smaller and smaller, and wondered if she would still be the wife of the richest, most powerful man in the county when she came home.

# Chapter 4

*The past: Elizabeth's sophomore year,
her first day at Whittington High*

Oblivious to the curious stares that followed her, Elizabeth pretended she was a secret princess, noble yet humble, as she strolled into the principal's office her first day of school at Whittington High. She sat gracefully to wait till her name was called. As she waited, more than one male teacher and student eyed her new womanly curves with approval, but she didn't let on that she noticed.

This was her chance to leave Bessie Mae behind, forever.

She'd worked hard to make sure her golden-brown hair swung sweet and shiny as she moved, and the clothes she was wearing looked like the ones worn by the popular girls. Nobody would ever know she'd taken the Greyhound into Atlanta to pick out the best the Goodwill and uptown thrift shops had to offer. Or that she'd cut them to style, then sewn them with perfect, even stitches under the light of a single dim bulb till they fit like they were custom-made—not too tight, but modestly close enough to make the most of her bustline and small waist. Her whole wardrobe had cost her only fifty dollars, but looked like thousands.

Now, here she was at last. She'd been planning for this day since her mother had announced her new job at the mill in Whittington, a job that came with a house in a new town, far from Greenville, where nobody knew them. A perfect chance for Elizabeth to start over and be who she wanted to be, not who she really was. A chance to hide the shame and poverty of her family.

Beautiful, brilliant, and unattainable, that's what she would be. Bessie Mae was dead, and in her place was Elizabeth, a paragon of virtue and intelligence, the kind of woman men wanted, but couldn't have. The kind of woman wealthy boys would marry.

"Miss Mooney," the school secretary announced, "Mr. Cowan will see you now." She motioned to the door with PRINCIPAL COWAN painted on the frosted glass.

Elizabeth rose with perfect poise and glided into the small office to face the first man she had to win over.

"Welcome, Miss Mooney. Welcome." Eyeing her up and down with appreciation, the principal motioned for her to sit. "I must say, I'm quite impressed with your transcripts from Greenville. Straight A's. Don't see many records like that."

He patted her file. "We're glad to have you in our student body." Glancing again at her impressive curves and narrow waist, he colored and smoothed his lapel. "May I ask, do you have any specific goals for your time with us?"

"Yes," she said with a careful mix of shyness and warmth. "I want to win a full academic scholarship to Emory and get my masters' in political science." Her whole plan depended on it.

The principal nodded with a mixture of skepticism and approval. "Nothing like setting your sights on the best. Good luck to you on that. If you keep up the good work, you might just make it." He leaned forward to press a button on his phone. "Phyllis, is Miss Mooney's student guide there yet?"

"Yes," crackled through the speaker.

"Then send her in." Mr. Cowan rose. "Welcome to Whittington High. All our new students have a guide to take them to their classes for the first day." He surveyed her again as she stood. "If you have any problems or questions after that, feel free to come by, and we'll do our best to iron things out." His expression said he hoped she would.

The door opened and a total nerd of a girl in thick glasses scurried in, carrying a canvas book bag printed with the school's tiger mascot. She granted Elizabeth a nervous wave. "Hi. I'm Cathy, your guide."

"Hi." Elizabeth smiled back warmly. She had a

soft spot for misfits, having been one herself for all those years. And she needed every friend she could get in this place. "Thanks for showing me around."

Cathy handed her the book bag. "Your teachers will give you your books."

"Thanks."

"Have a nice day," the principal dismissed, then stood in his doorway watching Elizabeth cross the offices and exit into the corridor.

Once she and Cathy were out in the hall, Elizabeth glided with perfect posture through the stream of students, her head held high, ignoring the frank looks of assessment from the girls and heated reactions of the boys.

It helped that she'd always had an eye for the finer things in life. She'd always watched and imitated how the rich people talked and dressed. Now she had a chance to put what she'd learned to use.

Here, in this new place, she'd make sure nobody would ever see the tiny, rundown mill house where she lived. Nobody would meet her useless, drunken father or her brawling older brothers. For all anyone at Whittington High knew, she had an ordinary family and a decent house. She knew how to deflect even the most persistent questions.

A woman of mystery, that's what she'd be.

As for her teachers and the school authorities,

41

Elizabeth had long since learned to forge her mother's signature and make believable excuses for her absence at parent-teacher conferences. She could handle that end of things.

As if she'd read Elizabeth's mind, Cathy asked, "Where do you live?"

Elizabeth cocked her head with interest. "Where do you?"

Cathy deflated. "On a farm at the edge of town. Bo-ring."

"Thank goodness for books," Elizabeth said. "They're a great way to escape boredom."

Cathy grinned, revealing a full set of railroad tracks, top and bottom. "How'd you know I like to read?"

"I can see you're intelligent," Elizabeth told her. "All intelligent people like to read."

"I think I'm going to like you," Cathy said.

Elizabeth nodded toward a covey of girls ahead who were fluttering around a tall, lanky, good-looking football player. A *very* good-looking football player, probably a senior. "What's that all about?"

Cathy gazed at the high school hero with a wistful sigh. "That's Howe Whittington and his usual harem."

*Him!* Bingo, and on her first day. It was an omen. Elizabeth's steps slowed, but she deliberately didn't look at the boy, just tossed out a disinterested, "Ummm."

"His family owns this town, and has for generations," Cathy murmured. "He's the last of his line, the biggest catch in Whittington, but his mother wants him to marry some rich Atlanta deb."

That's what *she* thought! Howe Whittington's mother didn't know about Elizabeth, and she wouldn't, if Elizabeth had anything to do with it, till it was too late.

Elizabeth waited till the crown prince of Whittington looked at her to turn away from him. "What's he like?" she asked Cathy in a whisper.

Cathy's eyes widened behind her glasses. "A total dreamboat," she whispered back, leaning in close. "Not spoiled at all. Treats everybody the same. He's even nice to the fat kids and nerds like me, and it's not put-on." She pivoted slightly to shoot him another adoring look, but Elizabeth stopped her. "He doesn't have a steady," Cathy confided. "Just plays the field. Every girl in school would kill to go with him."

Which was precisely why they wouldn't get him. Elizabeth had learned a lot in her short life, and she knew all too well that men want what they can't have. So she concentrated on Cathy. "Do you have any brothers and sisters?"

"One younger sister, in the eighth grade," Cathy said with regret. "She makes my life miserable."

43

Still ignoring Howe and his harem as they approached him, Elizabeth laughed at what Cathy had said, then heard the flutter of feminine conversation subside abruptly. Her side tingled with the sense that she was being stared at.

When she turned, Howe Whittington was peering right at her, his expression lucid with approval and curiosity. And then he smiled at her.

Ho-lee cow!

That dazzling grin transformed him from good-looking to drop-dead, sexy, *gorgeous*. Everyone else in the hallway seemed to disappear.

Ho-lee cow!

Elizabeth's insides did a flip. It took all her strength not to melt on the spot, but she somehow managed to keep her expression unaffected.

She'd definitely been run over by the love-train, which only made things harder.

It wouldn't be easy, acting blasé, but she had to let him chase her till she landed him, no matter how hard it was or how long it took.

So instead of responding to Howe's come-hither look, she lifted her eyebrows and bestowed her own sparkling smile on Cathy. "I don't have time for boys. I have to study. And I want to join the Drama Club. Come on. Show me to my first class."

She didn't even glance Howe's way as they passed, but deep in her heart, Elizabeth knew one thing: Howe Whittington was a hunk of a heartthrob, and she was going to marry him one day.

Four years later, Elizabeth made sure she was studying across the library table from Howe Whittington's usual spot at the Emory Library when he came in to study. She'd spent all her spare time in the first two months of college quietly learning his schedule. Fortunately, he was just as regimented as she was. Then she'd started coincidentally turning up where he was. Despite the girls who'd thrown themselves at him, Howe seemed just as obsessed with study as she was.

But she wasn't getting anywhere, and she'd waited long enough. Howe was between debs, and it was time to make her move.

As he always did on Thursday afternoons, he came into the section and dropped his books on the table, then pulled a bottle of water from his book bag.

Elizabeth kept right on studying. She had plenty of work to do. She was taking six courses and had to keep her grades up for the scholarship.

Howe took some time to settle in, then finally sat with his book open in front of him.

Eyes on her own books, Elizabeth arched her back with a soft moan and stretched, lifting her

arms high above her head, fingers interlocked.
Then she closed her eyes and counted.

*One, two, three, four . . .*

"Do I know you?" Howe asked. " 'Cause if I
don't, I'd sure like to."

This time, Elizabeth responded. "Actually,
we went to the same high school. I'm here on
scholarship."

His expression warmed. "Ah. Beautiful *and*
brilliant. I'm impressed."

She cocked her head with a skeptical, "Does
that line usually work for you with the other
girls?"

Howe chuckled. "The other girls I know aren't
usually brilliant, just beautiful, but that doesn't
make for good conversation. I'm not really into
creme rinses and the latest shopping news."

Elizabeth chuckled back.

Howe's eyes narrowed as he pointed her way.
"Wait. Don't tell me." He studied her face.
"Mason? Morgan? No, that's not it."

Elizabeth turned her attention back to her
book.

"You were homecoming queen," Howe
announced. "I saw the picture in the paper. And
you were head of the Beta Society. National
Merit Scholar. Perfect sixteen hundred on your
SATs."

She looked up. "How do you know all that?"

"My mother sends me the local paper every

week," he admitted. "So I can keep up with what's going on back home," he said with definite sarcasm, revealing that he wasn't too anxious to go back there.

Perfect. Neither was she. Elizabeth extended her hand. "Elizabeth Mooney," she offered.

"Elizabeth. Of course." Howe shook his head with a grin. "Every girl in town wanted to be you."

"Every girl in town wanted to *have* you," she said archly.

His eyes sparked with interest. "Except you." He slid down till they were facing each other across the table. "Why was that?"

"I didn't have time for boys," she said evenly. "I still don't. I want to have my Ph.D. by twenty-four and go somewhere far, far away from Whittington."

Howe grinned, melting her insides. "Me, too." He looked at her with deepened interest. "Don't you think you could make just a little time for me? We could plan our escape."

*Our* escape . . . Perfect, perfect, perfect. Elizabeth looked him up and down, then relented. "Well, maybe a little. But only a little."

Smug, he leaned forward. "How about dinner tonight? Anywhere in the city you'd like to go."

He was so adorable, it was all she could do to keep from jumping him across the table. But she forced herself to look at her math textbook. "Sorry. Test tomorrow."

"Shhhhh!" somebody hissed from the stacks.

Howe dropped his voice. "This weekend, then," he said with confidence. "Give me your number."

"I don't have one," she lied, then gathered up her books. "I'll see you around."

Howe looked slightly stunned to see her rise to leave. "How will I find you?"

She gave him a seductive look. "If you're as smart as I think you are, you'll find a way."

Then she glided away, heart pounding half out of her chest.

He didn't follow, but she wasn't worried. And sure enough, the next day when she came back to her dorm room, it was filled with a dozen vases of red rosebuds, and a single card, asking, "Dinner Friday at Blue Fish? Seven," with Howe's phone number.

Elizabeth flopped backward onto her bed, breathing in the scent of the roses, and laughed for joy. At long last, it had begun.

When Howe arrived at the dorm lobby to pick her up Friday night, he had on an expensive navy blazer, white shirt, camel pants, and a tie. Too good-looking to live. And a subtle hint of lime came from his freshly shaven face.

Elizabeth wore a simple skirt she'd made to go with a sweater from Loehmann's, and fake-crocodile flats. "Hi," she said. "How did you know I'd go?"

Howe looked smug. "Because I talked to your roommate, and she said Blue Fish was your favorite restaurant."

"She's wrong," Elizabeth said mildly.

Howe's confident expression fell.

"It's Bones," Elizabeth corrected. "There's nothing like a nice, thick slab of red meat to fortify a girl." Her slow delivery had Howe hanging on her every word.

He coughed slightly, then stroked his tie. "Okay then. Red meat it is."

Howe had one of those new radio phones in his BMW convertible, and he called the restaurant to make sure they'd have a table. That done, they settled for the drive.

"So," he said, "how is it you've been in Whittington all this time, and I know so little about you?"

It was an innocent enough question, but the answer was anything but. "I don't like to talk about myself," she said without disapproval. "What about you? What's it like, being the crown prince of Whittington?"

Howe laughed. "Nobody's ever called me that before," he said. "At least, not to my face."

Elizabeth smiled at his good humor. "So, what is it like, being you?"

He cocked a gentle half-smile. "Not nearly as much fun as everybody else seems to think," he confessed. "For one thing, my parents have

49

been after me forever to come back to Whittington and take over the bank."

Elizabeth studied him. "And you don't want to?"

"In a word, no." He grinned at the traffic ahead of them.

"What would you do instead?"

"I'm going to be a lawyer," he said with a mixture of pride and defiance, "a damned good one. And I'm going to make a difference, somewhere far from Whittington, Georgia."

"And marry a deb," Elizabeth added with a spark of humor.

"God, no. You sound like my mother."

"Don't you like debs?" she teased.

"They're all right, I guess," he answered. "Just not for me. Society stuff is so boring." He stopped at a red light. "What about you? What do you want to do?"

"Get my masters in poli sci and become an independent woman of means. And make a difference." It was most of the truth. She just left out the part about marrying him.

"What? No marriage? No family?" he teased.

She looked away. "Family things have been . . . painful. I'd rather not discuss it." Maybe she'd tell him someday, but not till they were married, or at least engaged.

Howe turned left into the restaurant driveway and stopped for the valet parking. When he came around to get her out, she looked up into his big, blue eyes and took his hand.

"Do you know how beautiful you are?" he asked, drawing her close to his side once she was on her feet.

"You're pretty darned good-looking yourself," she said, lightly elbowing him in the side, then stepping ahead. "C'mon." She pulled him toward the entrance. "Let's have some good red meat and talk about sex, religion, and politics."

Howe was laughing when they came inside. "Whittington," he told the host as he kept a possessive eye on her.

Magic. This was magic, and Elizabeth could tell it was the same for him.

Her hidden hopes took flight, making her feel free and fun and flirty for the first time she could remember.

All eyes turned their way as the maître d' led them to a secluded corner booth in the dark, cozy steak house.

When Howe slid into the booth to sit beside her, the air between them was charged with chemistry, but Elizabeth reminded herself to take her time. Their courtship needed to unfold, slowly and gently, till they could trust each other.

So instead of jumping Howe Whittington's bones at Bones, Elizabeth talked to him about favorite books and movies. They agreed on some and disagreed on others, laughing all the way through their shrimp cocktails. Then they ate steak and talked about campus life and politics. Then they ate some more and talked of faith and philosophy. He loved a good, fair argument just as much as she did, and soon, she felt as if they'd been friends forever.

Magic.

Then she turned the topic to him, and Howe told her about his childhood sins, sneaking out of the house and escaping to play Tom Sawyer. Rubbing itching powder into his mother's girdle. (Elizabeth wished she could have been there to see haughty Mrs. Whittington when the powder started working.) And the time Howe "borrowed" their black housekeeper's baby because he wanted a brother. Mrs. Whittington must have *loved* that one!

Elizabeth listened well and kept the conversation on him, fascinated to finally get a glimpse inside the man she'd longed for all those years. He was just as wonderful as Cathy had said that day she'd first seen him. Honest. Funny. Humble. Kind. Who wouldn't love a man like that?

They'd demolished half the huge steaks when he admitted, "I always used to wonder if I was popular for myself, or for my money. I still do."

He was worried about her, her motives. But so frank about it.

Elizabeth took a long swig of her iced water, the only thing she ever drank. Then she placed her hand over his. "Give people some credit,

52

Howe. Your money and your family come with the package and helped make you who you are." Her eyes met his over the dim little light on the table. "I like who you are very much. I'm sure your friends do, too."

Howe leaned close to kiss her, but she deftly evaded him by asking softly, "What's good for dessert here?"

She wanted the magic to last as long as it could, their courtship evolving, slow and easy. She wouldn't be rushed. And she reminded herself that men want what they can't have.

For the first time in her life, she was truly happy, and Howe Whittington was the reason why. She would make him happy, too. They'd escape together, for a sparkling new life together. God willing, for the rest of their lives.

# Chapter 5

## The present: Piedmont Hospital, Atlanta, Georgia

It was a stroke, and Howe got worse.

He let out another of those awful laughs in the chopper, but still didn't regain consciousness. When they reached the hospital, the paramedics whisked him to Trauma One, where the doctors Howe's mother had summoned were waiting.

In the ordered confusion of the ER, the doctors assured Elizabeth that Howe was getting the best care possible, then banished her to the waiting room, where she struggled to collect herself.

Her heart still hammering from adrenaline, she paced the dark blue carpet, oblivious to the decorated Christmas tree and the minor Sunday afternoon disasters that crowded the waiting room.

There shouldn't be Christmas decorations in the emergency room. Not when people might be dying.

Howe couldn't die.

But he might.

Should she call the children?

No. What good would it do at this point? They couldn't see him. And he might pull through. No need to frighten them unnecessarily. She'd wait till she had a verdict from the doctors.

Or he died.

In all her fantasies of being respectably free of their empty marriage, she'd never imagined that losing him would even affect her, much less send her into a tailspin, but it did. Now that widowhood stared her in the face, it terrified her. Elizabeth was a wife and mother, part of a couple. She had a place in Whittington as Howe's wife. Without him, she would lose that place. Elizabeth couldn't be alone. Not in that huge old house that had never quite felt like her own. Not in the town her husband's family had controlled for over two centuries. She just couldn't.

And anyway, Whittington wasn't big enough for two Whittington widows. Without Howe there to buffer her, his mother would eat Elizabeth alive.

Once, Elizabeth had dreamed of escaping, but now, she raged inside that her mother-in-law had stolen that dream from her and from Howe. And even worse, Elizabeth had let her. Where would she go if she left? What would she do?

Chest tight, she wrapped her arms across it as if to shield herself from what might happen. With every unfocused step, she marked out what she needed to do: don't panic; think. He's still alive. Hold on to that. He's still alive.

Whittington men lived well into their nineties, with all their faculties intact.

Except his father, of course, she reminded herself with a jolt, who simply hadn't woken up three weeks after his fifty-ninth birthday.

That sat her down, good and proper, a wave of nausea welling through her. She stared unseeing through the automatic glass doors into the ER parking lot, conjuring with crystalline clarity the day they'd gotten the news that Howe's daddy had died. She might as well have buried her own hopes for happily-ever-after in the casket with him.

Howe's mother had glommed on to her son, saying he couldn't leave her alone to run the bank. She'd been so pitiful and so insistent that she'd worn Howe down until he'd abandoned his own dreams for his mother's sake. His one act of defiance was taking Elizabeth to Baltimore to marry her, then showing up with her at the funeral, his grandmother's diamond weighting the hand he gripped through the service, his mother's pent-up outrage colder and more brittle than the three-carat stone.

Howe had leaned on her, then. Shared his sense of loss, his frustration at having to abandon his hopes of practicing law away from his mother's interference. He'd been so close to Elizabeth.

She'd loved him so, believed that their love was strong enough to weather anything.

She hadn't realized that the Howe who had captured her heart would slowly disappear as he assumed his father's place.

Now he was the same age his father had been when he died, and suffering the same catastrophe.

The cell phone rang in Elizabeth's stylishly huge leather purse, sending her half out of her skin as it jarred her back to the present. Assuming it was Howe's mother, she reluctantly rummaged past her day planner, checkbooks, makeup, coupons, lipsticks, and combs, finally locating it by the pale glow of the screen. *Insufficient information* showed there. "Hello?"

P.J.'s familiar voice answered with unexpected intensity. "How is he? Tell me. I need to know."

How had *he* found out?

His emphatic tone grated on her. "He's alive. For now. That's all I know." She caught herself casting a guilty glance around to make sure Howe's mother was nowhere in sight. Why was P.J. calling her there?

When he'd pressed her to leave Howe the week before, she'd made it clear that there could never be more than a casual friendship between them—she would never do anything to embarrass her children—but obviously, P.J. hadn't accepted that, despite his promise to honor her wishes. "I can't really talk now," she told him.

"I'm sorry," he soothed. "I know you must be upset. I just couldn't stand thinking of your being there, all by yourself, in the middle of this. How are you?"

He always said just the right thing, but this time, his shift in demeanor triggered unexpected suspicion. "How did you find out?"

"Howard Mason was with me at the club shooting a few holes, and his sister called and told him," he explained. "She got it on the Baptist prayer chain."

And so it was in Whittington. Nobody could stub a toe without the whole town's finding out. If hospitalization was required, the prayer chains cranked up, which, in Elizabeth's opinion, were a lot more about gossip than prayer.

Still, the good Lord knew Howe could use all the prayers he could get, but considering her husband's coldhearted business dealings, Elizabeth couldn't help wondering how many of those people might be hoping he'd die instead of live. She'd have thought P.J. would be one of them, but the concern in his voice had sounded genuine.

"Let me come sit with you," he urged.

"No!" That was all she needed. The grapevine would go wild. "I thought I made it clear at lunch, I will not embarrass my children or tolerate anyone who does, including you. Caesar's wife, P.J. I mean it."

"Sorry," he said without conviction. "I was only trying to help. I'll call later to—"

"No," she told him. "Please don't. Howe's mother is on her way. Everything's crazy here. I'll call you when the dust settles and I'm alone. Do not call. I can't handle any more complications right now."

There was a pregnant pause on the other end of the line before he said, "Is that what I am, now, a complication? Last Tuesday, you said you wanted to be friends. Friends help each other when there's trouble. I was only trying to help."

Please, God. Of all times for him to get territorial. To push things. He knew perfectly well what would happen if he showed up there.

Elizabeth refused to address the issue. "I'll call. It may be tomorrow. I don't know. But I'll call." Or not.

As she closed the phone and dropped it back into her bag, a tap on her shoulder sent a shard of guilty alarm through her. She whirled to find a tall, handsome man with prematurely gray temples and wearing scrubs and jogging shoes beside her.

"Mrs. Whittington?" he said.

"Yes."

"I'm Christopher Clare, your husband's neurosurgeon." His kind young face studied hers with concern. "Are you all right?"

Her worst fear tumbled from her. "Howe—he's not . . ."

"He's stable," he was quick to reassure her. "I won't minimize the situation. Our scans indicate that your husband has a tumor in his frontal cortex. The good news is, it's small and appears to be regular and contained. But the blood supply to the tumor ruptured, causing a stroke. We need to operate. They've taken him up and are prepping him now."

A brain tumor. *And* a stroke.

Elizabeth's heart turned inside out.

Was it hereditary? Charles! Her son. Would it—?

Dr. Clare proffered a clipboard holding a permission form with Howe's name printed at the top. "I know this is a lot to assimilate, but we're doing everything we can to pull him through with as little damage as possible."

Damage. Brain damage? Oh, God.

Dr. Clare handed her the clipboard. "This is the authorization form for the surgery. The procedure will be delicate because of the area that's involved, but so far, all his reflexes are normal, which is good. We won't be able to assess the full extent of any damage till he wakes up. If everything goes well, that could be in just a few days."

Elizabeth's pulse pounded in her ears, and everything around her suddenly seemed muted, far away. She stared at the permission form, two legal pages crammed with mouse-print spelling out reams of dire complications.

*Minimize* the damage.

God, no.

Elizabeth thought in black-and-white—Howe would be okay, or he would die. The thought that he might survive impaired hadn't occurred to her.

She wished with all her being for her strong, steady son Charles to lean on, but Charlottesville, Virginia, was a day away, by air or by car. Would it be selfish to call him in? He was scheduled to take his bar exams soon.

Patricia was closer in Athens, but all she would bring with her was drama, the last thing Elizabeth needed.

Elizabeth felt the doctor take gentle hold of her arm. "Perhaps you ought to sit down," he said, guiding her to an open seat. Then he sat with her, leaving an empty chair between them, and nodded toward the permission form. "Just sign at the *X*. I'll be happy to answer any questions you have."

Questions? She stared, uncomprehending, at the blocks of tiny print, and a bubble of ironic hysteria rose inside her. Was he kidding? Who could think of questions at a time like this, much less give informed consent?

When "the best neurosurgeon in the state" said somebody needed brain surgery, who in their right mind would say no?

Dr. Clare was being very patient, very kind. She had no right to take out her frustration on him, but really.

Brain damage. Brain damage. Brain damage.

Elizabeth had a searing vision of Howe restrained in a wheelchair, gaunt and drooling, his eyes vacant and a huge, livid scar across his shaved head.

Her breaths came in rapid pants, and she had to clamp her lips to keep from falling apart. She used to pray that he'd be kinder to her, notice her more, care for her, but all that paled to insignificance. *Please, God, don't let him have brain damage.* Howe would rather die than suffer such an indignity. Anything but that.

She gripped the clipboard and did her best to sign, but her usually perfect script came out a barely legible scrawl. The clipboard wobbled as she returned it, and the pen fell off.

"Don't worry," the doctor said, bending to retrieve it. "I'll get it."

Brain tumor. Brain tumor. Brain tumor.

Cancer? Was it cancer?

"Can I get you anything?" kind Dr. Clare asked.

"Just help my husband," she heard herself say.

"Someone will come take you to the intensive care waiting room, where you can use the phone and wait. I'll call you there as soon as we know anything." He scanned the crowded room. "Is anyone with you?"

"No." She needed to call Charles. Hands shaking, she groped for her cell phone. "I have to call my children. They'll want to know. My son Charles . . ." She took comfort in just saying his name. "I need my son." Where *was* the damned phone? "He's a senior at UVA law school," she rattled out. "Such a lovely campus. Howe went to Emory, but never got to take the bar because his father . . ." *Died.* Don't say *died.* "Howe had to take over the bank, instead. But Charles will practice. He'll make a wonderful lawyer."

She was babbling, but couldn't help it. Where *was* that phone? "My daughter's at Georgia, majoring in sorority. A freshman. She never answers when it's me. I'll have to leave a message." She finally felt the elusive phone and snatched it out. "There!"

"I have to go now, so I'll leave you to your calls." As the doctor rose, Sheriff Eddie Spruill's patrol car barreled around the corner from the front of the hospital, sirens blaring in violation of every municipal noise ordinance. Dr. Clare raised his voice to be heard. "I'll call when we know anything. This could take a while, so don't get nervous if you don't hear from me. I promise to let you know as soon as there's anything to tell."

Right behind him, Augusta Whittington made a beeline through the automatic doors.

"Christopher Clare!" She pointed at him as if he were an escaping felon. "Why aren't you taking care of my son?"

He acknowledged her with a nod, but didn't stop. "Hello, Mrs. Whittington. I'm on my way to do just that." He swiped an ID, then escaped into the emergency department, leaving Elizabeth to explain the situation to her mother-in-law.

Elizabeth faced Mrs. Whittington and motioned to the seat the doctor had vacated. "Sit down, Augusta." It was the first time she'd ever addressed Howe's mother with such familiarity, but since she was about to tell the woman her only child had a brain tumor, Elizabeth decided they should be on a first-name basis at last.

Surprisingly docile, Mrs. Whittington subsided, her back erect to brace herself for what she was about to hear. "It's a stroke, isn't it? I'm sure of it. That's what killed his father."

How could she be so sure? She hadn't allowed an autopsy. But Elizabeth was past such petty concerns. She had a dreadful bond to share. "Yes, it was a stroke. Caused by the blood supply to a small tumor in his frontal cortex." She pointed to the area the doctor had indicated above her eyebrow. "They're prepping Howe for surgery right now."

Augusta blanched, shooting to her feet with bald panic in her expression. "I have to see him."

Her blue-veined, manicured hands clenched. "They can't take him till I see him. I didn't get to say good-bye to his father. Dear God, let me have that, at least."

Elizabeth surprised herself by rising and putting her arms around the woman who had never thought her good enough for precious Howe. To her surprise, Augusta's stiff posture relented, but only a little. "He's probably in the operating room already," Elizabeth explained. "Dr. Clare just came out to tell me what was happening and have me sign the authorization."

Augusta glared at her with fierce determination, as if willing Howe to get well could make it so. "Chris Clare is the best, bar none. Howe will have the best."

"Thank you for calling Dr. Clare. And the others," Elizabeth said, surprised at how deeply she meant it. "And for the helicopter. The paramedics said it probably saved his life."

Before breaking free to straighten her already perfect silk shirtwaist, Augusta patted Elizabeth's arm—a sole gesture of affection in all the years they'd known each other. "My Howe deserves the best."

Under other circumstances, Elizabeth would have taken that as a subtle dig at her own undesirable origins, but in that place, in that dreadful hour, they were equals, and she rose above it. If Charles were the one in the operating room, she'd feel the same way Augusta felt about Howe.

A uniformed volunteer approached them from the hallway to the main hospital. "Mrs. Whittington?"

Both of them answered at once. "Yes?"

The woman looked from one to the other. "If you ladies will please follow me, I'll take you to the intensive care waiting room. Dr. Clare will call down from surgery as soon as he has anything to report, but his procedures can take a long time, so don't let that worry you. He's very meticulous, which is a good thing, when it's neurosurgery."

They followed through a series of spaces and hallways till the volunteer led them to a small room with cushioned chairs, a TV, and a desk that held a telephone. To Elizabeth's relief, there were no other people there.

At least their drama wouldn't play out in front of strangers.

After the volunteer left them alone, Augusta sank to a chair, her spine still unrelenting. "Thank God there's no one else in here."

"My thoughts, exactly." Elizabeth went to the TV and changed the program from *Judge Judy* to a nature show on PBS, then took a chair several seats away from her mother-in-law.

Silence stretched brittle between them till she remembered aloud, "Oh, God. The children." She started hunting for the phone again, which had been swallowed back into the bowels of her purse.

"You can call Charles," Augusta announced, opening her slim crocodile clutch. "I'll break the news to Patricia. She'll be heartbroken. You know how she adores her daddy." *Far more than she adores her mother,* Elizabeth silently finished for her, then let it go.

"Good idea." Frankly, Elizabeth dreaded telling Patricia. Unfortunately, her daughter took after Elizabeth's father—the life of the party, all impulse and emotions, and devil take the effect it had on anybody else. Elizabeth loved her, but despaired of her manipulative ways and lack of focus.

Augusta drew her cell phone from her purse and stared at it as if it were a snake.

Elizabeth volunteered, "Her number's—"

"I know her number," Augusta snapped. "It's just this contraption that takes me a minute." She dismissed Elizabeth with a waggle of her crowded gold charm bracelets. "Don't look over my shoulder. Call Charles."

Elizabeth couldn't let Charles get the news the way Howe had about his father. If they were going to lose Howe, she prayed there would be time for Charles to be there. She pressed speed dial for Charles's cell. To her vast relief, he answered.

"Hey, Mama. What's up?"

How could she tell him? "Your father's sick,

Charles," she said quietly. "He's in surgery at Piedmont. I think it would be best if you came home right away. Do I need to call the dean? I know your bar exam is just a few weeks from now, and—"

"I'll get the first plane out," he said, his tone clipped. "Don't worry about the bar exam. What is it, Mama? I want to know."

Always the straight shooter, her wonderful boy, as direct as his father was oblique. A strong boy. And good to the bone. "It's a tumor," she said, "a small one, in the front of his brain. The blood supply ruptured, causing a stroke, but the doctor said the mass appeared to be regular and contained." The possibility of cancer hung unspoken between them. "Your grandmother got us airlifted to Piedmont and called in Dr. Clare, a wonderful neurosurgeon."

The children didn't know much about their other grandmother, safely tucked away in a Clearwater condo provided by Howe, and Elizabeth meant to keep it that way. "Gamma says he's the best."

"Good." Charles's voice strengthened. "Don't worry, Mama. Dad will be all right. He always lands on his feet. You just hang in there till I get there. One of the guys can take me to the airport. I'll charter a plane if I have to." He'd gotten his pilot's license at sixteen, and his commercial license at eighteen. "I'll get Sam to meet me when I get to Atlanta." Charles's best friend, Sam, went to Emory.

"Don't speed," she cautioned. "And make sure the plane's safe. I couldn't stand it if something happened to you, too. I'll see you when you get here."

"I'll be careful." A brief pause. "Do you want me to call Patti?"

Elizabeth glanced over to see Augusta pressing the buttons on her cell. "Thanks, but Gamma's doing that for me."

"I'll see you soon. I love you, Mama-lama." He used the name he'd called her as a child, and it almost undid her.

"I love you, too." Her eyes welled with tears, not for herself, but for the loss her son was facing. Howe hadn't been a demonstrative father, but he'd been a good one, and Charles loved him. *Please, God, keep him safe. Keep them both safe.*

She closed the phone, suddenly feeling hollow.

"Patricia, this is your grandmother," Augusta enunciated. "Call me at once. There's been a family emergency. My cell phone number is . . ." She glared briefly at Elizabeth. "What in blazes is it? I never call myself."

"Four-oh-four, five-five-five, eight-eight-two-one," Elizabeth summoned from somewhere in the obscure reaches of her mind, though how she remembered was beyond her.

Augusta repeated the numbers, then said good-bye and held the phone out for a critical assessment before finding the disconnect button. "I don't know why that child doesn't answer. She might as well not have a cell phone."

Talk about the pot calling the kettle black. Augusta rarely even turned hers on, considering it beneath her to be at the beck and call of everybody no matter where she was.

Elizabeth glanced to the clock on the wall. Three-fifteen on a sunny Sunday December afternoon in Athens. Patricia could be anywhere.

Then she jumped when the phone in her hand rang. The screen showed her daughter's number. "Hello?"

"Mama?" Patricia's tone was the one she'd had when she was little and afraid, waking Elizabeth's maternal emotions. "What's wrong? Please tell me Daddy's okay."

"Oh, sweetheart," Elizabeth told her. "I'm so sorry, but your daddy's had a stroke. He's in surgery at Piedmont, but he's in the very best of hands. There was a small tumor at the front of his brain—"

Patricia lost it. "Oh, God! A stroke?" she sobbed out. "That's what killed Granddaddy! Daddy can't die. He can't. He's the only one besides Gamma who really loves me!" The last hit Elizabeth hard, square in the sternum. "He can't die, Mama. He can't. Don't let him."

Shaken, Elizabeth managed, "Sweetie, do you have a friend who can drive you down here?" Patricia was reckless under the best of circumstances. "I don't think you should drive right now, but I do think you need to come."

"Cathy!" Patricia shrieked away from the receiver. "Get your car! I need you to take me to Atlanta. My daddy's dying!"

For once, she wasn't exaggerating.

Her voice came back on the line. "I'm coming. Where? You said where?"

"Piedmont Hospital, at Peachtree and Collier. We're in the intensive care waiting room. But don't speed. There's time," Elizabeth said, unaware how prophetic that would turn out to be. "The doctor said the surgery could take hours and hours. Be safe, honey. Don't let anything bad happen to you."

"If Daddy dies," her daughter wailed, "I might as well die, too."

Elizabeth didn't even try to address that. "Just be safe, honey. I love you. We'll be waiting."

She ended the call, then turned to her waiting mother-in-law. "He can't die," she whispered, echoing Patricia's desperation, the tears overtaking her at last. "He can't." Grief for all they'd lost and all that never had been overtook her, and she broke down.

Augusta peered at her with consternation. "You love him?" Clearly, the idea didn't com-

71

pute. "Even after all these years? Even after . . . everything?"

So she knew about the hookers.

"God help me," Elizabeth managed through her tears, shocked by the truth of it. "I do." But how could she? She'd laid that all to rest so long ago.

Augusta rose and took the seat beside her. Awkward, she patted at her shoulder. "There, there. We mustn't make a spectacle. Howell wouldn't want us to. Dignity. We have to be strong for the children."

All the frustration of the past few hours suddenly found a focus, and Elizabeth turned on her mother-in-law. "Like you were for Howe when his father died? Do you have any idea how your coldness about that hurt him? Well, it did." Anger replaced the sorrow that had gripped her. "He hated you for that. He told me so." Augusta flinched, but Elizabeth took no satisfaction from it. "I hope my children do see me cry for their father. At least they'll know I cared what happened to him."

Her mother-in-law stood. "I refuse to listen to such hateful talk. Call me when you learn anything, and send Patricia to me. I'll be in the other waiting room." She left without a backward glance.

Even when attacked, she just gave orders.

Numb, Elizabeth sat back to wait, alone.

Two hours later, Patricia arrived. By then, Elizabeth had calmed down enough to comfort her daughter, then send her to her grandmother.

Another hour passed, during which Elizabeth escaped into a soggy sleep, curled in a chair in front of the droning TV. Then someone was shaking her. "Mrs. Whittington?"

She looked up to see Dr. Clare standing over her, a concerned look on his face. He'd said he'd call, but there he was, in person.

A chill settled to her marrow. "He's dead, isn't he?"

"No," Dr. Clare hastened to reassure her. "He's holding his own." He smiled. "Your husband is obviously a very strong man."

*Thank you, God!* Elizabeth crumpled in relief. She could almost believe that everything was going to be all right. Then the words *brain damage* brought her spine erect. "The damage . . . ?"

Dr. Clare met her frightened gaze with frankness. "The surgery went very well. The frozen section sent to the lab for immediate testing indicated that the tumor is benign and very slow-growing, but we'll have to wait for the biopsy results for confirmation. That should come in by Friday. The good news is, the growth was regular and well encapsulated. Could have been there for decades. As for what damage the rupture of the tumor's blood supply might have caused, we won't know for certain till your husband wakes up."

Elizabeth wanted to hope for the best, but was afraid to. "And when will that be?"

"Not for at least several days. We'll be keeping him sedated to try to minimize the swelling. Everybody reacts differently to this type of trauma. We'll just have to wait and see. Take it one day at a time."

"But he's out of the woods, so far?" she asked.

"So far, so good," he said, patting her upper arm. "Let's just pray it stays that way."

"When can we see him?"

"Once he's settled in ICU, the nurse will notify you when you can look in on him. After that, you might want to get a room nearby and get some rest, yourself. This is going to be a long week."

"His mother . . ." Elizabeth couldn't help putting herself in Augusta's shoes. "She really wants to see him. And our daughter." Why was she explaining? "Our son's on his way."

The doctor remained kind and patient. "As soon as he's settled and stable, you can each peek in on him, but he needs to rest."

As if he could in intensive care.

The doctor's pager went off, and he looked at the screen. "Sorry. I have another emergency." As he rose, he handed her a card. "Here's my PA's name and direct number. If you have any concerns or specific questions, please call him.

Families often see signs of trouble before the staff does, and I want to know right away if anything goes wrong." He rose to leave. "Now, if you'll excuse me . . ."

"Please, go. And thank you."

She'd scarcely been alone a minute, collecting herself before braving Augusta and Patricia, when Charles strode in and wrapped her in a warm bear hug. "Hey there, Mama-lama. What's the latest?"

Tears of gratitude and relief sheeted down her cheeks as she related what the doctor had just told her. "Now we just have to wait."

Charles rubbed his palms up and down her back, then gave her another, briefer, squeeze before he drew away. "Where's Patti? And Gamma?"

"Powwowed in the other waiting room." She didn't need to explain. Charles had long since wised up to the way things were, but he'd accepted the situation with a grace Elizabeth hadn't been able to muster. "Let's go tell them."

Her son took her hand, and fortified by his presence, she accompanied him into enemy territory to deliver the news.

Then they went, one by one, to see son, father, and husband lying pale and bandaged, connected by a maze of wires and tubes to monitors and IVs.

The blank peace of his expression gave them all comfort.

And then the waiting started.

At first, they all stayed at the hospital, taking turns getting food and necessities, fielding calls from church friends and Howe's employees and Women's Club and Garden Club and Sewing Club and Rotary members. And P.J., who seemed surprisingly concerned that Howe might not wake up, which seemed odd to Elizabeth, considering P.J.'s recent declaration of love.

Elizabeth told him, and everyone else, the same thing: Howe was holding his own, and they just had to wait for him to wake up.

Faithful servants Pearl and Thomas packed for the four of them and brought their things, then stood weeping quietly by Howe's bed before returning to watch over the houses back in Whittington.

But as the days wore on and Howe remained in his coma, the concerned calls and flowers slacked off, and Elizabeth took the doctor's advice and got them rooms at a nearby hotel. Augusta kept vigil on Wednesdays and Thursday nights. Charles took Tuesdays; Patricia took Sundays and Mondays, and Elizabeth sat up on Fridays and Saturdays. Their nights off were short, and the days at the hospital stretched longer and longer, but still, they saw no change.

And so their worlds were reduced to a small waiting room and one visit an hour beside a narrow bed in a tiny curtained space where the body of her husband lay.

Elizabeth did her best to distract herself and the children in the times between: reading, doing crossword puzzles, teaching Patricia to knit, and playing cards. She brought small Christmas gifts and treats for the dedicated staff, and did everything she could to make their jobs easier, but before she knew it, Christmas had come and gone, and the doctors moved Howe to a regular room, where she and the children and Augusta could offer him more stimulation to try to help him wake up.

After another two weeks passed with no change, the hospital social worker came in and said Howe needed to be moved to a long-term skilled-care facility.

Augusta and Patricia went ballistic, but blessedly, Charles took them out of the room so Elizabeth could have some peace to digest the idea that her husband was being sent to a nursing home.

"Did Dr. Clare order this?" she asked the woman.

"No, ma'am. Mr. Whittington's insurance did. They only pay for a certain number of days once he's stable." The woman was gentle with her, but what she was saying spawned a wave of frustration inside Elizabeth. "It's not just the insurance, though," the woman went on. "We have a shortage of beds, and those we have are needed for acute care. Once a patient no longer meets that criteria, we need to make the bed available for someone who does." She cocked her head in concern. "If you'd like, I could go over some of the options your insurance covers. There are many good facilities in the area. Or I could look into something closer to your home . . ."

Elizabeth flashed on a vision of long halls peopled by figures slumped in wheelchairs, surrounded by the stifling reek of stale urine and unwashed bodies and bad food.

"Mrs. Whittington?" the social worker said. "How can I help you best right now?"

Elizabeth knew it wasn't the woman's fault. She was just doing her job. But still, she wanted to slap her. Wanted to throw a screaming hissy fit, right then and there. But she didn't, because it might embarrass her children, and she'd vowed on the day they were born never to do so.

"I . . . Could you please just come back tomorrow? I want to check on some things before I make a decision." She would take him home. They had money for round-the-clock care. She could rent the equipment. Surely she could find someone to help out, some way to spare Howe the indignity of a nursing home.

The social worker hesitated, then relented. "Very well. I'll notify the financial office that you're assuming the cost of his care for now. I'll come back in the morning."

After she left, Elizabeth called Dr. Clare's PA immediately, but both he and the doctor were in surgery, so she left a message. It wasn't really an emergency.

But how could she possibly make all the arrangements to transfer Howe to the new facility in a day?

Overwhelmed, she sat beside her comatose husband and put her face in her hands and started to cry, from exhaustion as much as outrage.

If he wasn't going to wake up, maybe it would have been better if Howe had died.

The social worker reappeared at the door and knocked. "Mrs. Whittington?"

What now? Elizabeth looked up, wiping the tears from her cheeks. "Yes?"

"I just checked and found out a brand-new neurological hospital just opened near Emory, and it offers specialized long-term coma care. Cutting-edge. They're doing lots of studies using all the latest techniques, and word is, they're already getting some dramatic results."

Elizabeth latched on to that like a falling climber grabs a limb. "What's the name? Who do I call?" She groped for her cell phone.

The social worker read the phone number from a small piece of scratch paper, and Elizabeth stored it in her phone.

"Thank you. Thank you so much." Elizabeth let herself hope again, despite the shadow of permanent damage that still edged everything.

Then she heard a sound from the bed.

"Nnngh!"

She looked over and saw her husband shift his hand. "Howe!" His eyes were open. Just a little, but they were open, and the pupils were moving. "Dear God, he's waking up." She rang for the nurse, punching the button again and again, for the first time since they'd moved into the room.

"Yes, Mrs. Whittington?" blared over the speaker.

"Come quick. My husband's waking up."

"I'll be right there."

The social worker motioned to the corridor. "I saw your family at the end of the hallway. Would you like me to go tell them?"

"Please. And get the nurse." Elizabeth grasped Howe's hand. "Howe, can you hear me? It's Elizabeth. Wake up, Howe! Wake up."

His eyes remained slitted, but there was no further movement. His hand remained slack in hers.

"Squeeze my hand, Howe. Come on. You can do it. Squeeze my hand."

She thought she felt a faint pressure. Or was it just her imagination, willing her to believe it?

The nurse came in and checked the leads to his head and the monitors. "Let's see what we have here."

"He spoke," Elizabeth told her, her heart racing.

The nurse looked skeptical. "What did he say?"

"Well, it wasn't a word, or anything, but he made a sound and moved his hand. He hasn't done that before."

The nurse checked the tape from the EKG, and when she looked back up, Elizabeth saw pity in her eyes. "Patients who've been in Mr. Whittington's condition for this length of time rarely just wake up. Depending on the effects of their injuries, coming out of coma can be a long, gradual process, and sometimes a difficult one. Many move and make sounds, even open their eyes while they're still comatose. Some even respond to simple commands. But that doesn't necessarily indicate they're conscious."

Seeing Elizabeth's disappointment, she added, "We can take it as a hopeful sign that he might be beginning the process. Please call me if he shows any other signs. We're all rooting for him. And for you."

The door swished open, and the children preceded Augusta into the room.

"Daddy?" Patricia was flushed with excitement as she flew to take his hand. "Daddy, it's your Patti-girl. Open your eyes. Please, Daddy. We've all been so worried about you. Please open your eyes."

The nurse shot Elizabeth a sidelong glance,

then repeated what she'd just said, verbatim, making it sound canned to Elizabeth's ears.

She wondered how many times the woman had said the same thing to desperate families.

Elizabeth told the others that she'd decided to send Howe to the new hospital.

It came as no surprise when her mother-in-law balked. "Latest advances? What latest advances? Do you mean to make a guinea pig of my son? Well, I won't let you. We'll take him home, where he belongs. I can move in and help care for him."

Over Elizabeth's dead body! She managed to remain calm, but it wasn't easy. "I know you're worried about him, Augusta, but I'm his wife, and I think this is the best course for now."

Livid, her mother-in-law shot daggers in Elizabeth's direction. "Come, Patricia. The strain of all this has obviously affected your mother's ability to make rational decisions. I'll have a talk with Dr. Clare. I'm sure he'll agree with me that Howell will get the best care at home."

For once, Elizabeth didn't back down. "It doesn't matter what Dr. Clare thinks," she said with deadly calm. "I know you're frantic for Howe. We all are. But I'm his next of kin, and this decision is mine to make, not yours." She met Augusta's anger with quiet conviction. "I want him to go to the new hospital. If Dr. Clare won't refer him, I'll find someone who will." She knew Dr. Clare would cooperate, but wanted to make sure Augusta understood what was what. "There will be no more discussion about the matter. It's for the best. I'm sure of it."

"Oh, you're sure, are you?" Augusta glared at Elizabeth. "Some *stranger* tells you about this new place, and suddenly you're sure it's best for Howell?"

Charles stepped in to defend Elizabeth with, "I love you, Gamma, but if Mama wants to take Daddy there, we all need to respect her decision."

Augusta grabbed Patricia's elbow. "We'll just see about that. Come, Patricia."

Patricia cast her mother, then Howe, a troubled glance, then did as her grandmother commanded. "I'll call you later, Mama."

Charles regarded Elizabeth with concern. "Why don't you let me drop you off for dinner somewhere nearby? I'll come back and stay with Dad. It'll do you good to get away from here for a while."

She could use a nice, big salad, and getting out sounded great. "Good idea, but I think I'd rather walk. Clear my head." The exercise would do her good.

Charles's face clouded. "I don't know. This isn't Whittington, Mom. It's Atlanta, and it's starting to get dark. I don't think you should—"

Though she appreciated his concern, she'd have none of that. "I promise to stay out of dark alleys, but Houston's is just a couple of blocks away, and there are always plenty of people around. I'll be fine."

He frowned. "Call a cab for the ride back, at least. Please. To quote you, 'I couldn't stand it if something happened to you, too.' "

"I'll think about it." Which meant no. She needed to walk, to stretch her legs, to make a break for it, no matter how brief. She gave her son a hug. "I won't be long. Call if you need me . . . for anything." She paused in the doorway. "Want me to bring you something back?"

A law book in his hand, Charles settled beside his father to study. "Nope. I'll catch a buffalo burger later at Ted's Montana."

Downstairs, Elizabeth stepped out into the cold, clean air and exhaled the pall of the hospital, then breathed deep of the scent of pine and fresh-mown rye grass. It smelled like hope. Maybe the new hospital could help Howe and end the state of suspended animation they'd all been in.

At the end of the hospital's north wing, she crossed the driveway to the cut-through to Peachtree Street, then took the sidewalk toward Houston's, the Shepherd Center on her left. It felt good to stretch her legs.

As she neared the sign for the center, she became aware of pounding strides approaching from behind her. Before she could turn to register the jogger, she was crowded hard against the sign by a tall, hooded male figure.

Frozen with fear, she couldn't even scream.

"Didn't anybody ever tell you it isn't safe for a beautiful woman to walk alone in this town?" a gruff, familiar voice demanded.

"P.J.!" Elizabeth reared back in fury and flailed away at him. "You jerk! Didn't anybody ever tell you it's inexcusable to scare somebody half to death?"

"Whoa," he said, deftly evading the majority of her blows. "I didn't intend to scare you, just surprise you. I swear."

"You know what's paved with good intentions," she shouted. He tried to put his arm around her, but she didn't let him, stomping toward Houston's. "Leave me alone. I mean it! Scram."

"I'm sorry, Elizabeth. Really." He came up beside her, maintaining a respectful distance. "At least let me buy you dinner to make up for it. I promise, I'll behave."

After that juvenile stunt, Elizabeth wasn't in the mood for male company, period. "Just go home, P.J. I'm tired, and I'm hungry, and I didn't need this. Go home."

P.J. reached over and drew her close to his side, his touch gentle but insistent, and his tone convincing when he said, "Really, Elizabeth, I'm sorry. I was stupid. Insensitive. I never, ever want to scare or hurt you. Please, can you forgive

85

me?" Her posture relented before she could. Taking it as a sign, he cradled her in his arms. "I don't know what I'd do if you didn't forgive me."

Her anger let down, leaving her almost too exhausted to stand on her own. So she put her arm around his waist and leaned on his strength, giving him one last little poke in the stomach. "Okay. But you'll have to buy me an appetizer and dessert."

He stroked her back, his pace matching hers. "Okay. And it's a small price to pay for your company."

It felt so good to be with someone who valued her, even though he'd pulled that stupid stunt. But he was a guy, and guys did things like that. Except Howe. Howe never did anything rash. Maybe things would have been better if he had. "Believe it or not, P.J.," she said, "it's really good to see you. I get so lonely sitting by Howe's bed day after day."

P.J. gave her a squeeze. "I'll always be here for you. Always."

To her surprise, Elizabeth took great comfort in that. "Thanks. Let's eat."

# Chapter 6

Though the new facility worked diligently on Howe's body to keep his muscles from atrophying, after five months there, Elizabeth finally saw that he was losing ground. Charles, who had managed to graduate with flying colors and pass the bar in spite of everything, helped her summon up the courage to let the doctors try the experimental procedure they'd recommended.

P.J. had argued for it all along, saying she had to free herself from limbo so she could consider a new life with him. As the months had dragged by with nothing to do but sit beside Howe's bed and mull over the wreckage of their marriage, the prospect of freedom and a fresh start looked better and better.

But that wasn't why she decided to let the doctors experiment on her husband. Deep inside, something still bound her to Howe in a way he hadn't been bound to her for years. She made the decision for his sake, and the children's. If there was any hope they could have their father back, she had to take the chance.

So she was there by her husband's side the morning of June fifth when the first treatment was administered. She hadn't told the children, not wanting to disappoint them if the treatment failed. And she certainly hadn't told Augusta.

The doctors, residents and interns in tow, set up a camera to record what happened—or didn't —then warned her for the jillionth time that it often took several treatments to see results, and even then, reactions varied from minor to manic.

"Just do it," she said, worn out with second-guessing herself.

After the injections, Elizabeth took Howe's hand and settled in to wait and pray.

The doctors left a resident to monitor Howe's reaction. Quiet minutes ticked away, then stretched to hours, and nurses came in to change the videotapes, but nothing happened.

By the time two o'clock rolled by, both the resident and Elizabeth had begun to doze. Leaning forward, she laid her head on Howe's bed. She was just on the verge of tumbling down the rabbit hole to her usual, frustrating, busy dreams, when pain and motion brought her upright.

"Lillibuh," Howe gasped, gripping her arm so hard she almost cried out.

Thank God! He was awake! He could speak. He recognized her.

The resident summoned the others, who came running.

"Yes, it's me, Lillibet. I'm here." Howe had a future. *She* had a future, with him or without him. She leaned close and studied his face. His eyes communicated happy recognition mixed with fear and confusion.

By then, there were three doctors and as many nurses in the room, and they all started buzzing at once.

Howe let out a thundering fart, then looked at Elizabeth with glowing adoration, pulling her close. "God, I miss you," he said, kissing her hair as tears ran down his cheeks.

She couldn't believe he was so alert, so articulate. Maybe it really *was* a miracle.

"When was the last time we made love?" His voice was hoarse and insistent, loud enough for everyone to hear. "I want to make love to you, Lillibet."

After all those years, he gets the hots for her *now?*

On camera! In front of all those people, with more doctors and nurses crowding in every minute! Horrified, Elizabeth drew back, but Howe wouldn't let go of her hand. "Howe, you —you've been very ill," she stammered out. "You're in the hospital, and the doctors are here."

"I don't care where we are." He didn't look at the doctors. "Tell them to leave, so we can be alone. Lizzie"—Lizzie! Where had *that* come from?—"I want you more than anything in this world." One look at the sheet across his hips confirmed his statement, in spades.

Mortified, Elizabeth glanced to the doctors. "Is that normal?"

The dark-haired doctor in charge murmured back, "As we explained, a certain percentage of the patients have difficulty controlling their emotions and appetites at first."

Howe held on tighter with a plaintive, "Lizzie!"

"Do not call me 'Lizzie,' " she snapped at him. "I hate that name!"

Suppressing smiles, the other doctors and residents scribbled busily away on their notepads.

Howe tried to sit up, then collapsed against the pillows. "Whew. Feels like I've been hit by a train." He leered at her. "But I can still make love." He grabbed her hands and pulled. "C'mon, Lizzie. We're married. It's okay."

She'd prayed for years to get back the man he'd once been, but this wasn't the Howe she'd fallen in love with. He had never been so coarse and demanding. God only knew what he'd been doing with his whores all those years up in Atlanta, but he'd never talked about it.

Elizabeth tried to pull free of his grasp, but he was too strong. "Howe, let me go," she ordered. "You don't know what you're saying." How could he be so strong? Regardless of the physical therapy, he'd been in bed for months.

Stifled laughter erupted from some of the

underdoctors as many hands came forward to free her.

"No!" Howe protested when they pulled her loose, his expression burning as he fought them. "Lizzie, don't go. Don't leave me. I have to have you."

Elizabeth stepped back out of range and rubbed her arm. Howe hadn't wanted her since he'd moved out of their bedroom when Patti was a toddler! And what was with this *Lizzie* business? He'd never called her "Lizzie."

"Mr. Whittington," one of the doctors told him, "you're having a reaction to the treatment we just gave you. Try to rest. This compulsion will pass, I promise." Oh, really? How could he be sure? "Your wife is here, and she's not leaving, but you need to rest now. There's plenty of time for the two of you to be alone later."

"Wha . . . no." Howe wrestled against their restraining hands. "I need her *now*."

The neurologist drew Elizabeth safely out of range while the others kept Howe in his bed.

"Get off me," Howe protested, his strength failing as the adrenaline ebbed. "She's my wife. I want my wife. God, if I don't have her, my dick's going to explode!"

Oh, sweet Lord in heaven! Howe had never talked that way in his life!

"Sorry about that," the neurologist said. "We've

only seen this particular manifestation once before. You two must be very close."

"Not exactly," she said in a masterpiece of understatement. "My husband never talked that way in his life. Ever. No matter what, he was a gentleman."

"Lizzie," Howe said, his arm extended weakly her way. "Please. I need you." Then he went limp, along with the rising under the sheet.

Breathing hard, all of them watched Howe and waited for what came next, but when minutes passed with no further activity, they all relaxed a bit.

"He's sleeping now," the doctor said, indicating the EEG. "When he wakes up, we'll want to do a brain scan so we can compare it to the one we did last week."

Elizabeth straightened her clothes and tried to recover her decorum, which wasn't easy under the wry scrutiny of the watching medical corps.

Was there a male equivalent for the term *nymphomaniac?* "Is he going to be the way he just was when he wakes up again?" she asked. "Because if he is, I'd like to see some restraints. And a prescription for saltpeter."

The underdoctors exchanged amused glances.

What if he tried to jump her when nobody was around? As always, she projected the worst and tried to compensate for it. Howe had never liked condoms—birth control had always been her responsibility—so there was no telling what his whores had exposed him to.

"Is he out of the coma for good?" she asked the doctor.

"We can't be certain," he qualified, "but there's a high probability that he is. This is all so new. We're only talking forty-five patients over the past eight months who've responded to the drug so dramatically. But so far, those who have woken up with such high function haven't relapsed." He offered her a consoling nod. "There's an adjustment period for them, and for their families, that varies from patient to patient, but the results have been good."

Adjustment. That was putting it mildly.

Elizabeth smoothed her hair, compelled to explain, yet wishing she didn't feel the need. "My husband was a very dignified and private person. I'd hate to see him embarrass himself again." Or her.

*Lizzie,* for God's sakes.

*My dick's going to explode.* Really! Crass, crass, crass!

Howe Whittington had never, ever talked dirty. Never talked about sex at all. Recalling his outburst, Elizabeth felt a tiny, unexpected stab of lust awaken the part of her she'd long since put to sleep, which only upset her further.

No way was she having sex with him. Not till she knew he was safe.

This was the twenty-first century, and promiscuity like Howe's could kill.

Thank God the children hadn't been there.

Or his mother.

On second thought, it might have been fun to see the look on Augusta's face . . .

"Mrs. Whittington?" the doctor asked. "Are you all right?"

"I was just . . ." She bent close to the neurologist, feeling her face go hot. "Could you please do a complete STD test on my husband?" she murmured. "We haven't . . ."

"Oh." The doctor's eyebrows shot up, but he kept his response low. "Of course." He glanced at her in sympathy. "Of course. I'll let you both know when the results come in."

"Thank you," she said, doing her best to keep the others from overhearing, "but considering what my husband's been through, and the . . . unusual condition of his current mental state, would it be possible to discuss the results with me, instead?" Her cheeks prickled with heat. "I need to know if he's . . . *safe.*"

There it was again. That pesky stab of ancient desire, Lord help her.

The doctor considered briefly, frowning, then nodded. "It's bending things a bit, but under the circumstances, since he's clearly impaired, I think we could do that. As long as I tell him afterward, when he's more rational." He patted

Elizabeth on the shoulder, a gesture she read as patronizing. "Your husband's stroke occurred in the area of his brain that controls emotions and personality. His filters may have been damaged by the stroke. Many patients with injuries in that area of the brain experience similar problems, but they usually respond well to therapy and practice, over time."

That was some comfort, at least, but Elizabeth wasn't about to risk being ravaged in the meantime. "I just need to be safe. We can't exactly keep him in a condom, and you said sedatives weren't a good idea."

"We'll do another scan. If he continues to be so sexually agitated, I'll consult with an endocrinologist and see if we can regulate that," he offered. "Meanwhile, I'll order some restraints for the staff to use, if necessary."

"Thank you." Howe Whittington, chained to his bed because he lusted after his wife? Elizabeth sensed laughter from the cosmos, but she wasn't sure if it was coming from heaven or hell. Or if the joke was on her or Howe.

The doctor motioned for the Greek chorus to leave. "Your husband will probably sleep for several hours before waking up again," he said as the others filed out. "If he continues to improve, we may not need another treatment. Most patients start with shorter waking periods that gradually increase in length as they grow

95

stronger." He sounded scripted, detached. "Physically, your husband's going to need lots of good nutrition and PT before he's strong enough to go home. Mentally, he'll need long-term behavioral therapy to help him retrain his responses to the world around him. Do you have anyone you'd prefer to use?"

"No," she said. As if any of his family would ever consent to "air their dirty linen," even to a therapist. "Whoever you recommend. We can come to Atlanta for that." She didn't trust any-body in Whittington, HIPAA or no.

"I've been really impressed with the work Glen McAfee's done with our coma patients. Good man. We'll contact him and start that right away."

She wondered if she'd be included in any of those sessions or kept on the outside, the way she'd been kept on the outside of Howe's thoughts and feelings since they'd argued over the way he spoiled Patricia when she was just a toddler.

"If Mr. Whittington is hungry when he wakes up," the doctor concluded, "we'll remove the feeding tube and start him on some broth and Jell-O." He left her standing there to wonder who Howe would be when he next came to.

But thank God, he had woken up and didn't seem impaired. Just horny.

She needed to call the family.

Charles. She needed to tell Charles. Elizabeth retrieved her cell phone and speed-dialed his, even though he was probably still at work, clerking for one of Howe's favorite judges downtown.

"Mom?" he answered, concerned. She never called him at work. "What's happened?"

"Your father woke up." She wasn't going to be a perpetual caregiver to a coma patient. She wasn't going to be sentenced to widowhood under her mother-in-law's disapproving scrutiny. "I let them try the treatment, and he's out of the coma. It's amazing. He just woke up. He seems to have all his faculties." And then some.

No need to mention his temporary aberrations. Surely, those would pass.

"Mom, that's fabulous!" their son said with genuine relief. "Great. When can I see him?"

"Not right away," she hastened to say. "He's still not quite himself." That was an understatement and a half. "But you can see him soon."

Howe moaned again. "Lizzie?" He stirred. "Where's my Lizzie?" he murmured without opening his eyes. "I need my Lizzie."

Lord. Again with the Lizzie. Elizabeth lowered her voice. "I have to go. He's calling for me. The doctors said he'd be napping a lot, at first, but it's only sleep. I just wanted you to know. I love you, sweetie."

"You, too, Mama-lama." The line went dead.

97

"Lizzie," Howe pleaded louder, swiping at the IVs in his left arm with his right hand.

Temporary, she told herself. Once he was fully awake, he'd quit using that wretched nickname. It was almost as bad as the "Bessie Mae" she'd been before moving to Whittington at fourteen.

Nearing his bedside, Elizabeth glanced at the covers over his abdomen to make sure the coast was clear before getting within grabbing distance. Fortunately, he'd settled back into even breathing, his covers smooth.

She'd prayed for him to wake up, and God had granted her petition. But what was with the *Lizzie?* And his horniness?

"Lizzie, where are you?" Howe's brows drew together over an anxious frown, eyes still closed.

"I'm here," she murmured, bending over him, but still wary in case he grabbed her again. "I'm here, Howe."

He opened his eyes, blinking as if things were out of focus, his expression confused. Then he touched the tube running up his nostril and scowled, then coughed. "What happened?" he rasped. "My throat hurts, and I feel like my blood's molasses." He groped for her hand. "Everything's so bright. And the smells . . ."

It had been so long since they'd exchanged even simple touches that she felt dishonest taking his hand, but he grabbed hold for dear life and curled hers to his chest. "Lizzie," he croaked. "Lizard-breath. I need you."

Elizabeth couldn't have said which shocked her more: the fact that he'd said he needed her, or his calling her "Lizard-breath," a nickname from her favorite comic strip.

Howell had never, ever said he needed her. And if anybody had told her he read the funny papers, she'd have sworn it was a lie. The financial section, yes. But not the funnies. He'd long since become the most humorless man she knew.

"You had a stroke," she soothed, "but you're going to be fine."

How much should she tell him? She should have asked the doctor. "It will take some time. Just rest. You're weak."

Features clearing as his lids closed, he nodded but held on as if she were his one lifeline to consciousness.

Elizabeth stood there for several minutes before she tried to extract herself, but when she did, he roused again enough to resist. Maybe if she distracted him. "Are you hungry?" she asked, pulling free. "The doctor said if you're hungry, they could take out the tube and start giving you some clear liquids."

His blue eyes flew open. "God, yes. Get this tube out of me," he said, suddenly alert. "But forget the fluids." He grabbed the NG tube and started pulling it out, gagging in the process.

"Howell, stop that!" Elizabeth buzzed frantically for the nurse, then tried to stop him, but he swatted her away.

"Yes, Mrs. Whittington?" came over the intercom.

"He's pulling out his NG tube!" By the time she'd said it, he'd gotten the thing out completely and lapsed into a fit of coughing.

Fortunately, the tube seemed to have come out clean. There wasn't any blood. Elizabeth held his water close enough to sip. "Drink. Sip it slow."

Howe gasped, then did as she instructed. "Ah." He took another sip, followed by a hoarse, "Better."

His two swing-shift nurses appeared—Rachel and Mavis. "Mr. Whittington," the shorter, older Mavis challenged rhetorically, "what do you think you're doin'? Do not, and I mean do *not,* remove anything else from your body. Do I make myself clear?" She snatched the NG tube and shook it at him. "This could have gone very badly. Your family and your insurance company are paying through the nose for us to do those things for you." Pun intended? Mavis scowled. "If you want something, call us. Understand? Or do we need to put you into restraints?" She glared at him with her fists planted on her ample hips.

Howe had the good grace to look sheepish. "Sorry. I just couldn't stand having that tube in there anymore. It felt like a fire hose in my throat."

Not impressed, Nurse Mavis pointed to him in warning. "No more do-it-yourself, mister. Those IVs and that catheter stay till your doctor says they come out. And *we* do the takin' out, not you."

Howell let loose another brief spate of coughing, nodding and waving her away.

"All right, then." Silent Nurse Rachel in tow, Mavis hitched her uniformed booty back to the nurses' station.

Howe subsided into his pillow, clearly exhausted. "Remind me never to cross her again."

He closed his eyes for a few minutes, then roused, focusing on his surroundings for the first time. "Where am I, anyway?"

"At the new stroke center near Emory. You had a stroke. But you're fine now."

"Stroke," he murmured, drifting away. "My father had a stroke . . . He died."

"You're not going to die, Howell," Elizabeth told him. "You're going to be fine." She willed it for him. What they would do then, she didn't know. P.J. . . .

Howe didn't say anything else for another ten minutes, then woke with a start. "Man. I'm starving." He rubbed a hand across his stubbled jaw. "I want a chili dog from the Varsity." Hunger claimed his features, brightened by the prospect of junk food. "No, two. And a Glorified. And an order of rings. And fries. And a brownie. And a Big Orange." His stomach growled so loudly, it all but echoed. Then he let out another huge fart —and laughed!

Prim and proper Charles Howell Whittington II had not only farted but found it amusing. The world had turned upside down.

"Who are you," Elizabeth blurted out, "and what have you done with my husband?"

"It's me," he said with a boyish half-smile. "At least, I think it is. And God, am I hungry." He shot her a salacious glance. "I sure am glad to see you." He reached out with both hands, arms open. "C'mere, Lillibet. I'm as horny as I am hungry. The Varsity can wait. How 'bout a quickie?"

That tore it. "Not till you pass your AIDS test, and another one, six months later," she snapped just as the curtain swished open to reveal their son.

Charles froze, blinking in surprise while he took in the sight of his father's arms open wide to his mother, then stammered, "Uh, hey. I know you said to wait, but I couldn't. The judge gave me the rest of the day off when I told him." Charles hesitated. "Do you two need some privacy, because I could—"

102

"Charles!" Howe's attention shifted abruptly to his son, his eyes welling with tears as he sat up. "Son! By damn, come here. Give your dad a hug. God, it's good to see you."

Cussing and hugging? Charles shot Elizabeth a look of surprise, but she was so grateful for the distraction that she cocked her head for him to do as his father asked.

Howe enveloped the boy in a bear hug, all but pulling him off his feet. Tears streaming, Howe clapped Charles on the back. "How's my boy? You'll make a fine lawyer. Much better than I ever would have been. I'm so proud of you for getting into Emory law. So proud."

Unable to believe what she was hearing, Elizabeth felt her own eyes well. All his life, Charles had struggled to win his father's approval, but the most Howe had given him was an occasional *attaboy*. Like Augusta's, Howe's affections had been reserved for their daughter Patricia.

Howe thrust Charles to arm's length. "Look at this . . . *man* of ours, Lizzie. So handsome. So good. Can you believe he's ours?" Abruptly, Howe looked stricken. "I haven't been the father I should be. I have so much to make up to you, son." He searched Charles's shocked expression. "So much. But God's given me another chance. I know He's real, now. He spoke to me."

God spoke to him? Elizabeth must have fallen

down the rabbit hole, for real! Howe had always said people who thought God talked to them were crazy—including Jimmy Carter and George Bush.

"Can you forgive me, Charles?" Howe pleaded roughly. "Can I ever make it up to you?"

"Sure, Dad," Charles said gingerly. "Sure. We're okay." He shot Elizabeth a questioning glance. "Maybe you ought to lie back for a while and rest."

Howe nodded, releasing Charles. "I love you, son. I've loved you from the day you were born. You've never given me or your mother a minute of trouble. I love you."

To Elizabeth's knowledge, Howe hadn't said he loved their son since Charles was little.

Charles swallowed heavily, turning away.

Elizabeth didn't have to be clairvoyant to read his mind. Whatever had happened to his father, he was grateful.

Abruptly, Howe sat up again. "God, I've never been so hungry in my life. Charles, do you think you could go to the Varsity for me? I'm starving, and my tongue is set for some real food. Could you get me two chili dogs and a Glorified and some rings and fries and a Big Orange?"

Charles was skeptical. "Dad, don't you think you ought to start off a little easier? You haven't eaten any real food for more than six months."

Howe halted abruptly. "Six months?" He turned

to Elizabeth in dismay. "What's the date? How long have I been here?"

"It's June," she told him. "You were in the hospital for almost a month, then they transferred you here." She could see it was a lot to take in. "You've been here since January."

Stunned, Howe lay back down, then stared at his hand, flexing his fingers. "Whoa. Major sinking spell." Suddenly pale, he tried to lift his knees, but gave up after raising them only a few inches. "No wonder my legs don't work so well."

"You were pretty strong when you first woke up," she said dryly. "But the adrenaline's probably worn off." She just hoped the testosterone had.

"It won't take long to get back up and going," Charles reassured him. "You've had physical therapy every day here. Lots of it."

Howe shook his head. "Well, shit!"

Charles and Elizabeth stared at him in shock. "What did you just say?" Elizabeth heard herself ask.

Wide-eyed, Howe shook his head again in denial even as he said, "Fuck me!"

"Howell," Elizabeth scolded. Her father and brothers had worn the word out, but Howe had never, ever succumbed to such common talk, even in private. He'd always said cursing debased the one who did it even more than the ones who heard it, and she agreed.

"Sorry." Howe seemed perplexed. "I can't

believe I just said that. I never even *thought* that before, much less said it. Shit."

Elizabeth stiffened. "What's going on here?" Should she call the doctors?

"Damned if I know," Howe said, then clapped his hand over his mouth.

By then, Charles was having a hard time keeping a straight face, so he wasn't any help.

Ruffled, Elizabeth explained to Howe, "The doctor said there might be some emotional side effects, either from the stroke or from the experimental drugs they used to wake you up. Or maybe from the tumor." Oh, dear. She hadn't meant to say that last.

Howe's eyes widened. "Tumor? What tumor?"

So much for breaking it to him gently. "A small one, in your frontal cortex," she hastened to qualify. "Very slow-growing. *Not* malignant. They operated the day you were admitted, and got it all."

Howe reached up to feel his scalp and encountered the scar. He paled. "Shit! I had brain surgery?" His voice shook with alarm. "Shit!"

Elizabeth pressed the nurse's call button as she tried to reassure him with, "The tumor's blood supply ruptured, which caused the stroke. They took care of that, too. You're fine now. You're fine."

"I don't think so," her husband argued. "I can't control my language—or my appetites." She

106

followed his glance to the tented sheet above his groin. "I am *not* fine."

Nurse Mavis's voice crackled over the intercom. "What can we do for you, Mr. Whittington?"

"Roll back the clock six months," Howe snapped toward the microphone in the side rail of his bed.

"My husband wants some chili dogs from the Varsity," Elizabeth tattled. "And rings. And fries. And a Glorified and a brownie and a Big Orange." And never mind what else. Stroke or no stroke, no chance was he getting *that*.

"Men. I tell you," Mavis opined. "We cain't give him anything but liquids, but if y'all want to make a Varsity run, I cain't stop you," she said. "I'll be here to hold his head when he throws it all back up." She crackled off.

Some help. Elizabeth vowed to hold the woman to her word.

Charles moved close and took his father's hand. "It's okay, Dad. You're gonna be okay. Like you said: God gave you another chance. Try to focus on that."

Howe inhaled deeply, a range of emotions from fear to frustration to despair rippling across the face that had once been so impassive. He exhaled deeply. "You're right. You're right." The ravenous look reappeared. "But I really am starving. I'd kill for that Varsity order."

Charles and Elizabeth both froze at his choice

of words. Under the circumstances, they weren't sure whether to take him literally or not.

"Jeez, I didn't mean I could really kill somebody," Howe grumbled. "Lighten up." Something he hadn't done in a quarter of a century. "But I really want that food. Could you just get me the food, Charles? I may only be able to have a bite or two, but I want it."

Charles exchanged a pregnant glance with Elizabeth, then shrugged. "Okay. The Varsity it is. Be back within the hour."

Elizabeth shook her head as the door closed behind their son.

"Don't give me that look," Howe told her. "That's my mother's look. I hate that look."

Confrontation, from Howe? Elizabeth regarded him with a mixture of amazement and insult. "Kindly do not compare me to your mother."

"It just came out," he said. "I'm sorry." The words reflected more annoyance than repentance. He extended his hand. "Can I have the phone, please? I need to tell my mother I'm not in a coma anymore."

"Are you sure? I could call her for you." Lord only knew what he was liable to say. Then she'd be the one who had to deal with the aftermath.

"Yes, I'm sure." He was getting cranky. "I wouldn't want to inflict her on you. God knows, she's been nasty enough to you up till now." He waggled his hand for the phone.

Stunned, Elizabeth handed it over. In all their years of marriage, Howe had never said a word against his mother, much less taken Elizabeth's side on anything. He'd simply avoided conflict, telling Elizabeth she had to work things out with his mother on her own.

"Just punch star eleven, then the send button," she instructed.

He did so, then waited. "Mama? This is Howe. I'm awake." Elizabeth heard a very un-Augusta-like shriek of joy from the phone as Howe pulled it a safer distance from his eardrum. "But don't come see me yet," he all but yelled. "I'll call when I feel up to visitors. Not just yet."

A torrent of cultured Southern protest followed. "Mama," he said, "if you act like that, I'm going to hang up. I mean it. Do not come up here. And don't call Elizabeth. This is my decision, not hers." Pause, with more agitated mama-leakage. "Dammit, Mama. I'm going to hang up." Augusta's voice shifted lower and slower. "I don't know when I'm getting out," he said, shooting Elizabeth a questioning look.

She shook her head, mouthing *weeks.*

"Weeks. Maybe longer. I can't even walk, yet." He frowned when his mother resumed her tirade. "I'll call you tomorrow. I'm hanging up now, so I can call Patricia."

Oh, Lord. Elizabeth had completely forgotten Patricia. How Freudian was that?

Howe pulled the phone away from his ear again, and his mother's adamant instructions reached Elizabeth, clear as a bell.

"I'm hanging up now, Mama," he said. " 'Bye." Howe flipped the phone shut with a wince. "Shit. Is that how she talks to you?"

"When she talks to me. And you're not around."

"Damn. No wonder you can't stand her. If she wasn't my mother, I think I'd hate her, too." He peered at the phone, pressing the directory button, then punching the *p* key to summon Patricia's listing. "Ah. It all comes back." He pressed *send.* "And now for our darling daughter." He waited, then started to speak, only to pause abruptly, wait again, then finally say, "Patti-pie, it's Daddy. I'm awake now. Call me back on Mama's phone."

Since frankness seemed to be the new order, Elizabeth told him, "She never answers when it's me. I'm the mean mama."

Howe frowned. "That's not your fault. It's mine. But if I get a chance, I'll try to make it up to both of you."

If only Elizabeth could believe that. When had this change of heart happened, anyway? The man had just woken up.

The phone rang in his hand, causing both of them to jump. "Hello?" Howe opened it and paused. "Hello? Can you hear me?" Another pause. "Patti?" He checked the screen. "Caller rejected. No ID."

110

Oh, God. P.J. She'd blocked his number before the treatment, just in case.

A flush of adrenaline sent Elizabeth deadly still, her features blank.

Howe shrugged. "Whoever it was, they hung up." Suddenly fragile, he handed her the phone. "Whoa. Whiz-head." He closed his eyes, lips slightly parted. "Need a little nap."

And Elizabeth needed a new cell phone, pronto, with another number that she'd give only to P.J.

She almost dropped the thing when it rang again, but this time, Patricia's name and number flashed on the readout. Relief flooded her. "Hello? Patricia?"

"Where's Daddy?" her daughter demanded, clearly beside herself. "I want to talk to Daddy!"

"He's resting now, but he's out of the coma. I decided to try the treatment and it worked." Elizabeth would discuss the side effects later, before Patricia saw him. "I know he'd love to see you, sweetie."

"I'm on my way. Tell him I'm coming."

Elizabeth heard a horn blow in the background, and a screech of brakes. "Where are you?"

"I'm in Athens. I spent the night with Janie at her apartment. But I'm on my way to Daddy now."

"Slow down, honey. Take your time. It would

break your daddy's heart if you got in a wreck. He'll be here when you get here."

"Where are the cops when you need them?" Patricia complained. "This is an emergency. I need a police escort."

"This is not an emergency," Elizabeth scolded. She might as well be talking to the wall, and she knew it. "Patricia, you can't see your father if you're arrested for speeding. Remember, this would be your third offense. They'd pull your license on the spot and jail you."

"I sure will be glad when I can talk to Daddy again," Patricia grumbled, then hung up.

Consigning her to the care of heaven, Elizabeth did something she never had before: turned off the phone and removed the battery. Patricia was in for a surprise. And so was Augusta.

Half an hour later, the curtain swished open, and the smell of onion rings and chili blew in with Charles, his hands laden with three red-printed boxes and a loaded drink caddy.

Howe's eyes flew open. "Food. Thank God." He levitated to a sitting position. "Bring it on."

It took him a while, but he blissfully polished off a whole chili dog, half a Glorified burger, and half the fries and rings, washed down by the entire Big Orange.

And fifteen minutes later when he went green and bent double, Elizabeth summoned Mavis to hold his head when it all came up.

Patricia made her entrance an hour after that to find her father sleeping and Elizabeth dozing in the chair. "Whoa." She grimaced, pinching off her nose. "Who hurled Varsity?"

Howe smiled and opened his eyes. "I did, but it was worth every bite. C'mere, Patti-pie."

"Oh, Daddy!" She hurled herself into his arms. "I'm so glad you're back."

Crying, Howe stroked her hair. "Damn straight. Me, too. I love ya, Patti-pie."

Whether Patti would still be glad remained to be seen.

# Chapter 7

The minute Howe closed the door on the last guest from Patricia's second birthday party, Elizabeth sank into a club chair and threw her head back, eyes closed. "Thank God, it's over." What an ordeal.

All she'd wanted was to invite Patricia's Sunday school class for cake and ice cream, but Howe had turned the event into a three-ring circus, inviting half the town and hiring clowns and a pony ride, then having a caterer from Atlanta provide two separate buffets for both kids and parents—with at least a dozen servers—plus two bartenders.

To top it off, two-year-old Patricia ate so much cake and candy that she self-destructed amid an avalanche of wrapping paper, with a temper tantrum that would remain in the annals of Whittington history for generations. After Elizabeth finally got the child to sleep, she spent the rest of the afternoon trying to keep the children from hurting themselves or each other, while their parents got loaded inside.

*Not* her idea of a birthday party for a two-year-old.

"Howe, we cannot do this again," she groaned. "I can barely move."

Howe didn't answer. He hadn't wanted to talk to her since they'd argued over how he spoiled Patricia, leaving Elizabeth to be the heavy.

She sat up and looked toward the front door. "Howe?"

"I'm here," he said from the bar.

Servers came in and out of the kitchen, filling trays with dirty dishes and plastic bags with torn wrapping paper and festive birthday napkins.

"You didn't answer me," she said with annoyance.

Howe faced her squarely with a hefty scotch in hand. "You didn't ask me a question," he said in that maddeningly cool tone he used. "You made a statement. Statements don't require a response."

Here they went again. "I just . . . Howe, this wasn't a kids' birthday party," Elizabeth said, hearing it come out like a whine, which she hated. "Kids' birthdays are like the one we had for Charles: a few good friends, cake and ice cream, and some yard games." She sat forward, forcing her spine erect. "Please. Come sit down and talk to me. I want to understand what you're feeling."

Howe visibly recoiled. "What good would it do? You think one thing, I think another. We've

115

been over all this half a dozen times already. Elizabeth, we have a position to uphold in this town, and social obligations. And those include our daughter."

"But not Charles, apparently," Elizabeth shot back before she could stop herself.

Howe took a slug of scotch, his features hard. "Why are you complaining, anyway?" he accused. "You haven't had to lift a finger. The maid service cleaned the house for the party. The caterers will stay till everything's back in order. And the lawn crew is almost finished with the backyard."

"That's not the point," she repeated from their previous arguments. "Patricia isn't a princess. She's a child. She needs appropriate things in her life, appropriate boundaries. And she needs two parents who keep a unified front when it comes to discipline."

Howe rolled his eyes. "Here we go again." Another slug of scotch. "She's just a baby, and this is a home, not boot camp. Lighten up, Elizabeth." He set his drink on the table, then waited till the server left them alone. "I feel a cold coming on, so I'll be staying in Dad's suite for a while."

Elizabeth stilled. The opposite sides of their king-sized bed might as well have been in separate counties, for all the interaction they'd had lately, but she read something deeper in her husband's explanation for moving out, and it chilled her blood. "It's okay to stay. I can look after you." She hated to beg, but she didn't want to lose what little they still had together.

She knew about the hookers in town. She'd found some of the charge receipts, and traced down their origins. But they were merely sex objects. She refused to let them break up their marriage. Her children needed a father, a respectable home.

"We'll both sleep better this way," Howe said. "I know how my watching *The Tonight Show* bothers you. And I have to confess, your snoring bothers me."

That wasn't what this was about, and they both knew it! "Howe, please don't do this," she pleaded quietly. "We can work it out. Get help. Counseling . . ."

His expression steeled. "Elizabeth, you're always overreacting. My parents had separate rooms for as long as I can remember, but they were still close."

As opposite goalposts on a football field! "I was hoping our marriage would be better than theirs. Howe, I do love you." She stared into his eyes. "Do you love me anymore, at all?" There. After all the months of getting the cold shoulder, she'd come out and asked.

He regarded her as if she were one of the children. "Of course. You're making entirely too much of this, and you're tired. Go to bed, Elizabeth. You'll feel better in the morning, after a good night's sleep. We both will."

Elizabeth just sat there, wanting to hold on to their marriage the way it had been before Patricia was born. Howe had loved Charles, then. He'd laughed and played with him. He'd even laughed and made love to Elizabeth occasionally. But now he looked at her as only the mother of his children, and it broke her heart.

Separate bedrooms. Was that how it always ended up with people like the Whittingtons?

She'd known from the beginning that she shouldn't have fallen in love with him. Now she was paying the price. Elizabeth held her tears, determined to maintain some shred of dignity.

"Then I'll say good night." Slowly, she rose and went upstairs to her empty bed.

She cried a lot into her pillow that night. And in the nights to come. But eventually, she reconciled herself to the loss. And as the years passed, she came to see her room as her own private sanctuary. But she never lost the longing for the man she'd loved—a man who no longer existed.

# Chapter 8

## *The present*

Patricia burst into tears and threw herself into her father's arms. "Oh, Daddy. I was afraid it wasn't real, that you weren't really awake, but it's you. It's really you. I've missed you so much. I was so afraid."

Tears streaming, Howe stroked her long, expensively blonded hair. "It's me, baby girl," he choked out. "It's me. And I'm not going anywhere."

Patricia reared back to regard him with a mixture of surprise and dismay. "Daddy. You're crying."

Swiping at his reddened eyes, Howe exhaled a shuddering breath. "I seem to be doing a lot of that," he observed, wry. "And other things. But I'm still your dad, and I sure am glad to see you."

She laid her head gingerly back against his chest. "Not half as glad as I am to see you. I couldn't live without you and Gamma."

"Yes you could," he told her, "but you won't have to."

"No I couldn't." Now that Patricia knew things

were going to be all right, she put on the pouty face Elizabeth recognized all too well. "I've been so worried about you, I failed half my classes."

Ah, yes. Despite this miracle, Patricia was still Patricia. Elizabeth tucked her chin.

"You're not going to let Mama take my car away for that, are you?" the little opportunist wheedled.

Elizabeth braced herself for being undermined one more time, but Howe's response wasn't what she expected.

"Let's don't talk about any of that now," he said. "Let's just thank God that I'm here, and you're here, and Gamma and your mama are here." His face went sly as a little boy's. "And Charles brought me food from the Varsity."

"Which obviously you tossed," Patricia retorted with a dimpled smile that never failed to win him over.

"Without regret," Howe insisted. But the mere speaking of the word *regret* sent his features falling. "I have a lot of regrets, Patti-pie, but I plan to make them up, mostly to your mother and your brother. Things look . . ."—he struggled visibly to hold on to his composure—"very different to me now. I don't know how to—" He choked off, eyes welling as he looked to Elizabeth with profound apology. "God. How do people stand it, the guilt? I never felt this before. Ever." He looked away.

Howe? Guilty?

"It's horrible," he went on, more to himself than to them. "Goddamn." He turned to Elizabeth. "How can you even look at me? Shit."

Patricia's eyes widened with fear at his use of profanity. "Daddy?"

He covered his face with his hands. "Oh, God. How did I look myself in the mirror?"

Elizabeth couldn't have him blurting out some torrid confession, not in front of Patricia. She firmly drew her daughter away from the bed. "Daddy's had a rough day, honey. Let's go get a Coke and let him get some rest, now. He's not really himself just yet." Patricia looked back at the spectacle of her poker-faced father now in tears, but Elizabeth propelled her toward the door. "We'll look in on you later," she told the Alan Alda masquerading as her husband.

Howe swiped at the agony on his face. "Your mother's right. I'm not myself." He closed his eyes, bleak. "Do what Mama says, Patti. Go with your mama."

Patricia waited till they were in the hallway to balk. "What's the matter with him?" she demanded loudly, oblivious to everyone else in the vicinity, as usual. "You said he was okay, but he cries all the time. And he *cusses!*" she accused, as if it were all Elizabeth's fault.

"Patricia Augusta Whittington," Elizabeth scolded in a tight whisper, "you hush. He can

121

hear you." She dragged her daughter down the hall to the waiting area beside the elevators. When they were safely out of earshot, she sat Patricia on a large ottoman, nearing the end of her own rope. "Why do you talk to me that way? The man had a stroke, and brain surgery," she clipped out, grateful there was no one there to overhear. "And was in a coma for almost six months. But he woke up, and he's not a moron or paralyzed. It's a miracle he can even talk. So he cusses. So he cries. Big deal." A very big deal, actually, but not one she planned to go into with her daughter.

The shocks of the day finally got the best of her. "Have you once thought about how hard this has been on me?" she blurted out, hating herself for doing it. "I know you've been upset, but have you ever thought about anything besides what this has meant to you, and how you can use it as an excuse not to study or go to your classes?"

Patricia glared at her, lips compressed in a stubborn frown.

"Your father just came back from the dead," Elizabeth reminded her. "And the first thing you do is try to use him to keep from losing your car. I'm ashamed of you."

Elizabeth knew she should sit down and shut up, but Howe's lack of control seemed to be contagious. "I swear, Patricia," she vowed, her voice low but unsteady, "I'd shake you if I

122

thought it would bring any sense into you. You're not a child anymore. This isn't about you. It's about your father. And me. He has a lot of work ahead of him before he can even come home. I could use your help to get through this."

Years of adolescent resentment for Elizabeth's efforts at discipline finally came to a head. "You don't love him," Patricia retaliated. "You never did. Gamma told me. You just married him for his money."

Elizabeth's hand rose to slap her daughter, but she managed to hold back, curling it into an impotent fist. "That . . . is . . . not . . . true. I loved your father very much when I married him."

"No you didn't," her daughter accused. "You're a cold fish. I can't even remember your hugging him, or kissing him. Ever. I hate you, and so does Daddy, but he's too much of a gentleman to ever say it."

On that note, the elevator doors opened with a *ding* to reveal an agitated Augusta Whittington, uninvited and unwelcome.

"Gamma!" Patricia wailed, flying to her grand-mother.

Elizabeth expected the usual condemnation from Augusta, but saw fear, instead. "Patricia," Elizabeth said, "you've frightened your grand-mother." She approached her mother-in-law. "Howe is fine, but he's not quite himself yet. The doctors said there might be some emotional

123

side effects, but he's out of the coma and resting. We can thank God for that."

Patricia saw the relief on her grandmother's face and had the good grace to be apologetic. "Sorry, Gamma. I didn't mean to scare you. But he cusses. And he *cries*."

Augusta tucked her chin to hear such news, then shot Elizabeth a chilly look.

Elizabeth found herself wishing that Howe would cuss and cry all over the old bat. Served the old bitch right for what she'd told Patricia. But Elizabeth didn't give her mother-in-law the satisfaction of seeing her emotions. "He's very . . . *impulsive* at the moment. That's probably why Howe wanted to wait to see you," she said evenly.

"Nonsense," Augusta said. "I'm his mother. I have a right to see him." She turned, setting Patricia aside. "Stay here with your mother, Patricia. I'll see my son alone."

Even after all Howe had done, Elizabeth didn't have the heart to leave him emotionally naked and unprotected with his mother. "Wait here," she told her daughter. "I'm going with Gamma."

"But—" Patricia whined.

"Wait here," both women said at once, then exchanged territorial glances before heading back down the hall.

Elizabeth held the door open for Augusta, and the older woman glided in to stand rigid by the

124

bed where Howe was sleeping. "Howell, it's your mother," she announced. "Wake up."

His eyes flew open. "Mama!" Bursting into tears, he grabbed her and pulled her to him. "Goddamn, but it's good to see you!" He pounded her back. "So good. So good. I love you, Mama. I know I haven't told you in a long time, but I do."

Augusta acted as if a gorilla had gotten hold of her, eyes wide with alarm, her tone measured. "It's good to see you, too, Howell. Now, could you let me go, please? My osteoporosis . . ."

"Shit!" Howe released her, instantly repentant. "I was so excited, I forgot." But he didn't let her escape completely, capturing her hand in both of his.

Augusta looked constipated, deflecting with, "Now that you're awake, you must get well quickly. You're much needed at work. The bank needs you."

Howe chortled. "Screw the bank. I sold my soul for that place, and as far as I'm concerned, it can go straight to hell." Augusta's jaw dropped behind closed lips. "Don't worry, Mama," he reassured her. "The people I trained can run it just fine."

"Don't be absurd," she snapped, trying without success to reclaim her hand. "They'll steal us blind. You're the only one I can trust with our businesses. You know this."

"No I don't," he retorted. "And God knows, I wasn't trustworthy before this happened. Neither was Dad." A brief wash of disgust claimed his expression. "God, Mama, how did you stand it with all of Daddy's women? I hated him for it, but you never said a word. You just soldiered on."

Augusta almost choked, but Howe was oblivious. Elizabeth thanked God that Patricia wasn't there.

"I swore I would never do that to any wife of mine," Howe went on, "then I ended up doing the same thing." He shot Elizabeth a pained glance. "I'm so sorry, Lizzie. So sorry. I don't know why I did it. Maybe because you knew me too well. Wanted me to care. But I didn't have anything to give. You never gave me cause to do it. It was just the sex, I swear."

Augusta went so pale, Elizabeth thought she would faint. She'd have moved over to catch her, but her own feet seemed glued to the floor.

"I swear to God, Lizzie," Howe said to her, "I'll make it up to you. You've been a perfect wife. Perfect. And I've been a total shit."

Augusta inhaled sharply as if coming out of a trance, snatching her hand free to place it across her heart. "Such language," she spat out. "Such talk. Charles Howell Whittington the second, do not say one more word! Clearly, you are not in possession of your faculties." She glared down

126

her nose at him. "We shall never speak of such embarrassments again, is that clear? Never! Your father was human, but he had many fine qualities. I am shocked that you would dishonor his memory with such loose talk. Shocked."

Elizabeth watched in morbid fascination as Howe started leaking tears again. "Mama, it happened. We both know it. Dad screwed up. I screwed up." He swiped away the tears, clearly annoyed by his own lack of control. "Can't we be honest about it, for once? You've been so damned mean to Lizzie, but she never deserved it."

"Howell!" his mother shouted.

Oooh, hoo, hoo. Vindicated at last, Elizabeth thought her mother-in-law was going to stick her fingers in her ears and start singing, but she blustered instead, "That is enough. I am leaving." She turned to Elizabeth on her way out. "I'm taking Patricia home with me. Keep the children away from him till he's himself again."

The thing was, Elizabeth didn't want him to go back to being himself—she preferred the Howe he'd become.

"And don't let him use the phone," his mother ordered. "God knows what he might say." She pivoted, then marched out. "I won't be back till he's come to his senses."

Elizabeth watched her storm out, then turned back to Howe.

Rueful, he clasped his forehead, staring at the door. "There I go again. Fucked it up, entirely."

For the first time in memory, Elizabeth started laughing, laughing so hard she couldn't stop. It burst inside and rolled through her in waves, breaking up the scar tissue that had encased her soul. And Howe laughed with her.

# Chapter 9

The glow of that moment buoyed them both till that evening when Howe fell into a sound, natural sleep, and Elizabeth felt it was safe to leave him. But on her way out, she stopped by the nurses' station and explained that he was suffering from terminal impulsiveness and he preferred not to have any other visitors—including his mother and his children, to spare them further embarrassment—until he got a grip on things. As always, the nurses were kind and understanding (feisty Mavis had gotten off at three) and agreed to post a notice on the door with a list for visitors to sign.

The last thing Elizabeth wanted was to have to explain the situation to anybody else, so she resolved to screen her calls as she replaced the batteries so the hospital could reach her. But her cell phone rang as she strode briskly down the dark sidewalk toward the condo where she was staying, and she couldn't see the caller ID without her readers, which were, of course, in the bottom of her stylishly huge bag. It could be Howe or one of the children, so she answered. "Hello?"

"I heard," P.J. said dramatically.

She frowned. The Whittington grapevine was good, but not *that* good. "Heard what?"

"That he woke up."

"Who told you?" Was he bribing the nurses?

"That's not important. You might not believe this, Elizabeth, especially knowing how I feel about you, but I'm glad he's out of the coma, and I hope he does great. Then we can all get on with the rest of our lives."

Now was *not* the time to think about any of that. "P.J., it's not so simple. We're looking at a long haul, here. Lots of therapy. An extended convalescence. I can't talk about the future, now." She reached the stairs to the condo and suddenly felt exhausted as she climbed them. "My husband needs me." For now, at least, she had to do what she'd always done: be the good wife.

After a brief pause, P.J. said, "He's the luckiest bastard in the world to have you. But you don't have to go through this alone. I'll be here for you. I can't help how I feel about you, but friendship is better than nothing, so I'll be your friend. We'll sort the rest out later, once he's well."

Whatever *well* turned out to be.

Elizabeth sighed, entering the condo lobby. It felt good that somebody who wasn't brain-damaged loved her for who she was. "Thank you," she told P.J., pressing the up button on the elevator. "I'm home now, and worn to a frazzle. I'll call you soon."

"You never do," he said archly. "But that's okay. God knows, your plate's full. Get some rest, honey."

The term of endearment almost dissolved her. He'd never used one before. "You, too," she managed, eyes welling. "G'night."

The elevator doors opened, and she barely had the strength to step inside. When they closed, leaving her safe and alone, she burst into tears, then cried until she made it inside the generically decorated unit on the fourth floor.

When she finally crawled into bed, a flicker of a question darted through her mind, too swift to be addressed: How the hell *had* P.J. found out so quickly? Then she fell into a bottomless sleep.

There wasn't much laughing in the upcoming weeks. Howe's physical therapy was grueling, and he continued to blurt out whatever he thought or felt, with expletives, and weep, much to the dismay or shock of the staff and other patients. But daily counseling sessions gradually helped cut down on the cussing a little, at least.

Elizabeth still wasn't sure who the man inside Howe's body really was. She'd long ago prayed that God would restore her husband's love and affection for her, but not like this. This Howe wasn't the gentle, genteel boy she'd loved. This Howe was turning both their lives into one big, bad divine joke.

Be careful what you wish for.

Appalled by his own lack of ability to control what he did and said, Howe kept postponing seeing the children and his mother, leaving only Elizabeth to care for him seven days a week. As she always had, she remained the dutiful wife as far as anybody else was concerned. But inside, her frustration and weariness sparked the buried kernel of her anger to a tiny, white-hot sun that threw light on questions she'd never let herself ask. Questions like, "What have I really been doing with my life all these years?" And even more dangerous, "What would it be like to be happy?" Most dangerous of all, "Could I be happy with P.J.?"

Yet she dared not say anything, and never complained. Her cloak of long-suffering fit far too well to take it off.

Meanwhile back at the ranch, Augusta took over having the house cleaned and forwarding the mail to the condo. Charles, bless his heart, came to the condo every Tuesday and Thursday night with takeout from Elizabeth's favorite restaurants, then helped her with the mail and medical paperwork. Augusta had given Charles one of her rental houses in Morningside as a graduation-from-law-school gift, and he was full of anecdotes and gossip about clerking for the cranky old judge and doing over the house in his spare time. He never pressed about Howe, accepting her upbeat, nonspecific assurances that he was making progress and looking forward to being up for company again.

Patti had moved back in with her grandmother and resumed partying with her friends, but at least she answered Elizabeth's calls, eager for news of her father's progress, which she'd dubbed "the cussing quotient."

If it were only the cussing, Elizabeth would have been in better shape. But Howe was like a giant toddler, alternately winsome and frustrating, and she never knew from one minute to the next which he'd be. And even though he was definitely not the cold, distant man he'd been before the stroke, everything was still all about Howe, just as it had been before. But now, she wasn't sure how long she could take it anymore.

The whole thing was exhausting.

By the end of each day, she barely had energy to crawl back to the condo and go through the mail, then nuke supper and go to bed, so her dinners with P.J. grew fewer and farther between, and he worried aloud that she was shutting down emotionally.

Maybe she was, but it was the best she could do.

And so the days and weeks rolled by, insulated from their past realities and facing an uncertain —and ironic—future.

Despite Howe's progress, the pecker problem persisted. The man was well over fifty, but had no more control over the thing than a sixteen-year-old—not his own, charming sixteen-year-old self, but some sex-starved hormonal maniac with no sense of propriety. Sometimes all it took to set him off was saying "Hello."

Bing, up went the sheet. She could tell it embarrassed him, but regardless, the man was fixated. He hadn't jumped her bones, but he sure was gropey, and he was always trying to kiss her, even her hand.

Elizabeth had told him she was willing to let bygones be bygones and start over from scratch, and he'd said he understood, but apparently he didn't because he couldn't seem to keep his hands off her. She knew he wasn't accountable for what he did, but it angered her that he thought he had a right to even touch her, after everything he'd put her through. It made her even madder that he still had the power to anger her so. But for the children's sake, she put on a brave and patient face.

She'd tried dressing like a nun, but it didn't seem to matter.

At the rate they were going after a month, she decided it would be Christmas before she dared let him out in public. But the hospital and insurance company had other ideas. So, six weeks after Howell woke up, he walked out into the blazing July heat under his own steam, and Elizabeth took him home.

Blessedly, Patricia was in the Bahamas on a sorority trip she'd scheduled long before Howe's release, so they arrived home to find that Augusta had had the place scoured to within an inch of its life and smelling of Pine-Sol, her personal cleaning choice. Augusta had also made a few changes to the arrangement of the furniture and accessories, which was par for the course. She always had and always would consider the house more hers than Elizabeth's.

Suppressing a surge of anger when she saw the subtle changes, Elizabeth walked over and put her jade lion back where it belonged on the credenza.

Howell plunked down on the velvet bench beside it in the expansive Georgian foyer. "Whew. You wouldn't think an hour car ride could wear you out, but, d—sorry—" He staunched the cussword and substituted, "*Man*. I'm whipped." The appended apology had lately become a reflex when he cussed, which Elizabeth took as a good sign. At least he was becoming more aware of it, if only after the fact.

Elizabeth locked the front door and hooked the security chain, not against thieves—she never did that—but against her mother-in-law. "Would you like to lie down in the den for a while before going upstairs?" she offered, shifting the fresh flowers from the center of the credenza to the side, where she liked it, then moving both candlesticks to the other side where they belonged. "I could bring you some lunch on a tray."

Howe didn't respond, scanning the rooms. "Has this place always been like this?" He winced. "I don't remember disliking it, but it's so . . . *dark,* and heavy." Frowning, he sniffed the musty odor of ancient furniture and drapes. "So gloomy."

"You always said it was elegant," she told him, agreeing with his new assessment a hundred percent.

"Well, it doesn't look elegant to me now. It looks like closeout at a bad antiques shop." He frowned at the Victorian relics and heavy swagged moiré drapes in the parlor. "This was all here when we moved in?"

Elizabeth sat on the other side of the bench. "That, and more. We managed to get rid of some of it when your mother moved to your uncle's place." After that, Elizabeth had gradually relegated a few of the more objectionable remaining pieces to the attic, each of which Augusta noticed and asked if she'd sold.

Howe shook his head, taking it all in. "Damn —sorry. I vote we redecorate."

"Really?" Elizabeth had given up on ever getting the chance. Thrilled, she imagined what the tall, graceful windows would look like without the heavy drapes, the dark paper banished by pale green walls, and the heavy woodwork pristine white.

He grinned to see her so happy. "Really. Have at it, Lizzie." There was that blasted nickname again. "Whatever you want, as long as it's not dark and stuffy. We can afford it. Hell—sorry—we're rolling in money."

Not as much as before his stint in the center, but there was still plenty. Elizabeth remembered all the times she'd dreamed of renovating and updating the old place. "New kitchen and bathrooms?" They could finally get some decent insulation. "Thermal windows?" She could see it . . .

Then she realized what she was doing, and halted. Did she want to subject them both to a renovation if she was going to leave? P.J. had showed her what life could be like beyond the gossip and pettiness of Whittington. Beyond the reach of her mother-in-law. With someone who not only loved her, but cared what she felt and thought.

How did she know who Howe would end up being? What if he started slipping back into his old self? She couldn't go back to that, she realized. She couldn't.

Howe took her hand in both of his. "What's wrong? What did I say?"

"Nothing," she covered. "Your mother will go ballistic."

Relief brightened his expression. "Fuck Mama—sorry," he said. "She'll get over it." He squeezed her hand. "You scared me. Don't worry. I'll take care of Mama." He nodded toward the house they'd cohabited for the past thirty years. "You just make this place a home. It's never really seemed like home for you, has it?"

Seeing that he really cared, she felt a pang of emotion cut through her. "More of a home than the one I grew up in," she admitted frankly.

"Christ—sorry." He reacted to her flinch at the offensive profanity. "Sorry," he repeated with sincerity this time. "I completely forgot what you went through growing up." He shook his head, perplexed. "How could I forget something like that?" His brows gathered. "I've really been selfish, haven't I?"

Before the stroke, Howe would never have even considered asking such a question.

"Yes," she answered, unable to put into words the bitter cost of his monumental self-absorption.

"Sometimes, I feel like the old me is somebody else," he confided. "An evil twin. I have those memories, but I didn't *feel* anything then." His eyes lost focus. Clearly, the stroke hadn't damaged his verbal capacity or his ability to remember the way he'd felt. "Well, ambition, maybe. The fleeting thrill of the deal. And loneliness, but I had nobody to blame but myself for that."

Elizabeth sat silent. It was the most he had ever spoken to her of his feelings, and it frightened her. Caring about Howe had been far too dangerous for far too long for her to start doing it now.

"And lust," he went on. "Not love. Just lust, brief, and quickly spent. No entanglements. No demands." He gripped his chest as if in pain, guilt etched into his handsome features as he faced her. "Why did I throw you away?" She closed her eyes at the callous summary of what he'd done. "Why didn't you leave me?" he asked her.

"Because I had nowhere to go." She faced him squarely. "And I refused to shame our children. Every time my father beat my mother or embarrassed us all with his drinking and she forgave him, I swore I would make a better life for my children, and I have. I swore I would never shame them, and I won't."

Even by leaving Howe for P.J.? She couldn't think about that now. Focusing on Howe, she dismissed the thought.

She didn't know if her husband possessed the capacity to do what she asked him next, but she asked him anyway. "Howe, please don't make them ashamed of their father. I know Patricia resents me, but all teenaged girls resent their mothers. I can take it. But she idolizes you. Don't destroy that by telling her about the hookers." Elizabeth had thought herself beyond feeling when it came to that endless betrayal, but saying it aloud sent a hot stab of pain through her heart. "Confessing your sins might make you feel better, but it would destroy Patricia, and Charles. It's past history, and nobody's business but our own." And a long line of prostitutes, but if the family was lucky, he'd used an alias. "We have to figure out a way to get through this. Please don't make things worse by telling them."

He peered at her intensely. "I don't deserve you."

"Up till now, no," she said. "But you were my husband, and I made a promise to our children. Whether they know it or not doesn't matter. All that matters is what we do now."

He sagged against the dark wainscoting. "I *feel* everything now, times ten, and that includes regret. And anger at the man I was. And grief for what I've done to you and everyone else in my life. It's horrible. Horrible. How do people live with feelings like this? How did I live with this?"

Elizabeth didn't have the energy for any more angst. "Don't go all morbid on me." She stood. "Come on." She pulled his hand to help him up. Howe needed something to distract him from himself. Maybe they should do the place over, after all. "Come to the kitchen, and I'll tell you how I want to redo it."

He did another of his lightning about-faces. "Okay. It's the least I can do."

"We'll see how you feel about that when everything's torn up and the bills start coming in." She scanned the rooms and smiled with satisfaction. "I mean to gut this place, room by room, and bring it into the twenty-first century."

"Do we have any sauerkraut?" he asked cheerfully as they entered the kitchen. "I sure could use some hot dogs and sauerkraut."

"I'll see." Elizabeth shook her head. "Why you don't weigh a thousand pounds, eating the way you do, is beyond me."

Howe dazzled her with a smile. "Beats me. But I sure do like my food. And beer. Do we have any beer? Suddenly, I've got a taste for Heinekens."

An hour, a feast that would do a German proud, and eighteen mood changes later, Elizabeth followed Howe's labored progress onto the second-floor landing. Halfway across it, he stopped, frowning.

"What's the matter?"

He looked left to his master suite, then right to hers.

"Yours is over there," she reminded him. "Do you need any help?"

"I don't want to sleep by myself anymore," he declared.

Whoa, Nellie! Elizabeth stiffened.

"Especially not in there," he said, thumbing toward his rooms. "The place is like a cave, and there's no bathtub. I like baths, now." Registering her reaction, he hurried to qualify, "I'm not talking about sex or anything. I understand about your wanting to wait at least six months for the other AIDS test to clear before we even consider that, but I don't want to be alone." He was so earnest, so ingenuous. "Please. I promise not to hog the covers or squeeze the toothpaste in the middle."

But it was *her* room, and *her* bed! *Her* private retreat.

Seeing her resistance, he offered, "If you don't like it, I'll call the painters and have them redo the man-hole in there, but could we at least try it? I have these really bad dreams about the way I was before, and I hate waking up alone."

Too much information! He was playing on her sympathy. But since the stroke, she had to admit, the man couldn't seem to lie.

"I swear," he said, "I'll behave myself. One false move, and I'm out."

Elizabeth stiffened. Howe was the one who'd moved out of their bed, and it had broken her heart. Asking to move back now, because he was the lonely one, seemed bitterly ironic. Her room had become her sanctuary, and now he wanted to invade it.

She'd prayed so hard for Howe to come back

to her, all those long, lonely years ago. But not like this.

Still, she had to be certain her marriage was really over to think of leaving. That meant giving Howe a chance.

"All right," she said, prompting elation from him. "We can try it. But there have to be some ground rules." She pointed at him. "No groping, or you're out. No touching of any kind, without permission. One infraction, and you're out. No warnings. No second chances. Do I make myself clear?"

Howe nodded, undaunted. "Crystal." He lifted his palms to her. "No touching without permission." He shot her a brief leer. "No matter how much I want to."

Elizabeth rolled her eyes. She gave him one hour, and he'd be out. "And no farting," she added.

Howe looked stricken. "Lizzie! I don't do it on purpose."

"Don't call me 'Lizzie.' " She *hated* that name. "Gas-X," she ordered, pointing to her pristine white bathroom. "In the medicine cabinet. And no more sauerkraut. Or onion rings."

He granted her a smug smile. "Unless we both eat 'em. Then we can both fart under the sheets."

"I do not fart," she lied with impunity, then left to start calling architects. Elizabeth knew exactly how she wanted to redo everything, and

143

she wanted to make sure the renovations were well under way before Howe could change his mind.

That night, Howe kept to his side of the king-sized bed when she slipped in on the opposite edge wearing an opaque black-and-white print cotton sleep shirt that didn't give anything away. She had no intention of changing her routines at this point in life. If Howe didn't like it, he could go back to his room.

Still, she felt skittish as a girl, and couldn't help remembering some of the good times they'd shared in that same bed.

Best not to think of that. She had months before the second AIDS test made sex with Howe even conceivable. She'd taken a mild sleeping pill just to make sure she didn't give him any ideas, or get any herself.

After putting night cream on her lips, face, hands, and elbows, she lay on her back, pulled up the covers, put on her black satin sleep mask, then inserted the plastic bite guard she'd worn for ten years to keep from gritting her molars into bone dust.

"What's that?" Howe's voice perked with interest. "Lizzie, do you have *false teeth?*"

Exasperated, she pushed up one corner of the mask to glare at him. "No. Iss a bite guard," she snapped, then lowered the mask and turned her back to him.

He barked a laugh. "Makes you look like an alien when you talk."

"Thass strike one," she said over her shoulder.

"Sorry. Sorree," he muttered.

Glad she'd taken a sleeping pill, she didn't hear another word out of him till she woke to the smell of coffee.

"Lizzie," he cooed, his weight shifting the mattress close beside her. "Time to get uuup."

A pillow tucked under one knee and another close against her stomach, she shoved the mask off one eye to be greeted by glaring daylight and the jingly hum of the two air conditioners in her windows. "Wha time iss it?" she asked, releasing a cloud of dragon-mouth through the bite guard. Hungover from the sleeping pill, she remembered that she had a witness and pulled off the mask, palming the dental apparatus.

"Nine-thirty," Howe informed her, "and three architects and the cabinetmaker have already called back."

Noting his now-slender torso was minus the T-shirt he'd worn to bed, and the waistband of the navy silk pajamas Patricia had given him for Christmas, Elizabeth blushed like she'd woken up with a total stranger, which only annoyed her further.

"It ought to be against the law to be so chirpy before noon," she grumbled as she sat up. Yawning, she stretched to cover tucking the bite guard into the bedside table drawer. She'd sterilize it later.

Howe handed her a cup of coffee. "Welcome to the world."

"Do you have to talk?" she muttered. "New rule. No talking till after coffee. No noise of any kind."

Undaunted, he watched her sip her coffee as if she were a vision of freshness instead of a Susan Boyle impersonator. "At least you're awake," he teased. "You made plenty of noise last night. Your snoring woke me up several times."

Elizabeth glared at him in outrage. "I do *not* snore."

"Oh, yes you do," he countered with a smug smile. "Like a chain saw."

Was that why her mouth was always so dry when she woke up?

Mortified, she stammered. "Well, I . . . maybe the sleeping pill. But I do *not* snore."

"You always have. Even when we were newly-weds." He set her coffee on the bedside table, then tried to cuddle up beside her, but she resisted. "It's okay, Lizzie," he said. "It lets me know I'm not alone. And I can always get earplugs."

"I thought you were just making up an excuse when you said that was why you moved out," she blurted out.

She saw that he wished he could tell her it was, but this new Howe couldn't lie, even when he wanted to. "That was . . . Moving out didn't have anything to do with you, Lizzie. That was me. I couldn't . . ." Seeing the hurt and skepticism in her eyes, he stopped himself before he got in any deeper. "It wasn't you."

"Well, it sure felt like it." And suddenly, the pain felt all too fresh, resurrecting that bitter rejection. Elizabeth got out of bed and headed for refuge in the bathroom. "I don't think this is going to work out," she said from the doorway.

Crestfallen, Howe froze, making her wonder if he thought she meant *they* weren't going to work out. "You're kicking me out because I said you snore?"

"No," she said. "Yes. I don't know."

"Lizzie—"

"Don't call me 'Lizzie,' " she said, unconsciously investing all her fears and frustration into the obnoxious nickname. "I *hate* that name." Somehow, it had become an emblem of his selfishness, then and now. "I am *not* Lizzie, and I never will be. My name is Elizabeth!" She slammed the bathroom door, then sank to the toilet seat, angry that he'd told her about the snoring, and even angrier that the memory of his rejection had made her feel so small and impotent again.

The shadow of his feet blocked the east sun

shining under the door. "Elizabeth," he said, his voice carrying through the solid walnut panels. "I know you may not believe this, but I love you. I loved you deeply when we married, but after Dad died, coming back here and taking over the bank did something to me. There were some pretty dirty dealings. I tried to fix things, but ended up getting dragged in deeper. It . . . put my soul to sleep. But I'm not that man anymore, and I never will be." He may have meant it, but Elizabeth knew he might not be able to keep such a promise. "Don't push me away," he said. "I'm your husband. If you love me even a little, we can make this work."

Elizabeth could have lied to him and said she did, but she told the truth instead, hard as it was. "I don't know you, Howe. The man I fell in love with never cursed or took the Lord's name in vain." Tears sheeted down her cheeks. "The man I fell in love with slowly disappeared, leaving me alone in my bed to wonder who he was with, and what I'd done wrong, and whether our children would find out. I stopped loving that man a long time ago."

Elizabeth was willing to give Howe a chance, but she couldn't risk having her heart broken again. She wouldn't, so she wielded the truth like a weapon, to keep a safe distance between them. "Now you're like a toddler, all extremes. Exhausting. Dangerous, with complete disregard

148

for the consequences of what you're saying." She couldn't trust a man like that. "I don't even know you."

"But I know you," he said quietly. "At least let me try to be a real husband to you. A good husband to you. We had something good before we came back here, didn't we?"

When she didn't answer, he added, "For the kids, if nothing else, Lillibet." At last, the name she loved. "Just let me try."

This was too hard, too dangerous. "Go away, Howe," she told him.

They couldn't share a bed, not yet. Not till she knew who he turned out to be.

At least the way things had been before, she'd had some peace, some stability. They might even have grown old together and become allies in the end. Except for P.J.

Now she didn't know what to do.

She just knew she was tired. Tired of being the perfect wife for public consumption. Tired of pretending everything was fine when it wasn't. Tired of catering to all of Howe's whims and needs, seven days a week from dawn to dusk.

Tired of pretending she wasn't attracted to another man, a man who loved her enough to wait for her.

"I'm going downstairs," Howe told her, "but I love you, and I'm not going away. I'll do what it takes to be the husband you deserve, Elizabeth."

He might say that, but neither of them knew whether he could follow through.

Howe's voice tightened. "I'm still your husband."

"No you're not," she whispered as his footsteps retreated. "I don't know who you *are,* but you're not my husband."

# Chapter 10

Elizabeth seriously debated staying home from Sewing Circle—or "Whine and Cheese," as their husbands had dubbed it—but being cooped up with Howe was wearing on her, despite the welcome distraction of redecorating. So she went anyway, glad that it was at Mary's.

"Hey!" Mary greeted her with a glass of Portuguese white port and a warm smile. "I'm so glad you could make it. How's Howe?" She chuckled. "That sounds funny: How's Howe."

"Making progress," Elizabeth responded on reflex. It was the safe answer, what she always said. "Slowly." She took a drink of wine and felt its sweetness glow all the way down to her empty stomach.

Shoot. She'd meant to eat some crackers before she came.

Mary's warm smile reflected none of the skepticism Elizabeth's knee-jerk response had gotten from others. "Good. Come on back. Everybody else is here." She led Elizabeth toward her cozy den. "We were all so glad to hear that he was doing so well. Mrs. Whittington let us know that he's getting back to normal."

Whatever normal was anymore. Elizabeth just smiled.

In the den, Anne Kelly, Holly James, Carolyn Foreman, Elaine Mason, and Faith Harris were waiting. Holly jumped up to greet her with a wine-wary hug. "Hey there, girl! Is it true? Are you finally doing over that mausoleum you live in?"

Hallelujah. A safe topic. Elizabeth took another drink, then answered, "I always thought of it more as a funeral home." The frank comment brought everybody to attention. "And yes. I am finally, finally doing it over, with Howe's blessing. Actually, it was his idea."

Anne and Faith exchanged trenchant glances. "No guessing what your mother-in-law thinks about that," Anne observed.

Elizabeth took another slug of wine, warming to the company of these women she'd known for so many years. Maybe it was the wine, or maybe it was the isolation of the past few months, but she found herself wanting to trust them, at least a little, the way they'd trusted her. "Augusta is incensed, but for once, Howe put his foot down."

"God knows," Faith said, "it's about time."

"I heard Howe was . . . *different* now," Holly ventured.

How much of the truth did she dare reveal? "Nothing like almost dying to change your perspective," Elizabeth admitted. She chose her words carefully. "He's much more laid-back now. Much more demonstrative. It's . . . good."

"Couldn't tell from your expression," Carolyn challenged, "or your tone. What's the real scoop?"

Carolyn always had to push things. Enough was never enough with her.

"There are still some . . . issues," Elizabeth granted. "He tires easily, and he's . . . Well, for Howe, he's pretty emotional."

"Any emotion's emotional for Howe," Holly commented, then retracted. "No offense intended."

Elizabeth finished her wine. "None taken."

"So," Mary intercepted, "tell us about the renovations."

Grateful, Elizabeth said, "You can't believe the difference. So far, I've just taken down all the heavy drapes in the parlor and dining room and foyer, and had the wallpaper removed and all that dark molding primed to paint, but it's already transformed the whole place. Brought in so much light."

"What colors are you using?" Mary asked.

"A soft green for the walls, between a celadon and pale jade, and white for all the trim and wainscoting."

"Oh," Faith said. "That'll go so well with those marble fireplaces."

"Which is why she did it," Holly told her.

"What about the kitchen?" Elaine asked. "I don't know how you've managed all these years with it the way it was. Personally, I'd have gone stark ravin' crazy."

Elizabeth cocked a wry frown at her friend's frankness. "I'm working on a design. There's so much to fix, it takes time to get things done right." And it takes ten times more time if your husband insists on participating, but can't make up his mind.

Mary replaced her wine with a fresh goblet, something she didn't usually do. "Here you go, sweetie. After what you've been through, you deserve it, and then some."

She had a point. Elizabeth helped herself to some cheese and crackers first, but the pleasant buzz remained.

Holly leaned in conspiratorially. "So, what did Mrs. Whittington say about the changes?" She shot the others a wry smile. "Boy, would I have liked to be a fly on the wall to hear *that*."

Elizabeth couldn't suppress a satisfied chortle. "She said it was a travesty. Threatened to disown Howe if we did it." Once she'd started confiding, it didn't seem so hard. "Not that it would make any difference. Except for the bank, he's had their holdings separated for years."

Her candor prompted a brief exchange of surprised, but eager, expressions in the others. Elizabeth took another sip and went on. "Augusta badgered Howe for more than a week, but God bless 'im, he didn't budge. Told her she could do *her* house like a funeral parlor if she wanted to, but he wanted some light and life in his house, and that was that." She punctuated the last three words with a point of her finger. A giggle startled her by escaping, but she was on a roll. "So the next morning, she turns up, loaded for bear. Doesn't knock. Just lets herself in, like she always does, with the key that's supposed to be for emergencies."

Another sip. Boy, did she like this port.

The others sat mesmerized, waiting for her to go on.

"She's always sneakin' up on me," Elizabeth let slip. Ooo. Maybe she shouldn't have said that.

"So she let herself in . . ." Elaine prodded.

Elizabeth blinked and took a deep breath to chase the fuzzies from her head. But when she spoke, she sounded slightly swacked, even to herself. "Whoo, did she ever flip when she saw that woodwork painted. I thought she'd stroke out, on the spot."

Mary's lips folded inward, eyes widening, and Elizabeth realized what she'd said. "Oops. Bad choice of words. Strike that."

"What happened then?" Holly asked.

"Well, she tried to blame me, as usual," Elizabeth confided. "Said she knew it was all my idea, which it wasn't." Not that she hadn't

155

wanted to from the moment she'd walked into the place, but it was her husband's boyhood home, and he'd lost his father and had had to give up his career, so she hadn't wanted to make waves. "But Howe heard her fussin' me out, so he came and took up for me." Wonder of wonders. Satisfaction bled through to her expression. "He even told her to give him back the key and start calling before she came over."

The others hooted and hollered with glee, and Carolyn slapped her a high five. "Whoo! Yea, Howe. It's about time."

Elizabeth warmed to their approval. "They had a real knock-down, drag-out. She asked where the drapes were, and when Howe told her we had taken them down and weren't going to replace them, she said it was indecent, that perfect strangers could look in and see our private business. So Howe said they had no business looking, in the first place. Then *she* said she wanted the drapes so she could put them back up if he came to his senses." Elizabeth took another swig of sweet wine. "We hear that a lot these days, about when he comes back to his senses."

Man, Mary's sofa was comfortable. "And then *he* says he's putting them in a garage sale, along with the rest of the stuff we're getting rid of—what the kids don't want, though I doubt they'll want any of it. They both have decent taste." She shook her head from side to side, remembering

Augusta's reaction to *that*. "And then Augusta says she doesn't care if Howe is her son, there's no way she's letting him put the family's heirlooms out in the yard like some sharecropper, for every Tom, Dick, and Harry to 'paw through.' "

The girls all hissed and booed.

"So Howe says he can damn well have a garage sale if he wants to," Elizabeth went on with more alacrity, thanks to their encouragement, "because it's his stuff, not hers, and she gave it to us when she gave us the house." *Us,* he had said, for the first time ever.

Cheers erupted. "Yea, Howe!" "Woo-hoo!" "It's about time!"

Elizabeth realized abruptly that she'd said too much. But by then, she didn't really care. Tight as a tick, she stared unfocused into the middle distance.

All those years, her sewing circle had trusted her with their life crises. It certainly hadn't been very gracious of her not to trust them back. What harm could it do to tell them the truth about how Augusta had acted about the redecorating, anyway? Elizabeth had grinned and borne her mother-in-law's abuses in silence, and what good had it done her? Augusta had turned Patricia against Elizabeth, with no reason to do so.

It wasn't as if Elizabeth could be in any worse trouble with the woman. She'd already crossed the Rubicon by painting the woodwork.

"So what happened after Howe said you were having the garage sale anyway?" Anne prodded. "And I want first dibs, by the way."

"Y'all will get a special preview," Elizabeth promised.

"So what happened then?" Holly asked.

Elizabeth decided she might as well trust her friends with some more of the truth. "Well, after Howe said he'd have it anyway, the same thing happened that's been happening since he woke up. He started cussin' a blue streak, and Augusta got all huffy, and—"

"Howe, cussing?" Mary asked in disbelief. "Kyle said he never cussed, not even in the locker room."

Uh-oh. "I really didn't mean to tell that part." Too late. No sense trying to retract it. "Y'all please, don't tell anybody," she pleaded, praying that a miracle would happen and they wouldn't. "It's not his fault. Half the time, he doesn't even know he's doing it. It's from the stroke. That, or the medication they gave him to wake up. Or the surgery. Not that it matters which, really."

"Howe *cusses?*" Faith marveled.

"What does he say?" Holly prodded. She always pushed just one step too far.

"You name it," Elizabeth admitted. "But he's getting better—well, a little better. He apologizes. He's still just pretty . . ."

Faith laid a comforting hand on her leg. "Pretty what, sweetie?"

Oh, hell, why not tell them? Unlike Howe's past sins, his current condition wasn't a crime against God or mankind. Elizabeth wouldn't say anything about the crying. That would hurt his dignity, and a man had to have his dignity. Before the stroke, it was all Howe did have. "He's really *emotional*," she went on. "His moods can shift on a word. It all just . . . pops out." She gestured to emphasize the explosive nature of his new personality, and sloshed port onto the sofa. "Oh, gosh. I'm so sorry."

"It's microfiber," Mary dismissed. "Don't even give it a thought. And don't stop."

Faith's expression had congealed. "He hasn't hit you, has he? I don't care if he did have a stroke. You shouldn't be alone with him if he's—"

"No. Lord, no," Elizabeth hurried to correct. "No anger. He's just impulsive. Really, *really* impulsive. Not angry."

She saw the skepticism in their reaction. "Okay, well, he gets mad at his mother, but he certainly hasn't gotten *violent* or anything."

Elizabeth realized she'd said *way* too much. "I don't feel comfortable talking about this any-more. Please. Can we change the subject?"

Holly wasn't having any of that. "Oh, no you don't." Mary shot her a warning glance, but

Holly ignored it. "For the past twenty years, you've come to these meetings and listened to all our problems, but never once confided anything more important than the trials of teething or the frustrations of having two kids with chicken pox. Tonight, you finally opened up. That's a good thing, Elizabeth, not a bad one."

"It's not like you're criticizing your husband," Carolyn put in, "though God knows we've criticized ours plenty. And God knows, you've had cause enough to criticize Howe over the years, but didn't."

"And we admired that kind of loyalty," Elaine volunteered. "But please don't shut us out again."

Holly grew bolder with reinforcements. "She's right. Come on, Elizabeth. Do you think you're the only person in town who can keep a confidence? Don't you trust—"

"Holly." Mary tried to intervene. "Criticizing Elizabeth certainly won't make things—"

"Baloney." Holly dismissed the objection with a wave of her French-manicured hand. "I'm not criticizing Elizabeth. I'm just telling the truth." She turned back to Elizabeth, her manner softening. "Doesn't it get lonely in there with everything all bottled up inside you? Let us be your friends. Let us in."

Elizabeth killed her second (!) glass of port, then closed her eyes and did something she hadn't done since she and Howe were in college:

She confided her own feelings. "Oh, y'all, it's like living with a two-hundred-pound toddler. Happy one minute, depressed the next. Wanting me to help him, then wanting to do things himself. It wears me out. I mean, sometimes it's wonderful. He can be really sweet. But he's always *there,* right underfoot, and so demanding, without meaning to be. Wanting to know what I'm doing and why and how, every single second."

"I hear *that,*" Elaine said. "Harry was the same way when he first retired. Wouldn't leave me alone. Tried to tell me how to cook, for heaven's sake. Rearranged my whole pantry while I was at the grocery store, without asking. I still haven't found the capers." She shook her head. "Like to drove me nuts."

Elizabeth remembered. Elaine had threatened a divorce if he didn't find something constructive to do, so Harry had joined the Stephen ministry at church and stayed busy ever since. But Howe wasn't safe enough to let loose on the world. Not yet.

"These moods of Howe's," Mary asked. "The impulsiveness. Is it permanent?"

A heavy sigh escaped Elizabeth. "Who knows? Not the doctors. All they'll say is that he's making progress. When I pressed them for a prognosis, they said med school handed out diplomas, not crystal balls."

"Whoa," Faith said. "That's cold."

"Not really," Elizabeth allowed. "They were kind, but even doctors don't have all the answers."

"It's all so unfair," Carolyn told her. "You're the best person I know. Nobody in this whole, wide world deserves trouble less than you do. All those years with Howe's mama looking down her nose at you, when it should have been the other way around, and now this."

A huge lump formed in Elizabeth's chest. "Thanks." Oh, dear. She couldn't cry. Howe was the one who did the crying now, enough for both of them.

"Damn," Elaine piped up, "it would have been simpler if he'd just died, wouldn't it?"

Faith gasped in dismay at the same time Carolyn and Holly let out a stifled bark of laughter.

"Open mouth, insert foot," Anne scolded.

Elaine had the good grace to color up. "I'm not saying you, or anybody else, wants him to *die* or anything," she told Elizabeth, "but living in limbo like that . . ." She shook her head. "I'm just so sorry for you, sweetie."

"Thanks, but I'll be okay. Really," Elizabeth said, wishing she believed it. "Even impulsive, he's really a lot nicer than he was before. Just . . . so unpredictable. I never know what he's going to say. That's why we haven't gone out yet. It can be pretty embarrassing."

"Howe Whittington, old poker face himself?"

Holly said. "A blabbermouth?" Elizabeth winced to hear his predicament reduced to such a word. "I can't imagine."

"It's harder on him than it is on me," Elizabeth defended, wishing they could talk about something else. "Y'all," she pleaded, "please. I mean it. I don't want to talk about this anymore. I came here to get away from it."

"Oh." A light went on in Carolyn's expression. "I know what we can talk about that will cheer you up." A broad smile crossed her freckled face.

The others looked a bit confused, then their expressions cleared. "Oh, yeah." Faith nodded toward Holly. "Do you want to tell her, or should I?"

"You," Holly said, then pivoted to face Elizabeth across the coffee table. "Guess who's on the nominating committee for the Garden Club? *And* the Altar Guild."

"Who?" Elizabeth obliged.

"Me. And Faith. And Cassie Zellman." A nice girl who'd only been in for five years, making her fresh blood. "And Martha Dill." One of Augusta's old cronies.

The others peered at Elizabeth in expectation. She waited for the other shoe to drop, but when it didn't, she asked, "And?"

"And," Holly clarified, "that means that for the first time in eons, the committee consists of three of your friends and only one of your mother-in-law's."

Maybe it was the wine, but Elizabeth remained slow on the uptake. "And?"

They all grinned. "Guess who's been officially nominated for president—Garden Club *and* Altar Guild—by popular demand, and who hasn't?"

Uh-oh. "And who would that be?" Elizabeth asked, knowing the answer and not at all sure she liked it.

"You!" they announced, then produced confetti and toy horns from their seats, showering her to a tinny, dollar store fanfare. "*Not* your mother-in-law, at long, long last. The queen is dead, long live the queen!"

"Oh, y'all," Elizabeth said. "Really, I'm touched, and honored, but I . . . my plate is really full with Howe. And the renovations . . . I couldn't—"

Holly wagged a cautionary finger. "Oh, yes you could, and you should." The finger aimed at her. "You know perfectly well that the committee chairs do all the real work, and yours was the hardest." Flower show, one she'd chaired for over a decade. "Missy Bryan has agreed to take that over. All you have to do now is preside at meetings and go to district."

"Please. You have to take it," Elaine argued. "If you don't, there'll be mutiny. We haven't done anything new in ages. People are tired of the same old projects, the same old programs." The others nodded. "And you know better than anybody how many toes Howe's mama has stepped on in the last few years. Half the members have threatened to resign unless somebody else is elected. And you're the only one with guts enough to replace the woman."

"Please," Mary pleaded with exaggerated desperation. "Save us."

"Ooooh. I don't knoooow." They should at least have asked her. Elizabeth didn't like being set up. Still, they had a point. Everybody else in town was afraid of Augusta, and Elizabeth had already declared war by renovating the house. How much worse could things be?

"I'll have to think about it," she told them.

Holly's and Faith's faces fell. "Do you need three minutes or four?" Faith asked.

"Augusta will have a fit," Elizabeth hedged.

"She already did, over the house," Faith reminded her. "So she doesn't speak to you for another year or so. Would that be a bad thing?"

Not really. "I thought y'all felt so sorry for me, and here you go, doing this to me," Elizabeth grumbled.

Mary spoke up. "Oh, sweetie, we're not doing it to you. We're doing it *for* you. You've been under that woman's thumb too long. It's high time you stopped being crown princess of Whittington and assumed the throne. I know we'll all be

165

better for it. And I'm hoping you will be, too."

As Howe would say, *Damn*. "Well, when you put it that way," she conceded. "Okay." She raised a staying finger. "But if I need to quit, one of you has to swear you'll take over for me."

Holly and Faith pointed to each other and said in unison, "She'll do it."

Everybody started laughing, and the tension evaporated.

At least it would give her something to do besides nursemaid Howe twenty-four/seven. Elizabeth lifted her empty glass. "On that note, I'll have another glass of wine."

Mary frowned with concern at such unprecedented excess. "Only if you let me drive you home."

"Deal," Elizabeth agreed. Not that she meant to make a habit of it. But considering what she'd been through in the past six months, and what she'd just agreed to do for the next twelve, getting slightly snockered made a lot of sense. After all, she was among friends.

# Chapter 11

"I'm home!" Arms laden with groceries, Elizabeth entered the kitchen three weeks later to the mouthwatering smell of pot roast. No, something yummier than that. A hint of onion, and . . .

Howe had taken to cooking lately, an enterprise she'd encouraged, and he was actually getting pretty good at it. He'd even set the little breakfast table with the good china and silver, and cloth napkins.

She set the groceries on the cracked tile counter. "What's for lunch?"

"Shepherd's pie," he called from behind the closed door of his study. "With butterbeans, just like you like it."

Oh, yum. But if he kept cooking the way he had been for the past week, they'd both end up weighing three hundred pounds.

She started taking groceries out of the bag. "Smells great," she called toward the study. When he wasn't cooking or micromanaging the plumbers and painters, Howe had been spending a lot of time in there with the door closed. Maybe the forced togetherness was finally getting to him. Elizabeth assumed he'd been reading—she'd heard pages turning and the creak of his desk chair. She was just glad to have the rest of the house to herself while he was in there.

"Leave the groceries," he called through the study door, his voice accompanied by the rustle of papers and a dull thud from his desk drawer. "I'll put them away after we eat."

"I don't mind." She heard his door open as she took the cold things to the refrigerator and started loading them in. Bending to fill the hydrator, she sensed his approach, but jumped when his hands bracketed her fanny.

"Sorry," he said, lightly caressing her. "I didn't mean to scare you. I just . . ." She slipped from his grasp as he finished with a wry, "You're a very sexy woman, Elizabeth. Very, very sexy. And I'm a man. It's hard keeping my hands off you."

They'd been through this half a dozen times. Until he passed that second AIDS test in three months, getting frisky would be an exercise in frustration. Not that she wasn't tempted. He looked better than he had in decades, his classic features relaxed, his tall stature toned by physical therapy and a personal trainer.

She wished she could say the same about herself. Her once-impressive bustline had headed for her waistband, requiring her to abandon the sexy bras she used to wear in favor of industrial-strength support. And the ten pounds she'd gained with each of her children had slowly been joined by ten more. She still had her hourglass shape, only now it held an hour and a half.

Elizabeth abandoned the groceries, stepping safely out of reach to hang her purse by the door to the garage, where it belonged. A place for everything, and everything in its place.

Who would ever have imagined that a middle-aged woman like her would end up with *two* men vying for her affections?

The thought of P.J. made her miss him with surprising intensity. "I'm flattered, Howe," she told him. "Really I am." Despite her intention, annoyance crept into the words. "But you promised we'd take it slow."

At least P.J. respected her wishes, which was more than she could say for Howe, who kept having little "lapses" like this one.

"I know," Howe said. "I know. But slow doesn't mean we don't touch each other at all." When she turned, he was right behind her, and he took advantage of their proximity to pull her close. "We have to start somewhere."

Howe's personality may have changed, but the way he held her brought back how good it had once been between them with surprising clarity.

He cupped her head to his shoulder, and she felt her tension ebb away. How many years had she longed for this to happen?

Why couldn't she just accept what her husband

offered, flawed though it might be, and hope for happiness? Forget P.J. and do the right thing. She always did the right thing.

The trouble was, she didn't want to do the right thing anymore.

"Elizabeth, I love you," Howe said quietly. He drew back to look at her, his blue eyes clouding. "I'm trying to take it easy, but I *want* you. I want to . . ." Tensing, he let out a heavy sigh, frustration written on his still-handsome face. "If I could only . . ." He focused on her mouth, then bent his head to kiss her, his lips tentative at first, then harder and hungrier. But he didn't push inside her mouth, just focused all his yearning on her lips, his hands sliding around her to draw her fully to him.

She meant to pull away, but that chaste kiss awakened, quite abruptly, all she'd put to sleep so long ago. Suddenly, her breasts were breasts again, happy for the hard resistance of his chest. Her sides went smooth and hungry underneath his hands. And deep between her legs, a flutter heightened with his escalating heat and heartbeat.

God help her, she kissed him back and found herself suspended, out of time, catapulted to that place they'd known in the beginning, safe and set apart, abandoned to their flesh.

For the first time in a generation, she wanted her husband, wanted him inside her. Wanted to see this new Howe, this old Howe, cry with ecstasy above her as he stabbed away the pain and distance they had made. So she kissed him as lover, not as stranger, remembering the way it used to be.

She might have forgotten all her fears and let him have her, then and there, if the plumber hadn't barged in, saving her from herself.

"Ah, uh, hello?" the man said from the dining room doorway, his gaze averted. Elizabeth shied away from Howe like a sixteen-year-old caught in the act by her parents, a zap of humiliation instantly dousing the fire she'd felt.

Dazed, Howe reached after her with a disappointed groan before they both had the wherewithal to glare at the invader.

The plumber coughed. "Sorry, but we've got to turn off the water for the next hour or so."

At least he had the good grace to be embarrassed. He pulled an apologetic face, then backed away with, "So if y'all need to do any flushing, now's the time." He motioned toward nothing in particular. "Sorry to barge in, but folks get mad if I don't warn 'em. We'll give ya fifteen minutes to take care of business before we cut it off." He beat a hasty retreat.

The minute the plumber was safely out of sight, Howe turned and tried to pick up where they'd left off, but Elizabeth would have no more of that. "Don't even think it," she said, hurrying to the oven, where she got out the homely but delicious-smelling pie. "Sit down. This smells fabulous. Let's eat."

"To hell with lunch," Howe said, indignant. "I want to eat *you*."

Elizabeth halted with casserole in hand. "Howell Whittington," she whispered tightly, "I know I encouraged you, but where in the hell do you get off talking like that? Bite your tongue."

He peered at her with frustrated passion, his nostrils flaring. "I'd rather bite your—"

"Stop it, this minute," she scolded, slamming the Country French Corning Ware onto the hot pad between their places. "Get a grip on yourself." She sat and started to dish it up. "We are adults, not horny teenagers, and there are workmen in this house. Bad enough, that fool walked in on us. It'll be all over town before supper."

Howe accepted his serving with a smug smile. "So what if it is? What's wrong with kissing my wife in my own kitchen?"

"That wasn't just a kiss, and you know it." Elizabeth plopped a glorious blob of ground chuck with onions and gravy, mashed potatoes, and baby butterbeans onto her plate. "If he'd have come in thirty seconds later . . ." She snatched her napkin and unfolded it across her lap with a prim jerk. "We'd never live it down."

She pointed her fork at him. "I am *not* sleeping with you till you pass that second AIDS test, and that's that."

Howe just grinned, clearly unconvinced.

Elizabeth shoved a bite of pie into her mouth and promptly scalded the fur off her tongue. "Aaagh. Shit!" Damn. Now he had *her* cussing. Iced tea!

Howe winced as she gulped down half a glass. "You okay?"

She set the goblet firmly on the table, then blotted her mouth with the linen napkin. "Yes," she grumbled as she fanned her food.

"Gotta watch out," he said mildly, lifting a steaming bite. "Might be too hot to handle." He savored it as if it were the food of the gods.

Elizabeth exhaled, then changed the subject. "So, what did you do while I was shopping?"

Howe paused to study her, then ventured, "Talked to Harve. He called about Rotary. Said everybody wants me to come tomorrow."

Oh, Lord, no. She *bet* they did. Talk about a lamb to the slaughter.

Seeing her reaction, he clamped his lips into a straight line, his face betraying apprehension, deliberation, and assessment. "I've decided to go." He forked up another steaming bite. "The walls are starting to close in on me. I need to get out. Start doing things again. Getting back into life."

The thought of him out there, gushing and cussing and exposing their secrets, gave her cold chills, but she managed to keep from reacting with, "No, no, no, no, no!", which would have been the surest way to make him do the opposite.

She had to tread carefully, here. His self-control was improving, but he still had a long way to go. And he still cussed like a sailor, just followed it with a reflexive *sorry*.

"I see," she managed to say without betraying her alarm. "Are you sure you're ready?"

He shot her that same pregnant glance. Then his features cleared. "I prayed about it, and God wants me to go," he said calmly, as if such a statement were rational.

Whoa, Nellie! He'd talked about having a come-to-Jesus experience when he woke up from the coma, but this was a new wrinkle. "And exactly how," she asked as calmly as she could, "did you come to that conclusion?"

"He told me to go," he said, clearly aware of her skepticism. "When I was praying."

Firm in her personal belief that God was too busy running the universe to supervise the mundane events of our lives, Elizabeth didn't know whether to call the neurosurgeon, the psychiatrist, or a minister. Not *their* minister, of course. He was useless.

"God told you?" she repeated.

Howe exhaled heavily, shaking his head. "I knew you'd take it like that." He curled his lower lip over his upper. "Before this all happened, I'd have felt the same way if you told me God spoke to you, but it was real, Elizabeth. And I trust it."

Calm. She had to stay calm. "So God wants you to go to Rotary. Not *church,* but Rotary. Tomorrow."

He grinned. "When you put it that way, sounds bat-shit crazy, doesn't it?" Brows lifted, he let out a chuckle. "But yes, God wants me to go to Rotary. Tomorrow."

"He said that?" she pressed. "He said, 'Howe, I want you to go to Rotary tomorrow'?"

"Yep."

Where had she put the psychiatrist's number? "That's certainly interesting," she told her husband. "I'm curious. What does God sound like?"

Howe colored up. "I didn't mean I actually heard Him out loud, like I'd hear you," he qualified. He tapped his head. "I heard it inside, in my mind, but it was clear as a bell, and it was definitely God." He went back to eating.

The doctor would probably want to know particulars. "Does God sound like anybody we know?"

Howe narrowed his eyes at the sarcasm that leaked through despite her efforts to the contrary.

"Me," he said around his bite of pie. "My thought-voice."

"I see." Sweet mother of Murgatroyd.

He chased his food with a sip of tea, his expression clearing. "You think I'm crazy," he said with amusement, "but I'm not. For the first time in my life, I'm seeing things clearly, and I have God to thank for that." He wiped his mouth. "But don't worry, Lillibet," he said, fork poised. "I promise not to embarrass you. I'll never do that again."

Elizabeth had no idea how frank she should be with someone who was clearly off the tracks, but she had no intention of letting him humiliate their children. "I know you mean that, Howe," she said. "I'm just not sure you can keep that promise. As the Bible says, 'the spirit's willing, but the flesh is weak.' This town is a very small place, and you've stepped on a lot of toes over the years."

"Most of them," he interjected dryly, "but they've always been too afraid of me to retaliate. I know where all the bodies are buried." He sobered. "I'm not proud of that. Or of the other . . . sinful things I've done."

That kind of candor was as unprecedented as Howe's hotline to God. Still, she didn't let herself get sidetracked. "We both know there are plenty of people who would jump at the chance to embarrass you, or our family," she argued. "I can't

176

let that happen, Howe. *You* can't let that happen. Whatever our shortcomings might be, our children don't deserve to suffer for our mistakes."

He looked away. "The sins of the father." Then he faced her, regret in his eyes. "I have a lot of amends to make. Foremost, to you and the kids. But also to this town, and it's time for me to start."

Uh-oh. Making amends meant talking to people. About touchy subjects. No, no, no.

"Don't you think it would make more sense to try going to church, first?" she proposed. "As a test, to see how you manage. Just in for the service, then out, then home. I'd be there to help you, make sure things didn't . . ."—how should she put it?—"get out of hand."

He regarded her with the same look he used on his mother when she gave him orders, but this time, it was softened by compassion. "God wants me to do this, Elizabeth. He won't punish me for being obedient. I promise, it'll be fine."

Please. "Maybe you should talk to your counselor, first," she suggested.

"Can't," Howe said, undaunted. "He's out of pocket for the next week, and then it will be too late."

Frustrated, she argued, "Howe, think of the children. I know you wouldn't mean to, but surely you don't want to risk embarrassing them."

He chuckled. "We're their parents," he

countered. "All we have to do to embarrass them is breathe."

"I'm not talking about breathing," Elizabeth countered. "I'm talking about cussing. And crying at babies in commercials. Crying in general. And blurting out . . . inappropriate things."

Howe refused to be intimidated. "Why don't you come with me, then? As my . . . *handler.*"

Howe might be a changed man, but he was still a man, and he'd clearly made up his mind, whether it was his right mind or not. She briefly considered drugging him, but she didn't have anything on hand to use, and she didn't think the psychiatrist would consider Rotary Club enough reason to prescribe barbiturates.

Damn. "All right. I'll go. But you have to swear to me, on the Bible, that you will think before you open your mouth."

He peered at her in mock challenge. "And what if I don't?"

"Then I'll be forced to tie you up and keep you here," she said, only half joking.

He refused to take her seriously. "Well, I'm not supposed to swear anymore"—oh, *right*—"but I must say," he told her with a glint of lust, "the idea of having you tie me up sounds intriguing. As long as you have your way with me afterward."

"As if!" What was she going to *do* with him? "Stop acting like a sixteen-year-old and eat your dinner."

He waggled his brows her way. "Stop acting like my *mother* and eat yours."

Exasperated, Elizabeth sighed and took a big, comforting bite of warm shepherd's pie and said a prayer of her own. *Please, God, if you do care about our ordinary lives, don't let this Rotary thing go badly. Please, please, please, please, please.*

Maybe she was going batty, too, because she swore she could hear the distant echo of a laugh . . . in her own thought-voice.

Elizabeth braced herself as they got out of the car at Pappy's Restaurant. The parking lot was slammed, forcing them to go around back. Not a good sign.

She'd deliberately made them late so there wouldn't be time for Howe to circulate before the meal, and he was anxious to be inside. "Come on, Lillibet," he urged, shooting his cuffs from the sleeves of his Armani suit. "Hitch up your get-along."

*Hitch up your get-along.* "Since when do you speak *Hee Haw*?" she observed.

"Since I'm not a stick-in-the-mud anymore," he responded. He took her elbow and speeded up their pace. "At this rate, the buffet line will be so long, we might not get any stewed corn."

Pappy's stewed corn, deviled eggs, and home-grown tomatoes were the reason the Kiwanis

179

and Rotary clubs put up with the vintage-seventies, cheaply paneled meeting room.

Howe led Elizabeth between two of the many SUVs and deluxe pickups parked in front.

*Please, God, I'm begging, don't let this be a disaster.*

They weren't even halfway up the front stairs when a delegation came out to greet them, headed by Harve. "Howe! So glad you could make it!" He shook Elizabeth's hand. "And your lovely bride. Y'all come on in."

"Harve," she acknowledged as Howe did the same. "Tom. Good to see you, Adam. Phil."

The others said their hellos and shook hands, but Elizabeth had no illusion that the open curiosity in their expressions was sparked by concern. They were there to find out if the rumors about Howe were true.

Not that she'd heard any—she'd be the last one to know—but she knew Whittington.

Steeling herself, she gripped Howe's left hand in case she had to extract him quickly from a thorny situation.

The minute they walked into the restaurant, all conversation ceased and every eye turned to watch them.

Feeling as if she'd woken up naked in church, Elizabeth forced herself to smile as if nothing were amiss, but Howe said a cheerful, "Hi, everybody. Good to see you all."

180

The openly friendly remark from the same man who'd rarely granted anybody so much as a nod prompted a spattering of *hi*'s in response, and a rush of whispered comments.

Harve hustled them into the private dining room, where the same thing happened, only this time, the president, Frank Clopton, rapped his gavel loudly from the head table, then announced over the PA system, "Hi, everybody! Let's all give Howe Whittington a big Rotary hand to welcome him back."

As applause broke out, Elizabeth caught the irony and bold assessment on most of the expressions turned their way. But Howe acted like a gubernatorial candidate, calling out names, shaking hands, and greeting everybody he could get to. He tried to free his left hand from her grip more than once, obviously tempted to hug the few genuinely interested friends they encountered, but she refused to let go, sparing him that, at least.

Frank left his place at the head table and came back to welcome them personally. "Howe, great to see you looking so well. Back down to your fighting weight." He turned to Elizabeth. "I see you've been taking good care of him." He patted Elizabeth's back, patronizing. "What would we do without our little Rotary Annes?" he gushed.

Elizabeth managed not to snarl at the old blowhard.

"Come on," Frank insisted, taking hold of Howe's elbow. "Got a place for you both at the head table. You two are guests of honor."

Elizabeth shot Howe a panicked glance. She'd planned on sitting in back. By the door, in case they had to make a quick escape.

Howe registered her concern, then bent close to Frank's good ear to murmur, "Thanks. I appreciate that, but I'd rather keep a low profile, if that's okay with you. First time out, you know. We'll just sit back here."

Frank eyed him with skepticism, practically bellowing, "Since when does Howe Whittington turn down a spot at the head table?"

Uh-oh.

Elizabeth's mouth opened to respond, but Howe was quicker, leaning even closer to Frank's good ear. "Since Jesus and I had a little welcome-back meeting at the end of a coma. So cut me some slack, okay?"

Frank was struck dumb for at least ten seconds —a world record. Then he recovered with a flustered, "Well, at least let us get you to the head of the line." He tried to pull them forward, but Howe dug in, a hint of his old menace returning.

"We're just fine where we are." Howe extracted his elbow from Frank's grip with a jerk. Then he saw Robert Harris come in.

"Sorry to cut this short, Frank," Howe said, "but I need to talk to Robert about something."

182

Eyes on Robert, Howe dismissed the president with a nod. "Thanks for making me feel so welcome." He pointed in Robert's direction and barked a loud, "Robert! Wait up."

Everybody in the room went still. Howell Whittington never yelled. Ever. Much less chased anybody down. People came to him, not the other way around.

Shocked, Robert stopped in his tracks with a smile. "Howe. Great to see you."

"Thanks for rescuing me from Frank," Howe murmured.

"Anything I can do, you name it," Robert said quietly. "It's small enough repayment for—"

Howe cut him short, turning his back to the rest of the room to murmur, "Whoa, now. None of that. Remember, it's our little secret."

Robert colored. "Sorry. I just . . . Just thanks, for everything."

" 'Nuff said." Howe clapped him on the back. "Let's get in line while there's still some corn left."

"I need to speak to Phil Mason first," Robert deferred. "Y'all go ahead."

Elizabeth relaxed a little as they got in the buffet line. So far, so good. Howe hadn't self-destructed. Yet.

He let out a happy laugh, which was enough, by itself, to make half those present think the end times were upon them. Then he sobered abruptly.

Elizabeth followed his line of sight to see their ophthalmologist, Mark Leonard, come in, late as usual, and cut in line—as usual.

"Wups." Howe pulled free of her grasp. "Be right back. I need to have a word with Mark."

Uh-oh! Elizabeth hurried after him. "Wait for me," she whispered through a fixed smile as she chased him. "Remember. You promised."

Howe turned to her, his manner serious. "I know, but this conversation needs to be private."

"Then make an appointment," she shot back beneath a benign expression.

"I tried," he retorted. "He's booked solid for weeks. Just give us a minute. It won't take long."

No way was she cutting him loose. "Howell, you promised I could stay with you through this."

Nostrils flaring, he shot her a brief glare. "Damn, Lizzie—sorry," he muttered tightly. "I hate when you call me 'Howell.' You sound just like my mother."

"And I hate when you cuss and call me 'Lizzie.'" She leveled a quelling look at him. "I rest my case."

He let out an exasperated sigh, but relented. "Oh, all right. Come on." He took her hand. "But try to act like you can't hear what I tell him, okay?"

This did not bode well. "We'll see."

"Mark!" Howe hailed, drawing away from the

line to where the doctor stood. "A quick word?"

Mark sniffed—a constant affectation—glanced longingly at the fast-disappearing deviled eggs, then reluctantly came over, partially loaded plate in hand. "Just have a minute. I've got to eat and get back to the clinic. Got twelve lens correction surgeries this afternoon." He sniffed again, lifting a bent finger to his nostrils.

Howe placed a staying grip on the man's shoulder and didn't release it. "This won't take long." His voice dropped to a confidential tone as he drew Mark out of earshot of the others, with Elizabeth in tow. "I'd like to talk to you about canceling your appointments for a while and taking a vacation. You're not well. I know this. And I know why."

Elizabeth stilled. She'd heard rumors about Mark and cocaine, but he'd always seemed fully functional to her.

"This is total bullshit," Mark scoffed under his breath.

Howe's expression firmed. "You shouldn't be operating on anybody, Mark. We both know it. Take time to go get help, and I'll suspend all your payments—on the clinic, and the house. And the condo. They're all overleveraged, and there's no sense denying the reason. I pulled your credit reports. It's just a matter of time before this hits the fan," he said without a trace of gloating.

Mark glared at him, but didn't argue.

Howe regarded him with genuine compassion. "I got a second chance to put things right, and I want to give you one, too." He reached into his suit jacket and pulled out a thick envelope. "There's a good facility near Asheville that specializes in doctors. Once you're feeling better, we'll discuss getting you back on your feet financially." He proffered the envelope. "What do you say?"

"You bastard," Mark hissed. "That's blackmail."

Elizabeth agreed with him, but that was nothing new for the old Howe, which was ominous. But the new Howe was doing it for a good cause, which was confusing.

Howe smiled. "Call it whatever you want. I'd call it an offer you can't afford to refuse." He motioned to the Rotary banner. "Put it to the four-way test. What do you say?"

Mark turned his back to the roomful of curious men and muttered, "Talk about the pot calling the kettle black. Go to hell."

"Sorry," Howe answered. "Too late. Been there, done that, got the T-shirt." His eyes narrowed. "But I'll go to the medical board if I have to. We hold the mortgage on their place, too."

Mark went beet red. Trapped between his addiction and what Howe was forcing on him, he stood there quivering faintly, muscles flexed and bloody murder on his face. Then after what seemed like eons but was probably only a few seconds, he snatched the envelope and shoved his plate at Howe, spilling tossed salad on the worn carpet. "Here. Take my plate. I can't stay. I have to cancel my appointments. I feel a serious illness coming on."

"Good decision," Howe told him. "I'll be checking in later to see how you are. And praying for you."

"Goddamned hypocrite," Mark spat out under his breath, then pivoted and stalked out.

Howe inhaled, smiling as he turned back to Elizabeth. "That went well, don't you think?" He handed her the plate.

"I have no idea what to think," Elizabeth confessed. "I assume you came up with that one on your own."

"Nope." Howe pointed briefly upward. "That one was all His."

Now she *knew* he was crazy. "The last time I looked, God does not engage in blackmail," she clipped out.

Howe just laughed. "Oh, yeah? Try reading the prophets sometime."

He shepherded her back toward the buffet line. "Oh, look. Our spot has finally gotten to the deviled eggs, and there are still plenty left. And corn." He got them plates, then loaded up on fake crabmeat salad. Apparently, blackmail stimulated his appetite.

Then again, everything stimulated his appetite.

Elizabeth was afraid to ask, but couldn't help herself. "Anybody else you have to talk to?"

Howe shook his head, taking four deviled eggs. "Nope. All done."

She heaved a sigh of relief.

"For today, anyway," he told her. "Senator Robinson won't be here till next week." He served himself a fried chicken leg. "Now, *there's* a man who could use some encouragement to do the right thing."

Oh, Lord. What next?

# Chapter 12

Fortunately, the rest of the meeting was fairly uneventful, though Howe cried silently through the Pledge of Allegiance, said "Amen," three times during the Whittington Clean and Beautiful presentation, and escaped her to bear-hug several startled acquaintances on their way out. But all in all, it certainly could have been worse.

Elizabeth waited till he was safely ensconced in his study to take her cell phone up to the back balcony and call the psychiatrist, insisting on speaking to him as soon as possible.

When he called her back half an hour later, the psychiatrist wasn't amused to hear why she'd contacted him so urgently. Apparently, religious delusions didn't qualify as an emergency. He said it was great that Howe was getting in touch with his faith and feeling confident enough to get out and see people again. When she told the doctor about Frank and the eye surgeon, the man had actually laughed and said Howe was making real progress, which made her think the psychiatrist might be a fanatic, himself.

Next she called Patricia, who'd been staying with her grandmother since the sorority trip, and exchanged the usual platitudes. Then she called Charles at work, something she seldom did, but even though she couldn't tell him what had happened, she always felt better after hearing his voice. But all she got this time was his voice mail.

She'd just hung up, sitting there on the chaise in frustration, when her phone rang. Good. Charles had gotten her message. She said hello with anticipation.

"Hi," P.J. said. "How's it going, my friend?"

"Not so hot," she said without stopping to censor herself. She needed to talk to somebody, but she didn't dare trust P.J. with the truth. Maybe just a little of the truth. "It's hard. Howe is . . . he's really trying. I have to give him credit for that. But he's so different."

"Different good, or different bad?" he asked.

"Both," she answered honestly. "I have no idea how this is going to shake out. He means well —God knows, he means well."

"I'd say that's a change for the better," P.J. said with a definite edge.

What could she safely say? "He's taken up cooking. Pretty good at it."

"Howe, cooking?" She could just imagine the look on P.J.'s face. "Howe, cooking."

"I know. And he's been very hands-on with the renovations." And he thinks God talks to him, and he's blackmailing Rotarians, but the psychiatrist says that's a sign of progress.

190

"You sound discouraged," P.J. said.

"I'm just tired. This has gone on so long . . ."

"Why don't you make Patricia come help you?" he asked for the twentieth time. "She's old enough to take some of the burden—"

"It's not that. She'd come if I asked her, but Howe's . . ." She couldn't tell him that everything Howe thought came out, including the skeletons in their closet. Elizabeth had worked too hard to make sure those skeletons stayed dead-bolted in. "It's just not . . . prudent for him to be around the kids yet."

"God, Elizabeth," P.J. said sharply. "Has he done something to you? Are you afraid he'd hurt them? 'Cause if you are, you shouldn't be—"

"No, no. No," she corrected. "He's not the slightest bit violent." Why was everyone she confided in so quick to rush to that conclusion? Even at his worst, Howe had never lifted a finger against anybody.

Well, he had kicked the dresser in frustration a few times, but the only danger he posed was to the furniture. "It's complicated," she said. "I can't talk about it."

"Why not?" he prodded. "You can trust me. You said we could be friends. That's what friends are for. Elizabeth, you need to be able to talk to somebody."

"I've managed to get by so far without that,"

she said frankly. She took a deep breath. "I'm fine, really. I'll be fine."

"I can't stand thinking of you cooped up in that house," he said, "waiting on him hand and foot without any help. Let me send you a housekeeper, at least. Somebody good, and discreet."

She exhaled. "I appreciate your concern, really I do," she said, "but I'd rather handle things myself for now." As tempting as it would be to have more help, the last thing she needed was another stranger underfoot to worry about. "I have the cleaning service when I need them," she said. "But there's not much point till the renovations are done. There's dust and sawdust everywhere."

"I thought they hung plastic," P.J. said.

"They did, but the dust gets out anyway, and there are boxes and displaced furniture all over the place."

"So what harm would it do to have somebody come in and at least keep up with things?"

It was nice having somebody care how hard this had been on her. Howe meant well, but it was still all about him. "You sure are pushy," she chided good-naturedly.

"And you're martyring," P.J. chided good-naturedly right back.

He didn't know the half of it. But it shocked her to realize that martyring was all she knew how to do.

She heard the door to Howe's study open downstairs. "I have to go."

"I'm sending you a present," P.J. told her.

"No. Please—"

"Don't worry," he said, cheerful. "It'll come in a plain brown wrapper, none the wiser. Use it, Elizabeth. For yourself. You deserve it, and a lot more."

"No, really, I—"

" 'Bye." He hung up.

"Yo, Lillibet!" Howe hollered from the back stairway, clearly excited. "Guess what? We're all going to Disney World!"

Oh, Lord. "I'm coming!"

Three weeks later, despite Elizabeth's best efforts to get Howe to change his mind, he and Elizabeth rang the bell at his mother's to pick up Patricia for the flight to Orlando.

Elizabeth had argued for gradually acclimating the children to their father's new persona, but Howe had decided a boot-camp approach—albeit a *fun* boot camp—would be a more effective way to start over with their kids, so the trip was on.

Pearl opened the door with a huge grin. "Mr. Howe, it's so good to see you at long last. And lookin' so well!"

Howe enveloped her in a huge hug, lifting her off her swollen ankles. "How's my favorite treasure?"

"Here, now, you put me down," she fretted, flustered. " 'Fore you hurt yoself. Or me."

Howe eased her back onto her sensible shoes. "Don't worry about me. I'm better than I have been for the past twenty years." He waggled his eyebrows, leaning in close. "Don't you want to know why?"

Pearl straightened her always immaculate white apron. "Why is that, then?"

His eyes sparkled as he confided, " 'Cause I finally got born again."

Elizabeth rolled her eyes as Pearl burst into tears of joy.

"Have mercy, Jesus. My prayers have been answered!" Pearl grabbed Howe and started whacking his back. "Thank You, Jesus, for savin' this precious boy at last. Thank You, Jesus."

Augusta's voice cut across the foyer with an icy, "That's quite enough, Pearl. Don't encourage him." She approached from the family room. "You know as well as I do that Howell was baptized and brought up in the church." Augusta stopped beside the huge fresh flower arrangement in the vase on the circular table, her hands clasped before her. "Elizabeth," she acknowledged tersely. "Pearl, please tell Miss Patricia her—"

"Daddy?" Patricia erupted from the landing. "Daddy!" Laden with shoulder bags, her hair haphazardly caught up in a bright pink scrunchie, she ran down the stairs so fast Elizabeth was afraid she'd trip over her forty-dollar flip-flops. Though she was a woman full-grown, Patricia launched herself into her father's arms. "At last! I've missed you so much!"

"There's my girl," Howe managed through a fresh spate of tears. "There's my Patti-pie."

Elizabeth might as well not have existed, but she was accustomed to being ignored by her daughter.

"I can't believe I'm nineteen and going to Disney World for the first time," Patricia told Howe.

He swung her back and forth. "How do you think I feel? I'm fifty-nine." His voice broke. "Better late than never." He set her down. "First class, all the way. The works. We are gonna have us some good old-fashioned *fun.*"

Patricia reared back. "But I thought you were so sick," she said, grasping his arms to study him. "Too sick for me to come home." Her beautiful features set in a pout. "You don't look sick to me. You look great. Why didn't you want me at home?"

"Patricia, remember yourself," Augusta chided. "Your father almost died and was in a coma for six months. His injuries aren't visible. It's rude to question his decisions."

"I'm sorry, Daddy," Patricia told him.

He kissed her forehead, regret in his expression.

"That's okay, sweetie. I had a lot of adjustments to make, but I'm okay now, and we're all going to be together at last."

She giggled. "I can't wait to ride the teacups with you." Pulling her father, Patricia started for the door, oblivious to the two large suitcases they passed. "What made you decide on Disney World?"

"Patricia, honey," Elizabeth said. "Please take one of your suitcases. I'll get the other."

Howe extracted himself from their daughter's grasp. "No way," he said. "I'll get them both."

"Do you think that's wise, Howell?" his mother asked, her tone leaving no doubt that she thought it wasn't. "I can call Thomas."

"Mama, Thomas is eighty-three," Howe retorted. "I can handle these."

Augusta let out a disapproving sigh. "If you insist."

"No, Daddy, let me. Really." Patricia extended the handle on the larger one and pulled it toward the threshold. "It's on wheels." With a flash and a rumble, she was out the door and bumping down the brick stairway.

Howe picked up the smaller one up by its regular handle. "Well, I guess we're off." He walked over to give his mother a peck on the cheek. "Sorry we couldn't talk you into coming with us, Mama. You never know. You might have liked it."

Not a chance in hell, Elizabeth thought.

"Amusement parks are for children, Howell," his mother said as they exited onto the brick front porch. "And simpleminded ones, at that."

Howe looked at her with a sad smile. "So you said, Mama. See you in a week." He took Elizabeth's arm with his free hand. "Come on, Lillibet. Let's make up for lost time with the kids."

Augusta lifted her eyes heavenward with a sharp exhale. "Try to act your age, Howell."

His smile broadened. "Are you kidding? I've been old since I came back to this town. I'm ready to be young. Why do you think we're going to Disney World?"

Augusta shot Elizabeth a look of sympathy. "Do the best you can with him." Then she closed the door.

"Come on, Daddy," Patricia called from the front seat of their eco-pig Infiniti SUV. "Charles is already packed and sitting on his front porch downtown, waiting for us."

"On our way," Howe said with forced joviality.

Elizabeth had warned Howe that he couldn't undo a lifetime of distance with a trip to Disney World, but he hadn't listened. He'd just started crying and said he had to start somewhere with their children.

He opened the front passenger door. "Okay, Tinkerbell," he told a surprised Patricia. "Climb in back. I'd like to ride with your mama."

*That* was new. Usually, Patricia rode up front with her father, and Elizabeth rode in back with Charles. Elizabeth regarded Howe in mild amazement, and was rewarded with a sidelong hug.

"C'mon, Patti-pie," he urged their daughter.

"But Daddy," Patricia wheedled. "Mama's had you to herself for months and months." She frowned up at Elizabeth in challenge. "I always get to sit with Daddy. You don't mind, do you?"

Boy, was Patricia in for a surprise. For once, Elizabeth stuck up for herself. "Yes, honey, I do. Please do as your father asks."

In a snit, Patricia popped loose her seat belt. "Great." She stormed past Elizabeth to get into the rear seat, then slammed the door. "You must have brainwashed him."

Howe held the door for Elizabeth to get in front, then leaned over Elizabeth's shoulder to say to their daughter, "Patricia, I don't ever want to hear you use that tone with your mother again. You have no idea what I've put her through in the past seven months," he said sternly. "But even if I hadn't, you shouldn't ever be so rude to her. Is that clear?"

Patricia shot him a rebellious look. "Yes."

"Yes, what?" he pushed, confirming his parental stance.

"Yes, sir," she begrudged, smart enough not to push him further.

Surprised at how good it felt to have her husband stick up for her, Elizabeth sent Howe a grateful glance before he closed the door and put the luggage in the trunk.

Then, resolutely cheerful despite their sulking child, he got behind the wheel and leaned over to give Elizabeth an affectionate peck on the cheek. "Okay. We are off."

Elizabeth looked into the rearview mirror and saw Patricia's sullen expression change to one of wonder. "Mama, Daddy just kissed you," she said.

Elizabeth smiled. "That he did." Maybe this might not be such a bad idea, after all.

*If* Howe could keep their secrets to himself.

When they reached Charles's place, Howe waved to their son and told them, "You two wait here. I'll get him."

That earned a minor pout from Patricia, but Elizabeth watched with great interest as Howe walked up and hugged their son. "The place looks great, Charlie," he said, his voice rough with emotion. "Great. Who did you get to do the landscaping?"

Charles lit up like a lantern under his father's approval. "Nobody. Just me and Home Depot. And a lot of elbow grease." He moved awkwardly from his father's embrace to scan the lush plantings. "Amazing what you can get done when you don't have a social life."

Howe frowned in concern. "What happened to . . . ?"

"Celeste," Charles provided. "She dumped me three months ago, while you were in the hospital."

Howe looked abashed. "Sorry."

Charles shrugged. "It's okay. She was way too high-maintenance, anyway."

Howe nodded, scanning the yard. "Well, good riddance, then." He clapped Charles's back. "Her loss is the yard's gain. Looks professional. Everything's growing so well."

Charles beamed. "I used drought-tolerant native plantings, mostly, and put in drip irrigation."

"You must have inherited your mother's green thumb," Howe said.

Elizabeth watched the two of them stand there till the moment weighed too heavily with unspoken emotion and Howe reached for Charles's suitcase. "Here. Let me get this."

Charles whisked it from him. "No. I'll get it."

They headed for the car.

"Hey, Mama," Charles called on his way to the rear storage. "Hiya, Patti."

"Hi, yourself," she retorted, clearly not appreciating the shift of her constellation to son-centered.

Howe shot Elizabeth a pointed glance as he got in, then focused on the traffic while she settled back to see how things would shake out in the backseat. It felt odd, having both the kids in back.

Genial Charles tried to coax Patricia into conversation, but after a few terse answers, she put in her iPod and retreated.

So much for fun and togetherness.

Patricia didn't improve between there and Orlando, but Charles blossomed under his father's attention. The two sat together on the plane and talked law all the way to the hotel. Once they were in their suite at the Grand Floridian, Elizabeth wanted to take a rest, but Howe was far too excited.

The first shock came when he emerged from their bedroom in something so out of character that Patricia forgot to sulk. "Daddy," she exclaimed, "you're wearing shorts!"

Khakis were as casual as the old Howe had ever worn. And his legs were tanned! When had he managed that?

Howe followed her line of sight, then grinned. "Jany's Tanning Parlor."

Oh, Lord. Jany was one of the biggest gossips in town. When had he managed *that?*

Charles was more impressed with the garish Hawaiian shirt his father had on. "Cool shirt, Dad." He looked at the stylishly clunky sandals on Howe's feet. "Your wingtips must be rollin' in their grave. Are those Skechers?"

Howe cocked his finger like a gun. "You got it. All from the Internet."

Patricia was not impressed by the new, hip Howe. "It looks weird, on you."

Elizabeth agreed, but Howe wasn't intimidated. "Well, then, we're even," he said with a grin, prompting a startled chuckle from Charles. " 'Cause I think all that retro hippie stuff *you* wear looks even weirder. Whose idea was it to resurrect *that,* I'd like to know?"

Placing a hand to her chest just like Howe's mother, Patricia stared at him, appalled. "Daddy. Are you trying to hurt my feelings?"

"Nope." Howe stuck out his chin with a smile. "Nope. Just calling it like I see it. And anyway, you started it."

Lord. "I think I'll just lie down for a few minutes," Elizabeth suggested.

Howe's humor crumpled in dismay. "Aw, Lizzie, don't do that."

Charles and Patricia looked to each other in surprise, mouthing, *Lizzie?*

"This late in the day, the lines will be really short," Howe coaxed like a disappointed kid. "I want to go to the Magic Kingdom and ride Big Thunder Mountain Railroad. I've got us all Fast Passes."

Whatever they were. "You want to ride the kiddie train?" Elizabeth asked him.

"It's not a train," Charles corrected. "It's a roller coaster."

Pack her bags, the Lord was coming again.

202

Howe Whittington on a roller coaster. In shorts.

Patricia looked at her father as if he had just sprouted a tail. "Daddy?" She shot Elizabeth a worried glance.

"I'll go with you, Dad," Charles volunteered.

"Thanks, Charlie," Howe deferred, "but it wouldn't be the same without all of us." He reached over and swept Elizabeth into his arms. "Come on, Lillibet. Get your glad rags on and let's get out there and have us some all-American, A-one fun. The family that plays together stays together. Git a move on, girl." He swished her toward their room. "I'll buy you a margarita on the way to help you loosen up. How 'bout that?" He laughed like some bizarre sitcom character.

Charles appeared to find the whole situation highly amusing, but Patricia didn't. She shook her head in disbelief. "How long has he been like this?"

Elizabeth let out a brief sigh. "Oh, he's lots better than he was at first. We wouldn't be here if he wasn't."

"No wonder you didn't want him to see any-body," she said to Elizabeth.

"Hello," Howe said, gesturing between them. "I'm just brain damaged, not deaf. I can hear you."

Elizabeth nodded to her daughter. "Better get dressed. Once he makes up his mind, there's no changing it."

Patricia rolled her eyes on her way to her room. "I just hope we don't run into anybody I know."

For once, Elizabeth agreed wholeheartedly with her daughter. On her way to change, Elizabeth heard Charles say behind her, "Well, Dad, I don't care who we see. I like you a lot better this way than the way you were before."

"Thanks, son," Howe said with gratitude. "For what it's worth, I do, too. And so does God."

Oh, boy. There he went with the God thing again.

If that was the way things were going to go, Elizabeth would need *two* margaritas. At least.

Forty minutes and a jumbo premium margarita later, the four of them stood in line for the Big Thunder Mountain Railroad ride in Frontierland. Howe had tipped the attendant twenty dollars when they got to the head of the line to let them have the first two cars on the next run.

"Howe, really," Elizabeth murmured. "Why are you tipping these people to do their jobs? You already paid for the Fast Passes."

He gave her an exuberant side hug. "There you go again, being rational. We went over that in the bar. This trip isn't about being sensible. It's about having fun, and everybody knows that the best way to ride a roller coaster is in the first car, hands up."

"Aha," she said. "Since you're such an expert."

The man had never been to an amusement park in his life.

"That's why I'm here," he said, undaunted. "By the end of this week, I want to have ridden every single ride and seen every exhibit in this whole place, and you with me." Then he pinched her slacks-clad fanny, right out where everybody behind them could see.

Mortified, Elizabeth swatted his hand away, but he just put his arm around her and drew her back to his side, then turned to the people lined up behind them. "We're taking a poll, here," he shouted, causing Patricia to cringe. "How many of you have heard that the best way to ride a roller coaster is in the first car, hands up? Could we see a show of hands, please?"

Most of the kids and half the adults laughed and raised their hands.

Howe grinned. "Thank you!" He turned to Elizabeth. "See?"

Charles chuckled. "What's your favorite roller coaster, Dad?"

"This one."

"But you've never been here," Charles the lawyer argued.

"Never ridden a roller coaster, either," Howe told him.

Charles assessed him with a fresh eye. "You're kidding."

"Nope."

"Not even Six Flags?" It was right outside Atlanta.

"Your grandparents didn't believe in amusement parks," Howe clarified. "Dad thought they were embarrassing and ridiculous, and Mama thought they were too germy and dangerous." A faraway look claimed him. "I used to resent that, but now I realize why Mama was so overprotective. I was all she had." He cocked a wry smile at Charles. "Dad was present, but not present, if you get my drift," he confessed. "A lesson I learned all too well. But that's over now. This week, I'm going to be in the moment, if it kills me."

"Just as long as it doesn't kill us," Elizabeth observed dryly.

"Here we go, Mr. Whittington," the attendant said as the roller coaster barreled in. "Front car for you and Mrs. Whittington." He returned the twenty. "We don't accept tips, but thanks, anyway."

Elizabeth sighed and got in. What happened next became legend in their family.

Grinning like a ten-year-old as they rode up to the first big drop, Howe waited till they started down to raise his hands, then screamed his way through the *entire* ride like a maniac, hands up, all the way.

"Oh, my God," he said, breathless, as they came to a stop. "That was amazing. Amazing."

Windblown and spattered, Elizabeth wiped some of the water off her face, trying not to think of the chemicals and germs that were in it. "And wet."

Howe shook his head at her in disbelief. "How can you be so calm?" His fingers clawed. "All that fear and all that fun exploding inside you. My God. It's overwhelming. And fabulous."

Patricia tried to act like she didn't know them, but Howe turned around and stopped her from getting out. "No, wait. We've got to do this again." He waved to the boy who was helping people out. "Hey!"

The boy came over. "Yes, sir. Is there a problem?"

Howe dug for his wallet. "Fifty bucks if we don't have to get off."

"Daddy," Patricia complained, sheltering her face from view with her hand.

Howe ignored her, telling the attendant, "That was my very first roller-coaster ride, and it was the next best thing to sex." Patricia slunk lower in the seat, and Charles shot an anxious glance toward the retreating tourists. "Now I understand why scream therapy was so popular," Howe rattled on, oblivious. "I want to go again. Right away."

The attendant laughed. "Sorry, sir, but we don't take tips." He gestured to the other people. "We'd love to have you ride as much as you want, but everybody gets to take their turn at Disney World. It's only fair."

Abashed, Howe put away his money. "Sorry. You have a point." He stood and took Elizabeth's arm. "Come on, honey"—it was the first time she could ever remember his calling her that—"let's get back in line."

Elizabeth smoothed her damp, ruffled hair. "Once is quite enough for me. You go on. I'll just wait."

"*We'll* just wait," Patricia added.

"No. That won't work," Howe protested. "We all need to be together."

"I'll go with you," Charles volunteered.

Howe bent his knees in a dip worthy of a toddler. "C'mon, Lizzie." Elizabeth cringed. "You need to go again. You didn't do it right the first time." He aimed a pointed glance at Patricia. "And neither did you."

"Oh, really," Elizabeth said. "And how would you know?"

Howe grinned. " 'Cause you're not laughing. You should be laughing." He bracketed their shoulders to draw them in. "I can't remember either of you laughing in a long, long time," he said, suddenly wistful. "I had a lot to do with that, I'm sure, and I'm sorry. But I'd really, really like to see you laugh."

Something in the way he said it caught at Elizabeth's heart.

Howe bent forward to look Patricia in the eye. "How about it, princess? Could you let go and try to enjoy this with us? Please. For me?"

Patricia rolled her eyes, but relented. "I'll try. But if you mention"—her voice dropped—"*sex* again, all bets are off." She wiggled with an exaggerated shudder. "At your age. Ick!"

Charles laughed. "Way to go, Patti." He turned to Elizabeth. "How about it, Mama-lama? I'd love to see you laugh, too."

Elizabeth's chest tightened to see the compassion in Charles's face. It had been a long time since she'd laughed. Too long. When had she turned into the kind of person who worried more about messing up her hair or getting splashed than having fun on a roller coaster?

If she kept up that way, she'd end up turning into Howe's mother, God forbid. Dear Lord, she realized, she was practically there already! "I'll try, too," she promised, feeling some of the tension inside her begin to ease merely from saying it. "But don't expect miracles."

Howe took her hand and gave it a quick kiss, his eyes welling. "Too late. Already got one. We're all here together." His voice thickened with emotion, tears escaping. "That's a miracle, to me."

Patricia wasn't amused. "No crying, either, Daddy, or I'm outta here."

Howe swiped at his eyes as they neared the

front of the Fast Pass line again. "I'll try, baby, but you'll have to cut your old man some slack."

"Mr. Whittington," the boy he'd tried to bribe greeted him. "Glad to have you back so soon. Front car again?"

Elizabeth stepped between them. "Yes," she answered with a smile.

"Right this way, then."

This time, Elizabeth actually put her hands into the air and hollered all the way. And the next.

And pretty soon, they were all involved in the quest to see every attraction and ride every ride, no matter how juvenile, and Howe's enthusiasm was so contagious, Elizabeth started laughing again. So did Patricia.

Charles recorded it all on his digital camera. And they talked as they ate in the restaurants— about the rides at first, then about Charles's work and his renovations, and Patricia's friends and social life. And somewhere between Space Mountain and the Hall of Presidents, they started to feel like a real family.

And by week's end, Elizabeth was beginning to like the ridiculous, impulsive man who slept in the other bed of their hotel room.

If only they could have stayed there.

But reality forced them back to Whittington, and they weren't even in the house before everything unraveled.

# Chapter 13

Tanned and more relaxed than she could ever remember being, Elizabeth almost made it home on the glow of their vacation. But on the plane, Howe sat beside Patricia and informed her that she couldn't have her car back till she got a job —any job—and passed a quarter at the local community college. Unable to avoid eavesdropping, Elizabeth stifled a satisfied chortle to hear her husband's bombshell. Good for him!

Patti did her best to talk him out of it, but Howe didn't budge, so she sulked the rest of the way home, while Charles and Elizabeth chatted happily about his plans to redo the kitchen in his house.

When they got to Atlanta to drop Charles off, Patti asked him to put one of her suitcases in the seat so she could do her nails on the way home, then they left the city. Elizabeth noted the familiar landmarks on I-75 north from Midtown to Whittington with a growing sense of foreboding. Life in a bubble was one thing, but reality another, and reality was waiting, primed and loaded, back home.

Sure enough, no sooner had they crossed the

county line than Patricia stopped rummaging through her weekender and piped up with, "Daddy, could you drop me off at Gamma's so I can pick up the rest of my things? And my car?"

"Sure, to the rest of your things," Howe said lightly, then uttered a word their daughter had rarely heard from him. "No, to the car."

Elizabeth glanced in the rearview mirror to see outrage on their daughter's face. "But Daddy, I said I'd get a *job* like you wanted, even though it's perfectly absurd. We don't need the money."

"We went through all this on the plane," Howe said equably.

"Daddy," she protested. "You're not being fair. At least let me drive to school and my job. Judges let people with *DUIs* drive to work and school, for crying out loud."

"This isn't open to negotiation," he told her.

Patti didn't give up. "Please, Daddy. Be reasonable. I said I'd go to Grade Thirteen"—their local community college—"but how can I get to work or school if I don't have a car?"

Howe smiled. "One of us will take you and pick you up."

Patricia flounced against her seat, arms across her chest. "That is absurd. I'm in college. It would be mortifying to have my parents drive me. I have to be able to get places."

"Patti," Elizabeth reminded her, "we told you when we got you a car that you'd lose the keys if you flunked. You flunked *out*. At least we're willing to give the car back after you pass a quarter."

"Puh-leeze," Patricia said. "I know this is all Mama's idea," she said to Elizabeth, glaring at her in the rearview mirror. "You never want me to have any fun. To be young. All you care about is what people think."

"Patricia," Howe warned, "I told you, do not speak to your mother that way. This subject is closed. End of discussion."

Patricia's tone went sly. "Mama's always been jealous of me."

Elizabeth gasped to hear her daughter speak such a wounding truth so boldly.

Howe almost ran off the road. "Patricia!" he reprimanded, glaring at her reflection. "Apologize to your mother at once."

"Well, it's true," Patti retorted. "She's always picked on me because she knows you love me more than her."

Howe swerved onto the wide shoulder of the two-lane road, bloody murder on his face, then unlocked the doors and jumped out to jerk Patricia's door open. "Get out. Now!"

Elizabeth had never seen him so angry. For the first time in her life, she was afraid of what he might do. "Howe, let it go," she pleaded.

"Absolutely not," he declared.

Patricia recoiled, wide-eyed, as her father

leaned in and released her seat belt. "Ungrateful little shit," he muttered as he grabbed her arm and levitated her to the shoulder beside him. "You are coming with me, young lady."

Elizabeth erupted from the car to intervene, but Howe pulled Patricia onto the grass, away from her. "You are never, *ever* to speak of my wife"— his *wife,* not her mother—"that way again, do you understand?" he shouted.

Elizabeth hurried to them, alarms flashing, *anger, anger, anger.* Whittingtons didn't do anger —not overtly, anyway. Just the cold, withering kind. "Howe, it's all right," she told him. "Let it go."

He turned on her. "No, it's not all right." His face was livid. "This is my fault. I'm the one who spoiled her, and I'm putting a stop to it, right now. You don't deserve this, Elizabeth. All you've ever done is try to be a good wife and mother, even when I was undermining your efforts to instill a little discipline in her. It's about time she learned that the sun doesn't shine out of her ass."

Patricia regarded him with shock—and resentment. "Daddy!"

A car slowed, rolling down the passenger window. "Do you need help, ladies?" the well-dressed male driver asked her. "Is this man threatening you?"

Elizabeth said, "No," at the same instant Patricia said, "Yes."

"Patricia," Elizabeth scolded, then turned to

214

the Good Samaritan. "My daughter just had a temper tantrum, and my husband is trying to talk some sense into her." Lord. She was explaining their private embarrassment to a total stranger on the side of the road.

The man wasn't convinced. "You're sure?" Horns honked behind him as traffic began to back up, but he didn't budge.

Elizabeth approached his car. "It's okay, really. You know teenagers these days. She finally got on my husband's last nerve."

The man took in Patricia's petulant expression and nodded, his features clearing. "Been there, done that. Y'all have a nice day."

Elizabeth prayed there wasn't anybody they knew in the line of cars that started to go past.

Patricia burst into tears and wrenched free of her father. "You're not my father anymore! I hate you! I wish you'd *died* when you had that stroke. You're mean." She turned on Elizabeth. "I hate you both."

Howe recoiled, stunned.

Before they could stop her, Patti flew to the car, grabbed her suitcase from the seat, then flagged down a middle-aged woman in a dark sedan. "Help! I need a ride!"

Elizabeth and Howe rushed to intercept her, but before they could get to her, she was in the car and accelerating away, a steady line of traffic behind them.

They'd never catch up. "Howe," Elizabeth said, frantic, as she got back into the car opposite her husband. "Could you make out the license?"

"No," he said. "It was one of these alternate plates. Some college, I think. I don't even know if it was from Georgia." He cranked the engine and put on the blinker to get back on the road in pursuit.

Panic gripped Elizabeth. God knows what could happen. "What kind of car?"

"Mercury? Maybe a Ford." He inched closer to the line of slow-moving cars. "Damn. Why won't anybody let us in?"

Probably because they'd caused the bottleneck. Or thought Patricia was an escaping kidnap victim. "What color was the car? Black?"

"No," he said, "dark blue, I think."

They hadn't even gotten a decent description of the vehicle.

Elizabeth stuck her arm out the window and waved for somebody to let them in, desperate.

A woman in an SUV finally took pity.

"We need to call the police," Elizabeth told Howe, groping for her blasted cell phone. "Who knows what could happen to her, going off with a total stranger?"

Howe laid a staying hand on her arm. "Patti's not a minor. She left of her own free will. The police won't be interested till she's been gone three days."

Elizabeth covered her face with her hands. He was right.

Howe reached over to give her forearm a reassuring squeeze. "Nothing's going to happen to Patricia. Till she gets home, anyway. Then I plan to have a few words with her."

"How can you be so calm?" she argued.

"Because she took off with Betty Crocker, for one," he said, "not Ted Bundy. And because she's been in a lot worse situations than this and managed to take care of herself."

Elizabeth straightened. "What worse situations?"

"You don't want to know," he said. "But they worked out fine."

She should have known Patricia was confiding in Howe, not her, but it didn't feel good to be reminded. "But Howe, things are so crazy these days. What if—"

"She'll be okay," he affirmed. "Patti's spoiled, but she's not stupid. She can take care of herself."

Elizabeth sank back into her seat. "So what do we do now? Wait for a policeman to show up on our doorstep with bad news?"

Howe shook his head. "She'll probably be at Mama's when we get home. I'll give her some time to cool off, then I'll go talk to her and bring her home." Eyes forward, he briefly lost focus. "I'm sorry I called her a 'little shit.' It just came out."

"You couldn't help it," she told him. "It's nothing I haven't thought a million times. I just have the ability not to say it." An ability Howe still lacked, under pressure.

His tell-all face revealed remorse.

Elizabeth was glad he'd taken up for her, called her his wife with such passion when confronted by Patti's spiteful words. But it frightened her to think what it could end up costing. "I can't believe she said those hateful things to you."

"I can. And she meant them," he answered. "At the moment, anyway." He let out a sigh. "She got away with murder for a long time with me. It's going to take time to set things straight, but I will." He squeezed Elizabeth's hand. "I'm not going anywhere, and I'm not giving up."

He released her hand to press his fingers to his temple with a wince.

"Are you okay?" she asked. He'd done that several times in the past few days.

"Just a headache," he said. "Nothing a few Advil won't cure."

Elizabeth frowned in concern. "I'll call Dr. Clare. Maybe—"

"No, don't do that," he snapped, sounding more like the old Howe than he had since the stroke. "It's just a headache. People have headaches." He sniffed, forcing a smile. "Mine's named Patricia."

They rode the rest of the way home in silence.

Patricia wasn't there when they got to the house. Howe unloaded the car, then called the credit cards and canceled Patricia's, asking the companies to notify him immediately if she tried to use them. Later, he called his mother, but Patricia wasn't there.

When it came time for bed, Elizabeth tossed and turned for more than an hour, then put on her robe and crossed to Howe's room. She knocked on the door.

Howe opened it a few seconds later, looking tousled and appealing in his silk pajama pants. "What is it?" he asked in concern. "Did you hear from Patti?"

She shook her head, eyes welling. "No. I just . . ." She looked down toward her bare feet. "Could you come stay with me? I just don't want to be alone. I'm so worried about Patti, I—"

He circled her shoulders with his arms, drawing her close to his warmth. "Sure. Of course." They walked together across the dark landing toward her room. "And no monkey business. I promise."

That was a relief. "Thanks. I really appreciate it."

"Is it okay if I hold you till you go to sleep?" he asked her.

"More than okay." She needed the reassurance of touch.

Sometime that night, Patricia's car disappeared

from her grandmother's garage. When Augusta called to tell them the next morning, Howe explained what had happened. True to form, his mother blamed *him* for embarrassing and alienating the girl, then threatened to disown him if he reported the car as stolen.

Not wanting to go into it with her friends, Elizabeth skipped Sewing Circle and Altar Guild, claiming illness. But she knew she couldn't keep their situation a secret for long, just as she knew there would be plenty of people in town who'd be happy to see the high-and-mighty Whittingtons get yet another comeuppance.

Desperate, she even called her mother in Clearwater.

"Hi, Mama," she said after her mother's smoke-rasped hello.

"Well, glory be," her mother said with sarcasm. "The word has come from Olympus. To what do I owe this honor?"

Elizabeth had long since hardened to her mother's resentment. "Patricia's missing," she stated briskly. "Have you heard from her?"

Her mother paused. "Does she even know I exist?" she asked without accusation.

"Of course. She and Charles both know you're there." Elizabeth had waited till they asked about her family to explain that her father and brothers had been abusive alcoholics, and she and her mother had serious differences. True to

220

the Whittington code, neither Charles nor Patricia had pried or expressed an interest in meeting their "toxic" grandmother.

"I know Charles does," her mother said. "I've been gittin' a nice Christmas letter and Fruit of the Month from him for the last few years," her mother revealed, to Elizabeth's surprise. "He sends something to Liam in prison, too. Even offered to help him with parole, since Liam's been clean and sober all these years."

Stunned, Elizabeth froze in her seat. Charles knew about his uncle Liam?

Parole? Liam deserved to spend the rest of his life in prison. He'd beaten his wife to death in a drunken rage. The idea of her brother loose on the world gave Elizabeth the shivers.

"But I never heard a lick from that daughter of yours," her mother went on. "Charles mentions her in his letters. Sent some pictures, and all, but not a peep from her."

Reeling, Elizabeth didn't know whether to confront Charles or let the matter lie. The last thing she wanted was for her brother to be loose to hurt anyone else.

She struggled to collect herself. "Well, if Patricia contacts you, would you please try to find out where she is and let me know? We're worried sick."

"What happened?" her mother asked, suddenly canny. "Y'all have a fight?" A pregnant pause resonated between them. "It's not so easy when they get big and bossy, is it?" her mother gloated, clearly referring to Elizabeth's long-ago decision to escape her own family and better herself.

"Please, Mama," she clipped out, "just let me know if you hear from her."

"Okay," her mother said. "I reckon I owe you that much for keepin' me up. But it wouldn't kill you to call me occasionally when there's not some emergency, ya know. I could drop dead down here, and nobody would be the wiser except for the smell."

Same song, nine-thousandth verse. "The phone works both ways, Mama," Elizabeth said, a hint of annoyance creeping into her voice. "You could call me."

"Look out," her mother warned. "I might just do it."

"By all means, do."

"By all means, do," her mother imitated in an exaggeration of Elizabeth's carefully cultured accent.

" 'Bye, Mama." Elizabeth hung up.

She stared at the phone. Charles. Dear heaven. Should she call Charles about Liam?

"Who was that?" Howe asked, surprising her from behind. "You look upset."

"I am upset," she said, swiveling the kitchen stool to face him. "It was Mama."

"Oh." Howe's expression remained equable.

"I called on the off chance that Patricia might have tried to contact her. She hasn't." Should she tell him about Liam? "But Charles has been sending her Christmas updates and gift baskets."

Howe gripped her shoulder briefly. "Good for Charles."

"He's done the same with Liam. Charles has offered to help him with parole," she said in disbelief. *"Parole."*

"Your brother's been sober for a long time, Elizabeth," Howe said quietly.

She peered at him. "And how would you know that?"

He shrugged. "In my past life, I made it my business to find out anything that might affect our family. I've been keeping tabs on Liam all along. I did the same with your father and Jacob, before they died."

"You mean drank themselves to death, at long last," she corrected, the old bitterness surfacing.

Howe drew her from the stool, pulling her into a protective hug. "They're gone now. They can't hurt you anymore."

She leaned against his chest. "Liam can. I don't want Charles having anything to do with him. What if people found out?"

After a weighty pause, Howe let out a long breath. "Charles and I had a lot of time to talk in Florida. We ironed out a lot of things. He's a man, now, a good one, and nobody's fool." He chuckled. "He told me if I ever went back to being the way I was, he'd come for me, himself."

Howe sobered. "Whatever relationship he has with his uncle is up to him. It's not up to us. I promise you, Lillibet, it will only make things worse if we try to intervene."

"But if Liam gets out . . . Even if he has been sober, facing the real world, especially as an ex-convict, who knows—"

"If he gets out, we'll deal with it. Together." He drew back to lift her chin with his finger, meeting her fears with a calm, steady gaze. "I won't let anybody hurt you, Lillibet. I promise."

A throb of heart-deep pain loosed her next thought without her conscious participation. "You let Patricia hurt me. And your mother. For a long time." Lord! Where had *that* come from?

He winced. "Ouch. I deserve that. But I mean to change it, Lizzie, I swear."

She didn't even react to the name she hated. "I know. I know. I'm sorry. I'm just so worried about Patricia. It's not your fault."

He stilled, drawing her close again. "It is my fault. I spoiled her, then came down too hard on her, and she bolted. Not a moment goes by that I don't wish I could do it over. But we have to believe she's okay."

If only she could. "I'll call Charles and see if she's contacted him. And her friends."

He patted her back, then released her. "You do

that. With no credit cards, she's bound to turn up before too long."

Howe went to the cabinet for some Advil, something he'd been doing more often lately. He headed for the refrigerator for a bottle of spring water. "I've got some things to catch up on in my study."

"You've been spending a lot of time in there," Elizabeth ventured.

Guilt flashed across his face. "It . . . I've been . . . reading." She could see he wasn't being truthful. "It helps distract me."

A dozen possibilities crossed her mind, none of them good. "You're not . . . doing anything weird on the Internet in there, are you?"

His features cleared, to her relief. "No. God, no. Really, I've been reading. Pretty heavy stuff, actually."

At least she could see that was true. But where had his initial guilt come from? "Okay." Whatever it was, he would tell her eventually. He wasn't good at keeping secrets anymore.

He popped the Advil and washed them down.

"Are you okay?" she asked, even though she knew he didn't like to talk about it. "You've been having a lot of headaches lately."

He massaged his temples, then sighed. "I'm sure it's just stress, but I guess I ought to tell Dr. Clare. I'll call him."

"Good. And I'll start calling Patricia's girlfriends," she said. "Though how I can do it without setting off the grapevine, I can't imagine."

"Just tell them the truth," he advised. "We had a fight over her grades, and she left." He cocked a wry expression. "Like the good book says, the truth shall set you free."

The reference sent a random thought across her mind. "You're not reading the Bible in there, are you?" she asked, embarrassed that it sounded like an accusation. "I mean, you're not thinking about becoming a *minister* or anything?"

Howe laughed for the first time since Patricia had run away. "Lord, no. Quite the contrary."

Whatever that meant.

"Don't worry about dinner," he told her. "I'll make a salad later and do some steaks." Then he disappeared into his study.

Patricia called Charles first, not mentioning Liam or her mother, but he hadn't heard anything. After that she started contacting every one of Patricia's friends listed in her address book, without any luck.

Assuming they'd tell her if Patricia *had* contacted them.

She even scrounged up a sorority directory in Patricia's room and started calling girls she didn't know, but nobody she reached had heard anything. A few parents told her that a lot of the girls were vacationing, making Elizabeth wonder if

Patricia had joined any of them, but there was no way to reach them if she had.

By suppertime, Elizabeth had come up empty, and she and Howe shared a subdued meal.

That night, she dreamed Patricia was calling for help, but she couldn't find her. Frantic, she searched through more and more dire settings till she woke in a panic, drenched in sweat. Howe was sleeping soundly on his side of the bed, so she crept into the shower and cried under the cover of the noisy spray.

When he came in and found her, she was too miserable to notice that she was naked in front of him. He just quietly shucked off his pajama pants, then climbed in to hold her as she sobbed, his presence communicating more than words ever could. When the hot water ran tepid, he turned it off, then helped her out and dried her. Back in bed, he held her close, her wet hair against his chest, till they both, at last, fell asleep.

It was the closest she had felt to him since law school.

But the sun dawned on yet another day without word of their daughter. And another.

Meanwhile, Dr. Clare saw Howe and ran some tests, all of which came back normal, much to Elizabeth's relief. And Howe hired a skip tracer the bank had used, saying the man was very discreet and would find Patti soon.

But two more days passed, and the only calls

Elizabeth got were from her friends—predicated on thinly veiled excuses, which proved the gossip mill was onto Patti's disappearance—and a few from P.J. Elizabeth didn't mention Patti to him at first, feeling it would be disloyal, somehow. But he found out anyway.

Howe was in his study when her cell phone rang on the fifth morning since Patti had left. Seeing "unknown caller," Elizabeth wondered if it was P.J. or Patti and said a breathless, "Hello?"

"I just found out," P.J. said. "Why didn't you tell me? I could have hired a detective. Done something, anything, to help. I know you're frantic."

"Hold on." Elizabeth hurried to the side porch, safely out of earshot from Howe's study and the workmen. "Howe has somebody looking for her," she explained when she got there. "I just didn't . . . I appreciate your concern, but I really don't want to talk about it, if that's okay. I get sick to my stomach when I do."

"I never got to have kids," P.J. said. "Liza kept putting it off. Then my business went to hell, and she went with it, so no kids for me. I can't begin to imagine how awful this must be for you."

So much for not talking about it. "We'll be okay," Elizabeth told him, using the plural without thinking. "Howe's convinced she'll show up eventually, when she runs out of money."

"He would think of money," P.J. said, leveling the first direct criticism of Howe since he'd woken from his coma.

"It's not like that," Elizabeth defended. "He's not like that anymore. He's as worried as I am."

"Sorry," P.J. apologized. "I just can't help . . . the man has everything, including you. I'm jealous. I admit it."

"Don't be," Elizabeth told him. "Once I make sure Patti's okay, I might just strangle her. She's so . . ." Anger and frustration threatened to set her tongue loose at both ends, but she managed to get a grip on herself. "Trust me, you don't need to be jealous."

An uncomfortable silence lengthened between them. "What can I do to help?" he asked at last.

"Give me space," she said frankly. "I can't handle . . . the whole *us* thing. Not till I know Patti's safe. Maybe not even then. There's still so much to work out with Howe."

"Okay," he conceded. "But I'm here for you, Lillibet." The pet name rankled, coming from him. "I'm not going away."

As much as she hated to admit it, she didn't want him to, no matter how unrespectable that was. "I miss you," she confessed. "Miss our talks."

"I miss you, too," he said, his voice catching.

She exhaled heavily. "I'll call you when we find out anything."

"Okay."

She hung up, flashing on the feel of his arms around her and the heat in his eyes when he looked at her. Her insides did a flip.

Then she thought of Howe, holding her close as they both grieved their runaway daughter, and felt the old "bad girl" guilt she'd known as a child when her father had beaten her older brothers, yet never laid a hand on her.

"Hey," Howe said from behind her, sending Elizabeth half out of her skin. "I was looking for you. Dr. Clare said we could come in this afternoon to go over the test results."

"Good," she said, pocketing her cell phone, heart pounding. "I'll get my things."

Howe waggled his brows. "We can have lunch at the Varsity!"

"You and the Varsity," she said, grateful he hadn't noticed her reaction.

Dr. Clare showed them the MRIs and confirmed that nothing new was abnormal. Everything looked fine. Elizabeth was surprised by how elated she was to hear that Howe was all right. But her relief was tempered by growing dread about their missing daughter.

When the sixth day came and Patti still hadn't gotten in touch, Elizabeth broke down and called the police to report both their daughter and her car as missing.

True to Howe's prediction, the cops took the

report, but didn't seem concerned, especially after Elizabeth explained that they'd had a fight over the car.

Less than fifteen minutes after she got off the phone, Augusta called and royally chewed her out for "parading their family differences before the police, of all people, and trying to make a criminal out of her own flesh and blood."

Then she demanded to speak to Howe and railed on him, swearing on his father's grave that she'd never forgive them if anything happened to her granddaughter. After that, she gave them the silent treatment—a blessing, as far as Elizabeth was concerned.

As the days went on, even Howe's optimism flagged. He even begged off Rotary, saying he didn't feel well—his first successful white lie since the stroke.

Elizabeth didn't know whether to consider that a good sign or a bad one.

Worried and guilt-ridden, he retreated into himself and his study, reminding Elizabeth all too much of the way things had been before his illness.

Every time the phone rang, Elizabeth's heart leapt, hoping it would be their daughter. More than a week had passed without word when she answered yet another ring. "Hello?"

"May I please speak with my son?" Augusta's frosty voice asked.

Disappointed, Elizabeth went to his closed study door and tapped it lightly. "Phone, Howe. It's your mother."

"Thanks," came back through the door. She heard him pick up the extension. "Hello?"

She hadn't intended to eavesdrop, but before she hit the kill button, she heard Augusta say the one thing that kept her from hanging up.

"I have word of Patricia," Howe's mother told him.

"Thank God. Is she okay?" he said. "Where is she?"

"In jail, thanks to you, at Destin," Augusta snapped. "For stealing her own car. She called, asking me to bail her out. I've already engaged a lawyer there to do so, but if you pursue this ridiculous stolen-car business, I shall cut you off without a penny, Howell, and I mean it!"

"Of course we won't charge her," he said, ignoring the useless threat. "We just want her home."

"Thanks to you," his mother shot back, "she doesn't want to come home."

Elizabeth winced for Howe.

"Well, we want her here," he said, his tone firm. "She needs to learn that running away doesn't solve anything. Tell the lawyer not to bail her out. I'll take the first flight to Destin."

"Let me go, instead," Augusta said. "She's furious with you, and I don't blame her. She can stay at my house till both of you come to your senses."

Elizabeth gripped the phone and bit back, *No, no, no!*

"Mama," Howe said, "I really appreciate your offer, and I know you mean well, but I need to be the one to get her. And I need to drive her and the car back. It'll give me a chance to talk some sense into her."

After a bristling pause, Augusta said quietly, "Howell, though I suppose I can understand your recent efforts to provide more discipline in Patricia's life, I must ask if you've considered the fact that nineteen years of indulgence can't be undone in a matter of weeks, or even months."

"Yes, Mother," he answered. "I'm all too aware of that. I can't undo what happened, but she and I have to work this out between us. I wouldn't dream of putting you in the middle of this mess." That was one way of putting it. "I appreciate your concern, but helping her avoid this isn't helping. She needs to learn that there are consequences to her actions."

"Weren't you listening?" his mother scolded. "Regardless of your own change of mind and manners, Patricia is the same girl we both loved before your stroke." She left Elizabeth out of the equation, of course. "You may have changed overnight, but it's completely unreasonable to expect her to do so."

Ouch. Went for the jugular with that one.

"Let us handle this, Mama," Howe insisted. "Elizabeth and I are her parents, and we want what's best for her. You'll just have to trust us in this."

Yay, Howe, for including her.

He went on with, "And I don't want you bothering Elizabeth about any of this, either. In the future, if you have any criticism of me or my family, call me about it. Elizabeth has never done anything to justify the way you treat her, and I want it to stop, Mother. I mean it. I will not have you criticizing her anymore, tacitly or otherwise. If you do, I'll . . ."

Hardly believing her ears, Elizabeth held her breath, waiting for the rest.

"I'll tell everybody at Rotary that you wear a wig."

"You would not," Augusta breathed, aghast.

"Oh, yes I would. I even know where you buy them," Howe said, to Elizabeth's total surprise.

She'd wondered why her mother-in-law drove an hour every week, each way, to have her hair done in Atlanta, when it never looked that good.

"And we won't even discuss the Depends," Howe threatened further.

"Now you're sounding like your old self," Augusta accused.

Howe didn't take the bait. "Whatever," he said calmly. "But ease up on Elizabeth. And leave

Patricia to me. I mean it. Call off the lawyer."

"If you insist," she snapped. "You sound just like your father! Good-bye." She hung up.

"How was that?" Howe said over the dead air that followed.

"You knew I was listening?" Elizabeth exclaimed.

"I didn't hear you click off, and I didn't mind," he confessed. "It was thirty years late in coming, but I'm glad you heard."

"So am I."

"Good." She could almost hear him smile. "Can I take you out to lunch," he asked, "on the way to the airport? Say, the Varsity?"

"You and your Varsity."

Two hours and three chili dogs later, Elizabeth dropped him off at the Atlanta airport and said a prayer for traveling mercies. And a change of heart in their daughter—which would take a Red Sea miracle.

# Chapter 14

Howe and Patti arrived home late the next day. After a sullen hello and brief hug—clearly under duress—Patricia flew up to her room and slammed the door.

"That went well," Howe said dryly, "don't you think?" He made straight for the Advil in the cabinet over the dishwasher, and this time, Elizabeth didn't blame him.

He inhaled deeply. "Wow. Fried chicken."

"Homemade," she said, following him into the kitchen. "It helped to pass the time while y'all were on the road." She'd fixed Patricia's favorite supper: fried chicken, butter peas, rice and gravy, broccoli and hollandaise, deviled eggs, and sliced tomatoes from the garden. Elizabeth had cooked all day, glad for the distraction.

The way things had been going, Elizabeth had feared a policeman would turn up at the door to tell her they'd been in an accident. She took a tall glass from the cabinet. "So, how'd it go with Patti?" she asked above the raucous jangle of ice from the dispenser in the refrigerator door, followed by the mechanical whoosh of filtered water. She handed the glass to Howe.

"Could have been worse," he told her. "She

236

could have jumped from the speeding car on the Interstate."

"That bad, huh?" She handed him the glass.

His brows rose. "I kept telling myself to stay calm, that she was just testing me." He managed a wan smile. "You'd be proud of me. I didn't pull over once, and I hardly cussed at all. Only cried three times."

"That's an improvement," she acknowledged. "Especially under the circumstances."

He downed the Advil, then gulped half the water. "Well, at least she got it all out into the open. Said she wants to move out." He gulped the rest like a man who'd been lost in the desert. "Whew. Thirsty. Got any tea?"

Like all his other appetites since he'd woken up, his thirst consumed him in the moment, to the exclusion of everything else.

Elizabeth refilled the tumbler from the fresh-brewed pitcher of tea lightly sweetened with real sugar, just the way Patricia and Howe liked it, then prodded him back to the matter at hand with, "So what did you tell her?"

He drained half the glass. "I told her she wasn't a prisoner, but she'd have to do it with-out the car or any help from us. So she said she'd move in with Mama. When I said that wasn't going to happen, she called Mama."

"Who told her she could move in, I'm sure," Elizabeth said.

"No." He sank to a stool. "God bless her and her wig, Mama said she wasn't going to get in the middle."

Miracle of miracles. Never underestimate the power of blackmail, especially when it involved an old woman's vanity. "And?"

"And Patti went ballistic for about thirty miles, accusing us of turning her grandmother against her, then cried for another twenty over how cruel and heartless we were." He looked at Elizabeth with fresh assessment. "Is that how she's been with you all these years?"

"Only since she could talk," she replied evenly. "And only when you weren't around, of course." She got out the heirloom silverware she'd used for everyday since they'd moved in, a small act of defiance on her part.

Howe shook his head. "Whew. I had no idea." He got that tortured guilt look. "I should have known. Should have defended you. I'm amazed you can even speak to me."

She pulled three linen napkins from the drawer. "I loved you," she said, her use of the past tense sending a brief flicker of affront across his features.

"God, Lizzie, I'm so sorry I let her treat you that way."

Why did he always have to use that wretched name when he said something nice?

"So what happened next?" she asked, moving to set the breakfast table.

"I told her she could stay at home and work at the bank and go to school till she passed a quarter. Then she could have the car back, and her charge cards, as long as she used them responsibly."

"I'm sure that went over well," Elizabeth observed as she laid out their places. She'd even used Patricia's favorite peach-colored roses for the centerpiece.

"You can imagine," Howe said. "She called Charles and announced she was moving in with him." He shot her a brief sidelong glance. "I hadn't thought of that one. But thank goodness, Charles had the sense to turn her down." A smile flickered at the corners of his mouth. "I think he enjoyed that almost as much I did."

"Good for him." Elizabeth crossed to start taking out the food. Like most men, Howe couldn't keep his hands off the deviled eggs, but she'd made plenty and offered them up as consolation. "Here." She set the egg-shaped tray in front of him. "Have a couple of these to tide you over."

That brightened his mood considerably. "Don't mind if I do."

Elizabeth removed the clean kitchen towel that covered the platter of chicken with the same flourish her own mother had used when she was little.

Howe eyed the chicken, then her, with equal hunger.

"I missed you last night," she said quietly. Her bed had seemed too big and too empty without him.

"And honey, did I miss you. Patricia snores a lot louder than you do," he joked, but the desire in his eyes made her own insides do a flip. Especially when she flashed on seeing his lean body naked in the shower that night.

Everything was so mixed up. Because of P.J., she felt as if she were cheating to think of her husband that way.

Elizabeth headed for the back stair and called, "Patti! Supper! I made your favorites."

A muffled, "I'm not hungry," came down from the room above them.

Elizabeth's disappointment must have showed, because Howe got up with a firm, "I'll get her."

Elizabeth looked at the intimate table setting and the island laden with comfort food. "Wait. Do you have to?"

Howe laughed, a sound she was getting used to, and gave her an impulsive peck on the cheek. "Not if you don't want me to."

She didn't mind the kiss. Her hand caressed it into her skin. "I don't."

He looked at the ample spread. "It's a shame to waste any of this. Why don't we call the Harrises and see if they can come over?"

An impromptu dinner party? The old Howe would never have considered it. Neither would

240

Elizabeth, but they did have all that food . . . It was barely six. "Okay. I'll call Faith."

Elizabeth picked up the cordless phone and pressed the button for a dial tone. But instead of the tone, Patricia's voice leapt from the receiver. "Ohmygod, jail!" she emoted. "Me, in filthy, horrible jail, and it was all my parents' fault."

"How horrible was it?" her best friend Melanie asked in awe.

"Horrible. It smelled like pee, and people were *so* skanky. I was afraid I'd get an STD if I sat down. I called Gamma, but Daddy—"

"Patricia," Elizabeth interrupted, "please tell Melanie you'll call her back on your cell phone. I need to use this one."

Patti responded with an icy, "I can't. The battery went completely dead while I was in *jail,* and now it won't charge."

Elizabeth's frown prompted Howe to take the receiver. "Patti, hang up at once. I'll let you know when the line's free."

He listened for a second, then pressed the button and handed the phone to Elizabeth with a clear dial tone. "There you are, my dear."

Elizabeth had to admit, it felt awfully good to have Howe buffer her from Patti's contempt.

The Harrises were not only free, but seemed delighted to accept. When they rang the bell twenty minutes later, Elizabeth opened it to find them beaming over a basket of tomatoes.

"Hi," Faith said, suddenly shy. "We brought you some homegrown tomatoes."

"Thanks." Elizabeth accepted them with genuine appreciation. "Wow. These are gorgeous. The heat got mine, and now they're all watery and freckled."

Faith struggled for words. "It's so little, after all you've both done."

Eyes welling, Robert shook Howe's hand with both of his. "We don't know how to thank you both. I—"

"You don't have to." Howe clapped Robert's shoulder with his free hand. "I owe this town a lot of amends." Guiding them toward the kitchen, he shifted the subject to, "The guys at the bank tell me you're doing a great job with our rehabs."

Robert beamed. "Thanks. It's good to be working."

Howe grinned. "Speak for yourself." He leaned in closer for, "Frankly, I'm enjoying *not* working for a while."

"I love what you're doing with the house," Faith admired. "There's so much light in the living room and dining room, now. Painting the wainscoting made such a fabulous difference."

"Thanks." The dining room was the only one finished so far. "I hope y'all don't mind," she said as she led them past the twelve-foot-long banquet table toward the kitchen, where the breakfast nook was now set for four. "But we're eating in here tonight." It was the first time she'd ever served anyone but family there.

"Good," Faith said. "Frankly, your dining room has always intimidated me."

"Faith," Robert scolded.

Howe came to her defense. "Now that I think of it, that big old table is pretty pretentious." He lifted his brows for a wry, "Almost as pretentious as I was, isn't it?"

"You don't have to answer that," Elizabeth told their guests, with a brief warning glance at her husband.

Robert shifted his attention to the food. "I don't care where we eat," he said, "as long as I get to share some of this. What a spread. You've got all my favorites, and it smells great."

Elizabeth handed them their plates. "Good. Help yourselves." She thought about Patricia's refusal to come down and eat. "And have seconds. I don't want any leftovers."

Her daughter would be in for a surprise if she hoped to sneak any in the night.

Three hours and a pleasant evening of conversation later, the food and company were gone, and Elizabeth turned out the bedside table light, then climbed in opposite Howe with a satisfied sigh. "That was fun. We ought to do it more often."

"They're really nice people," he mused, as if he was realizing it for the first time.

"Yes, they are. Faith's always been adorable. And it's nice to get to know Robert better." In the past, they'd only seen the couple at big parties. Elizabeth reached across the distance between them to pat Howe's arm. "You did very well tonight."

"I did, didn't I?" He yawned, then slid to the middle of the bed, reaching for her. "How about a congratulatory hug?"

Hugs were nice. As long as that was all he tried. Elizabeth risked having to rebuff him and slid over to nestle alongside him, her arm across his chest. It felt good to be held, to fit her head to the shallow indentation of his shoulder.

"I hardly cussed at all tonight," he bragged.

"Hardly at all," she agreed. He'd even managed to avoid the topic of Patricia by talking about sports and the upcoming local referenda.

"And I only cried that once," he reminded her.

"That was okay," she said. "Robert did, too."

Robert had told them about a news interview with the father of a slain soldier. The grieving father had begged the press not to release graphic pictures of his dying son, but they'd published the photos, anyway. In the interview, the father said he wanted his son—whose military call sign was Holy Man—to be remembered for loving Christ more than anything, not for those horrendous photos.

Robert had said it was an example of how a

person of faith can bring light into even the darkest trials of life.

Hearing it, Elizabeth had choked up, herself.

"That story puts things in perspective, doesn't it?" Howe said. "About Patricia."

Elizabeth nodded, feeling warm and protected there beside him. Their family was alive and safe. That was all that really mattered.

Howe yawned hugely, then settled to quiet, even breathing. Just as she was drifting off to sleep, he muttered, "Oh, don't let me forget: there's a vestry meeting tomorrow morning, same time as your Altar Guild. We can ride together."

Elizabeth's eyes flew open, her body tensing. "Vestry? Are you sure you're ready for that? You know how heated those meetings can be." The church had split into two camps: those who wanted to keep the minister till he could retire (Augusta and her little band of cronies), and those who wanted to let him go for the good of the congregation (everybody else). "I don't really think it's a good idea to—"

"I need to go," Howe said firmly.

Uh-oh.

She closed her own eyes. "More instructions from God?"

He chuckled, followed by a crisp, "Um-hm."

"Oh, Lord. What now?"

He gave her shoulders a quick squeeze. "You'll see."

Elizabeth sat up, putting space between them. "What does that mean?"

A smug smile crossed his face in the dim light from the bathroom. "You'll see." Then he rolled over to his side of the bed, putting his back to her.

Sliding down to her pillow, Elizabeth said a heartfelt prayer that Howe would get a Holy Ghost dose of self-control. And divine wisdom. If he started talking about getting instructions from God . . . "Maybe I ought to stay home, then."

"Oh, I think you'll want to be there," he said lightly.

"You're not going to tell me, are you?" she asked with dread.

A cheery, "Nope," was her only answer. "G'night, Lizzie."

Again with the damned Lizzie. It always spelled trouble.

It wasn't easy getting to sleep after that, her mind spinning with what might happen at the vestry meeting, but eventually, Elizabeth wore herself out and slept. Till Patti woke them both up at two, slamming her door—on the way back from the kitchen, no doubt.

Howe and Elizabeth both chuckled from their respective sides of the bed.

If it wasn't for that vestry meeting in the morning, Elizabeth would have slept like a baby after that, but as it was, she tossed and turned, dreaming she was naked at Garden Club.

# Chapter 15

Elizabeth stopped short of the fellowship hall and straightened the curled collar of Howe's golf shirt. As far as she could remember, he'd never come to church so casually dressed, but she'd lost track of all the changes in this new version of her husband. "Remember what we talked about," she murmured. Well, *she'd* talked about on the way over. "Try not to make anybody uncomfortable. It's common courtesy."

He cocked a brow, clearly unmoved by her lecture on propriety. "People need to be made uncomfortable," he responded, "when they're not doing what they should be. Jesus did it all the time, especially to the religious types." He smoothed his placket. "The vestry needs to get a few things straight. To put our priorities where they belong."

Elizabeth frowned with worry and whispered a tight, "And you're the one to do it?" She looked right and left to make sure nobody could over-hear them. "What about God? Isn't *He* the one who's supposed to set things straight? Or don't you think He's capable of doing that without your personal assistance?"

Howe smiled. "Of course He can. But I asked Him to use me, and He gave me this job. Among others."

Oh, Lord. Had megalomania been one of the side effects on that treatment disclaimer she'd signed at the hospital? She couldn't remember. There had been so many.

"At least let me go with you to the meeting," she pressed yet again.

"No," he said, visibly annoyed by her refusal to accept his previous three refusals. "You need to go to *your* meeting," he repeated.

"Why do you keep saying that?" she asked. "Your mother can manage the Altar Guild perfectly well without me. She has for the last fifty years."

Howe rolled his eyes. "I know I've said this at least three times; I could hear my voice." He met her stubborn gaze with one of his own. "You're supposed to be at Altar Guild. I'll be fine. Go."

The side door opened and Sean Welch, treasurer of the vestry, came in. "Hey, there, Elizabeth. Howe," he said with forced amiability. "Good to have you back."

"Good to be back!" Howe responded. He started toward the fellowship hall as Sean passed them, but Elizabeth grabbed his shirt. "Wait," she said.

Howe's eyes narrowed as he removed her

hands from his shirt. "I'm going to my meeting now. See you later."

Damn. He wasn't going to budge. If she insisted, he'd probably make a scene. Ditto, if she followed him in.

She sighed. "This is against my better judgment, but okay. Have it your way." Maybe she could sneak out of Altar Guild later and check on him. She took a step toward the classroom where they met, then turned. "But I'll be there if you need me." Her voice dropped to a whisper. "And try not to cuss. Or cry."

He made a face, replying with a sarcastic, "Yes, mother."

Elizabeth's lips clamped flat at the one comment guaranteed to get her goat, then turned and strode away. Let him cook in his own juices, then.

She walked in, last of the twelve guild members present. A stickler for punctuality, Augusta greeted her with a grim smile and a frosty, "Good morning, Elizabeth. How nice of you to join us."

Faith patted the empty chair beside her. "Sit by me." Looking like something was definitely up, Anne and Elaine waved to her in welcome.

What was that about?

Augusta sniffed, glancing at the handwritten agenda in her lap as if she hadn't followed the same agenda at the very same meetings for five decades. "We have a lot to accomplish today," the queen decreed. "But let us begin with a prayer.

249

Sarah, would you please present our devotional?"

Elizabeth tried without success to focus when Sarah read a brief story from *Guideposts*, then led them in the Lord's Prayer, but all she could do was wonder what kind of trouble Howe was brewing.

"Amen." Augusta lifted her chin and called for the minutes of the last meeting, which her cohort and guild secretary Emily Bates was almost too blind to read.

Then eighty-eight-year-old Jane Hilliard gave the treasurer's report in her high, thready voice. "Last month, we had a balance of seven hundred thirty-six dollars and eighty-three cents in the active account, with an expenditure of fifty-one dollars to Jack's Cleaners for the altar cloths, and ninety-six dollars and twelve cents to Ames Church Supply for candles, bringing the balance to five hundred eighty-nine dollars and seventy-one cents."

She paused briefly to rest, then went on. "And in the Pipe Organ Fund"—Augusta's pet project —"we started the month with one hundred eighty-four thousand, nine hundred, sixty-seven dollars, and forty-one cents in the money market account, and accrued interest of nine hundred fifty-three dollars and seven cents, for a balance of one hundred eighty-five thousand, nine hundred twenty dollars, and forty-eight cents."

It wasn't enough that their small stone church had to have a new pipe organ, though the old one sounded fine to Elizabeth. Augusta insisted they have one to rival Spivey Hall's. Christ would probably come again before they got enough money for that, but nobody dared challenge the old bat.

"Is there any old business?" Augusta asked, prompting an odd outbreak of exchanged glances from Elizabeth's friends and the younger members of the guild. When no one answered, Augusta proceeded with, "Then we'll move on to new business, our annual elections."

Before Julia could raise her hand to nominate Augusta as she always did, Faith stood with unprecedented boldness and blurted out, "Augusta, you have dedicated yourself to many years of good and selfless service to this guild, for which we can't adequately express our gratitude. Because you have served so long and so faithfully, I and several other guild members think you have earned a rest. So I nominate Elizabeth as president."

Elizabeth tucked her chin as Emily scribbled away, recording the nomination, and everyone else looked to Augusta, who sat rigid, so taken aback she was speechless.

Anne stood. "I second."

Elaine stood, too. "I move we close the nominations."

Amazed, Elizabeth heard Christy, Julia's daughter, utter a firm, "I second."

It was a coup!

Augusta's eyes narrowed, her refined nostrils flaring. She turned to her cronies with a pregnant, "Two motions have been made and seconded. Any discussion?"

Emily remained silent as a chorus of protest rose from the old biddies flanking her, but only one spoke coherently. Ancient Joy Fisher twisted up the volume on her hearing aid and shouted, "What?"

"They want to take the guild away from me and give it to Elizabeth," Augusta said loudly, disdain dripping from Elizabeth's name. "What do you have to say about that?"

"Oh, well, all right then," Joy said, oblivious as ever. "Whatever you want. Elizabeth it is."

"Joy!" Emily scolded. "That gives them a majority."

Augusta exhaled in exasperation. Her mouth set in a grim line as she rose, uttering a scornful, "Well!" She straightened the peplum of her jacket with a decisive tug. "If that's the way things are, I am leaving." She glared at Elizabeth as if the whole thing were her fault. "I refuse to stay where I am not wanted. I resign."

Tenderhearted Faith grasped her forearm in an effort to keep her from going. "Please don't leave, Augusta. You are always welcome here." Only

Faith could say that without risking getting struck by lightning.

Augusta removed Faith's hand as if she were leprous. "Let's see how well you fare without me." With that, she sailed away.

"What's the matter with Augusta?" Joy demanded. "Is she sick?" Her droopy face drooped further. "I hope she's not sick. We need her for bridge this afternoon."

"She's not sick," Julia said, handing Joy her cane. "She's mad. Come on, Joy. I guess we'd better leave, too."

Glaring in accusation, Dorothy Prater joined them, but timid Sheila Cantrell murmured a furtive, "We're not resigning, though," on her way out.

Emily granted them a tentative wave. "I have to stay and take the minutes," she apologized.

Which left Elizabeth with a solid quorum of seven.

Holy cow! They could actually accomplish something new, at long last. Not that Elizabeth had any idea what to do first. Augusta had quelled so many good ideas over the years.

Once the old biddies were out of earshot, Anne laughed with glee and clapped. The sense of triumph in the room almost overrode Elizabeth's dread about how Augusta would retaliate. "Congratulations, Elizabeth," Anne told her. "You are now the chairman. I can hear the grapevine hummin' already."

Elizabeth sighed. "What have y'all gotten me into?"

"Only what you should have been for a long time," Elaine said with glee.

"It's gonna be great," Anne assured her. "This church is dyin' on the vine. We need some new ideas. New projects."

"A new minister," Julia muttered from her notes.

"But first, we have to get back to our elections," Elaine said. "I nominate Faith for treasurer."

"Then I nominate you for secretary," Faith retaliated.

"Oh, thank God," Emily muttered from her notes. "I hate this job."

While the others laughed, Elizabeth let out a long, hard breath, then assumed her new duties. "Okay. If we're going to do this, let's do it by the book. Elaine has nominated Faith as treasurer. Do I have a second?"

"I second," Emily said from her notes. She turned her thick glasses their way. "Jane will be thrilled to get out of it. She always has hated balancing checkbooks, but Augusta insisted— maybe because Jane always beats her at bridge."

Now that she was out from under Augusta's thumb, Emily was a real chatterbox.

"Well, I don't mind balancing checkbooks a bit," Faith said. "I'm good with accounts."

"All right then, we have a nomination for

254

treasurer and a second," Elizabeth said. "Any other nominations?" Nobody spoke up. "Okay, then. All in favor?" Everybody voted aye, including Faith. "Then it's unanimous."

Before Elizabeth knew it, a new slate of officers was in place.

She was about to bring up what they should do next when the door flew open and a flushed Hamp Myers motioned for her. "Elizabeth, I think you'd better come see about Howe."

Oh, Lord! She'd actually forgotten about him!

She'd known he'd get into trouble.

Everybody jumped up to follow as she made for the hallway, including Emily, who still had her notebook and pen in hand. "Don't write this down," Elizabeth told her as they headed for the sound of angry voices at the end of the long corridor.

The last thing she needed was to have Howe's latest escapade immortalized in the minutes.

"But we're not adjourned," Emily said in dismay.

Oh, for heaven's sake!

"I move we adjourn," Faith said.

"I second," Anne confirmed before the motion was out of her mouth.

"All in favor?" Elizabeth called as they neared the double doors.

"Aye," the women voted as Emily dutifully recorded.

"Then we're adjourned." Elizabeth pointed to the notebook. "Put that away."

255

She pushed open the doors to find the vestry meeting in shambles, a furious Keith McDonald gripping Howe by his shirt over the narrow table, and Howe declaring with red-faced obstinacy, "Don't argue with *me!* Take it up with God. Nowhere in the Bible does it condone the baptism of infants!"

"It never bothered you before now!" Keith retorted.

"I never read the *Bible* before," Howe retorted.

Meanwhile, the other ten vestry members either argued among themselves over the theological basis for infant baptism, or tried to calm Keith —who'd always been a hothead.

"It's a holy rite of the Episcopal Church!" Keith yelled into Howe's face. "If you don't like it, go somewhere else! Go be a . . . *Baptist,*" he said with scorn.

"Keith!" Elizabeth shouted in alarm. "Howe! Stop this at once!"

They both ignored her, too much testosterone over the dam already.

"I don't want to be a Baptist," Howe declared. "I want to be a proper Episcopalian, and when I see my church doing something it shouldn't, I have a right to speak out."

"Says you!" Keith snarled. "You may own everybody else in this town, but you don't own me, and you don't own this church!"

Why didn't the minister do something?

Elizabeth scanned the fracas. Where was he, anyway?

Sitting serenely at the far end of the table, looking for all the world as if he was enjoying the whole thing immensely.

"Do something!" she called to him, shifting his attention from the impending fisticuffs to her.

Still smiling, he shrugged. "I'm just ex officio. It's their meeting."

She turned to Faith. "Don't just stand there. Help me break this up." She motioned the rest of the guild to the other arguments that had broken out around them. "Y'all help, too." She headed around the table for Howe.

"The Organ Fund is for an organ!" Andy Henderson hollered at Jesse Lindstrom as Elizabeth passed. "We have no authority to spend it on some harebrained scheme, no matter what Howe said!"

"You call helping our members keep their houses a harebrained scheme?" Jesse argued right back, his neck scarlet.

Andy pointed to Howe. "Mortgage money that goes to *his* bank."

"You don't know that," Jesse countered. "Would you rather they lost their houses? What good's an organ if our own people are homeless? Anyway, the one we've got works plenty fine for that pitiful choir."

He had a point about the choir, but the vestry had no say about the Organ Fund.

"The Altar Guild controls the Organ Fund," Elizabeth told them, then grabbed Howe from behind and tried to drag him from Keith's clutches. But Keith continued to argue, holding tight to Howe's shirt. Elizabeth raised her voice. "Charles Howell Whittington the second, get a grip on yourself and stop this, this minute!"

He scowled, trying to wrest free of her. "Elizabeth, go back to the Altar Guild," he said curtly, in a manner she recognized all too well from his former self. "You're the president now, and I need you to swing this thing with the Organ Fund."

Elizabeth went numb, all the air sucked from her lungs as she realized Howe must have put her friends up to electing her so she could help with *his* agenda. She recoiled, letting go.

All his talk about changing, about telling the truth, but he'd kept that from her. He'd used her, just the way he had for so many years.

"We are in God's house!" Faith scolded Keith as she and Elaine tried to loosen his grip on Howe's shirt. "This is not how Christian men are supposed to act! Behave yourselves."

When that didn't get through to him, she hollered, "What would Jesus do?", which turned everybody's attention her way.

"Never mind Jesus," Elaine said, "what would *Mary Jane* say?", invoking his wife, a woman to be reckoned with.

Keith clipped his mouth shut and tucked his chin.

Elaine pried his hands from Howe's shirt at last. "You are *so* gonna be in the doghouse, mister," she threatened, "when Mary Jane hears about this."

Pointing at Howe, Keith turned to Father Jim. "Some priest you are! How dare you just sit there and let this . . . *idiot* question our Christianity and malign a sacred rite of this church? I'll have your job for this!"

"Now Keith," Father Jim soothed, "I know you're upset, but there's no cause to—"

"I didn't question your Christianity," Howe argued. "I just asked if you have a personal relationship with Jesus."

Oh, Lord. Elizabeth grabbed his arm, propelling him toward the door. "Howe, shut the hell up." Her unprecedented use of profanity erupted in a lull, eliciting wide-eyed surprise in the others.

"I wanted to talk about faith, not religion," Howe justified, "but Keith was so threatened that—"

Keith went almost purple. "I have been a member of this church since before you were born," he hollered, heading for Howe, "and you have the nerve to insinuate that I'm not spiritual? I've been on the *vestry* since 1967!"

The door and escape were within reach when Howe turned around to resume the argument. "I know," he said, "and you've done good service, Keith. I'm not talking about that. I'm talking about a spiritual *relationship* with God."

Keith glared at the others. "Are you all just going to stand there and let him do this? Isn't it enough that he owns everything and everybody in this town? Are you going to let him try to control what we believe, too? To hell with the mortgages he holds on our houses! He has no right!"

"I never said a word about any mortgages," Howe protested as Elizabeth tried to steer him back toward the exit. "I just wanted to help some of our members financially and discuss the spiritual life of this church, or more accurately, the lack of it!"

"You want to quote the Bible?" Keith fired back, "I'll quote the Bible: 'Thou shalt not judge.' How about that?" He headed for Howe. "And the Episcopal Church was *not* founded just because Henry the Eighth wanted to get a divorce and steal the Catholic Church's holdings!"

"Howe!" Elizabeth said. "Tell me you did not say such a thing."

He straightened, defensive. "Well, things had gotten pretty heated when I did. But it's historical fact."

Elaine tried to stifle a chortle of laughter, but wasn't successful.

"The hell it is!" Keith shot back. "Haven't you ever heard of a thing called 'the *Reformation*'?"

By that point, the observers looked like they were watching a tennis match at the club, with an occasional detour from Keith and Howe to Elizabeth.

"That is enough!" she yelled at the top of her lungs, whipping her cell phone from her purse and holding it up. "One more argument from either of you, and I am calling the police and pressing charges against both of you for disturbing the peace!"

Struck by one of his mercurial mood swings, Howe eyed her with open lust. "Whoo, Lizzie," he growled out, "you are so *hot* when you're hot like that."

In the brief pulse of shocked silence that followed, Elizabeth covered her face with her hands. Dear Lord. She had to get Howe out of there before he said anything else!

Elaine and Anne broke out laughing, along with half the men, defusing the situation at last.

"We are leaving," Elizabeth clipped out. "Now." She shoved him back toward the door with a force magnified by shame. "Before you embarrass us so much our children will never be able to show their faces in this town again."

"Okay, okay," Howe relented, then called back to Ernest Foster as if everything were perfectly normal. "Could you take over the meeting for me, Ernie? Gotta run."

They didn't wait to hear his answer.

# Chapter 16

After five minutes of frozen silence from Elizabeth on their way home, Howe looked over at her and said, "I had no intention of causing so much trouble. Really." He sighed. "A little trouble, yes. I mean, they needed shaking up a bit."

"A *bit?*" escaped her. Her hands tightened on the steering wheel. "And when were you planning to tell me about *your* plans for the Organ Fund?"

"Oh. That." He looked out the window. "Well, we had to get you elected, first."

"We? And who is *we?*"

"Well, I came up with the idea, but I called Elaine before your Whine and Cheese, and she thought it was great. She took the ball and ran with it."

"You called Elaine and set it up, without asking me if that was what *I* wanted?"

"Damn, Lizzie. You make it sound like some kind of evil plot. You've told me for decades that Mama wouldn't let the guild accomplish anything. I realized it was time that changed. So sue me."

"You should have talked to me, first," Elizabeth told him. "As it is, I feel used."

"Used?" He bristled. "I was only trying to protect you, so Mama wouldn't blame you."

Howe might be a changed man, but he still didn't get it. "Nice thought, Howe, but you know what they say about good intentions." She turned left past the town square, toward home. "I am your wife, not your child. You say you want things to be better between us, then you pull a stunt like this. You should have talked to me, first."

"But I told you, Mama would—"

"Forget Augusta," Elizabeth said. "She's always hated me and always will. I have a right to know when you're thinking of doing something that affects me." She turned onto their street. "If you want to fix our marriage, you can start by confiding in me. Trusting me with your plans. Taking my opinions into consideration. If you had, that disaster back there wouldn't have happened." She stabbed her pointer finger at him. "And don't try to tell me God had anything to do with what you did at that vestry meeting. It was pure chaos."

Howe looked back out the window as they turned onto the driveway. "Maybe it needed to happen. People got plenty mad at Jesus when he tried to put the emphasis back on faith instead of religion."

Elizabeth braked to an abrupt halt. "You are *not* Jesus!" She gathered her purse in a huff. "And Keith was right: the state of other people's souls is God's business, not yours." She threw open the door and tried to get out, only to be caught back by her seat belt. "Aaaagh!" She fumbled with the latch.

Howe reached over and laid a staying hand on her arm. "Elizabeth, I'm sorry. Please don't give up on me."

She shot him a skeptical glance and found the lines in his face deepened by doubt. "I did the wrong things for so long," he told her quietly. "I don't even remember how it started, but little by little, I put my soul to sleep. Stopped caring about anything good. Stopped feeling anything. I was dead inside. And now I'm alive. God gave me a second chance." His hand slid down her forearm to take hers. "I know it's been hard for you. But I'm really trying. I can't go back to stuffing everything into a black bag in the back of my brain. I feel things. I see things for what they are, and I have to tell the truth. I have to try, at least, to do the right thing."

Elizabeth looked at him. "What about us, Howe? Where do we fit into these grand notions of yours?" She was so tired from the past six months. So weary of trying to keep everything together. "You say you want to be a good husband to me. Well, good husbands don't humiliate their families. They don't go off half-cocked, alienating people. They don't cook up schemes and manipulate situations—in church or any- where else."

"Ouch." He frowned.

Elizabeth had to make him see, and deeply resented the necessity to do so. "Howe, do you ever think about me or the children when you're planning these things? Did you think about how your mother would feel about losing the only real authority she has left anymore?" Lord. She couldn't believe she was taking up for her mother-in-law. "Forget your reasons. Did it ever occur to you that what you did was selfish?"

He looked stricken, staring out the windshield.

Lord. Was she being just as selfish, wanting him to understand? The question gave her a headache. "I'm just asking you to talk to me when one of these ideas comes to you. Trust me." She unlatched her seat belt. "I know it won't be easy for you. We haven't talked for so long. But if you want this marriage to have a chance, you have to trust me."

Even as she said the words, she flashed on P.J.'s face, and felt ashamed. Do as I say, not as I do.

Howe nodded. "I've really screwed up, haven't I?"

That was something she never heard from the old Howe. "You meant well," she excused out of habit.

His brows drew together as he looked across their manicured lawn to the magnolias that flanked the yard. "Damn, I got it so wrong." His fist clenched in front of his belly. "Gives me this huge knot." He faced her. "I want so much to be the man I should be, but obviously I don't know who that is." He suddenly looked old, and defeated.

Elizabeth hadn't intended to punish the man. "Lord, Howe, it's not the end of the world." She was royally ticked off at him, but he looked so defeated. "I don't expect you to be perfect. Nobody does, not even God. I just want you to talk to me about things. No more plots." She exhaled sharply. "It feels way too much like before. I can't go back to the way things were before."

He winced. "Okay. No more plots." He unhooked his seat belt, a thoughtful expression replacing his discouraged one. "Okay."

They both got out. He turned to her and said across the hood of the car, "Sheesh. Maybe I *ought* to become a Baptist," in an effort to lighten things up. "Or better yet, a *Pentecostal*." He waggled his eyebrows at her. "What would you say to that?"

In spite of herself, Elizabeth had to laugh. "Your mother would have a heart attack."

He grinned, clearly glad to see her temper ease. "If I did, would you come with me?"

Lord, he could be winsome when he wanted to. "No. But feel free to try it if you want to. I just want to be there to see the look on your mother's face when you tell her. And Patti's."

"I'll talk to you about it before I do anything rash," he quipped.

The phone was ringing as they came inside. Probably Howe's mother calling to weigh in. Howe headed for the cordless receiver on the credenza. "I'll get it." He picked it up. "Hello?"

A surprised look claimed his features. "Oh, hi."

Not his mother.

He turned his back to Elizabeth, reminding her of many a suspicious phone call from the past.

Elizabeth's antennae went up.

"I guess that would be okay," Howe told the caller. "What time works for you?" He straightened. "Oh, really? Well, I don't see why not. I'm free." Pause. "Okay, then. Thirty minutes, it is." He hung up and replaced the receiver.

"And who was that?" she asked.

He turned, a mischievous look on his face. "The Baptist minister. He wants to have a chat."

Baptist minister, indeed. Was he lying?

Elizabeth didn't ask. She had no stomach for confrontation after the debacle at church.

Patricia clambered down from upstairs to halt on the landing and confront them. "Daddy! What have you *done?* I have never been so mortified in all my life! Five people have called me about it already."

"I guess the blood's in the water," Howe told Elizabeth dryly.

"I guess it is," she said. "And I'm leaving this one to you to clean up after."

As he headed up the stairs to do just that, Elizabeth's cell phone rang. She fished it out of her purse. *Out of area.* "Hello?"

"I just heard," P.J. told her. "Elizabeth, I'm concerned for your safety. The man's not right. I really think you should leave him. Or get him to leave. It can't be safe for you, the way things are."

Elizabeth bristled at his proprietary manner. "Who told you?" Did he have somebody from Whittington reporting to him?

"That doesn't matter," he dismissed.

"It matters to me," she retorted. Howe was loopy, but he wasn't dangerous. "I was there. You weren't." Why was she defending Howe?

"I heard the meeting ended up in a brawl," P.J. countered.

"That's nonsense," she said, surprised by her own protectiveness. "Tempers flared, but Howe didn't hurt anybody. All he did was challenge their hidebound attitudes and try to get them to help the hard-hit members of the church. It wasn't tactful, but it wasn't aggressive. Keith McDonald was the one who was aggressive. If he'd treated me the way he treated Howe, I'd have coldcocked the old blowhard, but Howe didn't."

P.J. chuckled. "I'll bet you would have."

Where was P.J., anyway? Listening over the transom at St. Andrew's? "How did you find out what happened so fast?" she demanded. "My car's not even cold from bringing him home. Where are you?"

"It doesn't matter where I am," he answered.

She'd tolerated that deflection one time too many. "When I ask you a question, it matters," she bit out, focusing all her frustrations on that. "And I expect a real answer. If you ever patronize me again by saying it doesn't matter, I'll hang up and block your number from every phone I can get hold of, and it will be the last you'll ever see or hear of me."

"Whoa," he soothed. "Sorry. Force of habit. I say that in business all the time, but I promise not to answer you that way ever again," he said. "I care about you, Elizabeth. What you're going through. How you feel. I want to see you. Help you."

He'd said the same thing so many times before, and she'd been drawn in by it, but this time, P.J.'s declaration of concern didn't ring true.

Elizabeth's phone beeped in, giving her a welcome excuse to end the conversation. "I have to go. I have another call."

P.J. didn't respond.

To her surprise, Augusta's name and number showed on the screen.

Elizabeth told P.J., "I've got my hands full, here. I'll get back to you once things have settled down, but I can't talk about any of this now, and I can't come to Atlanta. Please give me some space to get things straightened out."

His response was a cool, "If you insist. But I still don't like it that nobody's looking out for you in all this."

In the past, that would have made her feel appreciated. Now, it only made her feel pressured, for some reason. And annoyed. Maybe it was his paternalistic attitude. "I'm a big girl. I can look out for myself." She ended the call, and the phone beeped again.

Elizabeth looked at the phone's screen and considered not switching over to Augusta's call, but putting Augusta off only made the woman more vicious. So she braced herself and answered. "Hello."

"Elizabeth, this is your mother-in-law." Augusta's tone was brisk. "After that railroad job at guild, I vowed to wash my hands of you. But subsequent events have prompted me to reconsider for the sake of the family." That was new! Augusta never reconsidered anything. "For Patricia's sake," she went on, "I'm willing to put my feelings aside. The time has come for you and me to ally ourselves."

Elizabeth couldn't believe her ears. Augusta never forgave anyone after she'd written them off. The woman had half a dozen grudges older than Elizabeth, still as fresh as when some slight, real or imagined, had created them. "What would possibly make you want to do that, Augusta?" Elizabeth asked mildly.

"Howe is clearly ill. He must be sent where he can get help," her mother-in-law announced. "Somewhere he cannot humiliate the family, for as long as it takes him to come to his senses. No self-respecting man in his right mind would have done what he did at that vestry meeting. My lawyer is drawing up the commitment papers as we speak."

She couldn't be serious! "Augusta, while I agree Howe's behavior was embarrassing—and ill-advised—it was hardly grounds to have him put away."

"He insulted the vestry and every member of our church," his mother accused. "And he was violent!"

"He was not violent," Elizabeth defended. God only knew what people were saying. "I was there. Even when he was seriously provoked, he didn't get physical. Granted, there were some heated arguments going on, and Keith McDonald tried to get rough, but there was no violence."

"You're his wife," Augusta dismissed. "Of course you're going to put the best possible complexion on the matter, but our family name is being dragged through the mud all over town. This cannot continue."

Elizabeth decided she might as well be hung for a sheep as a lamb. "Augusta, Howe is your son. Why are you so quick to throw him under the bus? I should think you'd defend him, especially after what he's been through."

"Do not dare to lecture me about my own son, missy," Augusta ordered. "I'm only thinking of what's best for him. He'll thank me in the end. How will he feel after he comes to his senses if we let him run amok now?"

"What if he has come to his senses?" Elizabeth challenged. "What if this is the man he's going to be?"

Augusta had no answer for that.

"I'll admit," Elizabeth went on, "he's impulsive and lacks the filters the rest of us have. But he means so well, and he's heartfelt in his convictions."

"They're not convictions," Augusta minced out. "They're delusions."

Five minutes before, Elizabeth would have agreed with her assessment, but suddenly she realized she'd rather have this Howe, just the way he was, than the old one. "The last time I looked, we still had freedom of speech and religion. If what Howe did was insane, every evangelical in the country would be in an asylum."

"Maybe they should be," Augusta retorted. "And leave things to those of us with a proper sense of decorum."

What arrogance!

This was getting nowhere. "Augusta, I won't help you put Howe away. It's wrong."

"Then I'll have to take care of it on my own," she threatened. "And you know I have the means to do it."

Augusta was more connected than Georgia Power, especially in medical and judicial circles, so when she said she could do something, she could. Her threats were never idle.

"Try," Elizabeth threatened right back, "and I'll go to the media. I'll bet Dr. Phil or Oprah would love a story like this. Cruel banker wakes up born again and shakes up hidebound church. Maybe *The 700 Club*."

"You wouldn't," Augusta said.

"Try me."

Augusta's only response was to hang up.

Elizabeth took it as a victory, but she knew better than to think the matter was over. Augusta was sneaky.

Elizabeth decided to call Howe's lawyer and have him put things in place to counter any effort by Augusta to have Howe committed. Then she and Howe needed to talk. For all their sakes, he had to tone things down.

She'd just hung up from telling their lawyer

what was going on when the doorbell rang, and she answered to find not one, but two, beaming Baptist ministers on her doorstep.

"Good day, Mrs. Whittington," the senior pastor said. "I'm Pastor Lightman from First Baptist, and this is my associate, Pastor Graves. We called earlier."

So he hadn't been lying.

"Is Brother Howell available to speak with us?" the minister asked.

Only if she was present to make sure nothing else went wrong. "Come in. We're *both* looking forward to your visit."

She led the two men to the sitting room. "Please make yourselves comfortable." At least somebody would be. "I'll go get my husband." Only if he promised to behave himself. And not become a Baptist. That day, anyway.

Three hours of spirited theology later, Patricia showed up at the sitting room door and said Howe needed to take her to the mall. With a pained smile for the ministers, she assured them it was an emergency.

Worn out from trying to make sure Howe didn't go overboard and change churches without serious consideration, Elizabeth stood, signaling an end to the conversation. "Patti, your father will be with you in a minute." She turned to the ministers. "We'll have to continue this fascinating discussion another time, but thank you so much for coming."

Pastor Lightman pumped her hand with enthusiasm. "Indeed. I'll look forward to it."

Once they were gone, and Howe had ridden off with Patti behind the wheel of the family car, Elizabeth collapsed on the sofa in the family room and closed her eyes. What a day.

Any more like that one, and they'd have to commit *her.*

She must have dozed, but woke to a metallic taste in her mouth and the sound of the front door chimes.

Damn. What now?

After a deep sigh, she rose to find Augusta on the doorstep. Patti's emergency trip with her father suddenly made sense.

Damn, damn, damn. Elizabeth motioned her mother-in-law inside. "Come in, Augusta."

Her mother-in-law stepped inside and gasped in horror. "You have ruined the wainscoting," she accused. "And the windows are naked, for every burglar and common passerby to see in!"

Elizabeth smiled in satisfaction. "Yes. Howe insisted, and we love it." She motioned toward the kitchen. "I was just about to have a drink in the family room. A large one. Would you care to join me?"

Augusta nodded curtly. "I'll have a double sherry."

Elizabeth made the drinks while Augusta perched in a wing-backed chair. She waited to speak till Elizabeth handed her the sherry, then sat facing her. After a hefty swig, Augusta said, "I've come to plead with you to reconsider your position on Howe's hospitalization. Please, Elizabeth. Before he does something he'll regret for the rest of his life."

Something *Augusta* would regret.

Elizabeth started to launch into a defense of Howe's actions, but something in her mother-in-law's haunted expression reminded her of the way Howe had looked when Elizabeth had taken him to task for not considering her feelings before he did anything, and it occurred to her that she'd never granted Augusta the same courtesy. She'd always been too intimidated. Too defensive. So she'd judged Augusta just as harshly as Augusta had ever judged her.

The realization pricked her conscience deeply, bringing the thin, elegant woman into a fresh perspective. For the first time in all those years, she put herself in Augusta's place, and a sad place it was, indeed.

Seeing her sitting there, so rigid and fearful and angry, Elizabeth comprehended how isolated Howe's mother had always been. How lonely it must be to inspire only fear instead of friendship or affection in those closest to her. How empty, to be more obsessed with what people thought than with enjoying the blessings she had.

Not that anyone was responsible for that but Augusta.

Still, for the first time, Elizabeth actually felt pity for Howe's mother.

Not that being nice would get her anywhere with the woman. So Elizabeth decided to address the issue in terms Augusta could understand. "Augusta, I won't go into why it's wrong to try to commit Howe, which it is. I'll simply point out that it won't work. You haven't taken Howe into consideration in all this. I agree that his recent behavior is embarrassing, but he's not insane, and he's nobody's fool. He may not have practiced law, but he was one of the best they ever had in Moot Court at Emory."

Augusta's eyes lost focus, moving from side to side as she saw the glaring fault in her plan of action.

"If you try to commit him," Elizabeth concluded, "he'll fight it, and he'll win. Then the whole mess won't just be all over town; it'll be all over the news, even in Atlanta. So what would you have accomplished?"

Augusta drained her tiny goblet of sherry without flinching. "Much as I hate to admit it, Elizabeth, you have a point." Her posture sagged as she gripped the edge of her seat and stared unseeing at her great-grandmother's Oriental carpet. "This is all so . . . humiliating. I dare not show my face outside my door."

"Then don't," Elizabeth told her. "Take a trip with one of your friends. A royal tour of Scotland. Or Ireland. Better yet, take a *cruise*. Around the world, if you want. You can afford it. And don't come back till this blows over." She smiled. "It will blow over, Augusta. Howe's getting better every day," she said, ignoring the possibility that he might not be. "He just needs time. There's no reason for you to have to endure all the day-to-day ups and downs. Take a nice, long trip. He'll be better when you get back."

Augusta straightened, her eyes narrowing. "You're just trying to get rid of me."

Please. "No I'm not. I just want you to enjoy yourself for once. Be *happy*."

"I might expect such talk from you." Her mother-in-law set the empty sherry goblet decisively on the table beside her chair. "We are not put on this earth to be happy. We are put here to be righteous. To suffer and to sacrifice." She stood to glare down at Elizabeth.

"Oh, Augusta." Elizabeth rose. "Howe may be screwed up at the moment, but at least he realizes now how important it is to feel things. To laugh, and cry, and experience joy. I wish you could feel that, too."

"Rubbish." Augusta's thin lips pursed. "Now

he's got you spouting nonsense. I can see that this was a waste of my time. I'm leaving."

Elizabeth had an idea as she followed her mother-in-law toward the front door. "I'll bet Patti would love to travel with you, and it would be good for her to see more than her own little corner of the world. Maybe y'all could take a trip together."

Augusta lifted a haughty shoulder. "How convenient that would be for you, to have both of us out of the way." She looked Elizabeth up and down with disdain, but this time, her contempt had no power to sting. "Good-bye, Elizabeth." She darted a scornful glance around the renovation. "Do your best to keep Howell under control, before he destroys his reputation completely . . . and this house."

Elizabeth tempered her response with kindness, but spoke her mind. "I don't want a man who can be controlled, Augusta," she said. "Any more than I wanted to be controlled for all those years—by Howe and by you." She lifted her brows. "It was my fault. I let you both do it. But I know better now." She opened the front door. "I'm glad Howe's the way he is."

Saying it, she realized she meant it.

"Then you're as unstable as he is," Augusta snapped, sailing past her toward the car where poor Thomas was waiting behind the wheel.

"Good-bye, Augusta." For the first time in

more than a quarter of a century, Elizabeth closed the door on her mother-in-law without resentment. She actually didn't give a flying flip what the woman thought of her. For that, if for nothing else, everything that had happened since breakfast was worth it.

Without Augusta hanging over her like a vulture anymore, maybe Elizabeth really could work things out with Howe. Assuming he did get better . . . and didn't go off the deep end and become a televangelist, or anything.

But then what would she do about P.J.?

She didn't want to hurt him, but she realized she had to end it, clean.

Oddly, she felt no regret about it.

But she knew better than to think that P.J. would let her go easily. P.J. didn't let anything he cared about go easily.

Elizabeth decided to make herself another drink.

# Chapter 17

"Maybe we ought to skip church for a few weeks till things settle down," Elizabeth suggested over breakfast the next morning.

Howe bristled. "I know things didn't work out the way I'd planned at the vestry meeting, but I have no intention of hiding. I can work for change from within." Oh, Lord. "St. Andrew's is my church home and always has been. Regardless of how well the Baptist minister and I agree on theology, I have no intention of abandoning the Episcopal Church."

That was a relief.

"Unless God tells me to."

Oops. Spoke too soon.

Elizabeth focused on stirring her coffee, wondering if there was any connection between Howe's theological "revelation" and those long hours he'd spent holed up in his study. "Is that what you've been doing in your study all this time? Talking to God?"

Howe colored, suddenly intent on putting homemade strawberry jam on his toast. "Some of the time."

She waited to see if he'd go on, but he didn't,

so she asked outright. "What about the rest of the time?"

He frowned. "I'd rather not say. But I promise, it's not anything wrong."

Then why wouldn't he tell her?

"You're sure you're not thinking of going to seminary or anything, are you?" she asked as casually as she could manage.

Howe let out an undignified laugh that was half chortle, half snort. "God, no. I already told you."

Whew. The idea of being a minister's wife made her blood run cold. She was under enough scrutiny, as it was.

Howe cocked his head, considering. "Of course, if the Lord could make a minister out of Matthew, I guess he could make one out of me. Might not be a bad idea."

Oh, hell. She should never have brought it up.

He shot her a wicked grin. "Gotcha."

"That is not funny," she said mildly, relieved.

He gave her arm a brief, affectionate squeeze, sobering. "We were always dead serious about everything before, weren't we?"

That was an understatement. "Yep." She took a sip of her coffee.

"Damn. Sorry." He shook his head, pondering, then looked at her with dawning comprehension. "We never had *any* fun, did we?"

"You played *golf,*" she blurted out. "Wasn't that fun?" The sarcasm in her question made her feel like a shrew, but if they were going to make something of their marriage, the hookers had to be addressed eventually.

Guilt and remorse aged him before her eyes. "No," he said quietly. "It wasn't fun. Ever." Tears welled. "It was just . . . exercise. Release. No complications. No judgments. No connections."

She focused past him to the perfect garden that surrounded their perfect house. The summer had been the coolest in decades, with plenty of rain, so everything still looked fresh and green. But inside, she felt parched dry. "Is that supposed to make me feel better?"

"No." He covered her left hand with his. "There's no excuse for what I did. You never deserved it."

Elizabeth looked at his simple gold wedding band and wondered if he'd even bothered to take it off on those trips to Atlanta. Probably not.

"God, Lizzie, I'm so sorry," he told her. "I know that doesn't make up for what I did to you, but I mean it." Tears rolled down his cheeks, yet she couldn't count on that as a measure of his sincerity. He cried over everything from Puppy Chow commercials to the national anthem.

Howe tightened his grip on her hand. "Can we get past what I did?" he asked. "Can *you* get past it?"

"I don't know," she said honestly, wishing she hadn't brought it up. But she'd participated, by remaining silent. "Somehow, talking about it makes it all so real, so . . . sordid."

She pulled her hand into her lap to clasp the other. "I managed just fine pretending nothing was wrong. I did it for so long, I almost convinced myself." Odd, how easily she spoke the unspeakable. "The truth is, I knew I'd lost you long before that. Somehow, what we'd had together just . . . disappeared by degrees when we moved here."

"It was me," he said, "not you." He got up and walked to the bay window to stare outside, his voice reflecting off the glass. "When I took over for Dad, there were some seriously shady things going on at the bank. At first, I tried to fix things, but it was so complicated . . . I couldn't tell you about it without exposing you to the risk." He sighed. "Mama was adamant that we not make any major changes, and she was the principal shareholder. I tried to tell her we were past the gray area, but she wouldn't listen. The next thing I knew, I was in as deep as Dad had ever been. Little by little, I traded away my soul."

"I figured as much," Elizabeth said.

He turned, anguished. "Why didn't you leave me?"

"Where would I have gone if I did?" she shot back. "Everything I am, everything I had, was tied to you, to being your wife." What would she have done? "I couldn't have managed on my own, not with the children. And I knew you or Augusta would take them from me. I had nothing to fight that with."

The brief, self-critical flash on Howe's face was becoming familiar.

She went on. "But the main reason was, I refused to let what you did deprive our children of a whole family."

Howe swiped his palm over his forehead. "That's very noble, Elizabeth, but I don't want you to stay for them. They'll be okay. Thanks to you, they're both good kids, despite Patti's temper tantrums." Resolute, he bent to brace his hands on the table. "I've thought about this a lot. Prayed about it. I only want you to stay if you want me for your husband. If you can't commit to that, I'll give you your freedom." His voice roughened. "I'll explain it to the kids. Tell everybody it was my fault."

He bowed his head, as if the weight of what he was offering was too heavy. "I'll make sure you're comfortable. You could go anywhere you want. Be anything you want. No one would blame you, including me."

Elizabeth hadn't ever seriously considered taking off on her own. What would it be like, not having her familiar roles to fill? Who would she be, if not wife and mother?

The question scared her. She couldn't wrap her brain around the idea of being alone and free. But she wasn't ready to commit to staying, not without knowing who Howe would end up being . . .

P.J. popped into her mind, and she thought seriously about what life with him might be like. And when she did, she realized he was really another version of the old Howe—powerful, demanding, and insistent—just more attentive on the surface. She'd have a role with him, either as wife or lover, but she realized that would just be exchanging her old cage for another.

Howe was the one who'd offered her freedom.

He read the reservation in her eyes. "You don't have to make a decision now. I know neither of us can tell exactly how things are going to shake out with me, but one thing is certain: I'm not the selfish jackass I was before the stroke." Keith McDonald might take issue with that, along with most of the vestry. "I want you to be happy, even if that means I have to give you up."

Howe aimed a pained smile at her. "I love you, Elizabeth, more than I ever have. I want to spend the rest of my life with you, making you happy. Making it up to everybody for the things I did. I will; I swear it on my life."

She knew he meant it, but so did a child who wanted to please its parent. Elizabeth didn't want to be Howe's mother anymore. "You'll have to prove that, Howe. This time around, *you'll* have to win *me*."

"I did the first time," he protested.

"No you didn't. I just let you think you did," she said archly. "I decided to marry you the first day I saw you, when I was fourteen."

Howe smiled, his male pride inflated. "So that's how it was." He cocked his head at her. "How come I didn't notice you till we got to Emory?"

She chuckled, her mood lifting. "Because you were surrounded by every other girl in Whittington. And I was too busy being a paragon of virtue and intelligence, so I could win that scholarship and be the one you settled down with."

He straightened. "Wow. I am flattered."

"You should be."

"So now it's my turn." He switched on the radio, and the strains of "Sixteen Candles" filled the kitchen. "Okay, then." He drew her to her feet. "Hi. My name's Howe. May I have this dance?"

It was silly, but suddenly, Elizabeth felt almost shy. "Just this one."

He led her smoothly to the music, and their bodies remembered the long-ago time when they'd danced every day. "Did anybody ever tell you you're the most beautiful, smartest girl in this town?"

Elizabeth smiled. "All the time."

He executed a graceful dip. "May I take you to lunch?"

"I'll check my calendar." So this was what

happy felt like. She'd almost forgotten.

"How about Houston's on Peachtree?" he suggested blithely.

She almost lost her balance. Dear Lord, did he know about P.J.?

Before, it hadn't mattered if Howe found out. After all, she hadn't done anything wrong. But now, for some reason, she cared very much that her halo remain untarnished.

To her relief, he seemed oblivious to her reaction, and the new Howe was no good at hiding anything.

"Not Houston's," she managed. "I ate there so much when you were in the hospital, I got sick of it."

"Okay, then," he said easily, twirling her. "How about the Ritz?"

"Every girl loves lunch at the Ritz."

"Then it's a date." He pulled her close, his face near hers as their bodies shaped to each familiar curve and plane. For a minute, she thought he was going to kiss her. Hoped he was going to kiss her. Then the music ended, and he drew back with a grin, bowing. "I'll pick you up at eleven." He eyed her hungrily. "Wear something green. You look great in green."

Elizabeth actually blushed. She grabbed his shirt and pulled his face to hers to whisper, "Don't tell me what to wear." Then she went upstairs to find something green.

●  ●  ●

After a lovely lunch and a funny movie, Elizabeth was feeling so magnanimous, she talked Howe into calling the kids, then his mother, and inviting them for Sunday supper—something they'd never done. Howe had resisted at first, but when Elizabeth pointed out how lonely his mother must be, he relented.

She decided it was something they should do often.

When the doorbell rang that Sunday afternoon, she opened it to find Charles, looking trim and handsome in his Sunday suit, and bearing a hearty bunch of red alstroemerias.

Elizabeth chuckled as she accepted them. "Honey, you didn't have to do that."

He gave her a hug and a peck on the cheek. "I know I didn't. But I wanted to."

"Well, thank you. You know these are my favorites." She circled his waist. "But you're not company. You're family."

" 'Treat your family like company, and your company like family,' " he quoted. "I want y'all to come to my house for supper," he told her with pride, "but not till I finish with the yard. I'm hoping to be done by the end of the month."

Alerted by the doorbell, Patricia left the self-imposed exile of her room to come down and greet her brother. "I'm still mad at you for not letting me move in," she said evenly.

Charles gave her a bear hug, then started making fart noises by blowing on her neck.

"Aaagh! Charles, stop it!" Patti laughed in spite of herself, egged on by tickling from her brother. "Stop! Really, you are such a child." She escaped his clutches and straightened her peasant blouse. "I swear, Mother, no matter how old they get, men are still bratty little boys."

It was the first decent thing she'd said to Elizabeth since she'd come home, and it felt awfully good, even if Patti had called her "Mother" instead of "Mama." "You may be right."

Patti glanced at the empty table in the dining room. "I thought you said we were eating at four."

"We are," Elizabeth responded. "I thought it would be cozier in the kitchen."

"But Gamma always likes to eat in the dining room," Patricia argued.

"Gamma hates what we've done to the dining room," Elizabeth said evenly. "So I think she'll be more comfortable in the kitchen." Though Augusta probably hated what they'd done in the kitchen, too. But at least there was no painted wainscoting in that part of the house.

"Since when do you care whether Gamma's comfortable or not?" Patricia asked.

"Patti!" Charles scolded. "Now who's being a brat?"

"It's okay," Elizabeth said. "Patti, I'm not proud of the way I've treated your grandmother. I knew she disapproved of me, so I kept my distance. But I've realized how lonely she must be, and I want to try, at least, to make her feel more welcome."

Patricia looked at Elizabeth as if she'd just said she was Elvis Presley's love child.

Charles put his arm around Elizabeth's shoulders. "That's mighty big of you, Mama."

"No it's not. It's only right." She headed for the kitchen. "Your daddy's not the only one around here who can change."

Speak of the devil, just as they entered the kitchen, Howe came in from the door to the back hall. His face lit up at seeing his son. "Charles! You look great." He hugged him, then tapped a fist at Charles's newly trim stomach. "Join a gym?"

"Nope," Charles said with pride. "I've given up beer to save money for my house. And started digging holes every day. Huge holes. Then I've been filling them with topsoil and peat moss and manure. And planting bushes." He showed off his biceps. "Lots and lots of bushes: azaleas, gardenias, hydrangeas."

Elizabeth smiled as she placed the flowers into a vase, remembering the way he'd followed her around the garden when he was little, asking endless questions about what she was doing and why.

"But you're a lawyer, now," Patricia said. "And you work all those hours. Why don't you just hire somebody to do all that?"

Charles chuckled. "Because nobody would do it the way I want. At least, not the ones I could afford. And anyway, it helps me work off my frustrations from the office. And it gives me a sense of immediate gratification." He gave his sister's arm a friendly punch. "Not to mention getting me into shape."

The doorbell rang. Augusta.

Elizabeth braced herself. Kindness, no matter what.

"I'll get it," Howe offered.

Patti gave him a side-on hug. "I'll go with you."

When Elizabeth and Charles were alone in the kitchen, her son turned to her for a quiet, "How's it going, Mama? Really?"

"You mean, aside from the infamous vestry meeting?"

He laughed. "Boy, would I have liked to be a fly on the wall for that one." He looked at her askance. "Did Dad really punch Keith McDonald out?"

"Of course not," she said.

"That's a shame," Charles said. "The old blowhard sure could use it."

"Shhh. They're coming," she cautioned. "I don't want to upset your grandmother."

"Good luck with that one," Charles told her as the others approached. "Gamma!" He greeted her, taking her arthritic hands and leaning in for a brief peck. "You have to get Thomas to bring you up to see what I've done with the house."

Augusta warmed to his attention. "Did you get the bulbs I sent you?" She lifted a bejeweled finger. "They're my prized iris. You mustn't plant them till the fall."

"They came yesterday," Charles said warmly. "Thanks. And thanks for the planting instructions, and your special fertilizer." He risked a hug.

"The secret to beautiful bulbs is proper soil preparation," Augusta told him, tamping her cane on the last three words for emphasis. "And chicken wire just underneath the mulch, so the critters can't dig them up."

Charles grinned. "I'll follow your instructions to the letter."

Augusta acknowledged Elizabeth with a curt nod.

Before, Augusta's visits made Elizabeth feel like a declawed house cat facing down a wild raccoon, but this time she welcomed her mother-in-law with genuine sincerity. "I'm so glad you could come." She motioned to the table. "Charles, please help your grandmother to her seat." Elizabeth crossed to the new warming drawer. "Howe, would you pour the wine?" She turned to her daughter. "Patti, please help me bring over the food."

"That's sexist, you know," Patti said as she grudgingly complied. "You never ask Charles to help serve."

To Elizabeth's surprise, Augusta zeroed in on Patti with a terse, "Patricia, remember yourself. Help your mother."

"But Gamma—"

"Gamma, nothing." Augusta eased into the chair Charles held for her. "Polite young ladies do not speak that way to their elders." She eyed her granddaughter as Patti placed bowls of mashed potatoes and butter peas on the table. "I've been considering asking you to accompany me on a grand tour of Europe, but if this is the way you plan to act, I—"

"Europe?" Patti shrieked with joy.

You could have knocked Elizabeth over with a feather.

"Oh, Gamma," Patti said, "I'm *dying* to go to Europe. I'd *love* to go to Europe with you. I'll be a perfect lady, I swear."

"Perfect ladies don't swear," Augusta said with an actual hint of humor.

Howe stared at his mother in disbelief. Augusta hadn't even been west of the Mississippi, much less overseas. "Europe?"

Mistaking his reaction for disapproval, Patti sagged, crestfallen, into her chair. "My parents probably won't let me. I have to work at the bank and go to Grade Thirteen."

"I don't know about that," Elizabeth said as she laid the roast beef and gravy onto the table. "Touring Europe would certainly be educational."

She sat and put her napkin in her lap. "What do you think, Howe? I know we said Patti needed to work and go to school, but all that will be here when she gets back."

Hope bloomed in Patti's expression. "Please, Daddy. Pleeese."

Howe nodded to Elizabeth, graciously allowing her to take the credit with, "It's your mother's decision."

"I think it would be wonderful." Elizabeth smiled at Patti. "As long as you promise to buckle down to your studies once you get back."

"Oh, I will. Mama, thank you!" Patti exploded, practically tackling her with a hug. "Thank you, thank you, thank you."

Elizabeth savored the brief joy of Patti's gratitude and the feel of her daughter in her arms for the first time in so long.

Then Patti let go and plopped back into her seat, serving herself a huge dollop of mashed potatoes. "When can we leave?" She helped herself to butter peas. "Where are we going? How long will we be gone?"

Augusta actually smiled, and her face didn't crack. "We can go whenever we want. I thought the first of the month. That gives us two weeks to get ready and pack."

Augusta handed her plate to Howe for a serving of beef. "We'll have our own driver, with five-star accommodations, all the way."

She'd obviously done a lot of planning. "We'll start with four days in London, then on to Stratford and Bath and the Cotswolds. Then up to Scotland for the Isle of Skye and Inverness. Then on to Paris for four days, to see the museums. Then Switzerland and Prague. Then Italy. We'll be gone a month, in all."

"What a fabulous trip," Elizabeth said.

"I think this calls for a special blessing," Howe announced, taking Charles's and his mother's hands.

Augusta stared at his hand holding hers, then awkwardly took Patti's as they formed a circle and bowed their heads, something else they hadn't done before.

"Heavenly Father," Howe prayed, "We thank You for this meal and the hands that prepared it, and all the many blessings You have given us. Most of all, we thank You for this family, especially for Mama and the generous offer she's just made to share this special trip with Patti. I ask for protection and special blessings as they travel. Bring them home safe and sound. In the name of the Father, and the Son, and the Holy Spirit, amen."

Elizabeth felt herself relax. Augusta was right. A month without her or Patti to contend with would be a welcome respite for everyone. And Patti was so happy. Buoyed, Elizabeth started serving her plate.

"Well, Charles," Howe said as he did the same. "What's up with you besides the garden?"

Charles beamed. "It's not as exciting as Gamma's bombshell, but you know I've always wanted to get into politics. Well, a few of the movers and shakers I've met want me to run for mayor."

Howe almost choked. "Of Atlanta?"

"Oh, for heaven's sake," Augusta sputtered. "That is preposterous. Nobody white can get elected mayor of Atlanta."

Elizabeth raised her eyes heavenward at the comment, which was probably true but came across as racist.

"Damn, boy," Howe blustered. "Talk about a no-win job. That's almost as crazy as wanting to be president."

Charles smiled. "I might just want to do that, too, someday." He shrugged. "I've got to start somewhere. This is it."

"Cool," Patti told her brother. "But you know you don't stand a chance."

Charles laughed. "Oh, they don't expect me to win. They just think it would be good exposure. Get my name out there, and my face. It's strictly preliminary. I'll drop out before we get into the big bucks."

"Sounds like a plan," Elizabeth said.

"What then?" Howe asked.

"After I finish clerking, I'll go with the DA's

office; get my sea legs trying cases. Then I may run for state representative. After that, Congress. We'll see."

"I've never doubted for a minute that you'll go far in this world," Elizabeth told her son.

Howe stood, glass lifted. "I think this calls for a toast. To the *next* Charles Howell Whittington in the State House."

"Hear, hear," Augusta said as they rose and touched their glasses while Charles smiled with pride.

Just as they sat down, the phone rang. When Patti started to get up and answer it, Howe caught her arm. "They can leave a message. We're eating." After the fourth ring, the call service picked up.

But before thirty seconds had passed, the phone rang again. Patti shot a pleading look to her father, but Howe didn't budge. "This is the first time we've had dinner as a family since I came home, and we are not taking any calls."

The ringing stopped, then started again. Elizabeth decided to put an end to the disruptions. Closest to the phone, she rose. "I'll ask whoever it is to call back later." She crossed to the counter and saw "Insufficient data" on the cordless receiver's screen, then pushed the talk button. "Hello?"

"Thank God it's you."

P.J.! What was he doing, calling her at home?

"Are you all right? Has something happened?"

"I have to see you."

What was he thinking? Her mind raced. She had to cover. "I'm sorry, Anne," she said with deliberate calm, "but I'm having dinner with my family right now, so we'll have to go over that later."

"Meet me tomorrow," he insisted. "Houston's at noon."

He had some nerve. "I'm sorry, but that really won't work for me. I have to go now."

"If you don't come, I'll come to you."

He wouldn't! Elizabeth's heart pounded in panic. The others were watching her, wondering what was going on.

"Elizabeth, I don't make idle threats," P.J. said. "Meet me, or I'll come there and tell Howe how I feel about you."

"Why don't we go over that tomorrow?" she relented, furious at him for pulling such a stunt. "We could have lunch."

"I'll see you at noon." He hung up.

Elizabeth felt as if he'd pulled a plug and all the blood had run out of her.

Howe eyed her with a peculiar expression on his face. "What was that all about?"

Elizabeth focused on her plate as she sat. "Anne had some big idea for the Altar Guild." Damn. She did *not* just say that!

Howe winced as Augusta went stiff as a board.

299

Perfect. Nothing like rubbing salt in the wound.

Howe came to her rescue with, "So Charles, how can we help you out with this campaign?"

"Don't sock anybody in vestry meetings," Charles quipped. "And try to stay out of the papers." He looked to Elizabeth and his father. "But I don't need to worry about you two."

Unless P.J. turned up on their doorstep professing love for Elizabeth. It wouldn't matter that Elizabeth hadn't done anything. Everybody in Whittington would believe the worst, and the scandal would humiliate the whole family.

Holy heaven. What was she going to do?

# Chapter 18

The next morning, just to be on the safe side, Elizabeth told Howe something had come up, preempting her lunch with Anne. He could clearly tell that something was amiss, but he didn't press. "I'll be home by three," she said as she left. Did he suspect the truth? She couldn't tell from his newly shuttered expression.

On her way down to Atlanta, she wondered if it had ever been as hard for Howe to lie to her as it was for her to reciprocate. The thought made her even angrier at P.J. for making it necessary.

She would end it, pure and simple. Then she'd tell Howe the truth.

By the time she walked into the restaurant, she was feeling cold fury at P.J.

"Ah, Mrs. Whittington," the hostess said. "It's so nice to see you again."

Elizabeth faltered. How in blue-bloody hell did the woman know her name?

"Please follow me. Mr. Atkinson is already at your regular table."

Names? Regular table? Elizabeth had a bad feeling about this. Very bad.

She scanned the restaurant for any familiar faces, but didn't see any. Thank God.

P.J. rose when she reached the booth, leaning over to give her a very public peck on the cheek, but Elizabeth dodged him, sliding into her side with a glare of rebuke.

P.J. kept right on smiling as he sat to face her. "You look wonderful, as always."

The waitress came immediately. "Good afternoon, Mr. Atkinson. Mrs. Whittington."

Again with the names! P.J. had to be the one who'd told them. *Very* not good!

"And what may I bring you to drink, Mrs. Whittington?"

P.J. grinned. "Bring us your best bottle of champagne. We're celebrating."

"We are not," Elizabeth countered. "I'm not staying." She glared at the waitress. "Please leave us."

The waitress pulled a face and slipped away.

Elizabeth leaned across the polished table to murmur harshly above the din of the restaurant. "P.J., I cannot believe you'd pull something like this. Have you lost your mind? Surely you don't think this is going to win me over." She didn't pause for a response. "Because it's done just the opposite. So I'm ending it. Now. It's over."

He didn't react, just sat there, smiling with the confidence of a cat with its paw on a mouse's tail.

"Didn't you hear me?" she demanded. When he failed to respond, she tried another tack. "I've decided to try to make my marriage work. If you really care about me the way you say you do, you'll respect my decision."

P.J.'s expression hardened, intensifying the predatory gleam in his eyes. "Not if that decision is destructive. Howe's no good for you, Elizabeth. He can say he's changed all he wants, but underneath it, he's still the same man. He'll end up using you, just like he always did."

"I don't believe that," she defended.

"I can't let you do this," P.J. said. "You'll thank me in the end. I have no intention of giving up on what's best for you, ever, and what's best for you is me, not Howe. I can't let him have you."

At last, the truth. It hit Elizabeth like a semi. P.J. didn't love her. He wanted her, like some trophy.

But why her? He could have his pick of young and willing Atlanta babes.

Was it the chase? The fact that Elizabeth wasn't available?

"If I have to," he said smoothly, "I'll tell everybody about us."

"But there's nothing to tell."

His mouth curled into a cold smile that Elizabeth recognized all too well from Howe's past. "Do you really think people will believe that?" he asked.

Elizabeth's throat constricted. "P.J., that's crazy. You wouldn't."

He leveled a chilling stare at her. "Don't bet on it."

She had to think. Buy enough time to tell Howe the truth before P.J. lied to him. "I . . . I have to think about this."

"Don't take too long," P.J. warned.

A woman's voice sounded from behind her. "Elizabeth? Is that you?"

Adrenaline shot through Elizabeth as she turned to find Carole Thompson from Garden Club with her daughter Hannah. Blood rushed to her face. "Carole," she said, belying her alarm. "So good to see you."

P.J. rose. "We were just about to have some lunch. Please join us."

Carole shot a pointed glance from him to Elizabeth, then declined with a snide, "Thanks, but we wouldn't dream of intruding." She gave Elizabeth a subtle nudge. "Have fun."

"Actually, I was just leaving," Elizabeth said without looking at P.J. "Howe's had a minor emergency with the house. You know how renovations go."

The sommelier chose just that moment to arrive with the champagne in a bucket. "Your champagne. Enjoy."

Perfect.

Carole's eyebrows lifted as she shepherded her

daughter toward the next booth. "Come along, Hannah."

Elizabeth forced herself to turn back to P.J. "It was nice running into you, P.J., but as I said, I really do have to run."

P.J. took out his cell phone and waggled it in threat. "You're sure about that?"

"Yes." Elizabeth headed outside as fast as she could without attracting attention, groping for her own cell phone in her purse. Heart pounding, she reached the awning outside and hit speed-dial for her house.

Howe answered. "Hey there."

"Oh, thank God," she breathed out. "Howe, I need to talk to you."

He read the panic in her voice. "What is it? What's happened?"

"Nothing. Yet. But I have to tell you this in person." She picked a place halfway between Whittington and Buckhead. "I'm on my way home, now. Can you meet me at that little place where we used to eat in Crabapple?"

"Sure. Are you sure you're okay? You don't sound okay."

"I'm fine. Please, Howe. This is really important. Just grab your car keys and come. And don't answer the phone, no matter who it is. Just come."

"I'm on my way." She heard his cell phone ring in the background.

"Don't answer that," she pleaded.

"I won't." The ringing stopped. "I've turned it off," he said. "Be careful, Elizabeth. Drive safely."

"I will."

She didn't. She broke every speed limit between there and Crabapple, but didn't get caught—maybe because everybody else was doing the same thing.

Even so, Howe was waiting outside the little diner, which had gone out of business, when she drove up.

He got out of his car and came over to open her door. "There's a nice little park over there."

"Good idea." It was a lot more private than a restaurant.

He took her cold hand in his warm one to help her out.

Elizabeth had been rehearsing what she'd say all the way from Buckhead, but when she stood beside him, words failed her.

He didn't press. Just strolled toward a small gazebo with benches. "That looks like a nice spot."

Elizabeth nodded, a huge lump in her throat and a stone in her heart. Caught in a cycle of guilt and recrimination, she couldn't stop thinking she should have realized things could get messy when she first felt attracted to P.J. She should have realized what could happen.

How could she have been so weak?

When they reached the little gazebo, Howe sat facing her. "Okay. Let's have it. What's this important thing you have to tell me in person?"

She wrapped her arms across her chest, closing her eyes in shame. "I've been seeing someone." Oh, hell. She'd made it sound as bad as P.J.'s version. "I mean, just seeing someone. Not *seeing someone*."

She hated the hurt-child look in Howe's eyes, hated the fact that she'd put it there. The last thing in the world she wanted was to make anybody feel the way his unfaithfulness had made her feel, even Howe.

He bent forward as if she'd struck him from behind, bracing his arms on his thighs, hands fisted. "I . . ." He straightened, tears running down his cheeks. "I can't blame you. God knows, I gave you reason to turn elsewhere."

"It was stupid, but I was so lonely, and he made me feel important, desirable, for the first time in so long. But nothing happened, Howe," she said with passion. "I wouldn't let it. No matter what, I wouldn't let it."

He looked to the trees beyond them. "It didn't have to."

"Howe, you must believe me. Nothing happened."

"I believe you," he said, but there was no relief in his tortured expression.

"I tried to break it off today," she went on, "but he got angry. Threatened to lie and tell you

307

we'd had an affair, so he could break us up."

"Sounds like a real sonofabitch."

"I don't know," she said. "For some reason, he's obsessed with having me."

"I can't say I blame him," Howe admitted. "Who is he?"

"P.J. Atkinson." The fact that it was somebody they both knew seemed to strike him another blow. "We ran into each other a few times when I was shopping at Phipps, and we had lunch. All very casual. We just talked. Caught up on old times. Strictly on the up-and-up."

"But then," he prodded.

"Then you had your stroke. And the coma." She faced him. "It's not an excuse. I knew he cared about me more than I cared about him. But he made me feel like a woman again. He cared what I thought, how I felt." She hadn't meant for it to be an indictment of Howe's neglect, but it came out that way.

"Do you love him?" Howe asked, the question harsh.

"Not now." She saw his pained reaction at the implication that she once had, and felt compelled to explain. "I was attracted to him at first. And flattered. Maybe I thought I loved him in the beginning, but not now, not after seeing what he's capable of. I can't stand him, now."

"They say hate is the other side of love," Howe said, his voice tight.

"Not in this case. I'd be happy never to see him again."

"Maybe that's just because of the scandal he might cause," Howe said. Despite his own past sins, he was still a man, a man whose wife had been attracted to somebody else. He lapsed into troubled silence.

"I tried to discourage him," Elizabeth explained, "but the more I did, the more persistent he became. When he called me at supper yesterday, I knew I had to put a stop to it."

She reached the breaking point at last, and hot tears spilled down her cheeks. "Now he'll tell everybody we had an affair, which is a lie, and the whole thing will be an awful scandal, humiliating our children."

After all her years of silent sacrifice, she was the one, not Howe, who had destroyed their respectability.

Elizabeth covered her face with her hands and wept. "How could I have been so stupid? Now I've ruined everything. I'll never be able to face everybody."

Howe got up to sit beside her. "You haven't ruined everything." He drew her close, his hand stroking her hair as she sobbed mascara all over his golf shirt. "You were human. You were lonely." He exhaled heavily, as if to purge himself of pain. "I'd be the worst kind of hypocrite if I didn't forgive you, even if you'd slept with him." He rocked her gently, his voice filled with longing when he told her, "I love you, Elizabeth, but our marriage can't be based on duty or concern about what people think. Still, I'm human, too. I can't share you with another man."

"I don't want another man," she argued.

Howe went to the heart of the matter. "The question is, do you want me? Not because we're married, but because you really want me, as I am."

She should have said yes. Wanted to say yes. But the truth was, she couldn't.

"I see." He held her a little tighter for just a heartbeat, then eased his embrace.

"Howe, I just need time," she told him. "Is that so much to ask?"

"No. It's not." His brows smoothed. "I'll explain the truth to the kids before they hear from anybody else. After what I did to you, they'll understand."

Elizabeth sat up short. "You can't tell them about the hookers. Patti adores you. It would destroy her. And Charles . . ." She couldn't stand to see the new closeness between him and his father damaged. "He must never know. Boys need to look up to their fathers."

Howe brushed the hair back from her temple. "You're so good. I don't deserve you."

She deflated. "Yes you do. I guess we deserve each other."

He let out a dry laugh. "That suits me fine." He sobered. "I won't speak to the kids till I've tried to talk some sense into P.J. Maybe he'll listen to reason, man to man."

"God, how I wish he would." Elizabeth shook her head. "Just don't let things end up like the vestry meeting."

"Don't worry," he said, his mood lightening. "I won't."

"Howe," she said in a small voice, "I'm so sorry about all this."

"It's going to be all right," he soothed. "I promise." He pulled her to her feet. "Come on, honey. Let's go home."

Honey. She was beginning to like that. Elizabeth wiped her eyes, then clung to his side as they headed back for the car. "Maybe you and I should go to Europe," she suggested. "Tonight. Permanently."

Howe stopped in his tracks, peering at her. "Do you want to leave Whittington? Really?"

"I hate Whittington," she confessed. "I always have."

He frowned, trying to digest that little bombshell.

Elizabeth regretted adding that to the situation. "Don't mind me," she said. "I'm just dreading the gossip. But running away never solved anything."

She could see the wheels turning behind his eyes. "Sometimes running away works just fine," he told her. "Stepping back can make things clearer."

He pulled out his keys and carefully removed one from the ring. "I was going to tell you about this, but so many other things were going on that I—" He stopped himself. "No. That's not true. I was afraid to tell you, afraid you'd be angry, which you have every right to be." He placed the key into her palm and closed her hand around it. "This is the key to a foreclosure on Lake Blue Ridge that I bought when the bank took it back."

A cabin she'd never heard about, but Elizabeth was so accustomed to excusing things away when it came to Howe, she did it again by force of habit.

"I'm giving it to you," he said. "I'll have the lawyers transfer the deed tomorrow. I want you to go there and sort things out, get away from everything. I'll take care of things here: dealing with Mama and the kids, and the fallout if P.J. goes through with his threat." He read the resistance in her face. "P.J. can't manipulate you if he doesn't know where you are. You'll be safe there, free to rest and make up your mind without any pressure from anybody, including me." He looked at her with open desire. "Take as long as you need to decide what you want to do."

"But if I leave, won't people think—"

"I don't give a damn what people think," Howe shot back. "Lizzie, the truth is, I can't stand being so close to you and not having you. Especially

312

not now that I know there's somebody else who wants you just as much as I do. I can't treat you like a brother anymore, see you every day, have you in my bed, without being a real husband to you. I just can't do it."

At least he was honest about it, instead of trying to manipulate her into having sex with him.

Maybe she should go away, for both their sakes.

All her life, she'd worked so hard for respectability, first for herself, then for her children. She'd faced everything head-on and coped. But she was so weary of coping, of bearing up, no matter what.

Elizabeth tightened her grip on the key and wrapped her mind around the idea of escape, of answering to no one but herself—for the first time, ever. Of eating when she wanted, sleeping when she wanted, free of pressure. Of reading. Of resting. Maybe even finding some sanity. "All right. I'll go home and pack."

"Good." Howe took her elbow and started for the car. "I'll deposit two hundred thousand into your account. I don't want you to have to worry about anything while you're there. If that runs out, just call, and I'll transfer more." He offered her a pained smile. "I should have given you access to our money a long time ago. I'll take care of that while you're gone, too."

Elizabeth didn't know what to say, so she said nothing till they reached the cars. "What will you tell the children about where I am? And your mother?" Augusta would have a fit.

"I'll tell them, and everybody else, the truth: that I insisted you get away on your own to rest now that I'm strong enough to manage on my own."

"They won't believe you. Especially if P.J. spreads lies about me."

" 'Frankly, my dear,' " Howe quoted, " 'I don't give a damn.' "

"The kids will want to know where I am."

"You'll have your cell. Tell them as much or as little as you want to. It's your decision."

Her decision.

"Thank you for that," she said. "And for the cabin."

He cocked a crooked smile. "You can call me, whenever you want. We can still talk."

The trouble was, they'd talked already. He had, anyway.

Elizabeth was looking forward to not talking to anybody, for a long, long time.

# Chapter 19

When Elizabeth got home, she found Howe holed up in his study, and a note from Patti saying she'd gone shopping for her trip with Augusta. So Elizabeth was able to pack without interruption or explanation.

She tried not to think about what she was about to do, or why. She'd made her bed in a rut a quarter-of-a-century long, and the idea of climbing out was both exhilarating and terrifying. So she focused instead on selecting what to take with her. She didn't bring much, just the few really casual clothes she had. Most of her wardrobe was too dressy for the mountains. If she needed more clothes after she got there, she could always buy them.

She could buy anything she wanted, she realized with a tug of guilty satisfaction. As of the next banking day, she—Bessie Mae Mooney, from her train wreck of a family on the wrong side of the tracks—would be a woman of means, no longer a mere appendage to Howe's wealth and power. A woman with a lakeside cabin she'd never seen.

She still couldn't believe Howe had so casually

decided to give her a house. A fleeting shadow whispered that he might have parted with it so easily because the place was some moldy old shack that nobody wanted.

No. Howe reviewed every mortgage himself, and he'd never loan money on anything that wasn't priced right and extremely marketable.

Beyond that, she didn't let herself second-guess his gift, because experience had taught her, she might not like the answers.

She closed the suitcase on her clothes and realized she didn't even know what size sheets to bring, so she called the house line from her cell.

Howe picked up on the third ring. "Hi. Don't tell me you've already left."

"No, I'm upstairs packing. I just needed to know what size sheets to bring."

"You don't need to bring anything for the house. It's fully equipped." She heard him shift in his seat. "I called the caretaker to tell him you're coming. His wife's cleaning and changing the sheets as we speak. She's also putting break-fast food in the refrigerator, so you won't need to shop before you get there. The freezer and the pantry are already stocked."

Sounded pretty extravagant. Maybe the bank had used the place as a perk. "There's a care-taker?"

"More like a fixit man, really. He works for a

lot of the vacation people, but he's honest and reliable."

"Oh. Okay."

"Please let me know before you leave," he said. "I'd like to say good-bye. And I have a map for you. You can drive it easily in an hour and a half."

"I'll come by on my way out," she told him, wishing the leaving were already behind her, maybe because she'd always been the one left behind, never the one to go. " 'Bye."

Elizabeth found a couple of large plastic baskets and rounded up her favorite everyday things, including her pillows and lighted magnifying makeup mirror, then loaded them into her car. A quick tour of the kitchen produced her favorite tomato knife, her battery-powered can opener that crawled around the lid all by itself, and a few of the coffee mugs she liked.

Before she knew it, she was ready to walk out on the life she'd lived for the past twenty-five years. Maybe forever.

It wasn't easy, but she knew that it was what she needed to do.

She knocked on Howe's study door. "Howe?"

He came out into the hallway, the map and directions in his hand. Elizabeth's stomach tightened at the haggard look on his face. "Everything's packed," she told him.

Howe handed her the papers. "If anything's not clear, just call me." He placed his hands gently on her upper arms as she folded them into her purse. When she looked up, he asked, "May I kiss you good-bye?"

She nodded, a huge lump in her heart.

He kissed her gently at first, then his arms tightened around her, transmitting all his hunger and all his hopes into their embrace.

Maybe it was the fact that she was leaving, but Elizabeth responded without reservation, her own longing matching his till she forgot everything but what it felt like to want and be wanted.

Till Patti let out a startled, "Daddy! Please. Get a room!"

The two of them shot apart and pivoted to find their daughter and Augusta scowling at them in disapproval.

"Really, Howell," his mother said. "Show some self-control."

Elizabeth turned a brief look of regret and sadness his way. "I'll call you."

She walked up to Patti and gave her a big hug. "I love you, precious girl. Be nice to your father, and behave yourself."

Patti wriggled free of her. "Mom! I am not a little girl anymore."

Elizabeth walked over to Augusta and surprised her with a long hug. "I love you, too, Augusta." She actually meant it—at least a little. "I'm sorry I've been so distant. I knew I could never measure up to what you wanted for

318

Howe. But I'm so grateful Patti has you. Children need unqualified love from somewhere. God knows, I never got any from my family, but I'm so glad she has you."

Augusta remained as stiff as an armful of coat hangers, at a loss for words.

Elizabeth just kept right on hugging her. "And thanks so much for taking Patti to Europe. I hope y'all have a wonderful time. Don't let anything take that away from you, no matter what happens."

She finally let go, to Augusta's visible relief.

Patti frowned. "Mama, why are you acting so weird? You don't have cancer or anything, do you?"

"No. Nothing like that." Elizabeth hitched up her shoulder bag. "Well, I'm off." She looked to Howe. "I'll call to let you know I got there."

Tears welled in his eyes, but he managed not to cry, which was progress. "Thanks."

"Where's she going?" Patti asked her father as Elizabeth turned and headed for the rear door at the end of the hall.

"We'll talk about that later," she heard Howe say as she closed the door behind her.

Elizabeth didn't look back, and she didn't stop or let herself think till she was on the road and miles beyond Whittington. Then she started to cry. She cried all the way through Cumming, then past the rolling hills and horse farms on

Route 372. She didn't stop till she got to steep, quaint little Ball Ground. Numb, she blew her nose on some fast-food napkins from the glove compartment, then drove the rest of the way on 515, passing the usual mountain mix of raw Appalachian gravel pits, hardscrabble businesses, strip malls, and hyperquaint tourist attractions carved from the steepening terrain at Jasper and Cherry Log.

When she reached Blue Ridge, she pulled over and checked the directions, then turned off the main drag onto the old route that took her past the middle school, then onto progressively narrower roads that led to the final turnoff at Horse Point.

Catching glimpses of Lake Blue Ridge through the trees, she followed the private lane past an assortment of smaller, older houses and huge pseudo-Rockies McMansions. The closer she got to her house, the more curious she was about what she'd find. Near the end of the point, she spotted a single driveway with a small sign numbered "6969," matching the address on the directions. Massed white pines and rhododendrons obscured any view of the house.

"This must be the place," she said aloud.

Lord. She hadn't been alone for three hours, and she was already talking to herself.

She headed down the driveway for about three hundred feet, where the dense underbrush opened to reveal a beautiful, brown-shingled lakeside cottage with crisp white trim, cuddled by hydrangeas, rhododendron, and mountain laurel. The house was not too small and not too big, with a two-car garage, a big porch facing the lake, and a covered metal dock that sheltered a new-looking ski boat. Picture-perfect.

Elizabeth pulled into the open side of the garage to find a neat array of water sports equipment and yard implements hanging from the walls.

She turned off the ignition, then took out the door key. "Okay. Here we are." Refuge.

She made a mental note to have the locks changed as soon as possible. It wouldn't do to have somebody from the bank barge in on her.

She grabbed her purse and suitcase, then unlocked the door that led from the garage to the house. Inside the cottage, polished wood floors and a wall of sliding glass overlooking the lake defined the open floor plan. Subtle colors of nature were reflected in the plush area rugs and simple, masculine leather sofas and chairs.

To her surprise, the place wasn't musty at all, and clean as a whistle. Elizabeth set down her suitcase, then rummaged for her cell phone and was pleasantly surprised to find she had a good signal. After pressing speed dial for home, she heard Howe answer. "Hi. Is everything okay?"

"Perfect. The place is gorgeous."

He didn't respond for long seconds, which surprised her. "I . . . it's . . ." After another weighted pause, he said, "Thanks for letting me know you made it okay. Call if you need anything. Or if you just want to talk. I want to talk to you, Elizabeth. About a lot of things."

She wasn't ready for that, not yet, but she didn't want to hurt his feelings. "Thanks. I think I'd just like to spend some time here by myself, first."

To see if she could do it.

"Okay." Another pause. "I told the kids and Mama I'd sent you on a spa retreat for a month. I think they bought it. Patti was jealous, but Charles said you deserved it."

Elizabeth didn't know if it was a good sign or a bad one that Howe had pulled off his first big lie since the stroke. "Were you able to reach P.J.?"

"Yes."

The fact that he didn't elaborate spoke volumes. "No luck, huh?"

"We'll see." Whatever that was supposed to mean.

So much for wanting to talk about things. Awkward silence spread between them. "I guess I'll go now," she said.

"Okay."

" 'Bye."

" 'Bye." The line clicked dead, and she closed her phone.

Odd, how two people who had lived together for so long could be reduced to such strained monosyllables. Not that Howe had talked to her about anything that mattered before the stroke, but since he'd woken up, both of them were more aware of it.

Laying her purse on the dark granite counter-top, Elizabeth turned her attention back to the house, noting with approval the gas cooktop, double ovens, and French refrigerator in the well-appointed kitchen, and the flat-screen TV above the large stone fireplace.

Could they even get cable up there?

She spotted a remote control on the large ottoman and pointed it toward the TV. When she pressed the button, the gas logs burst into flame, making her laugh.

Further inspection turned up the TV remote on the mantel. This time, the screen came to life, revealing the satellite connection. She activated the channel guide, tuned to HGTV for company, then went to investigate the rest of the house.

Two identical master suites flanked the great room, both with heavenly king-sized beds that faced the lake, huge cedar closets with extra blankets and pillows, and spacious bathrooms with jetted soaking tubs and separate travertine marble steam showers with glass enclosures. The vanities were even stocked with basic necessities, and plush white cotton robes hung above matching slippers in his and hers sizes.

Elizabeth picked the suite on the right because it had a slightly better view of the lake.

That accomplished, she headed back to the kitchen, where she rummaged up a bottle of red wine and some crackers from the pantry, then helped herself to a block of fresh cheddar from the refrigerator.

Howe was right. The place was fully stocked.

*Her* place was fully stocked.

She poured herself a glass of wine, then rinsed a bowl of raspberries and took the food out onto the porch, where ceiling fans created just enough breeze to keep away the mosquitoes. Elizabeth settled into one of the comfortable white rockers and let the peace of the surroundings gradually silence the doubts and regrets that had chased her all the way there.

When it grew dark, she finished unloading the car, then locked the house and went to sleep, so sad and tired, she didn't wake up till morning sunlight slanted off the water and into her eyes.

Elizabeth stretched, feeling logy and disoriented in the luxurious bed. Something was wrong. Where was she, anyway?

Her hollow stomach howled as she opened her eyes to the unfamiliar surroundings and realized where she was, and why. The lump in her heart felt heavier than ever because she'd run away and left Howe to face the consequences of her stupidity. But the hurt, angry child inside her shot back that she'd covered for him for more than two decades. Let him see what it feels like.

Her stomach growled again.

Food. She needed food. And coffee.

She squinted at the digital clock on the bedside table. Nine A.M., August fifteenth.

It couldn't be the fifteenth. Not unless she'd slept for thirty-six hours straight.

Bathroom. Then food. Then she'd figure what she needed to do next.

She swung her legs off the bed and arched her back, yawning hugely. What she *wanted* to do next, she corrected as she made for the potty and relieved herself.

It was kind of scary, actually, not having anything to do. All the busyness of life in Whittington had kept her from having to look at that life too closely. At herself too closely. Now she had no distractions.

Lord, it was too early in the morning to start psychoanalyzing. She'd go nuts in no time if she started doing that.

Elizabeth donned the terry-cloth robe and caught a subtle whiff of perfume. Wow. That maid had thought of everything.

Enjoying the peace of the place, she made herself some bacon and eggs and coffee, then sat at the window and ate with *The Today Show* on for company. The weather was gorgeous, so she decided to check out Blue Ridge and find a locksmith.

Then she indulged in a long, hot soak in the bathtub and washed her hair. Since nobody she knew was going to see her, she didn't bother to blow-dry her usual smooth bob, but brushed through the damp waves, then caught them back with combs above her ears and scrunched in curls to air-dry.

She'd fluff it on the way to town.

She didn't even bother with foundation or eyeliner, just put concealer on the dark circles under her eyes, swiped on a little mascara, then rubbed some bronzer on her cheeks.

Defiant, she left her bra in the drawer and donned a thick cotton knit shell in a black, white, and brown print that concealed the evidence. Then she put on black knit travel pants and topped off the outfit with a chocolate-brown faux suede overshirt that matched her eyes.

The effect was very different from her usual carefully put-together outfits, but Elizabeth didn't care. Anonymity had its compensations. For the first time in memory, she wasn't trying to make an impression on anybody. She just wanted to blend in and disappear.

She found her way back to town without having to use the directions, then turned right on Depot

Street, where a sign said BUSINESS DISTRICT. To her left and right just before the railroad tracks, she saw blocks of quaint, refurbished brick storefronts. On the one-way street coming from her left, a vintage blue-and-white Rexall neon sign drew her attention to the plate-glass windows and sidewalk beneath it that were lavishly decorated for fall, even though August was the hottest month of the year in Georgia.

She crossed the tracks and turned left on Main past the two-story Coldwell Banker building and the Fannin County Court House, then turned left again so she could access the drugstore. Surely somebody there would be able to direct her to a good locksmith. She knew from Whittington that pharmacies were nerve central in any small town.

Sure enough, when she stepped inside onto the vintage beige small-tiled floor, she found three friendly ladies behind the counter. "Hi. Would you happen to have the date?"

The pretty, vivacious gray-haired clerk granted her a friendly smile. "I sure would. It's the fifteenth. Of August."

Lord. So the clock was right. Elizabeth really had slept away a whole day. "I'm new here," she said, "and I was wondering if anyone here could recommend a good locksmith."

The clerk's smile widened. "Welcome to Blue Ridge. We'd be happy to help." After consulting with the other clerk and the lady pharmacist, both of whom welcomed Elizabeth to the area, the gray-haired lady handed her a piece of paper with a name and a phone number. "He's real good, and completely trustworthy." Her blue eyes brightened with curiosity. "You on the lake?"

Elizabeth nodded, suddenly protective of her newfound anonymity "Yes. Thanks so much. Do you have a card for the pharmacy? In case I need a prescription."

"Got better than that." The helpful clerk handed her a map of Fannin County along with the card. "Anything else you need to know, just give us a call."

"Thanks so much. I will." Elizabeth took a step, then turned back to ask, "Is there any particular place the locals like to eat around here? I saw the fast-food places up on five fifteen, but I was wondering if there was somewhere local."

"A lot of folks like the Village, up on seventy-six."

"A lot go to McDonald's for the Senior Breakfast Specials," the other woman added.

Elizabeth wasn't looking for the geriatric breakfast club. She just wanted to get a feel for the place. "Thanks. I appreciate it."

Back in the car, she dialed the locksmith and got a recording, then left her cell number. That accomplished, she decided to drive around and get her bearings.

Three hours later, she had found everything there was to find from Blue Ridge to Jasper to Morganton. All in all, she preferred the old Main Street districts to the run-down repair shops and generically modern strip malls on 515.

Scrutinized by two local couples, she ate sparingly of a late buffet lunch at the Village, then found herself at sixes and sevens, and decided to buy some best sellers from Ingle's. Once in the store, she splurged on fresh raspberries and nectarines and avocados and gourmet chocolate coffee and macadamia nuts. When she got to the register and was writing her check, the middle-aged clerk asked if she had a local address. Elizabeth nodded. "Sixty-nine, sixty-nine Horse Point."

"Oh," the clerk said in surprise, looking her up and down as if she'd just announced she was from another planet.

"Is there a problem?" Elizabeth asked.

"Not for me, honey," the woman said, then bagged her groceries without further comment.

But as Elizabeth was leaving, she heard a murmur behind her and turned to see the clerk huddled with the girl from the next register, who looked at Elizabeth and said just loudly enough for her to make out, "She sure is old."

Uh-oh. Maybe she ought to be more careful about her hair and makeup next time.

Feeling exposed, she hurried to her car and

headed home. Once there, she vowed to sleep late, eat whatever she wanted whenever she wanted, and not speak to a soul—except the locksmith—till she'd read every book she'd bought.

The locksmith called that night, saying he knew the house, but couldn't come till after he got back from a fishing trip in ten days.

Elizabeth agreed, then settled into her retreat, putting a chair under the knob of the back door every night, just to be on the safe side.

True to Howe's promise, he transferred and recorded the deed to the house, then had it delivered by FedEx just three days after she'd arrived. She opened it to see that one of Howe's holding companies had granted her the title. The house was really hers.

At first, it was fun being there alone. Shutting away what might be going on back home, she lazed in a hot bath every morning, then read and napped and watched Ellen and Oprah and Dr. Phil and caught up on a dozen premium pay-per-view movies she'd wanted to see. She skipped lunch and had a simple supper by five, then took long, slow afternoon boat rides, and people enjoying their cocktails on their docks waved to her and spoke as she putted by.

Free of masculine supervision, she even got the hang of docking the boat without getting nervous.

Slowly, as the days wore on, she began to let herself think about what she wanted for the rest of her life, and she began to pray, in earnest, for some of that divine direction God had bestowed so amply on Howe. But the only voices she heard were her own, alternately condemning and excusing, or projecting extreme possibilities based on what she considered. So she bought a Bible and started reading through the Gospels to see what Jesus had to say.

She prayed for direction every time, but though the readings gave her peace, she still didn't know what to do.

The good news was, she had plenty of time to decide.

Then the locksmith came, and everything changed.

# Chapter 20

The day started so well. Two weeks after she arrived in Blue Ridge, Elizabeth woke to clear blue skies and a definite nip in the air that made her feel livelier than she had since spring, and a cool wind rustled loose the yellow poplar leaves that heralded the coming of fall.

She rooted a pair of fuzzy socks from the drawer, then wrapped up in her cozy robe and took her coffee out onto the porch, where she watched the choppy water dance in the sunlight. The whole scene was perfect.

Then the doorbell rang.

"Just a minute!" The locksmith wasn't supposed to be there till ten, and it was only nine. Elizabeth raced back inside. "I'll be right there," she hollered toward the back door as she flew toward her room to throw on some clothes and drag a comb through her hair.

He'd just have to take her the way God made her.

Sliding on her fuzzy socks, she made it to the door and composed herself to open it. "Who is it?"

"Locksmith. I'm a little early." Try, an *hour.* "Hope you don't mind."

Elizabeth opened the door to find a plump,

flannel-shirted man in jeans and a ball cap. She stepped back. "Hi. Please, come in." Oh, Lord; death breath. She hadn't brushed her teeth.

The locksmith didn't seem to notice. He picked up his large toolbox and came inside. "I been wonderin' what this place looked like inside. Real nice." He set the box on the floor as Elizabeth closed the door on the breeze that came in with him. "My cousin told me it sold. She works in the deeds room in town." He rubbed his hands together. "Turned off chilly last night. Next thing ya know, all the city folks'll be up to see the leaves."

Apparently, he didn't need her participation to carry on a conversation. "Let's see what ya got, here." He inspected the lock on the door, then went to the sliders. "Quality, all the way." He glanced at the double-hung windows in the kitchen and back walls. "Okay. Well, hyere's the thing. I can rekey the locks you got. *Or . . .*" He lifted a finger and leaned in as if he were letting her in on a secret. "I could replace 'em with some of them fancy new ones you can rekey any time you want, all by yourself. You can even open 'em by cell phone, which comes in pretty darned handy if you forget your key." He chuckled. " 'Course, that's taking bread out of my own pocket, but it's mighty convenient. I just did some at one of the Eaton places, and they like 'em a lot."

The Eatons, she had garnered, were old-line Fannin County gentry.

"I hadn't thought about replacing them completely," Elizabeth said. The newer locks sounded nice, but her experience with things electronic made her skeptical.

"Well, it's your call, of course." He hitched up his waistband under his beer gut. "I'd have to order them new ones, but I'd throw in rekeyin' the old ones till I could git 'em in for ya."

"I think I'd rather have you rekey the old ones, as soon as possible," she decided on the spot. "I have no idea how many keys the previous owners loaned out, so I'll sleep better when the locks are changed."

"I hear *that,*" he said, crouching to open his toolbox. He took out a small clear plastic case filled with tiny metal rods in different colors. "Wouldn't want any of them *love birds* turnin' up unexpected."

Elizabeth stilled. "Love birds?"

He peered at the tray of screwdrivers through his readers. "I reckon the real estate agent didn't tell you, but the locals call this place 'the Love Nest.' Some hotshot from Atlanta used to bring his fancy women up here, never the same one twice. Neighbors didn't like it much, but what can you do?"

Her house had been Howe's *love nest?* This gift she'd thought was so wonderful, so generous . . .

334

Oh, Lord, the bed. She'd *slept* in that bed, lolled around in it! Bathed in the same tub his hookers had soaked in! Eaten from the same dishes.

The perfume on that robe . . .

Disgust welled up inside her, leaving her queasy.

Son of a bitch bastard whore-loving, sorry-assed, lying . . . She couldn't think of anything bad enough to call him!

He should have told her. *Why* hadn't he told her? A lie of omission was a lie, just the same, so he was lying, just like he used to.

No way was she ever sleeping in that bed again! Or sitting on the furniture.

Oblivious, the locksmith started dismantling the back door lock. "Yer neighbors'll be glad to have a decent, respectable lady like you in the place, I can tell you."

Elizabeth wanted to throw something. She wanted to throw *everything* . . . into the lake! But if she did, she'd be branded a crazy woman. Not the way she wanted to start off in a new town.

Still, no way was she taking this lying down.

She'd get rid of every single tainted thing in the place, the lot of it. That's what she'd do. And have the maid bleach every square inch that was left. Then she'd redecorate the way she wanted and charge it all to Howe, sky's the limit. Assuming she could decide what she liked after twenty-five years of adapting to Howe's ancestors' tastes.

Maybe something minimal, but not masculine: feminine Zen.

"I find the furniture in this place doesn't suit my taste," she told the locksmith. "What do you think of it? Do you like it?"

He stopped what he was doing for a brief scan of the room. "It's mighty fancy," he said with a smile. "Looks like one of them high-priced condos in them decoratin' magazines my wife is always readin'." He pointed his screwdriver toward the flat-screen TV. "Now that TV is *nice*."

"I'll trade you, then," she said on impulse. "Everything in the place, lock, stock, and barrel, for rekeying what I have now, then replacing the locks with those fancy new ones. What do you say?"

He stood, hitching up his jeans again. "You're joshin' me now, ain't you?"

Elizabeth folded her arms over her chest. "I'm serious as World War Three. What do you say? Take it or leave it. All the same to me."

His lower jaw dropped behind pursed lips as he looked over the elegant, masculine furnishings again. "Truth is, the wife's got the house all done up country, like she likes it, and I need cash more'n I need stuff, even stuff this fancy. But I thank you for givin' me first shot."

"If you don't want it," she said, "I'll just give it all to somebody else." Her mind churned with possibilities. "What's your favorite local charity?"

The locksmith shrugged. "Wal, both ma girls play trombone in the band over to the high school. The boosters're always tryin' to raise money fer uniforms and trips and such."

Nothing more local than the band boosters. "Perfect. I'll donate it all to them, and they can have a sale."

He waggled his screwdriver at her. "Now, there's an idea that'd make a lot of folks mighty happy."

"Okay, then." Now that Elizabeth thought about it, she'd rather donate everything to a good cause, anyway. It would definitely up her stock in the community. "If you'll excuse me, then, I'll go call the high school." She would make it a condition that they come pick up everything immediately.

"You do that, now." The locksmith went back to work.

It took a lot of calls, but by the time the locksmith had finished, Elizabeth had arranged for the grateful band boosters to bring their trucks and their teenagers over that afternoon and empty the place. The principal had been delighted, offering to store everything at the gym till they could advertise the sale.

"How'd it go?" the locksmith asked as she came back from her bedroom.

"They're picking it all up this afternoon."

He let out a low whistle, handing her his bill, which was half what it would have cost in

Whittington. "I hate to be nosy, ma'am, but what'll you do with an empty house?"

"Buy an air mattress, then start shopping for furniture," she said briskly. She wrote his check, then handed it to him. "There you go. Thanks so much."

He handed her four keys. "Pleasure doin' business with you, ma'am."

After he left, Elizabeth bleached the bathroom from top to bottom, then called the caretaker and arranged for him and his wife to scour the whole place the next day.

Then she decided to make a run down to Town Center for the air mattress, linens, some decorating magazines, and a few basic necessities. Then she would sit with the empty house for a while—days if necessary—and decide exactly how to make the place feminine Zen.

Regardless of the house's past, it was hers, and she meant to make her mark there.

And hell would freeze over before Howe Whittington ever set foot in it again.

After three days of eating out and contemplating *Architectural Digest*, *Better Homes & Gardens*, and *Southern Living*, she still wasn't sure what she wanted, so she booked a room at the Ritz in Buckhead, then spent a week scouring the furniture stores and the Design Arts Center. But besides two king-sized Dux beds and frames, nothing spoke to her soul.

Maybe she didn't have any taste of her own.

Discouraged, she stocked up on fresh, hooker-free bed linens and beach robes at Macy's, then bought simple stainless silverware, glassware, and moss-green square dishes before heading back to Blue Ridge. She was almost there when a large freestanding store caught her attention with a huge sign advertising antiques and used furniture. On impulse, she pulled into the gravel parking lot and got out to browse the store's crowded interior, hoping for inspiration.

An immensely fat man behind the register didn't look up from doing a crossword puzzle when she came in. "Look around all you want," he mumbled. "Any questions, just ask."

So much for customer service. "Thanks."

Most of the so-called antiques were poor quality that probably only dated back to the twenties or thirties, and the used furniture ran toward heavy Mediterranean or massive Ethan Allen seventies bedroom sets. There were lots of ponderous overstuffed sofas, chairs, and recliners. Nothing that interested her. But just when she decided to leave, she spotted the top of a hutch in the far back of the room, almost obscured by stacked dressers.

Elizabeth threaded through the piled-up furniture for a better look. What she found when she got there made her heart beat fast. The tall hutch looked like native cherry, free of even the smallest imperfection, its doors, sides, and top so artfully fitted they looked like single planks. Only age and TLC could produce a finish like that, the same rich, reddish brown as the shingles on her house.

Clearly, the clean lines and perfect proportions had been produced by a skilled but naïve craftsman. Each shelf above the base cabinet was hand-beaded, and each plank of the tongue-and-groove back had been perfectly sanded and fitted.

Elizabeth hadn't considered using anything rustic, but the piece looked like it had been made for the big wall facing the fireplace, and suddenly she could see the room furnished with comfortable white sofas with clean lines, and soft, sculptured white rugs on the floors, the final effect finished off by minimal accents she could change with the seasons.

Perfect, perfect, perfect.

She couldn't find a price tag, but knew it wouldn't come cheap. Not that it mattered.

Concealing her enthusiasm, she went back up to the register and said to the proprietor, "I noticed that cherry hutch in the back, but it didn't have a price."

The man looked up, almost resentful. "That one's consignment. Been here forever because the owner wants so much for it. It's a good piece, I'll grant you. Owner said her umpty-great-granddaddy from Charleston made it way back before the Revolution, and it got rescued from a fire during the Civil War. 'Course, there's no way to verify that."

Elizabeth frowned, wondering if he was playing her or telling the truth.

The man went on with, "The lady who owns it had to sell her place and move to assisted living. She made me put a real high reserve on it. Frankly, I think she's senile. I'da made her take it back, but she's got no place to put it anymore."

"Just for curiosity, how much is it, anyway?" Elizabeth asked.

He sized her up, and Elizabeth was glad she had on casual clothes. Then he looked back down to his crossword puzzle. "Fifteen thousand, and not a penny less. Take it or leave it."

Elizabeth laughed. The piece might very well fetch that at some high-end antiques store in Atlanta, but without provenance, he had some nerve asking that much. And she certainly didn't want to be branded a patsy by the locals. "Never mind, then." She started to leave.

"Wait." He let out an exasperated sigh. "Lady, I'd like nothing better than to sell you that hutch, but . . . Just hang on a second." He picked up the phone, then flipped through a roller file on the desk behind him. "Let me call the owner and see if I can do any good." He punched in the number, then turned back to

341

ask her, "How much would you be willin' to pay?"

"Twelve," she said off the top of her head.

He lifted a finger and said into the phone, "Hello, Miz Berry? It's Hal down at the furniture store." He spoke louder, "Hal! At the store! I got somebody interested in that hutch! How much do you want for it?"

He frowned, then yelled, "That cherry hutch you wanted me to sell!" He rolled his eyes, covering the mouthpiece to whisper to Elizabeth, "Now she doesn't even remember it." He hollered into the receiver again, "Is your granddaughter there?"

Relief eased his expression. "Could I speak to her, please?" he shouted. After a brief pause, he spoke normally. "Hey, it's Hal at the furniture store. Your grandma left a cherry hutch here on consignment, and I got somebody interested. Would you take twelve thousand for it?" He frowned. "Well, your grandma said that, but we got no proof." His eyes narrowed. "Eight years, at least. And I only got one other serious offer, a whole lot less than this one." Pause. "Okay. See what you can do with her. I'll wait."

Elizabeth watched as he sat back down behind the counter, his back turned to her.

She really wanted that piece.

"She will?" The man turned a broad smile to Elizabeth. "Then it's a deal. You can pick the check up next week. 'Bye, now." He hung up. "Ma'am, you just bought yourself a hutch."

"Will you take a check?" she asked. "I have plenty of ID." Seeing his frown, she reached into her wallet and pulled out her platinum Visa. "Or would you rather take a charge?"

He stood and snatched the card with amazing speed for a man of his bulk. "Visa's fine."

"When can you deliver it?" she asked as he started writing up her receipt.

"I'll have to hire at least two people to help me with it." He shot her a defiant glance. "It'll cost you."

"How much?"

"Depends on where you live."

"I live out on Horse Point at Lake Blue Ridge, number sixty-nine, sixty-nine."

His assessing look turned to a leer. "Oh. *That* place."

Elizabeth straightened in indignation. "No, not *that* place anymore. Now it's *my* place."

"Delivery'll be two hundred," he had the gall to say, probably because she was on the lake.

If she let him gouge her, the whole town would think she was a patsy. "Really? In that case, I think I'll have to reconsider the whole thing." She leaned over and plucked her charge card from the counter. "I'll just take that."

"Wait," he said, palms lifted in surrender. "How about a hunnerd? It'll cost me that for the gas and the muscle, honest to God."

Elizabeth smiled. "That's more like it. We have a deal." She handed him her card. "When can you deliver it?"

"Soon as I can get somebody," he said. "If you'll leave me your number, I'll call."

"I'd like it as soon as possible." Once it was in place, she could measure for the sofas.

She whistled the rest of the way home.

Four days later, the beds were delivered and installed, and after sleeping on hers, Elizabeth decided they were worth every penny.

The day after that, her hutch arrived.

"We tried it with just two of us, but that danged thing's so big and heavy, we had to get two more," Hal explained as the four movers gingerly unloaded the hutch, now shrouded in dusty packing quilts. They managed to get it to the back door, but it was so tall, they had to take off the quilts to get it through. Elizabeth watched nervously from the living room, holding her breath as they struggled to get it inside without banging the top on the doorjamb. Once they finally made it into the kitchen, they all heaved a sigh of relief.

Then the movers turned the back of the piece toward her to take it into the living room, and Elizabeth gasped.

The back had been burned, some places so deeply that she was surprised it hadn't come through to the other side. "Wait. This is damaged," she said. "I never would have bought it if I'd seen this."

The men shot each other troubled glances. "You'll have to take that up with Hal, ma'am," the older one said. "He's out in the truck."

Elizabeth couldn't believe he hadn't told her about the damage. "Would you please go get him?"

Several minutes passed before a wheezing Hal labored through the back door. "Jake says there's a problem?" he challenged, clearly not happy.

"I paid for a perfect piece," she said. "I'm afraid you'll have to take this back. You never told me it had been burned."

"All respect, Miz Whittington, but I did. I told you about that fire it was saved from."

"That's not the same as telling me it was burned," she argued.

"Ma'am, those planks are almost two inches thick. Even burned, there's still an inch of good wood in 'em. The piece is sound." When he saw that she wasn't convinced, his tone softened. "Nothing that old is perfect. Take it from me, anyway, perfection is boring."

Her life back in Whittington certainly had been.

Hal gestured toward the breakfront. "Those burns are part of the character of the piece. Makes it interesting. And anyway, who's going to see them?"

He had a point.

Elizabeth debated making him take it back on principle. But the hutch was still gorgeous.

Maybe she'd been destined to fall in love with the thing, for she, too, had her own hidden scars.

Hal nodded toward the high, blank wall of the dining area. "Just let the men put it where you want it and see what you think," he proposed, "before you make up your mind, okay?"

It was a reasonable enough request. "Okay."

They moved the hutch into place, and sure enough, it balanced the fireplace as if it had been custom-made for that exact spot, and the light from the lake warmed the finish, bringing out every detail. There was just enough wall showing above the piece and space for a chair on either side, perfectly framing its placement.

Hal and the perspiring movers turned hopeful expressions her way. "What do you think?" he asked.

"I think you should have told me it was burned," she said. "But I'll keep it."

That was one decision she *could* make.

As for whether or not to go back to her marriage —and to Whittington—that was another matter. She was still mad at Howe for not telling her the house's history, but she had enough sense not to let that override all the good things he'd done.

For now, she was content to make the place her own. The rest, she decided not to decide,

346

which, for her, the compulsive fixer of all things, was progress.

Happy with the new focal point of her décor despite its hidden imperfections, she thanked a very relieved Hal, then tipped the movers and saw them out. Alone at last, she settled on the raised hearth and savored this first, impressive evidence of her very own style.

But she wouldn't have been so happy if she'd known what was going on back in Whittington.

# Chapter 21

Howe was deep into what he was reading, at last, when the doorbell rang.

Blast. How was he supposed to concentrate?

For the third time that week, he seriously considered hiring a housekeeper.

The problem was, who? All the good ones were hired, even with the economy the way it was, and a lingering bit of his old self didn't trust opening his life and their home to a complete stranger.

With Elizabeth gone, he'd realized what a huge job it was to keep up the place, even with a cleaning service once a week.

The blasted bell rang again. "Coming," he called into the intercom, then left the study.

There was no mistaking the silhouette in the leaded-glass front door. It was female.

Here we go again.

Howe opened the door to find Cassie Benefield, the mother of one of Patti's friends, standing there dressed to kill in deep cleavage and spiked heels, holding a warm chicken casserole with her name and phone number etched into the tinfoil on top. "Hi, Howe. With

Elizabeth gone, I thought you might need something to eat."

"Thanks, Cassie," he said, accepting the casserole, but not asking her in. "That's very nice of you. I'll tell her. I know she'll appreciate your looking after me."

Cassie looked past him to the empty house. "Must be awfully lonely in this big old place all by yourself, with Patti in Europe with your mama." She placed a hand suggestively on his chest. "Why don't you let me come in and heat that up for you?" In case he hadn't gotten the message, she added a sultry, "I'm really good at heating things up."

Some friend, Howe thought, but managed to keep from saying it. "Gee, I appreciate that, but I've already eaten." It was a lie, but he had no choice. He'd already fended off a harem's worth of Elizabeth's acquaintances who had brought him food and offered to keep him company, and there was no doubt as to what kind of company they meant.

He'd talked the whole situation over with Father Jim, who'd absolved him of the lies, but they still bothered Howe. Probably because he could now lie so easily and convincingly, making him wonder if he was slipping back into the way he'd been before.

Confronted with yet another predatory female, he started to close the door. "I'll tell Elizabeth you came by," he repeated. "Thanks." For nothing.

Nonplussed, Cassie waved to him with shiny red talons. "Call if you get lonely. My number's on the tinfoil."

"You betcha." Howe was lonely, all right, but for Elizabeth, not some desperate housewife. The truth was, he was miserable without his wife, which proved his old world had indeed turned upside down.

The trouble with having emotions was that they had him. Yes, the highs were high, but the lows—and the loneliness—were lower than low. And he was awfully lonely. And horny.

Time for another session on the treadmill. If that didn't calm things down, he'd work with free weights. The good news was, he was looking really good. The bad news was, Elizabeth wasn't there to see it.

Howe wondered if she was lonely without him, or just relieved.

He carried the casserole back to the kitchen and opened the refrigerator, which was still full of casseroles the others had brought, some of them getting moldy. Even the chest freezer was full.

He needed to clean the refrigerator out, but he'd been so busy supervising the renovations and working in his study that he hadn't had the time.

He had to find a housekeeper. That was all

there was to it. Somebody mature and meticulous who could take phone messages and ward off female visitors. Maybe an agency in Atlanta could send somebody reliable.

He took out a bowl and spooned the warm chicken and broccoli casserole into it, then got a beer and headed back to his study. If he didn't get more studying done, he'd never make the deadline he'd set for himself, and he definitely didn't want to have to go through all this again.

He'd just gotten settled when the phone rang. He looked at the caller ID, but it wasn't Elizabeth. Damn. "Hello?"

"May I please speak to Elizabeth?" a woman's voice asked.

Why did he feel compelled to answer? He knew better. "I'm sorry, she's not in. May I take a message?"

"Gosh, I really needed to talk to her. This is her friend Louise from church. Do you know when she'll be back?"

Howe gave the woman an F for originality. The whole town knew Elizabeth was gone, and it was obvious from the femme fatales circling overhead that nobody was buying the spa story. "I'm sorry, she didn't say when she'd be back." Or if she'd be back. "I'd be happy to take a message."

"I . . ." The woman paused for effect. "I just really need to talk to somebody, and she's always been so helpful. And discreet."

Howe didn't volunteer to substitute, just started counting to see how it long it took for what came next.

He'd only reached five when she asked, "Do you think it would be okay if I talked to you, just a little? I'd really appreciate it."

Bingo. "I'm afraid you caught me in the middle of something. I—"

"Oh, it won't take long. And really, I could use a man's perspective. It's about my husband. I think he's cheating on me, but if I ask him, and he isn't, he may never forgive me."

No originality whatsoever.

Howe had tried dodging the subject with some of the other women who'd called him with the same ruse, but it had only drawn things out, so he took the bull by the horns. "The question is, what do you plan to do after you ask him?" he said. "If he *is* cheating, he's been lying to you, and he'll probably just deny it. If he says he's not, how will you know it's the truth? Frankly, I think you should go to a counselor and figure out what you really want out of the marriage, either way. Ellis Jackson is a good one. But that's just my opinion."

Clearly not what she'd been expecting. "Oh."

"I'll tell Elizabeth you called." Not. "Gotta go."

Dodged that bullet, one more time.

Howe wondered how long it was going to take

before these women realized he wasn't back on the market.

The next day at Rotary Club, Howe was cornered by Louise's husband Mitch and another good old boy, Sam, whose wife had sought Howe's "advice."

"Howe, old buddy," Mitch grumbled, "what the hell you been doin' talking to my wife?"

"And mine," Sam challenged.

"And where in hell do you get off tellin' her we need to go to some *counselor?*" Mitch finished.

"Yeah," his buddy echoed.

"Well," Howe said evenly, "I didn't call them. They called me. Seems Elizabeth is the Dear Abby of Whittington, but with her gone, I ended up as stand-in." He smiled as if the two men had just paid him a compliment, then leaned closer to them to confide, "Maybe y'all ought to pay more attention to your wives, and less to your girlfriends. Of course, I didn't mention the girlfriends to your wives. Didn't want to upset them. But if I were you, I'd go to the counselor, and I'd participate. Maybe then your wives will stop calling me."

"Oh, right," Sam scoffed. "Everybody in town knows Elizabeth left you, and why."

That stung, but Howe managed to hang on to his smile. "Actually, that's not accurate. I gave her a nice, long retreat to rest and pamper herself.

God knows, she earned it, looking after me for all these months." He straightened. "And God also knows, I've got plenty to make up to Elizabeth for, so I'm doing my best to be the good man she deserves." He clapped Mitch on the back. "I'm living proof that nobody's beyond redemption. If I can reform, so can y'all." He grinned. "Take it from me, there's something to be said for being able to face yourself in the mirror."

"Bull," Mitch said. "You talk to my wife again, and I'm comin' after you."

Howe's smile congealed. "You talk to me like that again, and I'm calling your loans."

Mitch blanched. Like most people in the current economy, both he and Sam had made more than a few late payments, which was grounds for foreclosure.

Howe considered it divine providence that he held the paper on every reprobate in the county, and he wouldn't shrink from using that to accomplish good. His family had suffered enough from Howe's past sins. He had no intention of letting some blowhard like Mitch or Sam embarrass them further.

"You, too, Sam," Howe warned.

Sam sneered. "Ah. There's the old Howe we all know."

On the way home, Howe decided to put a stop to all the female attention. So he showed up, unannounced, at the Women's Club the next day. The president—plump, graying Susan Connor—glided over with a look of pleased surprise. "Howe, it's wonderful to see you. How well you look." As the others looked on, whispering among themselves, she took his arm, openly admiring his flat stomach and newly thickened biceps. "Just delicious." After a glance at his ass, she focused on his face. "There must be some mix-up, though. I don't have you scheduled to speak today."

"Actually, I'd just like to make a brief announcement, if there's room on your agenda," he said, flashing his old charm. He scanned the women present, noting that almost all of the ones who'd called or come to him were there. One even blew him a kiss. Lord. "It won't take long, I promise."

"I don't see why not. Is it something to do with the bank?"

"Nope." He diverted the conversation with, "How are those three grandsons of yours? Elizabeth tells me they're all playing football now."

The grandparent diversion worked every time. Susan's face lit up. "Can you believe it? Seems they were just babies, and now they're in the annual football parade. They're so cute in their little uniforms. But I can't say so, of course. They want to be *tough*."

"Do you have any photos?" Howe said. "I'd love to see them."

"Do I ever. Right here in my bag." She reached into her bag on the nearby head table, then produced a two-inch-thick stack of pictures.

Grateful for a safe diversion, Howe oohed and aahed until it was time to start, and he found a seat near the back of the room.

After the previous minutes and treasurer's report, Susan motioned her gavel in Howe's direction. "Before we move on to old business, we have a request from a very good friend of the Women's Club. Howe Whittington would like to make a brief announcement."

All eyes turned his way as the women pivoted in their chairs.

Howe stood. He'd planned exactly what he meant to say, and he wanted to get it right. "First, thank you for allowing me to intrude on your meeting. Since the Women's Club is the heartbeat of Whittington, I figured this was the best place to reach most of you lovely ladies." He made bold eye contact with the ones who'd come on to him. "First, I'd like to thank those of you who've brought me food while Elizabeth is on vacation. It's all wonderful, and I really appreciate it. But my refrigerator and freezer are full, so you can all stand down when it comes to that. I have enough to last me for the next six months."

A chuckle rippled through the audience.

"Second, I have to eat some crow, here." He glanced down. "For a long time, I was nobody's idea of a model citizen, and an even worse husband to my devoted wife Elizabeth. But now that God has given me another chance at life, I plan to do everything I can to make it up to her."

Half the audience made a dreamy "awww" face, while the rest reacted with visible consternation.

"So," he went on, "though I'm flattered that some of you have felt comfortable calling me and coming by to visit, I'd be a lot more comfortable if you didn't anymore. I'd hate for anybody to get the wrong idea, especially Elizabeth." He faced them squarely. "No matter what you might hear or think, I love my wife, and I don't ever want her to be worried on my account again. Ever."

The spurned exhaled as one in exasperation, while the rest of the women applauded.

Susan grasped her gavel to her bosom. "God bless you, Howe. Would that all our husbands would be so thoughtful."

Howe bowed. "Thank you for your time and attention." Then he escaped before anybody could corner him, pleased with how well things had gone.

But by the time he got home, an emotional rebound had sent his spirits plummeting. The house—and his life—seemed so empty without

Elizabeth that he broke down and called her for the first time since she'd left.

When she answered, he hardly gave her space to say hello before launching into, "I know I said I'd give you time to think, but I really need to talk to you."

"You should have talked to me before I came up here," she snapped. "I found out this was your *love nest* from the locksmith, a fact that everybody in this town was aware of but me."

"Damn." He should have. She was perfectly justified in being angry. "I wanted to tell you, but I was afraid you wouldn't accept the place if I did."

"So you just didn't tell me. How convenient." Her pause bristled with hostility. "Not telling the truth is the same as lying, Howe. I've had a crawful of that, and I won't take it anymore. If you want a relationship with me, you have to tell me the truth, even when it's messy."

"I will." Why hadn't he just told her? It was his old self who'd used that place, not the man he was now. "I swear. From now on, it's the truth, the whole truth, and nothing but the truth. That's why I called you. Things have been pretty . . . *messy* around here since you left."

Her tone shifted. "How, messy? Dirty house, messy, or trouble, messy?"

"Both, but the house, I can deal with." He owed her the truth. "The rest . . . Nobody bought

358

the spa story, so a lot of your so-called friends have been showing up on the doorstep with casseroles, offering to keep me company."

To his amazement, Elizabeth laughed. "Who? Tell."

It certainly wasn't the reaction he'd expected. He tucked his chin, offended that she wasn't the least bit threatened. "Wouldn't you rather know if I was tempted?"

"If you were tempted," she countered, "you wouldn't have told me. Who were they? And what did they bring?"

"Chicken casseroles, mostly," he said. "Sarah Williams was the first."

"That doesn't surprise me. She always has hated me for marrying you."

"Why?" That was ridiculous. "I never even dated her."

"You were the catch of the century. A lot of girls in Whittington took to their beds when we eloped," Elizabeth told him. "So did their mothers."

Howe mimicked a breathy starlet's voice. "That makes me feel like a piece of meat."

"Who else put the mash on you?" she prodded.

Maybe she did care, and was making a blacklist. Howe smiled, then named off as many as he could remember. "And that's not counting the phone calls," he said.

"They *called* you, too?"

"Not the same ones," he said.

"Lord. What did they say?"

"They started out asking for you, then said they needed advice about their husbands," he explained. "I tried to get off the line, but they were crafty."

Elizabeth laughed again. God, it was good to hear. "That is *so* lame. Do they think you're a moron?"

"Apparently," he said, missing her more with each passing word.

"So, what did you tell them?"

"To go to a counselor to figure out what they wanted from their marriages. I recommended the one I'm seeing."

A long pause strained the silence between them. "I guess you'd like for me to figure out what I want from this marriage, too," she said at last, her voice subdued, "wouldn't you?"

He hadn't realized it when he'd placed the call, but she was dead right. "I know you want honesty, and I'm going to do a lot better with that. As for the rest . . . I don't want to pressure you. I can wait. It's not easy; I miss you like hell. But take the time you need."

When she didn't respond, he said, "I figured out a way to get your so-called friends to leave me alone."

"And what was that?" she asked with obvious trepidation.

"I went to the Women's Club meeting this morning and asked them to back off."

"Charles Howell Whittington the second, you did not!" Elizabeth exploded.

Uh-oh. "I did."

"If you ever want to speak to me again, you will tell me every word you said," she ordered. "Exactly. And do not leave anything out." She muttered, "I cannot believe you did that."

So Howe told her. By the time he'd finished, Elizabeth had calmed down.

"That was very diplomatic," she said. "And very, very sweet."

"I meant it."

After another extended pause, she said quietly, "I was really furious at you for not telling me the truth about this place."

At least she used the past tense. "I'm really sorry, Lillibet. It was stupid. And I can't promise you I won't ever do anything stupid again, but I will try to be honest, even when it hurts." He couldn't help making at least one excuse. "I just wanted you to have a safe place to think things over." Even as he said it, he realized his motives hadn't been quite so pure.

"That's not the whole truth," he owned up. "I wanted to know where you were, somewhere I could picture you." Stupid. And selfish. "That was selfish of me."

The silence from her end tightened his chest,

and he gripped the phone with both hands, aching for her solid, calming presence. "I miss you so much, Elizabeth. Without you, this is just a big, empty house."

She didn't respond, which only made it worse. He'd promised not to pressure her, but that was just what he was doing.

At last, she spoke. "Lonely enough to make you look for comfort elsewhere?"

"No." The word came quick and sure. "Just lonely enough to make me miserable. I try to keep busy with the renovations and another project I'm working on, but without you, none of it means very much."

"You can call me," she offered, softening. "It's okay."

"That would help a lot."

"But don't talk to any more of my so-called friends," she advised, a welcome hint of jealousy in her tone.

"I told you, I asked them to back off."

"Some people don't take no for an answer," she said. "Now, they'll probably call to tell you what a wonderful thing you did today. If they do, let the message pick up, then you can block their numbers."

"Tried it. They just come over . . . with a chicken casserole."

She chuckled, breaking the tension.

"I'm hiring a housekeeper," he announced.

"Somebody mean and matronly. Let her deal with it."

"Sounds like a plan to me."

Don't hang up. "You know, I never appreciated how much work this place is till you left," he said. "I didn't appreciate a lot of things you did, but I do now."

"That's good to hear."

The next pause stretched awkwardly between them.

"Well, I guess I'd better go," she said. "They're delivering the new sofas today, and I don't want to tie up the phone."

But the house was fully—and expensively— furnished. "New sofas?"

"Yes, sir," she said. "When I found out every-body in town called this place 'the *Love Nest*' " —Howe winced—"I got so furious knowing those women had been here, *slept* here, touched everything, that I wanted to throw every bit of it into the lake. Especially the beds."

Damn. He'd never even considered the whole bed thing. "Did you?"

"I was tempted," she admitted, "but no. I gave everything—and I mean everything—to the band boosters, instead. They raised six thousand dollars auctioning it all off."

It had cost fifty, but Howe had no intention of bringing that up. "So what are you doing for furniture?" he asked.

"Haven't you looked at the Visa bill?"

Howe tucked his chin. "Hazel does all that at the bank," he told her. "Why?"

"Let's just say I finally got to decorate a place the way *I* like it."

Howe made a mental note to check the bill. However expensive it was, he couldn't very well blame Elizabeth. "Splurge all you want, and enjoy it."

"I will, but I don't need your permission to do it," she shot back.

She'd gotten feisty up there on her own, and it turned Howe on.

Another awkward pause settled between them.

"I really have to go now," she said.

It was so hard letting her go, he couldn't be the one to say good-bye. "Thanks for taking my call. I promise not to abuse the privilege."

" 'Bye."

The line went dead.

Howe hung up and made straight for the treadmill and ran till he was too exhausted to think, then took a long, hot shower and cried like a baby.

At least he wasn't bawling in public anymore.

The next Sunday at church, Father Jim surprised the congregation by preaching on what an inspiration it had been to work with Howe and see his new dedication to his faith and their parish.

Surprised, Howe shifted uncomfortably in his seat, knowing what Paul must have felt like when he referred to himself as chief among sinners.

The priest went on to paint vivid pictures of the changed lives of the disciples, both before and after Christ's death. Then he confessed that he had lost his fire and been phoning it in for the past few years, for fear of offending anyone. But seeing Howe's new beginning had made him decide to make a new one of his own. Then he challenged the congregation to examine their own lives and pick one area, just one at first, where they would start afresh with a new commitment to their own relationships with God and the spiritual growth of their church. He concluded by asking for their help along the way in his journey of renewal, and promising to help them in theirs.

It was the best sermon the man had ever given, and Howe's mother wasn't there to hear it.

After the service, several of the members who'd given Howe the cold shoulder since the vestry meeting came up and shook his hand as he waited to tell the minister what a great job he'd done.

When Howe reached Father Jim at his usual postservice greeting place at the back of the sanctuary, the priest enveloped him in a hug, clapping his back.

"Great job, Father," Howe told him. "Really great. You need to be careful, though. I might get the big-head."

The minister's eyes were rimmed with red when he drew back. "Your trust and willingness and enthusiasm made me realize how far I'd fallen from the joy of service I once had."

Howe faltered. "I never intended to imply that you—"

"You did exactly what God wanted you to do," the priest interrupted, "and I'm grateful. Thanks to God's mercy, we can *both* start over exactly where we are."

If only Elizabeth could, too.

Father Jim smiled in sympathy. "How much longer till Patti and your mother get home?"

"Wednesday," Howe said. Till then, he'd rattle around in that big place like a marble in a steamer trunk.

Father Jim smiled in sympathy. "Why don't you come by for lunch after this? I know Nancy would love to see you." He leaned in close again. "And I promise, she won't make a pass at you."

Howe chuckled. He could use some company. And something besides chicken casserole to eat. "It's a date." That took care of Sunday. Now all he had to do was take care of the rest of the time till Elizabeth rendered a verdict on their marriage.

He knew better than to let himself think beyond that.

Meanwhile, he'd have to tell Patti something about where her mother was when she got back, before the rumors reached her. The question was, what?

# Chapter 22

The next Wednesday, Howe and a host of others waited for the arriving passengers at the top of the escalators in the main concourse of Hartsfield-Jackson, and was surprised to see Patti emerge from the elevator, instead, pushing his mother in a wheelchair.

Howe rushed over to help. His mother's baleful expression dared him to mention the chair, so he didn't.

"There're my girls! I sure did miss you two." Howe confined himself to bear-hugging Patti. "Hey, Patti-pie. How was Europe?"

"Fabulous, Daddy. Fabulous. I can't wait for you to see the pictures. We stayed in real castles. They were so gorgeous. And our drivers were so nice. They were licensed tour guides, too, so they all knew everything about what we saw, and took us to these great little out-of-the-way places." Brimming with all she'd seen, she launched into a detailed travelogue as they headed for baggage claim.

When they got there, Howe asked Patti to find out which carousel their luggage would be on, then waited till she was gone to crouch beside his mother and ask, "Mama, are you okay?" Her color was terrible, and she appeared to be in pain.

"I'm eighty-five years old and just took a whirl-wind tour of Europe with a nineteen-year-old," she snapped. "Not to mention the fact that I've just spent seven hours flying home. I have a right to be tired."

"When was the last time you had a physical?" he asked.

"None of your business."

Patti came back, pointing to the nearby baggage carousel. "It's coming in on that one."

No bags had shown up yet, which came as no surprise. The Atlanta airport was so busy, it could take an hour to get your luggage.

Howe didn't let his mother off that easily. "Mama, you need to have a physical every year."

"Yes, she does," Patti chimed in.

"I do not," his mother protested. "They just run a million expensive tests, then tell me I'm old and try to drug me. There's no point."

Howe looked more closely at her, concerned. "Mama, you're not well. I can see it."

"She has stomachaches all the time," Patti tattled.

Howe's mother glared up at her. "That was just the unfamiliar food."

"Which you hardly ate," Patti countered.

"Can you blame me?" her grandmother said. She turned her head, refusing to look at either of them. "Patricia, I *told* you not to tell him."

Patti leaned down to her level. "I don't care. You need to go to the doctor, Gamma. I know you, and this is more than a case of Napoleon's revenge."

Haughty, Howe's mother tamped her cane on the floor beside her. "I am a grown woman of sound mind, and fully capable of making my own health decisions." She used the side of the cane to move Patti out of her personal space. "Now change the subject. You're ruining our homecoming."

As she always did, Patti gave in to her grandmother and shifted back to telling Howe about their trip.

He let the matter drop, but only till his mother had a chance to rest. Then, if she wasn't greatly improved, he'd insist she see someone.

After they'd dropped his mother off back in Whittington, Howe took Patti home with him.

They hadn't taken two steps into the kitchen when she put her hands on her hips and said, "Gross, Daddy. How can you eat in here?" She pulled off a paper towel and mopped up some baked-bean juice he'd spilled trying to use the hand-crank can opener. "What happened to the cleaning service?"

"They went out of business." Murphy's Law: Elizabeth left, and the service went out of business. "I got a handwritten note on an index card in the mail last week."

Patti shook her head. "Mama's gonna have a fit if she comes home to find it like this." She crossed to the refrigerator. "Is there anything to eat?"

"Ah . . ."

She opened the French doors to find the shelves packed with casseroles and other care packages in take-along containers, most of them bearing the donor's name and phone number. "What in the world?"

"Your mother's friends are trying to keep me from starving while she's gone," he said.

Patti opened one and recoiled from the moldy food inside. "Eeyew. Gross." She dropped it into the garbage. Two more similar specimens followed. "Daddy, you should have frozen what you couldn't eat. Everything in here is rotten."

Hence, the baked beans. "I did freeze stuff, but I ran out of room."

Patti opened the two freezer drawers and found them crammed full. "Good grief. Do they think you're destitute, or what?"

"Beats me."

She stilled, then turned, her expression wary. "When is Mama coming home, anyway?" Her blue eyes begged him to tell her everything was okay, and her mother would be home soon.

If only he could. "I don't know, honey. That's up to your mother."

Patti sank to the stool. "Daddy, she didn't *leave* us, did she?"

Howe took the stool beside her. "No. I asked her to go. I wanted her to have time to think things over." He looked down at the floor. "Patti, I'm not proud of the man I was before my stroke. I did some terrible things to your mother, but she endured it because she loved me, and you and Charles. She never complained, just made the best home she could for all of us."

"I know that Gamma doesn't like her," Patti confessed, steering the conversation away from those terrible things he'd mentioned. "And I know why. Charles told me, about her family and all." Patti touched his arm. "I should have been nicer to Mama."

"We all should have."

"Charles was," Patti said. "He's always been sweet to Mama." Her voice thickened with tears. "All my friends love Mama. Why couldn't I?" She answered her own question. "I just always felt like she wanted me to be perfect, and I can't be. I'm not like her."

Howe put his arm around her. "Patti, this is not your fault. It's mine. I should have helped your mother with discipline, but you were the only person in the world who adored me, and I was selfish. I didn't want to mess that up, so I left all the hard parts to your mother. That was wrong of me."

He summoned his courage for the rest. It hadn't been an easy decision, but after long prayer and thinking, he'd realized he needed to own up to what he'd been and ask his children's forgiveness. He'd already talked to Charles, who had suspected the truth all along. But this was his baby, who idolized him. He took a deep breath, then got it out. "Patti, I was unfaithful to your mother for many years."

Patti pulled back. "That's not true. You're lying."

"I wish it wasn't true, but it is," he said, meeting her stricken gaze with anguish. "Not only that, but I shut her out of my heart and my life."

Patti slid off the stool, putting distance between them. "Why?" she demanded. "What did she do? She must have driven you away. She's so demanding."

"She didn't do anything wrong," he said, emphatic. "She just loved me, warts and all, and I betrayed her. The guiltier I felt, the more I shut her out."

"I don't believe this," Patti told him, turning her eyes to the ceiling. "You're just saying this because of the stroke. That's it."

"I'm saying this because you have a right to know the truth about your father," Howe said sternly. "You've misjudged your mother, Patti. She's the most loving, caring person I've ever met, and she deserves better, from both of us.

She's been terribly, terribly lonely, trying to keep this a secret."

Hurt warred with revulsion and denial in Patti's face.

Unable to face it, Howe braced his elbows on the granite island and leaned forward, threading his fingers through his hair. "Elizabeth deserves so much more than I've given her. I've changed, and I want a chance to make it up to her. The last thing I want to do is let her go, but I asked her to take some time by herself because I wanted her to have her freedom, Patti, even if that means I'll have to live the rest of my life without her."

"Daddy." Tears streamed down Patti's face, and suddenly she wasn't a wild woman, but a small, vulnerable child. "She'll come back. I know she will. You said she loves us. She'll come back."

The hardest part was yet to come. He walked over and hugged his daughter, as if his arms could protect her from what he had to say next. He leaned his cheek against her hair. "We're not the only ones who love her, sweetie."

Patti went stiff. "What do you mean?"

"There's somebody else who loves her."

"Oh, God," Pattie lashed out. "She cheated on *you*."

"No." His arms tightened to keep her from running away before he could explain. "She'd never do that. It isn't in her. But she was lonely, and he paid attention to her. Sought her out. Listened to her problems. Made her feel important. Everything I should have been doing, but didn't."

"How do you know she didn't sleep with him?" Patti asked, her voice harsh. "You lied to her all those years. Maybe she's lying to you, now." She wrested free of him, her fingers braced on her temples as she paced in circles. "This is a nightmare, a freakin' nightmare. I come home, and find out my Norman Rockwell family is really some cheap, filthy reality show."

"No it's not," Howe said. "Our family is what we make of it. So far, my past sins have been private, and your mother wants to keep it that way. I'm the one who told her I didn't want to be married unless she could love me the way I am now."

Every nerve and flaw exposed, he turned to Patti. "I love your mother more than my life, but it would kill me to know she only came back out of duty or some misguided effort to keep up appearances. I've hurt her enough already."

"So you're just going to hand her over to that other guy?" Patti said, tears streaming down her cheeks. "If you love her, why don't you fight for her?" She grabbed his arm, shaking him. "Daddy, you need to fight for her. Tell her you're sorry, that you'll make it up to her. Let her know how much you love her."

He laid a staying hand on hers. "I did."

She cried harder. "I'll make Gamma be nice to her. I don't know how, but I will."

Howe embraced her, hating the pain he'd caused. "Honey, this has to be your mother's decision. Whatever she chooses, she deserves your love."

Patti collapsed against his chest and sobbed. "Don't let her go, Daddy. Don't let her."

If only it was that simple.

The damned doorbell rang, and Patti pushed him away. "Answer it," she choked out. "It's probably some so-called friend of Mama's trying to hook up with you." Seeing his shock, she swiped at her nose. "I'm not an idiot, you know. I saw their phone numbers on all their casseroles."

Howe moved toward her. "Never mind the door. They'll go away. I don't want to leave you like this."

Patti raised her palms to ward him off. "Go. I need to be by myself." She headed for the back stairs. "I'm going to my room."

Reluctantly, Howe watched her leave, then headed for the front door.

The silhouette in the leaded glass was definitely *not* a woman's. It was male, and large, too tall and broad shouldered to be Mitch or any of the other "Dear Abby" husbands.

He opened the door to find P.J. Atkinson on

the doorstep, and the man was spitting nails. "Where is she?" P.J. demanded, pushing past him. "Elizabeth would never have broken off with me unless you forced her to! Now she's disappeared. None of her friends knows where she is. What have you done with her?"

"I haven't done anything to her," Howe said. "Not that it's any of your business."

"It is my business," P.J. shot back. "She's mine, not yours. And if you don't tell me where she is, I'm filing a missing persons report."

"Be my guest," Howe said. "She'll just call the police and tell them she's fine. And she doesn't want to see you. Or me."

P.J. went livid. "You may have ruined me by foreclosing on my developments in ninety-one, but it's payback time. I stole your wife. She's mine, body and soul, and I do mean body."

"She never did that, and you know it," Howe growled out. "I always knew you were sleazy, so it doesn't surprise me that you took advantage of a lonely, vulnerable woman. But Elizabeth told me all about it, and I know there was no affair."

"Oh, right," P.J. scoffed. "Just like you never used every hooker in Atlanta for the past twenty years."

A gasp from the stairway turned both their attentions to Patti, who stood, stunned, on the landing. "Hookers?" She searched Howe's face. "You went to hookers?"

"Patti, go to your room," Howe ordered. "Now."

"Yes, Patti, go to your room," P.J. mocked. "We wouldn't want you to find out the truth about your mother." He went sly. "Never mind that your daddy's a whoremonger, and your mother slept with me."

"Your mother did no such thing, Patti," Howe barked out, then pivoted on P.J. "You sorry, low-life bastard. You're just mad because Elizabeth saw through you and told you to get lost. Now I'm telling you the same thing. Get lost."

"Make me," P.J. taunted.

"You're trespassing. Get off my property. And leave my family alone, or you'll regret it," Howe threatened.

P.J. laughed, a harsh, ironic sound. "Oh, I don't think so."

Howe shoved him, hard, toward the open door. "Out, or I'll call the cops."

P.J. shoved him right back, reclaiming his place. "Oh, by all means, call them. But be sure to tell them why I'm here. If you don't, I will. I think this town will be very interested to know that the high-and-mighty hypocrite Howe Whittington has been cuckolded by the likes of me." He leered. "I think she told you about our affair, and you refused to let her go, then did something to her. At least, that's what I plan to tell the media. Who cares where she really is, or why? The word will be out."

378

Howe had never hit anybody in his life, but without even engaging his brain, he landed a bone-crushing haymaker to the lying sonofabitch's face that sent P.J. onto his rear.

"Daddy!" Patti shrieked, clamoring down the stairs as Howe shook his throbbing hand.

The next thing Howe knew, P.J. was getting up, his lip split and bloody murder in his eye. "You pansy-assed chickenshit. I'll mop the floor with you." He charged, but Howe deftly stepped aside, which only made P.J. madder.

"Stop it! Both of you!" Patti ordered, but both men were beyond hearing her.

P.J. cocked a fist and barreled toward Howe, who evaded him again.

"How can you claim to love Elizabeth," Howe shouted, "then say those things about her?"

An evil grin spread across P.J.'s face as he swiped the blood from his lip. "I never said I loved her. I just *used* her to get even with you, and it was sweet."

Howe hit him again. This time, P.J. came back with a solid blow to Howe's stomach, then a deadly right hook that rattled his brains, sending him sprawling against the foyer table, then onto the black-and-white tiles. By some miracle, his great-grandmother's huge crystal vase didn't fall off the table, but turned over, scattering silk flowers and the gallon of clear glass marbles that held them all over the floor.

Howe got up, then went right back down again as he slipped on the marbles.

P.J. dodged them on his way toward Howe, clearly intending to kick him when he was down.

"Stop it!" Patti grabbed the nearest implement —an umbrella—then launched herself halfway across the room with a single, adrenaline-powered leap onto P.J.'s back like a rabid cat, flailing away with every word. "You . . . leave . . . my . . . father . . . alone! And . . . shut . . . your . . . lying . . . mouth . . . about . . . my . . . mother!"

Howe managed to regain his feet as P.J. spun around, trying to shake her off, but Patti gripped his hair and gave his ear a vicious twist. "Damn!" P.J. roared. "Get this bitch-brat off me!"

By God, Patti was ferocious, but she was going to get hurt. "Patti," Howe shouted through her blood-haze. "Let go! I can handle this." He dodged the marbles and grabbed her, but she whacked his hand loose with the umbrella, which stung like hell.

Then she resumed whaling away on P.J. "I . . . am . . . not . . . done . . . with . . . you," she roared at P.J., sounding like a Klingon warrior.

Whoa!

"What the hell is going on here?" a male voice said from behind them.

All three of them turned to see Charles standing in the open doorway with his startled employer.

"Judge Etheridge!" Howe said.

Everybody froze, then Patti slipped off P.J.'s back, giving him one last jab with the umbrella for good measure. In response, he side-armed Howe back into the marbles. As Howe fell, he took P.J. with him, and somehow all three of them ended up on their asses amid the silk flowers.

Patti grabbed a white gladiola and smacked P.J. across the face like a knight wielding his gauntlet. "Bastard."

"Quit that." Howe snatched the flower to prevent further mayhem. "It's over." He helped her to her feet as P.J. got up. "Sorry, Judge," Howe said. "This man pushed his way into our home and refused to leave."

"Do I need to call 911?" the judge asked, clearly entertained.

P.J. glared at Howe. "You haven't heard the end of this. I meant what I said." He tried to storm out, but the effect was lost because he had to tiptoe through the marbles.

Charles turned to Howe with a grim, "Was that the guy?"

Howe didn't answer. "Judge, I apologize about all this. When I tried to push him out of the house, things got physical, and Patti jumped into the fray."

"I'm glad she's not mad at me," the judge quipped. He bowed slightly to Patti. "Well done, young lady."

Her cool restored, Patti made a brief curtsy, followed by a dazzling smile. "Thenk yew." She straightened her peasant blouse. "I found it very . . . empowering."

"You were lucky he didn't hurt you," Charles scolded. "You should have called the cops."

"I couldn't," she said. "He threatened to . . ." She shot a troubled glance the judge's way and didn't finish.

"The important thing is, he's gone," Howe intercepted. "If you'll give us a minute, Judge, we'll clean up this mess, and I'll fix you something to drink." He rubbed his sore jaw where P.J. had connected. "I could use a double."

"I'm the one who should apologize," the judge responded. "Charles drove me down to speak to the county bar association, and I convinced him to drop by on our way back. We should have called."

"Nonsense," Howe dismissed. "Your arrival was divine providence. Nothing like a judge as a witness to stop a fight."

"Glad to be of service." The judge motioned Charles back toward the car. "Come on, Charles. Let's head back to the office." He nodded toward Howe. "This'll stay between us. Unless you need me to testify."

"I'm sure that won't be necessary," Howe assured him.

"Don't bank on it," the judge said. "Atkinson's pretty vindictive. I've seen him in action."

So the judge knew P.J. "I'll bear that in mind."

Howe saw them out to their car, then came back to find Patti crying and sweeping up the marbles. "Aw, honey, it's over." He took the broom and hugged her. "Everything's okay. Don't cry."

"I just hate this, all of it," she said.

"I know. So do I."

"We have to tell Gamma about those awful lies before somebody else does," Patti moaned out. "Like, *now.*"

"I know. I'll do it."

She wiped her eyes. "No. Let me. Gamma listens to me." She exhaled, looking old beyond her years, and it made him sad to see it. "Then I want to go see Mama and tell her it's all right. Where is she?"

Howe was through hiding things. "I had a house in the mountains where I used to go when I was up to no good," he told her. "I gave it to your mother, so she'd have a place of her own. It's on Lake Blue Ridge."

"I'll tell Gamma first, then go up tomorrow."

"Patti," he told her. "You were very brave to defend me. I'm proud of you. But I don't want you fighting my battles with your mother."

"I won't, Daddy. This is about me and her." She handed him the broom. "But first, I'm going to Gamma's, then I'm getting a double cheeseburger and fries. Then I'm going to bed."

"Sounds like a plan."

She grabbed her purse from the credenza. "Can I take your car?"

He nodded, tossing her the keys. She took three steps, then turned back to say, "I love you, Daddy. I hate what you did, but I still love you."

He didn't deserve such grace. "I love you, too."

And she was gone, leaving him alone in the house once more.

# Chapter 23

On her way back from the point with an armful of fresh pine boughs, Elizabeth was enjoying the cool weather when she saw Howe's car disappear down her driveway.

She stopped in her tracks on the graveled path. He wouldn't come without calling unless something awful had happened.

To Patti? Oh, God.

Dropping the branches, she sprinted for the house faster than she knew she could run. When she neared his parked car, she barely had enough breath to call his name, but she didn't get an answer. Hands shaking so hard she could hardly work the key, she let herself into the house. "Howe?"

Movement drew her eye to the front porch, where she spotted not Howe, but her daughter.

"Patti!" Relief erased the distance between them. The next thing she knew, Elizabeth was on the porch and whirling her daughter in an ecstatic hug. "Ohmygod, when I saw the car, I thought something must have happened to you, and your father was afraid to tell me over the phone."

"I didn't mean to scare you, Mama." Patti

hugged her back just as hard. "I just wanted to surprise you." The look she gave Elizabeth was without artifice or resentment. "Is it okay if I stay?"

"More than okay," Elizabeth said. Something big must have happened for Patti to be so affectionate. Part of Elizabeth wanted to believe her daughter had changed, but another part wondered what her daughter was up to. "That would be fabulous." Elizabeth kept her arm around Patti's shoulders as they went inside. "There's a second master suite you can have all to yourself."

Unnaturally clingy, Patti clasped her arms around Elizabeth's waist. "This is beautiful, Mama," she admired. "Did it come this way?"

Elizabeth smiled. "Nope. I did the whole place over, right down to the napkins."

Patti pulled free of Elizabeth to run her hand across the hutch. "I probably would have, too. Considering."

Elizabeth stilled. "Considering what?"

Patti turned, her expression matter-of-fact. "What Daddy used it for before he gave it to you."

Stunned, Elizabeth subsided onto the arm of the club chair behind her. "Who told you about that?"

"Daddy did." Patti regarded her with a maturity and compassion Elizabeth had never seen. "He told me everything. About everything,

386

including that idiot guy who came to our house and told lies about you."

Elizabeth gasped. "P.J. came to our *house?*" No, no, no!

Patti nodded. "Yesterday, right after Daddy picked me and Gamma up at the airport."

Oh, Lord. "Was Gamma there when he came?"

"No, but I was." Patti beamed in triumph. "Don't worry, though. Daddy defended you. Then, when the guy threatened to lie to everybody, Daddy *socked* him right in the face. Split his lip and put him *on his ass*." She pointed to the floor for emphasis. "But then he knocked Daddy down and was gonna kick him, so I jumped on his back and beat the bastard with an umbrella." She hardly seemed traumatized. "It was very cool. But then Charles and the judge came in and ruined everything."

"Judge Etheridge?" Howe hadn't called to tell her.

Of course, Elizabeth could understand why.

"Once there were witnesses, the guy left." Patti sighed, inspecting the hutch. "The judge even offered to testify against the guy, but Daddy said that wouldn't be necessary." She faced Elizabeth. "That guy *was* lying," she asked in a very small voice, "wasn't he?"

Elizabeth had never anticipated having this conversation with her daughter. But after what Patti had seen, there was no point in trying to cover anything up. "I did see him for a while," she admitted. "Strictly platonic, at first. Then he started pressuring me for an affair, so I broke it off." How stupid she'd been. "Nothing happened."

She'd known better, but had seen him anyway. "I can't believe he actually came to our house and got into a fight with your father." She felt sick, just thinking about it. "I guess I learned the hard way that it's not safe to play with fire."

"Hell, Mama," Patti said. "Who could blame you? Daddy burned down the whole freakin' forest."

That was one way of putting it.

At least Patti didn't blame her. Elizabeth exhaled, long and slow. "I'm just sorry P.J.'s lies might get out and embarrass you and your brother. I've worked so hard since I married your father to be respectable, no matter what. I still can't believe I jeopardized that for a little male attention. I blew it."

Patti came over and gave her a hug. "So you're human. Frankly, I find that a relief. It isn't easy being the daughter of a perfect mother." She wasn't complaining, just stating a fact, and it gave Elizabeth a new perspective on how things looked from Patti's side.

"I've had a lot of time to think about things up here," Elizabeth said. "I've taken a long, hard look at myself. Back home, I kept myself so

388

busy, I never had to do that. But I should have.

"My own family was so awful," she went on, "I always swore I'd do my best to make ours perfect. To be a perfect mother and a perfect wife, with perfect children. But all that did was make me, and your father, miserable. And you. Perfection is a cruel master, for everybody concerned." Elizabeth stroked her daughter's hair. "I'm so sorry, honey. I want to be your mother, not your warden."

Patti let out a wry chuckle. "Does this mean I can have my car back?"

Elizabeth smiled. Couldn't blame a kid for trying. "Sure. Soon as you pass a quarter at school, it's yours."

"Ah, yes," Patti said without rancor. "School." She stilled. "Actually, I'd like to talk to you about that."

Uh-oh.

"Mama, I know you and Daddy always wanted me to go to college"—here it came—"and I can understand that. I really do. But we all know I'm not cut out for academics."

"I thought you liked being at Georgia," Elizabeth said.

"I love everything about it, except for the classes," Patti admitted. "I did okay at first, because I took the easy courses. But last quarter I had to take core academics." A weighted pause followed. "I didn't fail because I didn't try, Mama. I failed because statistics and French and college algebra are too hard for me."

Elizabeth frowned, wondering if she was being conned. But Patti sounded so sincere.

"I'm not saying I didn't party," Patti admitted. "I did, but only on Fridays and Saturdays. The rest of the time, I really studied. Honest to God, Mama, I did. You can ask anybody in my sorority. They even tutored me, but I just didn't get it." She sounded so discouraged. "I'm not smart like Charles, Mama. I'm no good at memorizing stuff, and tests make me so nervous, I can't remember half of what I did get. It's so embarrassing, doing your best and failing, anyway."

"Oh, Patti." Elizabeth had never even considered the fact that Patti might not be able to do the work. She'd just assumed that partying and socializing had gotten in the way. "I had no idea."

"How could you know?" Patti said. "I sure didn't want to tell you I was too stupid for college. I'd rather you thought I was partying."

"Wow." Elizabeth's expectations for her daughter did a global shift. "If you don't go to college, what would you do?" She needed to rephrase that. "What would you *like* to do? Or have you thought that far?"

Patti got up and crossed the rug to sit facing Elizabeth, her face animated. "I have thought about it. A lot." She paused for effect. "I'd like to

390

go to art school. A good one. Believe it or not, I found out in art class that I'm really good with painting and design. I mean, I always did well with stuff like that, but my professor was amazing, and she taught me so much." She waggled her hand. "Not the computer kind of art. The real stuff. And I love decorating magazines. Maybe I could be a designer." Elizabeth hadn't seen Patti so excited about anything since she was little. "Or even a builder. I've dreamed up a zillion imaginary houses in my head."

"Is there any particular school that interests you?" Elizabeth asked. "We could go look at some together, if you'd like."

"I'd like." Patti smiled, hands gripping her knees. "I wish we could have talked like this a long time ago."

"Me, too. But I guess we get there when we get there. At least we can do it now."

"I'm glad we don't have any more secrets to hide," Patti said. Testing the new bridge between them, she shifted to the subject that had hovered over them since she'd arrived. "I understand why you kept what Daddy was doing a secret. I know you were just trying to protect us. But now that Charles and I know, and Daddy's changed, you don't have to worry anymore, no matter what that awful guy says. We're all gonna be okay."

"I wish I could believe that."

"Believe it." Patti turned a sad smile toward

Elizabeth. "All the way up here, I was thinking about how I've treated you. I was such a brat. But that's over. If Daddy can change, so can I." Her voice broke. "I know I made your life miserable. Can you forgive me?"

How many years had Elizabeth ached to hear those words? Now that she did, she prayed that she and Patti could find a way to get along through the ups and downs to come. "Of course I forgive you." Though she hated what had brought them to this, she was glad for the change it had made in her daughter. Patti had grown up. "You need to forgive your daddy, too."

"If he was still cheating, I don't think I could," Patti said. "But he's so different now, it's easy to let go of all that stuff. He's still a dope, though, for sending you away."

"If he hadn't," Elizabeth said, "we wouldn't be having this conversation. So it's all good. We can all start over and try to do better."

Patti peered at her, serious. "Can *you* forgive Daddy?" she asked. "Is that why you haven't come home?"

"It wasn't easy," Elizabeth admitted, "but I have forgiven him. The thing is, I'm still not sure what the right thing is for me and your daddy."

"That's easy," Patti said. "The right thing is for you to come home. We all love you, and we miss you."

That didn't include her mother-in-law. Elizabeth

shuddered to think how Augusta would react if P.J. spread his lies.

As if she'd read Elizabeth's mind, Patti said, "I told Gamma what happened. All of it."

Oh, Lord. "And?"

Patti shrugged. "At first, she got mad at Daddy for telling me what he'd done. Then she blamed you. That made me mad, so I told her it wasn't your fault. Then I said she had to be nice to you, or I'd quit coming to see her."

"Oh, sweetie," Elizabeth said, "I really appreciate your taking up for me, but I don't ever want to come between you and Gamma. She loves you so much, and she's so lonely."

"Well, she'd better behave herself," Patti declared. "Or else."

"Now you sound just like her," Elizabeth teased.

Patti laughed. "Oh, God, no. Spare me." Then she sobered. "Gamma knows everything now, and she knows we don't believe what that guy said. We can all hold our heads high, no matter what anybody says. So you can come home."

"Oh, honey. I wish it were that simple, but it's not." How could she explain what she wasn't sure of, herself? "I love your daddy, but life with him is life in Whittington, and I'm not ready to go back to that." She decided to be completely honest with her daughter. "I'm not sure I'll ever be."

"Then we'll move!" Patti said. "We can do that. People move all the time." She brightened.

"Daddy's loaded. We could get an apartment in Manhattan. Or a place in Hawaii. Or even better, Santa Barbara. It's gorgeous. I've seen it on TV."

Patti's enthusiasm lifted Elizabeth's spirits, but it didn't change anything. "I'll think about it. Meanwhile, would you like to help me bring in some pine branches? I dropped an armful up on the road when I saw your daddy's car and thought the worst."

"I'm really sorry I scared you," Patti repeated as she followed Elizabeth toward the back door.

"Forget it. The important thing is, you're here, and that makes me very, very happy." Elizabeth opened the door to a breeze scented with the promise of fall. "When we get back, I'll cook supper."

"I'll help you," Patti volunteered for the first time since she was seven.

"Great." If things kept up this way, maybe they could even be friends. "I'm so glad you're here."

And Elizabeth was, for all of two weeks.

Patti brought out her pictures from Europe and told Elizabeth all about the trip. Even though Augusta hadn't been up to snuff, the two of them had had a really good time.

Howe continued to call every few days, and they agreed that art school was a good idea for Patti. When he said his mother wasn't doing well, Elizabeth couldn't help wondering if

Patti's ultimatum was to blame, but she didn't say so.

So far, P.J. hadn't showed up again, and Howe said there was no evidence he'd followed through on his threats. As a matter of fact, P.J. had been blessedly silent.

Once those issues had been discussed, their conversations degenerated into stilted chats. Hearing the loneliness in Howe's voice, Elizabeth felt guiltier every time she hung up.

Away from the bad influence of her party-hardy friends, Patti read and took long walks with her mother, admitting she was tired of boozing and didn't want to screw up her life. Elizabeth did her best to be supportive without offering solutions. Patti had to find those for herself. There were meetings she could go to. They both knew it.

Day by day, their relationship entered new ground. They looked up art schools on Patti's laptop and planned to visit them after the new year. But as the days grew shorter and colder, Patti grew restless and started going out at night. It didn't take a rocket scientist to figure out she was partying with the locals.

Then, two weeks after their big heart-to-heart talk with its promises of new beginnings, Elizabeth got up at three in the morning and headed to the refrigerator for some cold water. Entering the darkened living room, she was met by the reek of booze and turned to find Patti, missing a shoe, passed out cold on the couch. Elizabeth tried to rouse her, but Patti just grumbled, then belched hugely—releasing another miasma of whiskey breath—and swatted her away.

So Elizabeth covered her with a quilt and sat watching her daughter in the darkness, praying about what she should do.

If she told Howe, he would probably want to come get Patti and lay down the law, but Elizabeth knew enough to know that wouldn't work. Yet she couldn't have Patti driving drunk, either. The mountain roads were treacherous enough in the dark, cold sober. She might kill someone—or herself.

Elizabeth didn't want to ruin their newfound relationship, but she'd have to address this, somehow. Shivering and discouraged, she went to bed.

The next morning when Patti emerged, haggard, from her room at eleven, Elizabeth decided to give her some time to wake up before broaching the subject. "How about some breakfast?"

"My stomach's a little shady." Patti winced against the morning sun. "I think I'll just have some cereal."

"Okay." Elizabeth made her own bacon and eggs, ignoring Patti's occasional frown at the strong aromas. She set her plate on the counter. "Coffee?"

Patti lifted a staying hand, gingerly shaking her head.

Elizabeth poured her own, hoping that Patti's hangover was awful enough to act as a deterrent.

Patti sat down, leaving a stool between them. "I know what you're thinking," she said in the surly tone Elizabeth recognized all too well.

"You do? That's a pretty neat trick," Elizabeth responded, doing her best to keep from sounding sarcastic. "Should I alert the media?"

"Very funny," Patti grumbled, but her mood lightened a little. She focused on her cereal as the kitchen clock ticked away five minutes of quiet.

"I was stupid last night," she said at last, the sullenness gone. "I met this cute guy, and he invited me and some girls from Atlanta to a party at his parents' weekend place. Once I got there, he started flirting with me. Then this local girl challenged me to do some shooters." She rolled her eyes. "I don't know why I felt like I had to keep up. I knew I had to drive home. But I kept on drinking, and next thing I knew, the guy was driving me home in Daddy's car."

She frowned, her eyes losing focus. "He could have been anybody, a *rapist*," she said with chilling insight. "And I was in the car with him." Stricken, she turned to Elizabeth. "How could I be so stupid?"

Elizabeth was afraid to ask what came next,

but she had to know. "Did he do anything to you? Hurt you?"

"No." Thank God, thank God. "I was lucky," Patti said. "He was a really nice guy. Not that he'll ever want to see *me* again."

Sick with relief, Elizabeth covered her mouth to keep from lecturing Patti.

"I vaguely remember another car following us down the driveway," Patti went on. "I guess they took him back home." Her eyes narrowed. "I think it was those girls from Atlanta. I remember hearing them laugh at me when he helped me out of the car."

Elizabeth didn't know whether to wring Patti's neck or kiss her for being okay.

"Why did I *do* that?" Patti demanded. "Why *do* I do that?"

Please, God, Elizabeth prayed, tell me what to say. She gripped her coffee mug. "Only you can answer that question, honey," her voice said. "The real question is, what do you plan to do next?" Elizabeth struggled to keep from trying to control the situation. Or enabling. Or criticizing. "I'm really proud of you for telling me."

The good Lord knew, Elizabeth couldn't throw stones. She'd made her own stupid mistakes with P.J.

"There's help, sweetie," she offered. "All kinds of it. Support groups of people who've been where you are and gotten past it. Don't let the labels throw you. Just focus on the help."

Patti didn't argue, which Elizabeth took as a good sign. "Or if that doesn't work for you," Elizabeth went on, "maybe you could try talking to a specialist. We could find a good one who works with people your age." Patti nodded. "The only thing that won't work is doing nothing. It's your choice, honey, how to handle this."

Patti stared out over the lake. "I wish I could start over, knowing what I know now about you and Daddy. I would have done things differently."

Elizabeth got up to pour herself another coffee. "Not possible," she said. "But what you do next, that *is* possible. It can be as good or as bad as you make it." She sat beside her daughter. "We're lucky, you know. We still *have* choices, both of us. A lot of people don't."

Patti shot her a nobody-wants-to-hear-it-could-be-worse look.

Elizabeth focused on the lake—and keeping her mouth shut.

Then an idea bloomed, whole and perfect, in her mind. "How would you like to take a little trip? To your grandmother's."

"Gamma's?"

"No, your other grandmother's," Elizabeth said. "I think it might be helpful to you."

Patti peered at the lake as she considered. "Okay," she said, "but only if I get to do the driving."

Elizabeth waved a hand in dismissal. "We'll fly. First class. And rent a convertible when we get there. How about that?"

Patti grinned. "Only if I get to drive the convertible."

"Only if you're sober," Elizabeth said, half serious.

"Trust me," Patti said. "It'll be a long time before I can face tequila again."

Good.

Energized, Elizabeth got up. "Come on, honey, let's pack. I'll call Delta."

"This'll be fun." Patti stopped halfway to her room. "Mama, do you realize, this will be our very first trip together, just the two of us?"

Could that be? "You're right," Elizabeth said.

Maybe God had told her what to do, after all.

Twenty-four hours later, Elizabeth watched the sights of Clearwater, Florida, go by as Patti followed the rented convertible's GPS toward the retirement center where Elizabeth's mother lived.

"How long has it been since you've seen her?" Patti asked.

Elizabeth was ashamed to answer. "Not since we moved her into the condo. Ten, no, twelve years ago."

"How was she, then?"

"She was pretty crabby when we moved her

into the condo," Elizabeth said. And drunk. But she'd let Patti find that out for herself. "Like I said, moving is hard for old people. She would have stayed in that filthy, roach-infested apartment of hers forever, if we'd let her."

"Isn't she glad she moved, now that she's settled?"

"I can't remember my mother ever being glad about anything, except when I told her I'd married your daddy. But then she turned right around and complained because we eloped." As if her parents could have afforded a wedding, in the first place. Much less stayed sober long enough to keep from humiliating everybody involved. "She's always fussing at me when I call her."

"Why? You'd think she'd be glad to hear from you."

Elizabeth focused on the glimpses of the Gulf between houses and condo towers. "She's mad because I abandoned her."

"But you didn't," Patti argued. "You said on the plane, you and Daddy support her."

Elizabeth had filled Patti in on the bare facts of her family, but left out the sordid details. "We do support her financially, but that's not the same thing." Elizabeth adjusted her sunglasses. "I couldn't handle the chaos, so I cut her off emotionally." As coldly and completely as Howe had cut Elizabeth off because of his guilt.

"Oh."

"Turn right in fifty meters," the GPS said, "on Sunshine Lane."

"What should I call her?" Patti asked.

Elizabeth brushed a windblown curl out of her eye. "I don't know. What does Charles call her?"

"He didn't say."

"You could ask her what she wants you to call her, I guess," Elizabeth suggested.

Patti pulled up to the ten-story condo. "Here we are. This is nice." She parked in a visitor's space, then reached to the floorboard behind Elizabeth. Patti had insisted on bringing red roses, because Elizabeth had said they were her mother's favorite.

"Remember, she can be pretty negative," Elizabeth warned for the third time. "Don't take it personally. She's like the French: they can't stand anybody, including each other."

"You already told me," Patti said. "Mama, it's going to be okay."

Elizabeth wondered if this was a good idea, after all. "I just don't want you to have unrealistic expectations."

"I don't." Patti held the door for her, scanning the lobby. "*Very* nice."

"We picked it because they have independent, assisted, and skilled care in the same complex. Like I said, moving can be really traumatic for the elderly, especially when their health is failing."

They got into the elevator, and Patti pressed the eighth-floor button. "How old is she?"

"The same age as Gamma, but she's not in nearly as good shape."

"Speaking of Gamma," Patti said, "I'm really worried about her. Every day when I call her, she sounds sicker, but she won't go to the doctor."

"It's hard to see somebody you love make destructive choices," Elizabeth said.

"I get the double meaning, there," Patti said. "Way obvious."

The bell rang, and the elevator opened.

They stopped in front of the door Elizabeth hadn't seen since she'd gratefully closed it on her complaining mother twelve years before.

Patti motioned for her to ring the bell.

Elizabeth motioned for her to do it. Her mother had been so grumpy when she'd called to say they were coming that suddenly Elizabeth had cold feet.

Flat-mouthed, Patti obliged.

"I'm comin'," a gravelly voice called from inside. "Hold your horses."

The door opened to reveal Elizabeth's mother in a clean housecoat, her hair neatly combed, and her expression remarkably clear. Unless Elizabeth was mistaken, she was sober!

"So this is her," her mother said, looking Patti up and down. She focused on the flowers. "Did somebody die?"

A joke? Had her mother made a joke? "Mama, this is Patti," Elizabeth introduced. "Patti, this is your grandmother."

"Hi." Patti extended the flowers. "These are for you. Mama said they were your favorites."

"Oh, she did, did she?" Her mother accepted them. "I guess I'll have to let you in, then." They followed her to the front of the efficiency unit, which was surprisingly tidy. She pointed to the sofa. "Sit. I'll put these in water."

It was the most cordial her mother had been in memory.

"What would you like me to call you?" Patti asked over the sound of running water as her grandmother filled a vase.

"What?" Her grandmother turned off the water and plunked the vase on the breakfast bar between them.

"What would you like me to call you?" Patti repeated, louder.

"I'm not deaf," Elizabeth's mother retorted. She put the flowers into the water, then dropped heavily into the recliner. "That brother of yours calls me 'Bop.' God knows why."

"If you don't like 'Bop,' " Patti offered, "I could call you something else."

Elizabeth's mother sniffed. "It's as good as anything, I reckon."

The three of them sat there, an awkward silence stretching between them.

This certainly wasn't the object lesson Elizabeth had planned. She'd expected to find her mother drunk, as usual. "Mama, you're looking really wonderful," she said.

Bop looked to Patti. "What she really means is, she's shocked to find me sober."

Patti compressed a smile.

"If she'da come to see me sooner," Bop grumbled, "she'da known I've been clean and sober for *the last six years.*"

"Mama, that's wonderful," Elizabeth said. "I'm so proud of you."

Her mother still didn't look at her, just spoke to Patti. "That's somethin' I never expected to hear come out of *her* mouth." She frowned, eyes narrowing at Patti. "You drink, little girl?"

Patti went red, looking down at the carpet. "Yes, ma'am, I do."

"Take it from me," Bop said, "it'll steal your soul, and cost you everything good and decent in your life." She waggled a gnarled finger Patti's way. "Like it or not, you come from a rat's nest of alcoholics. It's in the genes." She straightened. "My daddy was a drunk. His daddy was a drunk. I married one, and got to be one myself. Raised two of 'em. Buried one at thirty-two. The other one's in jail for killin', drunk. He's sober now, but that don't help that poor wife of his he kilt. Bessie Mae hyere's the only sober one in the lot of us."

405

Patti turned hardened eyes to Elizabeth. "Did you talk to her about what happened?"

"She didn't talk to me about *squat!*" Bop said. "I see that chip on yer shoulder. And that look, same as I seen whenever I asked Bessie Mae's daddy not to drink. Same as I seen in the mirror when yer mama asked me to quit." She leaned forward. "You be smart, little girl. Us Mooneys ortn'ta drink, period."

Patti exhaled heavily, defensive. "But you managed to quit."

"Only when it was that, or die. The fear of hell was what done it for me, but you're young. You got money, a family you can be proud of. Your mama, she never had anything but grief from us. I don't blame her for runnin' away."

"I should have come back to see you, Mama," Elizabeth said. "I'm sorry."

At last, her mother looked at her. "Sorry, sorry, sorry. Everybody's sorry. Forget sorry. Take me to Red Lobster."

Elizabeth and Patti both laughed, and to Elizabeth's amazement, her mother did, too.

"Save that shock for when you git the bill," her mother said as she got up. "I'm gittin' the Ultimate Feast. Lobster, shrimp, *and* crab legs. Plus a shrimp cocktail." She nudged Patti with her elbow. "Only kind of cocktail I git anymore, thank You, Jesus." She turned a baleful eye at Elizabeth. "And I'm gittin' key lime pie, too. So there."

Elizabeth looked at her mother in wonder. "But Mama, this is Clearwater. Wouldn't you rather go to one of the great local seafood restaurants?"

Bop frowned and said to Patti, "Is she deaf? Did I say Red Lobster, or did I say Red Lobster?"

Grinning, Patti confirmed, "You said Red Lobster."

Bop waggled a finger toward the breakfast bar. "Hand me my purse." When Elizabeth obliged, she said, "Don't let it give you any ideas, now. I ain't payin' fer a thing. You go twelve years without comin' to see me, you can damn well pick up the tab." She looked to Patti. "I been wantin' to surprise her with bein' sober for six damn years. But did she come? Hell, no."

Bop took Patti's arm. "Okay, missy. Let's hear it."

"Hear what?"

"You tell me," Bop said. "Way I see it, we've got about nineteen years to catch up on, not to mention whatever you might want to know about me." She headed out the door. " 'Course, I cain't guarantee my accuracy. Killed too many gray cells with the booze, but I'll do my best." She waved toward Elizabeth. "Close the door behind us."

Still holding on to Patti's arm, Bop punched the button at the elevator. "I figure we got at least a week's worth of talkin' to do. Meanwhile, you can take me to Walmart to get some new housecoats.

And CVS. I been out of Metamucil so long, you could pave a highway with what's stuck in my guts."

Patti snorted a laugh.

Lord. Elizabeth's mother might be sober, but she was still her mother.

Four days later, they'd taken Bop to every discount store in town, plus the optometrist for new glasses, plus bingo at the VFW, and dozens of other minor errands. They'd just come back from lunch and a trip to Publix when Elizabeth's cell phone rang, and Howe's number showed on the screen. "Hello?"

"Elizabeth," he said, his voice breaking, "you and Patti need to come home. Now. To Whittington."

# Chapter 24

Elizabeth's stomach tightened. "Howe. What's happened?"

"It's Mama. She got so sick, I literally carried her, kicking and fighting, to the emergency room." His voice broke. "It's pancreatic cancer."

For all the times Elizabeth had wished her mother-in-law gone, she felt only pity for Augusta now. So much time wasted in fear and negativity, and now her life was over. "Oh, Howe. I'm so sorry."

Patti would be devastated.

Seeing Elizabeth's expression, Patti halted her conversation with Bop in mid-sentence. "Mama, what is it?"

"We'll take the first plane out," Elizabeth told Howe, then hung up to give the news to her daughter. "Sweetie, I'm so sorry, but Gamma's really sick. We need to go home right away."

"Figures," Bop complained. "I finally git y'all down hyere, and that woman upstages me."

Elizabeth frowned. "Mama, she's really sick."

"What is it?" Patti asked, clearly fearing the answer.

There was no way to make the truth any easier.

"Pancreatic cancer," Elizabeth said gently. "I'm so sorry, honey."

Patti burst into tears. "Oh, God. I *knew* she was sick! I should have *made* her go to the doctor." She swiped her cheeks, struggling to get control of herself. "Pancreatic . . . that's bad, isn't it? Really, really bad. If only I'd—"

Elizabeth wrapped her in a comforting hug. "Oh, sweetie, it's not your fault. She wouldn't let any of us help her. Hard as it is, the decision was hers to make, not ours."

"She's dying, isn't she?" Patti pulled free of Elizabeth. "I should have realized it. Done something."

At Augusta's age, with that kind of cancer, it wouldn't have made much difference, but Elizabeth saw no purpose in saying so. "Let's get home first and talk to the doctors before we go there, okay?" she soothed.

Bop shot her a knowing look. "Yer mama's right," she said, giving Patti a brief, rough hug. Then she pushed her away with a gruff, "Now, you run on and pack. But don't fergit to call me when ya git back home, little girlie, ya hear? It don't have to be every day, but every other will do."

Patti wiped her eyes. "Okay. I will." She lifted her chin. "I love you, Bop."

Bop's eyes reddened. "Wal, I love ya', too," she said gruffly. "And yer mama. Now git back home." She hustled Patti toward the door, but Elizabeth could see Bop could hardly bear to let them go.

It struck Elizabeth as divinely ironic that Patti had gotten to know her other grandmother just as she was losing Gamma. "I'll call you, Mama, to let you know when we're home safe." She hugged her mother, noting how frail she felt in her arms. "I love you." She hadn't said it since she was a child. Hadn't felt it since then, until that moment.

Her mother stilled, holding on, then shooed her out. "G'won, now. Git."

Four hours later, Elizabeth and Patti walked into Augusta's room at Piedmont Hospital, where she lay, looking dead already, with an IV hooked up to her arm.

Howe rose from the chair beside her bed, so thin and haggard that Elizabeth felt guilty for leaving him to fend for himself.

"Daddy." Patti rushed into his arms. "How is she?"

"She's dying," Augusta said sharply, "but still present and accounted for, so kindly do not speak of me in the third person when I am present." She extended her hands toward Patti. "Now come give Gamma a kiss."

"Oh, Gamma." Patti leaned over the bed to embrace her grandmother very carefully. "Don't talk like that. They have treatments, and we can—"

Augusta softened, stroking back Patti's hair. "Dear one, I am eighty-five years old, and I have no desire to spend my last days on this earth sick as a cat from treatments that can't do a thing but prolong my misery. So I've asked them to make me comfortable and let me go home."

"But Gamma," Patti argued, silent tears sheeting her cheeks, "you can't just give up."

"Do not tell me what I can and cannot do," Augusta scolded. "I'm sick, not incompetent." She shot Howe a withering look. "If your father had just left me alone the way I wanted, I could have died at home, in peace, by now. But no, he had to butt in, and here I am."

"She's still full of vinegar," Howe said with more than a touch of affection, "no matter how sick she is."

"Well, what do you expect me to do?" his mother demanded. "Turn into some namby-pamby, begging forgiveness just because I'm facing my maker? Well, I have news for you all: I'm still the same person I always was, and you —and God, for that matter—might as well accept that."

Augusta was still definitely Augusta.

Elizabeth said a brief prayer for compassion. "Is there anything I can do for you, Augusta? Just name it."

A brittle gleam shone in her mother-in-law's eyes. "Yes, now that you mention it." She shot a

412

sly look toward Howe. "You can come back to Whittington, where you belong. And have your annual Christmas party early this year. *And* invite P.J. Atkinson."

Patti gasped. "Gamma. That's crazy."

Surely the woman couldn't be serious. "I'll move home," Elizabeth agreed—for the moment, anyway. "But the party . . . and P.J.—Augusta, that doesn't make sense."

"You asked if you could do anything, and that's what I want you to do," her mother-in-law challenged. "You've already humiliated this family, then run off and abandoned my son. Now I'm giving you a chance to make up for it. Come back and face it with your head held high. That's my dying wish. Refuse, and I'll tell everybody in town you cheated on my son."

"Gamma!" Patti protested. "Don't threaten Mama that way. She didn't do anything wrong, and you know it."

"I most certainly do not," her grandmother snapped, "but that's irrelevant, at this point. What matters is that she and your father show a united front." She glared at Elizabeth. "Well? What is it? Have the party and spit in that tale-carrying fool's eye, or face the consequences."

"Mama," Howe interjected, "it's not fair to—"

"Who said anything about fair?" his mother said. "News flash, Howell: Life isn't fair. Neither is death, but here I lie. So don't talk to me about

413

fair. Either honor my dying wish, or get out of here and don't bother coming to my funeral."

A funeral Augusta had planned in ostentatious detail, in writing, and prepaid when she turned eighty.

Howe shot a troubled look to Elizabeth.

The crazy thing was, Augusta had a point. There were bound to be rumors. If Howe and she faced everyone, together, it might put an end to at least some of the speculation. "All right. I'll have the party."

"And invite P.J.," Augusta commanded.

Elizabeth exhaled sharply. "All right."

"Mama," Patti said, "you cannot give some huge party when Gamma's *dying*. It's disrespectful."

Augusta scowled at her. "I vow, Patricia, you can be tiresome at times. Didn't you hear a word I said?"

"But Gamma—"

"But Gamma, nothing." Augusta straightened in her hospital bed. "This is what I want, and I expect you to help your mother. She's going to have her hands full with me upstairs dying while the rest of Whittington is in the parlor."

Elizabeth almost choked. "Upstairs?" Oh, Lord.

Augusta straightened the sleeve of her silk bed jacket. "That's what I said." She met Elizabeth's surprise with iron will. "Howe was born in that house, and I've decided to die there, not in that Johnny-come-lately place I was forced into when you two married."

In light of the circumstances, Elizabeth didn't contradict her, but Augusta had moved out of her own accord—thank God.

"Or in some hospital or death-hotel they call a hospice facility." Augusta arched her eyebrows. "Don't look so shocked. I can afford help—around the clock, if need be. I can take the west suite." Howe's.

She looked to Patti. "And I'll expect you and your brother to be there till I'm gone, as well."

"But Mama," Howe said, "Charles works downtown. The commute is—"

"Thousands of other people do it every day. He can do it for me, for a few weeks." She leveled a smug look at Howe. "Anyway, he's already agreed. And Pearl is getting their rooms ready, as we speak."

Leave it to Augusta to take over Elizabeth's home without notice or permission. She'd never really surrendered it, anyway.

"Sounds like you've planned everything out," Elizabeth said, doing her best to keep resentment from her tone.

"Somebody has to," her mother-in-law snapped. "You left."

"Well, I'm back," Elizabeth said.

"Good," Augusta said with satisfaction. "Just make sure you don't get in my way."

Even dying, Elizabeth's mother-in-law did as she damned well pleased.

*Lord, help me love this woman somehow. I sure can't do it on my own.*

That night, back in her own bed, Elizabeth was just about to doze off when Howe sat down beside her on the bed. "Lillibet? Are you asleep?"

"You're home." She roused, foggy. "Augusta—she's not . . ."

"No." Howe sat on the edge of the bed, his silhouette striking in the dim light from the bathroom. "I really appreciate your coming home." He'd already told her, several times.

She reached out to stroke his arm, longing for the comfort of his presence in her bed and her heart. "It feels good to be here." To her surprise, it was true, even with their day of reckoning ahead.

"I was wondering if it would be okay for us to sleep together," he said, his voice deep and even.

Elizabeth welcomed the warmth of his presence in her bed. She'd had enough time alone, so she pulled back the covers on his side. "Sure. Climb in."

He got in, then drew her to his side. Her head fit perfectly against his chest as he stroked her hair. "I know I told you to take all the time you needed to make a decision about us, but I can't help wanting you. I want to hold you and please you till everything else goes away for both of us."

416

Part of Elizabeth was afraid to respond, but the rest was just as lonely as he was, and just as hungry to forget everything and lose herself in lovemaking.

He ran his hand down her torso, savoring her body like a sculptor approving his masterpiece. Then he brushed his lips across her temple, sending a frisson of desire through her. "God, Lillibet, I love you so much. Let me love you." He kissed her gently, his breath warm against her skin as his lips trailed lower to whisper against her skin. "It doesn't matter if you don't love me back. Could you just pretend, for a while, that you do?"

She could. She could even love him, if she let herself believe he was who he seemed to be.

Did it really matter what happened next month, or even next week? Somehow, they'd managed to come to that moment, and she wanted him, too, with all the desire she'd kept pent up inside her over the long, lonely years.

They were married. He was hers and she was his.

Why had she been so afraid of that?

Because there were consequences. "Howe, the test . . ."

"It came back two weeks ago, clean," he said, his voice sultry, his groin swollen against her leg. "I'd never risk your health, Lillibet. Not now, or ever. But it's safe."

417

Of its own will, her palm trailed down his flat stomach to caress the evidence of his arousal, and he gasped, then kissed her with all the fervor of their courtship, and Elizabeth let herself be carried back, willingly sacrificing the future to the present.

And so he loved her, not with the brief and reckless passion of their youth, but with a growing heat that swelled and exploded like a nova, leaving her spent and sated as ripples of pleasure pulsed through her. She waited till he had fallen asleep to whisper, "I love you, too," tears of fear and joy escaping the corner of her eye to wet his skin. "I always have, even when I didn't want to."

And for the first time since they'd lost each other, they slept entwined, at peace for that one night, at least.

The next morning, Elizabeth's phone rang off the hook with "welcome home" greetings and invitations from Sewing Circle and Altar Guild and Garden Club. Touched by the genuine out-pouring of affection, Elizabeth realized how many real friends she did have in Whittington, but she dodged their invitations, pleading Augusta's poor health. She still wasn't ready to jump back into things full bore. Not yet. But she did let everyone know that Augusta had asked them to have their annual party early.

That accomplished, she set about getting the

fully renovated house ready for Augusta and making arrangements for the party. Since the theme of the party would be harvest instead of Christmas, Elizabeth dispatched Patti to shop the wholesalers in Atlanta. In her element at last, Patti transformed the house into a tasteful fairyland of autumn splendor. And every day, Elizabeth's true friends came by with food or flowers or brief words of encouragement, even though she'd dropped out of their lives and stopped returning their calls when she went to Blue Ridge. Their acceptance and kindness made Elizabeth see Whittington not as a cage, but a haven where she was cared for and respected.

And the next thing she knew, almost a month had passed, and Howe's suite had become a hospital room where Augusta was ensconced with a full retinue of nurses and hospice care. And Charles was commuting an hour and a half each way to Atlanta while Elizabeth ran the house and made the final preparations for the big event that felt more like an impending execution than a celebration.

Now, with the party only three hours away, Elizabeth stood in the beautifully decorated living room, checking to make sure everything was ready, while Pearl and Thomas finished the food in the kitchen.

Howe sneaked up behind her and put his arms around her. "Maybe we both ought to head for

Blue Ridge and let the chips fall where they may," he teased, nuzzling her neck.

Elizabeth wasn't amused. Despite the fact that they were man and wife again, she still felt territorial about the house in the mountains. It was the one thing in the world that was truly hers— a Fortress of Solitude, where no boys were allowed, especially Howe.

Howe sensed her reaction and turned her to face him. "What?"

"I . . ." He was still so vulnerable, especially since his mother had grown weaker and weaker without making peace with him or anybody else. "Let's not talk about Blue Ridge. This party is hard enough without adding that to the mix."

He propped his chin on her head, drawing her close. "It's going to be all right, Elizabeth. No matter what happens tonight, we have each other, and our children. Just think about that."

She leaned into him. She'd worried so much about the future, but what good had it done her? Too weary to do it anymore, she finally let go. No matter what happened at the party, tomorrow would come, and they'd face it together. Augusta would die, and they would face that, too.

"Howe," she said, "I'm so sorry your mother hasn't . . . I mean, I know you've tried to make peace with her these past few weeks. I'm sorry she hasn't been willing to do that." Maybe that

420

was how Augusta expressed her fear and anguish over dying, by trying to control those around her when she couldn't control what was happening to her. "I know it's been hard on you."

"Not as hard as it would have been without you," he said.

Howe released her, waggling his eyebrows salaciously. "I've got an idea. Why don't we go upstairs and take a little *nap* before the party?"

Elizabeth had to laugh. "Lord. You are insatiable." Not that she hadn't enjoyed it. She looked at him with narrowed eyes and whispered, "You're not taking anything, are you?"

Howe smiled. "Don't have to." He gave her rear a grab. "Maybe it was the stroke, but I'm ready Freddie."

Elizabeth swatted his hand away. "Quit that," she said mildly. "We don't have time for a *nap*."

"Now, that's what I like to see," Charles said from the foyer.

Elizabeth colored with embarrassment, but Howe beamed. "Hey, son. Did the judge let you off early?"

Charles grinned. "Yep. But only if I promised he could come to the party."

"Charles, you did not tell him P.J. was coming," Elizabeth scolded.

Her son wasn't intimidated. "Mama, don't you know it's a crime to lie to a federal judge?"

"Yes," she shot back, "but I also know you

should never volunteer anything that might be incriminating. Especially to your mother."

"Touché," Howe said.

Elizabeth headed for the stairs. "Help your daddy light the fires. I'm going upstairs to do my hair and change."

True to form, Miss Emily Watson arrived half an hour early, but this time, Charles was there to charm her, then invite her up to visit with Augusta.

Elizabeth's friends came next, all of them right on time and supportive. The rest of Augusta's cronies were close behind, along with the ones who were hoping for Elizabeth's and Howe's comeuppance. And the merely curious filled out the guest list, so within thirty minutes of the time on the engraved invitations, everybody who was anybody in Whittington had arrived and started chatting, their eyes on the door as if they knew P.J. was coming.

Meanwhile, Augusta's cronies made their pilgrimages to her bedside in twos and threes. With Patti as her lady-in-waiting, Augusta held court in her best pink bed jacket, her mood even crankier than usual, probably because she'd insisted on cutting back the morphine so she'd be awake for her company.

Howe and Elizabeth circulated through the gathering downstairs, visiting and encouraging their guests to eat and drink, but the atmosphere was brittle as diamonds. Elizabeth felt as if she were in one of those dreams where she was naked, but nobody had noticed . . . yet. Both she and Howe kept looking toward the door as if death himself were going to turn up any minute.

A lot was said, but what wasn't being said hung over their guests like a pall, waiting to descend.

Then the bell rang, and Pearl opened the door to reveal P.J., a dark glitter in his eye and a scowl on his face.

Conversation halted abruptly as all eyes turned his way, then shifted from him to Elizabeth and Howe, then back to P.J.

Elizabeth stopped breathing, the throbbing of her pulse the only sound in the silence.

Pearl tried to close the door on P.J., but he grabbed the edge and forced himself past her. "I was invited," he said loudly.

Oh, Lord. He'd been drinking.

Elizabeth felt Howe and Charles move in to flank her, and the judge was close behind. Howe took her cold, quaking hand in his.

"I need to see Howe and Elizabeth," P.J. said loudly. "I have something to say to them, and I want everybody in this room to hear it."

He was so angry.

Elizabeth felt the corner of her mouth start to flutter, and covered it with her free hand.

Grim, Howe looked P.J. square in the eye as he approached. "Hello, P.J." His arm slid protectively around Elizabeth's waist.

"You," P.J. said with contempt.

Elizabeth braced herself for the worst.

"I . . ." P.J. seemed as if he couldn't make the words come out, then finally managed, "I owe you both an apology."

Elizabeth stilled, wondering if she'd heard correctly.

P.J. glared at Howe with hatred. "I did my best to steal your wife, but she wouldn't have anything to do with me, so I shot my mouth off, but none of what I said was true, and I apologize." He pointed a shaking finger toward Howe. "And be sure you tell your mother I said so."

Then he pivoted and stormed out the door.

After a heartbeat of silence, pandemonium erupted all around them, but Howe and Elizabeth stood staring at each other in amazement.

The judge and Charles hee-hawed.

"Am I hallucinating," Howe asked her, "or did he just admit he lied and apologize?"

"He did." But why?

They both voiced the same thought in unison. "Mama," and "Augusta."

As P.J.'s Mercedes SUV roared away with a squeal of tires, Howe and Elizabeth flew upstairs together and burst into Augusta's room.

"Patti," Howe said, "go downstairs to help your brother with our guests. We need to talk to Gamma."

No fool, Patti looked from her father to her

grandmother's smug expression. "Why? What happened?"

"Your brother will tell you." Howe turned to the nurse. "Please excuse us."

"Yes, sir," the nurse said as she rose. "Just call if you need me. I'll be right outside."

"Not too close," Howe cautioned. There had been enough gossip already.

They waited till the door was closed to flank Augusta's bed.

"How did you do it, Mama?"

Augusta smoothed her bed jacket, focusing on the rosebud buttons. "I simply convinced him it was in his best interest to tell the truth and apologize. Publicly."

"But how?" Elizabeth demanded.

Augusta shot her a brief, critical glance. "You can't very well expect me to sit idly by after Patti told me about his coming over and making such a scene. So I called the boy and explained that if he didn't recant and apologize, *publicly,* I would tell his dying father that he's not his father."

What? That didn't compute. "Who's not whose father?"

Augusta glared at Elizabeth as if she were a simpleton. "P.J.'s father is not P.J.'s father."

Howe scowled. "And how would you know that?"

"I make it a habit to know everything that

425

concerns me and mine," Augusta told them evenly, keeping her voice low enough not to be overheard. "And the fact is, P.J.'s mother was having an affair with your father when she got pregnant. Of course, I never discussed the matter with your father. It would have been demeaning." Howe stood, stunned, as she went on. "I wasn't sure whose child the boy was till the DNA tests were available, then I confirmed it with a blood test," Augusta said calmly. "I needed to be forearmed, if it ever came to light."

"And P.J. agreed to the test?" Howe asked in disbelief.

"For heaven's sake, no. Do you think I'm a fool?" Augusta winced briefly in physical pain, then resumed. "I had Dr. Collins take the sample when he did P.J.'s physical, then I sent the sample off myself, under a made-up name, with some of your father's hair from his baby book."

This was absolutely Machiavellian.

"How in hell did you get Dr. Collins to do that?" Howe demanded. "He could lose his license for doing that."

"Everyone has his Achilles' heel," Howe's mother gloated. "Including Dr. Collins." She looked from Howe to Elizabeth. "Well, don't thank me all at once."

"P.J. Atkinson is my *brother?*" Howe sank to the chair the nurse had been sitting in.

"Half brother," his mother corrected. "But I

wouldn't advise making anything of it. The man clearly takes after his mother. Worthless, the both of them."

Howe stared unseeing into the middle distance. "I have a brother."

"Lower your voice," Augusta cautioned. "I didn't tell you to have you blabbing it all over town. For your sake, and the family's, I expect you to keep that in confidence." She suddenly looked frail and weak. "Your father is dead and gone, Howell. Do not besmirch his memory."

Howe turned to Elizabeth. "P.J. Atkinson is my *brother*."

"Apparently so." Elizabeth didn't know what else to say.

"Now you've worn me out," Augusta fussed. "Go back to your guests, and send in that nurse. I want some morphine."

Howe leaned over and kissed his mother's forehead. "Thank you, Mama. For everything."

She waved him off. "You're my son. I love you. Now go on and leave me in peace."

They did as she asked, then sent in the nurse. On the way back down the stairs, Howe took Elizabeth's hand and gave it a squeeze. "C'mon, Lizzie. Let's party."

"Don't call me Lizzie," she said. "I told you, I hate that name."

Howe waggled his eyebrows at her. "Nobody's perfect, Lillibet, and that includes me. You're gonna get Lizzied from time to time. Might as well get used to it."

He looked so young and winsome when he said it, she couldn't suppress a chuckle. Suddenly the world looked welcoming and new with possibilities.

Charles made straight for Elizabeth when they entered the parlor, and Patti went for Howe. "Mama," Charles said, "I don't know how that happened, and I don't care. I'm just glad it did."

"Me, too." Patti gave her father a peck. "I'm going back up to check on Gamma."

"I'm afraid we wore her out," Elizabeth said.

"Don't worry, I'll stay with her." Patti regarded her parents with affection. "It's so good to see you together." Then she headed for the stairs.

"Charles, put on some dancin' music," Howe told him. "Something slow. I want to dance with your mother."

"Comin' right up," their son said.

"In the Still of the Night" came through the speakers over the rumble of conversation, and Howe led Elizabeth into an easy box-step. "We are going to have a good time at our own party, my darling." He twirled her, then bent close to whisper in her ear, "Then I am going to run these people out, and the real celebration is going to start."

Elizabeth couldn't wait. And celebrate they did, first with everybody who was anybody in

Whittington watching two people in love, then behind closed doors, just the two of them. Twice.

But the next morning when they woke to the rest of their lives together, Augusta didn't.

# Chapter 25

Patti came in at dawn and told them. To Elizabeth's surprise, she wasn't crying.

"I was with her, Mama," she said, almost in wonder. "I woke up at three, and just felt like I needed to check on her, and when I got there, she was hardly breathing. I called the nurse, but Gamma grabbed my hand and said no." She lost focus, reliving it. "Her eyes were almost black. She held my hand and said she was ready for it to be over. Then she closed her eyes." Patti sank to the bed beside Elizabeth. "At first, I thought she was asleep. Then I realized her chest wasn't moving. So I called the nurse, and she got her stethoscope and said Gamma's heart had stopped. Just like that. Gamma said she was ready, and she died."

Elizabeth gathered her daughter close. "Oh, sweetie. I'm so sorry. I know how much you loved her."

His face grim, Howe got up quietly and put on his robe.

"I know it was selfish of me," Patti said, "but I asked the nurse not to say anything to anybody, and sent her away. Then I sat there, holding

Gamma's hand, remembering all the fun we'd had together." She drew back to peer at Elizabeth. "I don't know why, but it felt . . . holy, being there when her soul left her body. Holding her hand till it was cold, and the sun came up." A single tear escaped. "She never did let go."

"Oh, honey."

Howe kissed the top of Patti's head on his way out. "I'll call Flanigan's."

Patti reached after her father. "Gamma has everything written out, just the way she wants it. She talked about it a lot. The file is on her desk."

Howe nodded, hesitating with his hand on the doorknob, as if to delay the inevitable. "I know," he said, his voice gruff.

He'd come a long way in controlling his emotions to remain so composed. "Have you told Charles?" he asked.

"Not yet," Patti answered. "I wanted to tell y'all, first."

"I'll do that," Howe said. "I need something to do." He left, carefully closing the door behind him.

Suddenly deflated, Patti yawned, then curled up in the bed beside Elizabeth. "Can I take a nap in here with you?"

Elizabeth stroked her shoulder. "Of course you can. C'mere."

Patti nuzzled in close the way she used to after

431

she'd had a bad dream as a little girl, then fell asleep.

Lying there with her, Elizabeth digested the fact that Augusta was dead, at last.

Elizabeth had expected to feel some relief when it happened, but she didn't. All she felt was sympathy for Patti and Howe. Augusta's death had left a big hole in their lives, and a surprising one in Elizabeth's. She couldn't imagine what life was going to feel like without Augusta second-guessing her every move. The shocking thing was, she might even miss the woman.

And the wonderful thing was, now that it was finally over, she could let go and forgive the lifetime of criticism Augusta had levied on her.

Howe insisted on coordinating all the funeral arrangements himself from his study, the door closed. Meanwhile, Patti helped Elizabeth take down the decorations and get ready for the reception after the funeral. There was something cathartic about putting the house in order themselves, wiping away the past with the dust on the surfaces and furniture. At Augusta's instructions, they stopped the clocks in the front rooms at the hour of her death and covered the mirrors in black silk.

At the reading of the will on Monday, they found out that Augusta had topped off the

Organ Fund at St. Andrew's, stipulating that the funds could only be used for that purpose, and left fifty thousand each to Pearl and Thomas. The rest—half a million in cash, her house, and her fifty-one percent interest in the bank—she'd divided between Howe, Patti, and Charles, which came as no surprise to Elizabeth.

What did surprise her was Howe's response.

He calmly asked the lawyer to put half the value of the shares his mother had left him into Elizabeth's account, with the hearty approval of the children.

Touched, she told him, "Howe, I don't need your money."

"You earned it, Lillibet," he said, "and then some. More than that, I want you to be independent and secure, so you'll always be free to choose what you need."

Elizabeth's heart glowed. "I made my choice. You know that."

Howe smiled with pride, his eyes welling. "Then make this one. Take the money."

Elizabeth shrugged. If that was what he wanted . . . "Okay. Just don't ask me to have anything to do with the bank."

"Speaking of the bank," Howe said, glancing down. "There's something I need to tell you all." He looked squarely at each of them, then said, "I've had a really good offer for my shares of the bank, and I've decided to take it. It's something I've been working on for some time, but I didn't want to upset Mama."

Elizabeth was happy to hear it, but worried that he hadn't told her. He'd promised to tell her the truth.

"Dad," Charles said, "if it's too much for you because of the stroke, I can come take over for you."

"Lord, no, son," Howe said. "That's the last thing I want. Y'all are free to do what you wish with your shares. I've got a very good reason for selling mine." He shot Elizabeth a shy expression. "I just found out last week that I have another job."

Something *else* major he'd neglected to mention? "Howe!"

Howe smiled. "I passed the bar. I'm going to be a lawyer, at last."

Charles jumped up and started pounding his father's shoulder. "Dad, that's great! Better than great! That's fabulous! What kind of law?"

"Don't know yet," Howe confessed.

Patti leapt into Howe's lap and kissed his cheek. "Whatever you do, you'll be great at it. I just know you will."

So that's what Howe had been doing in the study all those months! Studying. "Why didn't you tell me?" Elizabeth asked, ecstatic and angry at the same time.

He shrugged. "I was afraid I'd fail." His chin

rose. "I didn't want you to know if I couldn't hack it."

It was the life they'd both dreamed of in college. "Honey, I'm so proud for you. But you should have told me."

He grinned. "I just did."

The lawyer cleared his throat. "Well, this has certainly been an eventful reading." He straightened the paperwork. "Allow me to be the first to welcome you into the profession, Howe, though I can't say I'm looking forward to the competition."

Howe nodded. "Don't worry. There's plenty of pro bono work to keep me busy in this town."

The lawyer nodded in approval, his chin dimpling, then rose. "There was a time when I wouldn't have done this, but I'd like to shake your hand." He extended his hand.

Howe got up to take Ben's hand into both of his own and pump it. "Thank you, Ben. I'll do my best to justify your respect."

Elizabeth stood, dazed. So much had happened so quickly since Saturday night. She felt as if some cosmic force had ordered the misaligned dominoes of her life and tipped them into place.

"God has blessed me far more than I deserve," Howe said, putting a name to that force.

She took her place at her husband's side. "Thank you, Ben."

The lawyer smiled. "I'll transfer those funds

as soon as they become available," he told her.

Funny. Being independently wealthy didn't feel any different.

"I want to sell my shares, too," Patti said on impulse. "I'm going to art school," she announced to the lawyer.

"Congratulations," he told her. "This is a big day, all round."

"Come on, everybody," Charles said. "Now that I'm a man of means, lunch is on me. We'll drink a toast to Gamma."

"That we will," Elizabeth said, knowing that Gamma was rolling in her grave.

Wednesday evening, Patti and Elizabeth dressed in black, with only pearls for adornment (Augusta's instructions), and joined Howe and Charles in their best dark suits to sit visitation with Pearl and Thomas beside the cloying blanket of roses and orchids Augusta had ordered for her closed mahogany casket with silver fittings.

And it was there, at last, that Augusta's chickens came home to roost.

Everybody she had slighted, insulted, or terrorized stayed away, leaving just her three closest friends, plus the people who came for Elizabeth's and the children's sake, or Rotary, to trickle in and sign the guest book. Only a few arrangements and sprays had been delivered, from Garden Club or Altar Guild or the Women's

Club. The largest and most impressive was a spray from Pearl and Thomas, but the parlor Augusta had reserved seemed big and empty by evening's end. Just before they left, the judge arrived to pay his respects to Howe, but Elizabeth counted only twenty signatures in the book, including his.

The next night was even more sparsely attended, but Augusta's three best friends stayed for longer, complaining bitterly the whole time about who wasn't there.

By the third and final session on Friday night before the funeral, the family sat alone beside the casket.

The children took it in stride, but Howe didn't. They'd only been there for ten minutes, without a single visitor, when he told Elizabeth he had some phone calls to make, and asked Thomas to take him home.

"What's up with Daddy?" Patti asked, concerned, after he'd gone.

"I guess he's upset that people aren't respecting Gamma the way he thinks they should," Elizabeth answered.

"Gamma was good to Dad and Patti and me," Charles said frankly, "but she stepped on a lot of toes in this town. There's no getting around that."

"Hyere, now, Mister Charles," Pearl chided. "Yore grammaw was good to me and Thomas, too. Don't you go speakin' ill of the dead. It tempts the Lord's vengeance. Miz Augusta, she had her own hurts aplenty in this life, and she done the best she could. Ain't no cause fer people to stay away from her funeral."

"Pearl, she made a lot of people mad," Charles insisted.

Patti sighed. "You're right. Still, it's sad."

Elizabeth knew she was talking about more than visitation. "Yes, honey, it is."

Only Augusta's best friends and Father Jim showed up. The minister thanked the family for the new pipe organ, which had been ordered according to Augusta's instructions. Then he prayed a sweet prayer of thanksgiving for Augusta's devotion to the church and generosity, and made his farewell.

When they got home, Howe was holed up in his study and didn't come to bed till late.

Elizabeth rolled over in the darkened room when he got into bed. "Are you okay?"

"Yeah. I just . . ." He let out a forced sigh.

"What?" she prodded gently. He'd come a long way since he'd woken up blurting out everything that came to mind, but she almost preferred that to brooding. "Howe, please don't keep things from me. We've had too much of that, already."

He leaned over and gave her a peck. "Just this one more thing," he said. "I need for everyone to

438

come to the funeral. Not for Mama—she's gone —but for me."

"Why is it so important to you?" she asked. Augusta was the one who'd alienated everybody. Howe had been making amends for his own bad behavior ever since he'd woken up.

He turned his back and pulled the covers up over his shoulder. "You'll see tomorrow."

And with that, he went to sleep.

The next morning, he was no more forthcoming. Antsy, he bolted his breakfast, then retreated into his study till it was time to dress.

He'd hardly said ten words before the four of them got into the long black limo Augusta had ordered for the trip to the church.

It wasn't easy, but Elizabeth didn't prod Howe. Whatever was on his mind, she'd find out soon enough. But nothing prepared her for what they confronted when they walked into the sanctuary at St. Andrew's.

# Chapter 26

Two identical mahogany coffins flanked Augusta's flower-laden one.

"Daddy," Patti accused in a tight whisper, "what is this? Who's in those other coffins?" She pointed to them in anger. "Gamma didn't say anything about this. She wanted her own funeral, just for herself."

"Patti, honey," Howe said gently but firmly, "funerals are for the living, not the dead. Gamma's not here, but we are. I want you to trust me about this. If you're still mad at me after it's over, then I guess you'll be mad at me. But Gamma was my mother. I'm the one who has to make the decisions about her service."

"It's not right," Patti protested, drawing attention from the people who had begun to file into the church.

"Patti, keep your voice down," Elizabeth cautioned. "You know the last thing your grandmother would have wanted is for you to make a scene." She shot a reassuring glance to Howe. "We need to trust your father's judgment."

Howe responded with a look of gratitude.

"Come on," Charles whispered, taking his sister by the arm and steering her into the front pew where Pearl and Thomas were waiting. "Just settle down. Dad knows what he's doing."

"Since when?" Patti hissed, then clamped her mouth shut in consternation as her brother pressed her into the pew.

"Since he woke up," Charles whispered back, then knelt on the prayer rest.

Patti flounced to her knees beside him, but kept silent.

Elizabeth sure hoped Howe knew what he was doing. And she was dying to know who was in those extra coffins.

Elizabeth's Sewing Circle arrived en masse and sat in the pew behind her, offering gentle touches and words of consolation, with no questions asked, but they didn't have to say any-thing about the three coffins. Elizabeth could sense their unspoken shock and curiosity.

Slowly, the church began to fill, and with every arrival, a new set of whispers emerged. The organ began to play, but the organist clearly wasn't the virtuoso Augusta had contracted for. The hymns came out in odd phrases, with more than a few missed notes.

Appalled, Patti slipped out the side aisle and headed for the hidden organ to see what had gone wrong. After a whispered conference that resulted in a slew of missed notes, she returned to tell Elizabeth that the other organist had called in sick at the last minute. Unable to get anyone else to fill in, the funeral director had been forced to press his teenaged cousin into service.

Elizabeth winced with every wrong note along with the rest of the congregation. It would have been funny, if it wasn't so awful.

But fate wasn't through getting even with Augusta yet. Only three altos and one bass from the choir processed down the aisle at the start of the communion service, providing a very lop-sided version of "How Great Thou Art."

Elizabeth dared not look back for fear she'd see someone laugh and join them. So she bit her lips and did her best to remain dignified.

Unfazed, Father Tim began the rite of communion first, instead of the funeral service, a departure from the usual order of service, but the familiar litany—and the absence of music—settled things down. Till the soloist from the Atlanta Chorale was supposed to sing the Lord's Prayer, and instead of her trained voice, Miss Emily Mason's thready, geriatric soprano struggled through the PA system with as pitiful a rendition as ever was attempted.

Patti grabbed Charles's arm so hard, he pried it off with a grimace of rebuke.

Meanwhile, Howe finally registered what a disaster the service had become. Lips curled inward, his rigid posture wavered as his eyes widened and nostrils flared.

Lord. If he started laughing, she'd be done for.

Elizabeth's mouth pruned up, and she gripped her fists so tight her nails bit into her palms, hoping the pain would offset the deadly urge to laugh.

For the moment, it worked. Just thirty more minutes. If she could get through that, it would all be behind them.

When Father Jim and the acolytes came to the front of the aisle and offered the Lord's Supper, Elizabeth took a healthy swig of the strong communion wine, hoping it would calm her down, but all it did was soak straight into her empty stomach lining, leaving her with a brief buzz.

She offered up a sincere prayer for composure, and managed to settle down for the remainder of the ritual.

Then it was time for the eulogy, and Father Jim looked down from the pulpit to say, "First, I'd like to thank you all for showing your love and support for Miss Augusta's family by coming here today to commemorate her life. What a glorious comfort it is to know that despite all our human failings, we Christians have the assurance of God's mercy through Christ. Miss Augusta was a devoted member of this church, and we have all benefited from her service and generosity. In her final will and testament, she donated the remainder of the funds needed to provide a new pipe organ for our sanctuary. And in a separate provision she made just before her death, she endowed the salary for an organist and minister of music."

The need for which was glaringly evident in the day's proceedings.

"So we owe her a great debt of gratitude," Father Jim continued, "and were blessed by her presence, despite the human frailties we all share. Thanks be to God. " He nodded to Howe. "And now, her son Howe has asked to share a few words about his mother."

Howe slipped into the aisle before Elizabeth could reach over to give him a reassuring touch. He passed between the coffins, then met Father Jim on his way to the pulpit and shook his hand. "Thank you, Father."

Then he mounted the shallow stone stairs to the pulpit and looked across the congregation. "Thank you all for coming," he began. "I know I had to bend a few elbows to get you all here, but there's something important I need to say, and I wanted you all to hear it." Howe glanced at the coffins. "I know you're all wondering why there are three coffins here."

And who was in them!

He faced the congregation with calm and assurance. "The one in the middle holds my mother's mortal remains." He paused, looking down on it with regret.

Then he shifted his focus to the one beside it. "The one on the left holds the woman she might have been if life had been different, and she had made different choices. My mother tried so hard to be the perfect wife, a paragon of virtue. But she only ended up making a prison of her own skin, the smallest prison in the world." His mouth crumpled briefly. "This coffin holds all the joy she never knew. All the love she hid away inside her. All the laughter we never heard. All the kindness she never got to give."

Patti gripped Charles's hand and groped for Elizabeth's till she found it.

You could hear a pin drop as Howe went on. "But, like many women of her generation, my mother felt she had to keep up appearances, no matter what happened. She bore the indignities of her life by hiding behind a wall that isolated her from those of us who loved her, as well as those she feared. A wall that isolated her from her better self and all the simple pleasures of this life, except for her beloved grandchildren."

He faced Elizabeth. "She did it to protect herself and her marriage, and it was contagious. After my father died and I came back to Whittington, I found myself doing the same thing. What I felt, I suppressed. What I feared, I controlled. What I wanted, I took. For that, I owe a lot of you a humble apology."

A murmur rippled through the congregation in response.

A wry smile eased Howe's expression. "It took a stroke and a brain tumor to wake me up, and I thank God for both, because they brought me to God, and to the truth. While I was crying and hugging and cussing and being jerked around by my emotions and my appetites like a two-year-old, I saw how wrong I'd been."

Elizabeth was so proud of him, she felt her chest would explode.

"God gave me another chance," Howe said, "and I mean to make the best of it."

He pointed to the last coffin. "That third coffin is for the man I was. The selfish, greedy, soulless, heartless man I let myself become every time I cut corners in business, or turned my back on those in need around me, or betrayed the family who loved me." He struggled to maintain control. "Thank God, that man is gone. I'm burying him beside my mother, and I pray he stays buried forever."

Gripping the edge of the pulpit, Howe scanned the congregation. "It's never too late to make things right. If I can do it, anybody can. Don't waste the chances you still have."

Elizabeth heard sniffs behind her.

Howe looked to his mother's coffin, head

bowed. "Don't let there be an empty coffin beside yours for the person you might have been." In the resounding silence that followed, he left the pulpit.

Patti clung to Elizabeth and her brother, then all three of them reached out to Howe as he took his place in the pew while Father Jim concluded the service.

Nobody noticed the pitiful choir or its accompaniment at the recessional. They were too moved by Howe's message, and the minute Father Jim pronounced the benediction from the back of the church, the whole congregation erupted in a surge of support.

Elizabeth's friends enveloped her with hugs and praise for Howe's turnaround, and most of the men present came up and shook Howe's hand in wordless approval till the funeral director shepherded the family to the front of the aisle, where Howe and Charles joined the pallbearers in taking not just Augusta's, but the other two coffins to the three waiting hearses outside.

Elizabeth caught up with Howe after the last casket was shut into the hearse. "You're not really going to bury those, are you?"

"Only Mama's." He put his arm around her shoulder and leaned in close so no one would overhear what he said next. "Just between you and me, I'm donating the other two to needy veterans, along with a dozen more."

Elizabeth smiled, slipping her arm around his waist. "I like that. It's a nice memorial for Augusta."

He drew her toward the waiting limousine. "Come on. Let's go bury the past."

"Sounds like a plan." And they did.

Once their sins were laid to rest with Augusta, the life they shared was fun and maddening and glorious and true and frustrating and unpredictable. And that suited Elizabeth just fine. So fine, in fact, that she sometimes invited Howe up to Blue Ridge. But only sometimes.

**Center Point Publishing**
600 Brooks Road ● PO Box 1
Thorndike ME 04986-0001 USA

**(207) 568-3717**

**US & Canada:**
**1 800 929-9108**
www.centerpointlargeprint.com